I

'A darkly humorous, keenly observed blend of millennial drift and murder mystery from a razor-sharp writer' *Red*

'I absolutely loved it ... It made me really think about identity, who we are and why we do what we do. Such a beautiful book' Emma Gannon

'O'Donoghue establishes herself as one of the most exciting young Irish writers on the literary scene. Her acerbic wit is matched by her sharp-eyed observations, resulting in a piece of fiction that is dark, gripping and beautifully written' Louise O'Neill

'I was so hooked on this beautiful, funny story of homecoming and self-discovery I didn't want to put it down. The characters are wonderfully drawn, and the sense of place is so compelling – it is a mystery, a fireside yarn' Keith Stuart

'A dark yet joyous novel about family and friendship' *Grazia*

'Put this book somewhere safe, because it is set to be one of those you spend your life reading over and over – discovering new moments and new lessons each time ... I think *Scenes of a Graphic Nature* – blisteringly funny and clever – is O'Donoghue's best work yet. Raw, heartfelt and incredibly compelling, I can't recommend this enough' Lucy Vine

'Absolutely loved it. It's an absorbing blend of quarter-life crisis mixed with a bit of mystery' *Irish Tatler*

'A witty story of second-generation immigrants trying to belong, *Scenes of a Graphic Nature* grapples with love, friendship and identity' *Heat*

'An intriguing read, raising questions about what stories should be told, when and by whom' *Scotsman*

CAROLINE O'DONOGHUE is an Irish author, journalist and host of the award-winning podcast *Sentimental Garbage*. She has contributed to *Grazia*, *Irish Times*, *Irish Examiner*, *Buzzfeed*, *Vice* and *The Times*. Her first novel, *Promising Young Women*, was shortlisted for the Irish Book Awards' Newcomer of the Year and the Kate O'Brien Award. Her first novel for young adults, *All Our Hidden Gifts*, will be published in 2021. She was born in Cork but currently lives in London with her partner and a terrier with chronic eye problems.

*Also by Caroline O'Donoghue*

Promising Young Women

# Caroline O'Donoghue

# Scenes of a Graphic Nature

virago

VIRAGO

First published in Great Britain in 2020 by Virago Press
This edition published in 2021 by Virago Press

1 3 5 7 9 10 8 6 4 2

A CIP catalogue record for this book
is available from the British Library.

ISBN 978-0-349-00997-1

Typeset in Bembo by M Rules
Printed and bound in Great Britain by
Clays Ltd, Elcograf S.p.A.

Papers used by Virago are from well-managed forests
and other responsible sources.

Virago Press
An imprint of
Little, Brown Book Group
Carmelite House
50 Victoria Embankment
London EC4Y 0DZ

An Hachette UK Company
www.hachette.co.uk

www.virago.co.uk

To Ella Risbridger, 'for the agreeable fact
of her continuing presence which in twenty
years I have never presumed to expect'

# PART ONE

As sad misfortune came over me
Which caused me to stray from the land
Far away from me friends and relations
Betrayed by the black velvet band

*'The Black Velvet Band'*,
TRADITIONAL IRISH FOLK SONG

# I

'Connor Cronin was a pudgy boy,' he muses. 'And he made for a pudgy corpse.'

My father's voice is tinny coming out of the cheap speaker, made worse because the batteries are almost gone. His voice is still good, though, his Kerry accent joyful and compact as a grape.

'Boy' is pronounced 'biy'. 'Corpse' is pronounced 'karps'.

'Are you sure you want to say that, Dad?'

'Say what?'

'Do you want to go on the record, calling a little dead boy "fat"?'

'I said "pudgy". It's a story detail, Charlie. Stories need details. Otherwise it's just a big long list of things that happened.'

The Dictaphone picks up my long outward sigh. I hate myself for sighing. For being so vividly exasperated by my own father, who was just trying to answer a question, after all.

I should have been nicer. I should *be* nicer. I press my ear closer to the tiny speaker as though it were a seashell or a stringed-up tin can.

'I just don't think it's very . . . '

'What? *Politically correct?*'

'Don't say it like that.'

'Like what?'

'Like there's something weak about not wanting to hurt people.'

I click down the big plastic 'stop' button on my old Dictaphone. I bought it the year I turned twenty-five, when Laura went travelling and I had moved home. I was supposed to have gone with her, but my dad's cancer – which, we had been promised, would be zapped quickly by chemotherapy, and be in the rear-view mirror of our lives before we knew it – came back.

The cancer and I have spent the last four years boomeranging to my father's bedside. I have been tailing this disease like an undercover cop, furiously taking notes on its progress and letting my twenties slip by in the process. I've tried to be productive. It's what you do. 'Life is what happens when you're making other plans.' People love telling me this, particularly as they are making other plans.

I used the time at home to write scripts, and to interrogate my dad in daily interviews about his childhood in Clipim, a small island off the west coast of Ireland. Interviews that made him feel famous, and me feel like there was a point to me being home in the first place. I thought, as the creative one in the family, it was my job to be my father's biographer. To preserve the official record of his unusual and tragic life story. Soon, the two activities started to bleed into one another. What was the point of me writing endless, never-to-be-commissioned screenplays, when there was a real story sitting right in front of me?

By the time Laura was back from her year abroad, I had both the script and the grant funding to make the movie that would eventually become *It Takes a Village*.

It took two years. Two years of sharing everything, from the microwave-ready meals to cigarettes to the mildewed, queen-sized bed that we were half-certain had bed bugs.

If I had known it would end so quickly, I would have treasured it more.

Now, Laura's gone again. Lost in the undertow of heterosexual commitment and surprise weekends in Belgium; leaving me to mope around our old bedsit like a ghost. I still seem to spend most of my time in Essex, hanging around my parents' house, listening to old recordings of my dad telling me about his early years and trying to believe that it is possible to beat cancer for a third time.

I have memorised my father's childhood so well that my own feels like tracing paper over a much stronger image. His earliest memories are ones of drama, death and destruction. My earliest memories are of hearing about it.

*Pudgy.* What a word to use. Festive and jolly and sweet.

I press 'play' again. I can hear my dad – sounding rudely, obnoxiously healthy, despite it being his second bite of the cancer cherry – tutting me under his breath.

'Charlie, my love,' he says, a little song in his voice, the song that always creeps back in when he's convinced of his own moral fortitude and wants to be playful about it, 'if you think you can get through a story like *this* without upsetting people, then . . .'

The little light on the Dictaphone fades from traffic-light red to a dull cherry, and then to grey. The battery finally runs out, and I don't get to hear what happens when you think you can't upset people.

There's noise downstairs. Mum is home. She always forgets to take bags to the supermarket and never wants to buy them when she's there, so she ends up stacking tins of beans and packets of ravioli into her arms, then releasing it all on to the kitchen table like a jewel thief emptying a pillowcase.

'Charlie!' she calls.

I peep through the door of my old bedroom. I listen to her movements and creep out as light-footed as I can, judging her mood by her voice.

'Charlie, are you up there? Come on, there's a load of shopping.'

I come down, comfortable that this is about food and not about Dad.

'Hey,' I say, 'you weren't gone long.'

My mum is short, like me, and blonde, not like me. She moves around the kitchen, hunched and defensive as an armadillo, not really registering my presence. I start packing Greek yogurt and raw chicken into the fridge, then scooping out the rotting bananas in the fruit bowl to replace them with fresh ones.

'Keep them,' she instructs.

'But they're vile.'

'Banana bread.'

'I have never once seen you make banana bread.'

'Dad loves it. We can make it tonight and bring it up to him tomorrow.'

I start packing Fruit n' Nut into the long cupboard where the dry things are kept. I say nothing.

'I'm heading up in a minute. You're coming, aren't you?'

'Of course I'm coming.'

The words come out of my mouth like thumbtacks.

'I just need to shower first.'

She looks me up and down for the first time today. 'It's almost two, you know.'

'I was up late working last night.'

'Working? On what?'

'Film stuff.'

'You might be better off looking for something closer to an actual job.'

'This is my *actual job*.'

She raises her eyebrows, that being the dignity of her answer.

'Are you coming or aren't you? You can't come looking like that.'

'I'll be super quick. I promise.'

I'm not super quick, though. I get out of the shower and sit on the edge of my bed, tapping out messages to Laura.

**Do we have any more festivals coming up?xx**

'Charlie!' Mum calls up the stairs. 'Are you coming or not?'

'Two seconds!' I yell back from behind the door, conscious that she'll see me in my towel and know that it won't be two seconds.

'Make your bed, tidy your room.'

'Well, do you want me to come quickly or do you want me to make my bed and tidy my room?'

'WHAT?'

'I said, do you want me to—'

'I CAN'T HEAR YOU; I'LL BE IN THE CAR.'

Laura texts back.

**Brighton Brave in September, Cornwall Film Fest in Nov xx**

September. Five months away. I can feel the time stretching out like hot tar in front of me. What am I supposed to *do* with myself?

Since Laura moved out of our flat to live with Mike, our time together has become sporadic. At first the distance felt like it could be good for our friendship. She would habitually return to West Norwood, fling herself back on our queen-size bed, and take long drags on her cigarette while complaining that Mike wouldn't let her smoke indoors. I learned to love this version of us. There was no choice *but* to. It was like Laura was the child of some phantom divorce. That I was the fun, Saturday parent she thought about all week.

I let her use anything as an ashtray: jars, mugs, a cereal bowl that I hadn't sipped the milk out of yet. Then one day, eight weeks after she moved out, she walked into our old room and didn't immediately fall backwards on to the unmade bed. She picked up a mug on my nightstand.

'You know there's a cigarette butt in this, right?'

Now, we only seem to see each other when it's about the film. We had a rash of festival appearances back in November, all at least an hour outside of London, all introduced by the organiser as 'the third annual Somerset Shine Film Festival' with an air of genuine amazement that they had managed to put on a festival not just once but three times.

Mum's sounding her 'hurry the fuck on' beep: three short beeps and two really, really, long ones. I pull on a T-shirt and run out to the car, my hair wet and hanging in stunted clumps around my neck.

'Charlie,' my mum says, in a tone she found when she started taking me to mass and hasn't stopped using since, 'you're almost thirty. Do I really have to tell you to wear a bra to the hospital?'

'I only *just* turned twenty-nine, and I'm like ... half an A-cup. Bras are purely ornamental for me.'

'And the hair, Charlie. Really. Do you want all Dad's pals to think you're some kind of ... skag head?'

'I'm sure they're probably too focused on their own cancer to think about it, honestly,' I reply, wondering where she learned the phrase 'skag head'.

We go quiet then, because I said cancer, and Mum prefers to be euphemistic with this kind of thing. 'The C Word' is preferable, but 'Dad's trouble' is what she uses herself.

I clear my throat. 'I was thinking,' I eventually volunteer, 'maybe I could load up my old iPod for Dad. Give him something to listen to when he's in there.'

'That sounds like a good idea,' she says, indifferent and apolitical as a UN summit.

'Yeah,' I say awkwardly. 'I'll put on all the old Irish showbands he loves so much. Joe Dolan. Luke Kelly. The Dubliners. All that.'

Her mouth goes tight.

'Now you don't want to depress him, Charlie.'

'Why would that *depress* him? He loves that stuff.'

She presses her lips together like she is trying to even out her lipstick, but doesn't say anything.

It's a funny thing, the Irishness in our house. Growing up, it pervaded everything emotionally but it touched nothing physically. Dad's mum had been a widow, and when she died before I was born, he lost all reason to go to Ireland. He had no old friends, no surviving playmates: just the gruesome honour of being the last boy of his generation to survive the disaster in the old schoolhouse.

'Maybe Frank Sinatra?' she says finally.

When we get to the hospital, he's asleep, but not deeply. This is the thing with people in hospitals. It's almost impossible for them to get a full, unbroken night of sleep. They're woken up either by nurses' checks or by their room-mates, resulting in a perpetual, day-long doze that is interrupted by meals, visitors and habitual prodding by whoever's on call.

His eyes are closed and his lips are slightly parted, mouthing out a low, quiet snore. He has a pyjama shirt on but the buttons aren't done up, so I can see tufts of his chest hair. I sit on the edge of the bed, lowering my weight on to it carefully, as if there are delicate china figurines under the duvet. He wakes up, smiles at me, and takes my hand into both of his.

'My love,' he says, and his voice is hoarse with tenderness and phlegm.

'Hi, Dad. How are you feeling?'

'I'm all right, pet. Another awful night.'

'Did Corned Beef keep you up?'

He gives a long, purposeful side-eye to the bed next to him, a look that is utterly lost as the curtain is drawn around it.

'You're feckin' right he did. All this moaning and groaning and waking up and calling the nurse. Appalling behaviour.'

Corned Beef is an eighty-something man who has been sharing a room with Dad for about a week now. He refuses to eat anything the hospital provides, instead asking his grown-up kids to bring in packets and packets of the stuff. He has loud nightmares, which Dad resents him for. My dad resents anyone who gives evidence of having a subconscious. Unless they are suffering from PTSD – and even then, the PTSD must be gained specifically from having fought in a war – they are, according to him, taking the piss. He is a big fan of that Freud quote about how the Irish are impervious to psychoanalysis, and brings it up a lot, usually in conjunction with: 'Well, Charlie, *I* never needed any therapy, and think about what happened to *me* . . .'

When he is finished giving the plastic curtain a filthy look, he asks me how I am, and how work is at the cafe, and whether there's any news about the film.

'We're still waiting to hear back from a bunch of festivals,' I say, my voice falsely chipper. 'But we're getting a really good response so far.'

'Is Laura doing any more of them panels?'

I feel my ears go red. 'I don't know.'

'She should. She was so good at the last one. Wasn't she, Sharon?'

Mum walks in with food from the Tesco Express down the road and starts unloading plastic containers of pesto pasta salad and Walkers Sensations crisps. My mum is the kind of person who is still very impressed by Sensations crisps, believing they can elevate any kind of situation to the status of informal dinner party among close friends.

'Who's this? Laura?' Mum asks, shuffling the crisps into a bowl. 'Is she still working at Channel 4?'

Address isn't the only thing that's changed with Laura recently. It isn't that Laura is necessarily better than me, it's just that her skill set is more marketable. In the hopeful window of time after Uni but before cancer, we were both working as runners on movie sets. They were jobs set up by our University to prove to other applicants that over 90 per cent of graduates really *did* go on to have careers in the entertainment industry. The reality, however, was that we were just warm bodies, barely trusted to knock on dressing-room doors to remind actors of their call times.

Laura was good at it, though. She came back from travelling and was remembered fondly by everyone, sailing right into a job as a camera assistant. Now she's making great money at a production company, working the camera for the kind of reality shows you see on Channel 5 in the middle of the day.

I am making lattes in The Blue Door, a cafe a hundred yards from our old flat.

'She is,' I answer, even though she doesn't work at Channel 4. I stuff five crisps into my mouth.

'Do you think she could get you a job, then?'

To tell the truth, I've sort of wondered that myself. I had assumed that as Laura started getting jobs, she'd naturally find one for me. We are co-creators, after all.

I could tell my parents this – that I am as confused by my lack of employment prospects as they are – and maybe I would if it was just me and Dad. But to tell Mum that I have hurt feelings would give her fuel for a grudge, and there's nothing she loves more than a grudge.

I pretend not to hear and start looking around the room for inspiration. I don't usually have a problem talking to my dad but there's something about coming to see a sick person in hospital that mutes you. You can't be too glum, or ask too many questions about cancer, because it brings the whole mood down. You can't be too up either, though. Last time, I chatted happily to Dad for an hour about a film I'd seen at The Prince Charles, and then got a hissed lecture in the car home about reminding him of things he wasn't able to do.

'He gets it into his head that he's well enough to go to the pictures with you,' she said. 'And then he gets himself all worked up asking the doctors to let him sign out.'

So, we live in the neutral. How soft his new pyjamas are. How good the Tesco own-brand stuff has become. How useful Spotify is. It gets difficult. I have never been an especially good small-talk person, but small-talk in a hospital is the shit worst.

I spy a book next to his bed and grab it, delighted by the familiar cover. It's *Harry Potter and the Prisoner of Azkaban*. I pick up the dog-eared old copy that he brought from home and see CHARLOTTE REGAN written at the front in light pencil. It's like running into an old friend in a foreign country.

'I can't believe you're rereading this!'

'Comfort reading,' he says, grinning. 'To get me through the night with Corned Beef. I've decided to reread the whole series while I'm in here. The first one's still brilliant but *Chamber of Secrets* is a bit shite.'

My dad was one of those grown-ups that read *Harry Potter* when it first came out, even before all the newspapers were saying how weird it was. We used to queue up for the midnight releases at Waterstones; we saw all the films together. His favourite was *Goblet of Fire* because it opens with Ireland in the finals of the Quidditch World Cup.

'I remember us reading the first one together,' he says, as I thumb through the old copy. 'Do you remember the first page, Charlie? Of the first book?'

'Uh ...'

'The Boy Who Lived,' he says, before I have a chance to come up with an answer. 'And I thought, *That's a bit like me, isn't it?*'

He laughs then, a thin yellow throaty laugh.

'Or, it was.'

I hear the hollow click of Mum sucking her teeth, the signal of a forthcoming talking-to in the car home.

I now have to re-address *Harry Potter* as a neutral topic, because ultimately, *Harry Potter* is a story about a magical boy who survives something tragic for no good reason. That is why my father likes it. Because he survived tragedy for no good reason, and then went through life dazed by the blow. Yet touched – yes, touched does feel like the right word – with a certain sense of destiny. An understanding that whatever planet governs supreme misfortune had cycled out of his orbit, and he had been spared. Unblemished. Alive.

My father is dying, and I don't know what to do about it.

# 2

They say that carbon monoxide poisoning is directly responsible for at least half of Victorian ghost sightings.

The symptoms of poisoning include pressure on your chest, hallucinations, drowsiness, amnesia and dread. Carbon monoxide is ghost juice. It creates everything that the human body needs to genuinely believe that it is surrounded by supernatural ill will. You might throw all your hats into the bath, and then wake up fifteen hours later with the solution that the ghost must have done it. If you catch the poison early enough, it becomes a ghost story. If you don't, you become the ghost.

The oil burner in Clipim schoolhouse had been installed in the early fifties, a hand-me-down from the local Big House who had been using it to heat their stables. This is an image that one journalist reporting for a November 1963 edition of *The Munster Express* seemed particularly captured by. 'What was good enough for English horses was good enough for Irish children,' the copy read.

This statement was republished in article after article, essay after essay, leading to the eventual folk myth that the young people of Clipim were educated in a stable. This is something my father comes back to a lot in our recordings. The eighteen children of Clipim died in a schoolhouse, a proper one, and not a stable. It's the burner that was the issue. The English ex-pats had simply donated it with no concern for how old it was, how loose the pipes already were, how a single knock of a child's foot could have turned a one-room cottage into a kind of Lilliputian graveyard. It was a carelessness, my dad said, that was typical of the English aristocrats living in Ireland during the time.

'But, Dad,' I interrupt, 'okay, the English didn't check the burner was safe before donating it, but ... the people running the school didn't check, either? Wasn't it just as much *their* responsibility?'

Dad sniffed. 'Ah, now. They wouldn't have had that kind of know-how at all. We were deliberately kept ignorant, Charlie. Pig ignorant.'

'Sure, but I don't know if that completely erases ... '

'Think of the Famine, pet. They hooked us on the spuds. And then, when the spuds were gone, there was nothing, and they made us into criminals. It was like crack in America in the 1980s.'

It was not the first time my father compared the Famine to the war on drugs, nor would it be the last.

The faulty burner ate through the oxygen in the room in big, greedy gulps, and because the chimney was stuffed up with newspaper from the previous winter, there was no space for new air to dilute the atmosphere. Dad had been called home before lunch to help his mother on her smallholding, and by the end of the day Emma Casey and her eighteen students were dead.

My dad has the ghost story. His classmates are the ghosts.

By the time the news had reached *The Irish Times*, half of the children had already been buried. Clipim was an inward little place, where not much was reported to the mainland, and so it was the undertakers who noticed first.

The island is off the coast of Kerry, as west of Ireland as you can possibly get, and was not big enough to have more than one funeral home or more than one graveyard. This made the tragedy of 11 November 1963 an administrative one as well as an emotional one. Father Matthew, the parish priest, gently encouraged the parents to send their dead to other places where they had family. Many of the bodies ended up in Waterford, and some settled in Cork, but the undertakers were a surprisingly communicative profession – most funeral homes being family-run businesses, and many being related by blood or marriage – and they talked. Eventually, the papers became involved. After that, most people moved away. It seemed the best way to deal with things.

The few newspaper clippings my dad still has are pasted into an autograph book he once got free with a copy of the *Sun*. The cover is blue and says 'Guess Who I Met?' and inside are articles about him Pritt-Sticked on to stiff card. The journalists who wrote about the story did so with disgust, astonishment and a cranky resentment towards Clipim itself. How uncivilised was this town, to have one schoolhouse and a chimney stuffed with newspaper? Just who were these cowboys, who allowed eighteen children to die slowly over the course of a school day? Clipim became an emblem of rural Ireland at its most disturbing. Clip was careless, backward, stuck in the past, and it was primarily populated by Kerrymen who didn't have the good sense to educate their children in safety. It helped bolster a stereotype about Kerry that already existed, and like so many stereotypes, it became very hard to let go of.

And the teacher. Well, she was another matter entirely.

Emma Casey, a plain-looking girl from the mainland who had to be brought over because they had no one literate enough on the island to teach in the first place. She had been ill for weeks before the accident, sick with a lung infection she had supposedly got from teaching in the damp old building to begin with. My dad's memories of her are patchy. 'Pale thing,' he says. 'Bit of a drip.'

Every article, every TV item, every snippet of story seems to pose the same question: just who *are* these people?

No one ever really got to find out, because before the country was even done mourning, and before the journalists had finished gathering information on it, John F. Kennedy was assassinated, and everything and everyone in Ireland stopped.

When I wrote the script, I tried to find a way to get around the JFK thing. To just not mention it, if I could. It seemed so obvious. The last thing I wanted was a load of pretend Irish people dabbing their eyes and whispering about how Kennedy, *their* Kennedy, a *Catholic* president, an *Irish* Catholic president, had been shot down before their very eyes, in the prime of his life, at the height of his presidency. He had *just* visited, after all, back in June. Including it would pull focus from the main story, the same way it pulled focus from Clipim back in 1963.

'You don't understand, Charlie,' Dad had said, when I showed him the first draft. 'He was our Obama. Bigger than Obama, even, because at least Obama had JFK to be compared to. But JFK paved the way for JFK. There is no story without JFK.'

Of course there is a story without JFK. But in my dad's eyes, the film is about himself, and to him, there is no 'him' without JFK. In his head, their fates are bound so tightly that he is not sure when one begins and the other ends. In my father's brain, the story goes: 'I survived a tragedy, so John F. Kennedy was shot in the head', not: 'I survived a tragedy, *and* John F. Kennedy was shot in the head'.

But there was no getting around it, in the end. Ireland was on the turn of something in 1963. Kennedy visited. The Beatles visited. George Harrison was on the news, talking about his Irish cousins. There was hot energy coming out of the country, a firing away from the Church and towards some undecided mid-point on the horizon. It felt best not to dwell on things, and so the country moved on from the Clipim tragedy. How much sadness can one place take? There was a silent, national pact between the people of Ireland: *Let's not ruin the momentum*.

We manage to skim over the 'boy who lived' awkwardness and on to easier areas. I read him some *Harry Potter*, and eventually we managed to drift back into our old dynamic, losing ourselves in myths and stories grander than our own. We go from *Harry Potter* to *Lord of the Rings*, from Peter Jackson to Steven Spielberg, from *ET* to *The Color Purple*. When Dad eventually gets tired of animated conversation, he lies back on his pillow, insisting that he is only resting his eyes and not sleeping.

'Whoopi Goldberg,' he says.

'Gary Cooper,' I respond.

'Christoph Waltz.'

'William Wyler.'

He furrows his brow. 'You have me stuck on W's now.'

Mum gets bored of The Initial Game quickly. She wanders around the ward, making chit-chat with the wives of other sick people, curious to see how forthcoming they will be about the details of how cancer has ruined their lives. Eventually, she leaves the room to make a phone call. She comes back an hour later with another shopping bag from Tesco, having compulsively purchased all the items that have been marked down because they expire tomorrow. This is how my mother relaxes.

My dad has started to ask about film festivals again. He generally asks about how *It Takes a Village* is doing at least three or four times per visit. The drugs aren't doing anything to his memory. He just likes hearing about himself.

'Have you talked to any movie types? Producers? Directors? Best boys?'

'Uh, a few.'

'And is there any interest from America? They love the Irish over there. I think it would do really well in America.'

My father is obsessed with America. He is convinced the feeling is mutual. He is constantly telling me how much Americans love and want to be Irish, apparently to the point where they are willing to abandon all logic and reason and give me ten million pounds for my film.

'It doesn't really work that way, Dad.'

'Did you give anyone your business card?'

'I don't have a business card.'

'Well, there's your problem then.'

It's hard not to hold this against him. It's not that *It Takes a Village* is doing badly: by the standard of most no-budget independent cinema, it's doing pretty well. We've even sold out a couple of festival screenings. If he would just let me tell the story, he could be impressed by it, instead of disappointed that it doesn't fulfil the picture of success he has in his head.

'One woman cried when she saw it,' I try again. 'She said it was a mature, quiet film. Remarkable. Her word. *Remarkable.*'

Dad perks up again. 'Who was she? Another industry type?'

'No. She was just a person.'

'Well. She's right. It *is* remarkable, isn't it? Isn't it, Sharon?' He gestures to Mum, who is getting twitchy.

'Well, at the very least, it has been an adventure, hasn't it?' says Mum. She has started stuffing the empty crisp packets into one another, indicating that it's time to go. 'And even if it comes to nothing, you've still had a lovely time with all of it.'

'I mean, the adventure is just *starting*,' I say, making no attempt to hide my peevishness. 'We still have more festivals.'

She scrunches up the rubbish loudly and stuffs it into plastic bags, and I raise my voice to meet it.

'And there are still festivals we haven't even heard back from yet.'

'Of course.'

Her face is fixed to a false mildness. She looks at me with a detached, lipless smile. A 'let's finish this in the car' smile.

'Honestly,' I go on, 'I might have to quit working at The Blue Door this summer; I'm going to be spending so much time on the road.'

The lie tastes sour on my tongue, like under-ripe blackberries. We have nothing until September, but she doesn't know that.

'Not really, though, Charlie?'

'Why not? It's just a cafe.'

'It's steady work.'

'I'll have steady work soon. In an industry that's actually relevant.'

She gives an exaggerated shrug, one intended for some invisible audience she always seems to be playing to when she's frustrated with me.

'*What?*'

'Nothing.'

'Tell me.'

'I just don't want to be ten years into my retirement and still worrying about you.'

*Alone.* That's what she's not saying. She doesn't want to have to worry about me alone. Worrying about a child with your husband of thirty years is one thing; worrying about your child as a widow is something else entirely.

We're silent in the car home. Silent all evening. I make a tuna sandwich for dinner and eat it in my old bedroom, and she eats a yellow-sticker pot of red pepper hummus while watching a True Movie about a woman who donates her kidney to her son and then he dies anyway. She loves this kind of thing. She will not watch an actual film but she will inhale three of these in one sitting. Presumably it's why she married my father, The Tragedy Man.

We have never quite learned how to relax around each other. There's a density to our silences, one that fills the whole house with a tropical dread. Once she asks me if I want tea; once I ask her if she wants tea. We are both thinking the same thing: *This is what it will be like when he is gone.*

I suspect we had mutually assumed that our strained relationship was a result of my teenage years and her menopause, which had dovetailed around the same time. But when Dad first got sick and I moved up from London to play the dutiful daughter, the atmosphere between us was even worse than when I was fifteen and she was having hot flushes. Which is really saying something.

In my room I start adding people in the film industry on LinkedIn. Most of them are connected to Laura, none of whom has the slightest clue who I am, but I add them anyway in the hopes that a producer will mistake me for someone who is well connected. I Google myself. I Google my film. I Google Laura. I watch YouTube interviews with Mike Leigh.

I log in and out of my online banking. I have £21.05. I flush, even though there's no one else in the room. I spend a lot of time trying to remind myself that being poor is synonymous with being young (or, young-ish) and creative. It's a part of my story, or it will be when I'm successful. I picture myself in the future, regaling a table of ethnically and sexually diverse artists about how I used to find bristles in my mouth because I didn't have the money for a new toothbrush. It makes me feel better. Some of the time.

When I get my next cup of tea, I notice that Mum has fallen asleep in front of the TV, so I take her cup and rinse it. I turn the volume down slightly, but not enough so her ears will register the difference. The huge blue light of the screen bounces off her highlights, and for a moment, she looks soft. I almost feel like touching her. She was always the oldest mum at the school gates, something I wouldn't have noticed if she hadn't gone to such pains to conceal it from everyone. Her fiftieth birthday passed unremarked upon; her sixtieth must have passed already. I know that her younger sister, Aunt Eleanor, is fifty-five, because Aunt Eleanor has birthday parties like a normal person.

Satisfied that she's asleep, I open my laptop again. I log out of CharlieReganDirector@gmail.com and into LottieMinxxx@yahoo.co.uk. There's only one email waiting for me, even though I haven't checked it in a week.

> Hey baby girl ... loved the video you made me. So fucking hottt, but could you be sucking on something for the next one? Love those tiny little tits xxxxx could do $200 for a new video or $50 for a photo set? 4–6 high res imgs would be fine xxx

They're always like this. When I temped in an office last year, someone told me that managers learn to give criticism by using the 'shit sandwich' method. You say one nice thing, one piece of critique, and then end on a nice thing. The few men I make videos for all have a thing for girls with small boobs and skinny hips, so that's what they compliment me on. They think we've come together over a shared appreciation of my deficiencies, as if I were an unusual hobby. A ship built inside a bottle.

I unzip my bag to see if my camera is charged. It is.

> Could do a set for you right now. $170. Xx

He's emailing from somewhere in America so won't respond right away. I know the answer will be yes, though. It always is.

I didn't bring my make-up bag with me, so I wander into

Mum and Dad's room. Mum's selection is nowhere near as good as Laura's but it does the job when it has to. Crusty Max Factor concealer, lipstick the colour of rotting plums, blush that goes on like dust from a chalk board. I remember how Laura and I used to obsess over creating the perfect 'smoky eye', watching YouTube tutorials before big nights out.

'You have a face that's good for make-up,' she used to say, while soft brushes flickered on my face, the bridge of her hand resting warmly on my cheek.

'Are you saying I'd make a good "before and after" picture?'

'Yes, Charlie, that's exactly what I'm saying.'

She always said that I should learn to take a compliment. Instead, I learned something else: how to apply make-up in such a way that you don't feel like yourself any more.

I find an old eyeshadow palette, all blues and navies, and top it off with some liquid liner I had in my bag. I comb my brows into place, colouring them with a soft, nutty brown lip-liner that I'm pretty sure hasn't been opened since the nineties. I turn my camera on, and look around for something to suck. There's a Mitchum deodorant bottle that might do the trick. I test it around my newly glossy mouth. Fine.

Maybe I can use the money to buy me and Laura a big boozy lunch. She doesn't know about any of this. The porn, I mean. Laura's parents are so rich that she never thinks to question why a person might have no money one week and a windfall the next.

When we were at Uni, there was a real explosion in selling your tits online for cash, particularly among the few women on our filmmaking course. These were girls who knew their way around a camera, and it was generally accepted that if you kept your face out of the pictures, no harm could really come of it. I never bothered participating, partly for feminist reasons, but mostly because there's not a lot of money in being anonymous *and* flat-chested.

Eventually, the bubble burst. The bottom fell out of the top, as it were. Too many girls were doing it and pretty soon a picture of your breasts (nipples uncovered) with your face cropped out couldn't buy you a pint and a sandwich. Nipples covered wouldn't get you a bag of crisps.

But faces. Faces is where the money is. And my face – even though it's a flat, muddy-eyed, sloppy-mouthed face – netted me some quick cash when Dad was first in and out of hospital and I had to keep cancelling job interviews to grab the train home. Plus, it felt transgressive and rebellious to create a porn studio in my bedroom while my mother asked me pointed questions about what I was going to 'do' with my degree. And why else do you get a film degree, if not to feel transgressive and rebellious?

I text Laura.

**You around Saturday? xx**

# 3

Mum is all sunshine the next morning, hyper and bustling and determined to be useful. She pulls back the curtains while I'm still in bed. I scramble around, blearily trying to make sure that the debris from last night's photo shoot is covered up. *Please don't pick up the deodorant bottle.*

'You got a letter,' she says.

'From who?'

'Well, *I* don't know,' she says, the 'duh' implicit. 'But it's thick. And it's not junk mail. Did you apply to one of those postgraduate courses I told you about?'

I still get everything sent to my parents' house. Even letters. I'm pretty sure my mother steams open at least half of my post before she hands it to me, but given the regularity with which post goes missing in my building, it's worth it. The amount of times I've come through the hallway to find the doors on the postboxes broken open, their flimsy locks waving like hitchhikers' thumbs, have been too many to count.

'Where is it, then?'

'Downstairs. Kitchen.'

'You couldn't have just brought it up?'

'You know I don't open post upstairs. It just creates clutter.'

I pull on my hoodie and make my way to the breakfast table.

The envelope is thick, like my mother said it was. I squint

at the stamps. The Queen is curiously absent from this letter. Instead, a small brown bird. Mum walks into the room with freshly ironed pyjamas for Dad.

'It's from Ireland,' she says neutrally.

'You've looked at it?'

'I just saw the bird. I wasn't holding it over the kettle or anything.'

We stand there for a moment, looking at the letter as though it came from another planet.

I never went to Ireland, but I went to Catholic school. Even on this, my dad would flip-flop constantly. He himself was an atheist: he stood outside the church during my Communion, waited in the pub for my Confirmation. 'Why did you *send* me if you weren't even going to join in?' I whinged. I couldn't fathom the point of religion unless it was going to bring me closer to him.

'It was a notion I had,' he would reply. 'Anyway, everyone needs something to fight against.'

He taught me words and phrases *as Gaeilge* when the mood took him. I still repeat them to myself around the house, loose nouns that lack the context of grammar or basic sentence formation. I whispered '*bainne*' to the milk and '*ispiní*' to the sausages. We ate no Irish meals, wore no Claddagh rings, but Dad always talked about our family as though it were as much Irish as it was English. It was like he wanted to remind everyone where he came from, but didn't want to be reminded of it himself. His adolescence – the period after the accident, but before he moved to England – was almost never spoken about.

All the same, it was something that Dad and I had that Mum didn't have. We were Irish, and she was English. She was from Waddington and had one sister and no stories.

I open the envelope, and a chubby brochure for the Cork Film Festival slides out.

Dear Charlotte Regan,

Many thanks for your application and your interest in our festival. Our panel very much enjoyed your debut feature, *It Takes a Village*, and I am delighted to invite you to participate in the Cork Film Festival programme, running 1–20 May.

Your film has been selected to run in our Young Voices of Ireland category, alongside three other entries, detailed in the programme attached. The screening will take place at the Triskel Arts Centre on Friday 4 May at 2 p.m. sharp. You are permitted to bring one guest. Subsequent tickets can be purchased from our box office.

Warmly yours,

Kate McKenna

Programme Director

Cork Film Festival

I yelp and show Mum the letter.

'That's only three weeks away,' she says, and for a moment I think she's about to congratulate me. 'Maybe someone else dropped out.'

I start walking away from her, realising that it's pointless to discuss this with my mother and still feel proud of myself.

'You're not *going*, are you?'

I take the letter to my room. Lying on my bed, I can't stop grinning as I read the letter over and over.

Me and Laura are going to *Ireland*. The place I've been hearing about and defining myself by for my entire life, but have never actually visited. Ireland! I hold the letter up to my face, trying to detect a smell, a mood, anything that marks it with destiny.

The worst thing about going to an all-girls Catholic school in England wasn't the nuns, or the constant preparing for some kind of elaborate mass, or the homophobia. It was the fact that everyone else was second-generation Irish too, and better at doing it than I was. They went to Wexford or Donegal or Mayo on their school holidays. They all talked about how their uncles were killed in the Troubles, and how the family still held a mass for them every year. And then there was me, the person with the most tragically Irish back-story of all, and I hadn't even been. I bothered my parents about it constantly, but I always got the same line: *If we're going to leave the country, Charlie, then we're going to leave it for a bit of sun.*

Of course, the older I got the more I realised that the girls in my class were visiting family in Ireland, and that without living relatives, we were spiritually without a visa. Once I got old enough to go by myself, I was either too poor to afford a holiday or too preoccupied by Dad's illness to leave the country. Anything could happen, after all. He could take a turn for the worse, and where would I be? On a fucking jolly.

It's one of the many things that make me wish for siblings. I have a wealth of imaginary siblings, each with their own specific function. There's Dee, the reliable married older sister who drives down from Manchester whenever there's a problem; Andrew, my silly handsome younger brother with a range of dumb girlfriends; Simon, the careful, quiet brother, the one who is in the middle with me and is gay or, in some fantasies, trans. I told Laura about my imaginary siblings once and she teased me, calling it 'the cutest thing I have ever heard'.

'Do you only children ever think about anything that isn't being only children?'

Downstairs, I can feel tremors of my mother's anxiety rising through the floorboards. She's always baulked at Dad's and my talk of Irishness, and was icily disapproving of me interviewing him when he first got sick. She didn't see the point of remembering, much less recording, the Clipim disaster, which feels rich for a woman who spends every evening gawping at dramatised versions of true-life stories on the Hallmark Channel.

When I show Dad later that day, he's so excited that he loses the line in his arm.

'I like to talk with my hands,' he tells the nurse who graciously reattaches it for him. 'My daughter has just won a prize, you see. For her film.'

He is excited, and so goes heavy on the 'u' in film. *Filum*.

'Dad, I haven't won a prize. I'm just in the running.'

'Her film is about me,' he says and the nurse nods warmly at me.

'We've heard all about you,' she says in a softly Caribbean voice.

'Joy is from an island too,' my dad says, as if this clarifies the matter. 'It's why we're such good friends, isn't it, Joy?'

When his nurse leaves, he reads the letter again. First to himself, then out loud. When he's done, he reaches out to squeeze my shoulder.

'Well, look at that. Look at that,' he says, eyes shining. He is in an emotional mood today and I wonder if they have given him morphine again. 'You'll have to go, of course. I know Cork isn't Dublin, Charlie, but it's a great town. As a Kerryman I'm not supposed to say that, but it is. Very arty. They'll appreciate it there, Charlie. They'll get it the way the Brits just won't.'

'Colm. She can't *go*.'

Mum is in the doorway again with yet more snacks. I'm starting to wonder whether she prefers the staff at Tesco Express to me and Dad.

'What are you on about, Sharon? She has to go. It's her homecoming.'

'Ireland isn't her home. She's never bloody been there. She's an English girl, raised in England. And you're too sick.'

I bite my lip. What remains of my teenage instinct wants to remind them that I am almost thirty years old, merely home for a few days to see my sick father, and that it's not up to them whether I go to Ireland or not. But Mum does have a point: I can't just run off to Ireland when Dad is lying in hospital. Can I?

'I'm not *too sick*,' Dad says, bringing his hand down on the tray where a half-eaten Hoisin duck wrap sits. 'And anyway, it's Charlie who's going, not me. And I'm not going anywhere. She'll get back and I'll still be rotting away here, listening to that *miserable fucker* next to me.'

Corned Beef looks over at us, startled. Dad's voice is loud now. He is irritable, cranky and definitely not on morphine. My dad doesn't ever swear, and certainly not in public. His accent is getting stronger. It's been doing that, since he got sick. When I was a kid and he was working on building sites, I hardly ever noticed his Irish accent. He said he learned to hide it in the 1970s, when he briefly lived in Birmingham and the Irish were, in his words, 'public enemy number one'. He experimented with being Canadian, because he couldn't do a proper American accent, and back then nobody really knew what Canadians sounded like.

The last few years have changed all that. In the early stages of his sickness he started sewing the threadbare fringe of an accent back into his voice. If you're listening for it, you can hear it growing across the eleven recorded interviews that formed my script. I liked to think that talking about Ireland encouraged him to sound more Irish.

'Charlie, if you have to cut the top off a turnip and ride it there, you're going to Cork,' he insists, before turning back to Mum. 'She can't keep sitting around waiting for her life to start. Running down here on weekends. Never going out with anyone, never going out with friends, no romances. Christ, Sharon, do you want to keep us both prisoner?'

Mum starts digging her thumbnail into the armrest on her chair. She is in the good armchair, the one for wives and next of kin. It's made of red plastic leather and isn't comfortable, but comes with a certain level of status that her character won't expand to fit. There is a long, long silence as Mum looks at her hands and Dad looks at his duck wrap. Eventually, she brings her finger to her face and wipes away a fat, mortified tear.

This isn't fair and I know it isn't. Mum is the one who made him get check-ups. Mum was the one who suspected that the cancer had come back. Mum made every appointment, pushed every doctor, called about MRI results while Dad carried on as if everything was ordinary. And he resented her for it.

Eventually, I start to speak.

'Mum's right. I shouldn't be planning trips. Not while you're in here. Not while everything's so . . . '

'Charlie,' he says, suddenly exhausted. 'You have to go. See Cork. Tell me what it's like. I haven't been there since 1971. For the love of God, if not for yourself, then go so I can have something new to think about. Don't say you don't have the money. I'll give you a couple hundred.'

'I could even visit Clip,' I say. 'It wouldn't be too long a journey from Cork to Clip, would it, Dad?'

He shakes his head. 'That miserable old rock? I wouldn't bother. The ferry hardly runs any more, anyway.'

'But people live there, don't they?'

'Clipim is three old men with four teeth between them. Trust me. It's not somewhere you want to visit. You'd only be wasting your time.'

Mum has started unpacking pyjamas from the Bag for Life she brought in earlier.

'These are clean,' she says, as if the conversation were not still happening.

'Get her money out of the Credit Union, will you, Shar? You will, won't you?'

She nods without looking at us. 'I will.'

Later that night, Mum leaves her debit card on the kitchen table with a Post-it on it that just says 'flights', her way of saying that she will support the trip financially if not morally. The Ryanair flights might only cost £70 a head, but it's still not the kind of money my parents are able to part with lightly. Mum had been working in the John Lewis in Chelmsford before this most recent sickness, and the loss of income was heavy on her lifestyle. By 'lifestyle', I mean: 'ability to throw away bananas without worrying'.

I take down the card details anyway. There's no winning with some people, and I could wait a lifetime to win with her.

# 4

For a brief time during Uni, I went through a phase of hating my father. Or, at least saying I did. My heart was never really in it. I loved my dad, and he so badly loved me. Has always loved me.

'Fuck my dad,' I'd say, for no reason, regardless of whether or not dads were part of the conversation. It felt like a powerful thing to say, and it was never challenged by the other gay girls that I hung out with.

'Fuck *my* dad,' my friend Liz would counter, doubling down on the aggression, making the hatred feel communal and sisterly. We were all reading Valerie Solanas at the time, and were fans of her theory that the purpose of fathers was to 'corrode the world with maleness'. I don't think any of us had a real problem with our dads, particularly. I think we just liked saying the word 'corrode'.

I had met Liz and Aisha after attending a Freshers' Week queer night that was almost exclusively attended by boys. They were skinny and shiny-eyed and determined to throw off the shackles of their homophobic small towns, and equally determined to tell you about it. We stood and watched and waited for the other girls to show up, and when they didn't, we decided to make friends with each other. It never quite worked. Our energies were too similar. The three of us had grown up nervous and lonely, and we resented spending our

Uni days gazing into mirror reflections of that alienation. But still, it was something.

'Fuck my dad *and* my mum,' Aisha would finally finish, and we would each issue a low, damp laugh to show that it was time for us to walk to the vending machine.

When I got back from Christmas break, I found out that Aisha and Liz were together, and that I was on my own again. I wasn't supposed to be, not technically: they were constantly reassuring me that this changed nothing, that they would still come to those painful queer club nights, that we would still go inter-railing that summer. Nonetheless, one Wednesday in February, I found myself swaying alone to La Roux's 'Bulletproof' with one eye on the door, waiting for them, or anyone, to show up and save me.

And then I saw her.

She was wearing a policewoman's outfit from Ann Summers, and she was surrounded by lads. Not the Bambi-featured, beautiful nineteen-year-old boys that I was used to seeing at the queer nights, but *lads*. Men-in-training. Huge country boys who I only ever saw queuing for breakfast sandwiches at the petrol station opposite my halls, and who were perpetually eating or shouting or drinking bottles of Lucozade. They were exploding through the dance floor, evidently furious at whatever club they had just been kicked out of, and determined to take it out on us. They formed one of those rugby huddles in the middle of the room, booming the lyrics tunelessly.

'THIS TIME MAYBE. I'LL BE—'

The girl dipped in and out of my vision, blonde hair flowing out of her plastic black cap. She was dancing with a boy. She was going to the bar. She was looking for a lighter, miming the flicking action with her hands.

'BULLETTTTTTTT PROOF.'

I remember thinking of Valerie Solanas then. The woman

who shot Andy Warhol, and who wanted an all-woman soci-
ety. I could feel myself tapping into the same rage that must
have driven her. Why do they get everything? Why do they
get to be everywhere? Can't there be this one thing, just for us?

I shoved a boy. He shoved me back. I elbowed him in the
ribs, and turned to go. He stopped me, wrapped his arms
around my torso, and picked me up. He spun me around and
around, the sweat soaking through his shirt and on to my
body, the smell of Lynx, ketchup and Hugo Boss smearing
on to my skin. I wanted to be sick.

'Jez!' I heard a voice say. 'Put that girl *down*.'

He looked over his shoulder but seemed unwilling to give
up so easily. I wriggled my head free. It was the girl. The
policewoman.

'I'm only having a laugh, Laura,' the boy said defensively.

Without a word, she sprang forward, attached herself to him
in an involuntary piggyback, and – very deliberately – bit him
on the side of the face. He screamed, released me, called her
a rabid cunt, and went to report the matter to the other men.

She grabbed my hand.

'Are you okay?'

That's how I met Laura.

After a brief, crushed cigarette in the too-full smoking area
we left and went to a shisha bar. It felt like a wildly exciting
thing to do, to even think of doing.

'Can we just ... do that?' I asked, not exactly sure
what I meant.

'Oh.' She nodded, looking down at her police officer cos-
play. 'You're right. Give me your jacket? They probably won't
mind. But, y'know. Respect for their culture.'

I was delighted that Laura thought I was respectful of
shisha code of conduct (the existence of which I knew nothing) and delirious that she would want to wear my coat. I
slunk it off my shoulders and gave it to her.

'God, you're so tiny. Lucky bitch. My tits explode out of everything, especially when I'm on my period. They're like rocks, right now.'

She briefly looked at her breasts as though they were two troublesome goats, perpetually stuck in the fence at the edge of her property. We went inside. No one minded about the policewoman's outfit. We ate dates and drank sweet tea until three in the morning, the taste like perfume in my mouth.

I hold off on telling Laura about the Cork Film Festival until I see her for lunch on Saturday. This is mostly because every meeting with Laura lately is so peppered by her endless stream of Exciting News that I have learned to hold some of my news back to make it seem like there's stuff going on in my life, too.

It's not how I'm used to communicating with her. After that first night in the shisha bar our friendship became a round-the-clock commitment. For a long time, I assumed that Laura's interest in me was as fleeting as her interest in the boys she had saved me from, and so treated her presence in my life as though I were a small city that had somehow ended up hosting the Olympic Games.

I stretched every resource I had to facilitate her: going to parties I would never usually go to, societies I was too terrified to join, student protests where I had no idea what, exactly, I was marching against. We ran *Venus in Film*, a feminist film newsletter that ran for three issues and mostly consisted of Laura furiously re-explaining the Bechdel test and me tentatively writing about why films like *Hocus Pocus* were 'secretly feminist'. We loved feminism as long as things were 'secretly' feminist, because it saved us the intellectual rigour of having to read books like *The Second Sex* or *The Feminine Mystique*, which nobody wanted to do. We felt the same way about indie filmmakers. It was far better to dig through the films we had already seen and find new meaning in them because it saved us from the jealousy of watching people whose careers were blossoming in real time. It was not a good newsletter.

In second year we became housemates and it became clear that, for whatever reason, Laura was here to stay. We spent every moment together in our scummy little house-share, took all the same classes, had all the same ambitions. We never wanted to date the same gender, so there was never any romantic overlap. She was more interested in the tech side of filmmaking, while I was more into the writing, so we never fought over scripts or camera angles. We sailed along in happy codependence for all of Uni, and then spent a few years in a house-share in Clapham with six other twenty-one-year-olds who self-defined as artists. We all made short films together with equipment stolen from our runner jobs. We told ourselves it was okay, because it was for our art. Each of us was convinced that *Toilet: The Talk Show* – a show where we took turns to interview each other while on the loo – was the height of gonzo-style filmmaking, and would definitely become a YouTube sensation. If we ever bothered to upload it to YouTube, that is.

Eventually, people started to move out. They got sick of being poor, so they moved in with their boyfriends or they moved home. Laura and I were disgusted. We knew that we had traded our right to economic solvency when we made the decision to become artists. But we also knew that what we got in the trade was much more valuable: the ability to make our early twenties last as long as we wanted them to. We interviewed new housemates based on who was talented and we wanted to sleep with, which worked beautifully for a while. When we got bored of being the 'legacy tenants', we decided to share a one-room place in West Norwood, where we made *Village*.

But now, post-Clapham, post-Laura in West Norwood,

post-my utter failure to move through life at the same veloc-
ity as she seems able to, everything is different. Strange.
Strained. I try to pretend I don't know why, and that it has
nothing to do with the night before she moved out, back in
October. When the dynamic in our relationship began its
slow shift from deeply intimate to affectionately casual.

I meet her at The Water Poet, because it's near Shoreditch
High Street and therefore mere minutes from her new front
door. She's still twenty minutes late, her long blonde hair in
a Dutch-girl plait around the crown of her head. I wave at
her and get halfway out of my seat, wondering if I should
get up and give her a big hug like old friends are meant to.
*It's only been two weeks, Charlie, since you last saw her,* I remind
myself. *You saw her at a wedding literally two weeks ago. Relax.*
The end result is a cramped half-hug that makes me look like
Quasimodo hurling himself at Esmeralda.

'All right, Heidi!' I say, motioning at her hair. 'How's
it going?'

'What?' she replies, already opening the menu. She fingers
her head. 'Oh. This. Sorry, my hair was greasy, so I thought
I'd pin it up off my face. Bit minging, but you know.'

I have literally seen bridesmaids with worse than hair this,
but I let it go.

'So what's going on? Any news?'

Of course. There's news. There's always news, but before
she tells it to me, she has to produce a loud, lip-flapping
exhale that lets me know just how exhausting and tedious
her activities are.

'Christ, where to start? Well, we've just wrapped on
*Britain's Deadliest Plants*, which was what you can charitably
call 'an experience'. Honestly, mate, you'd think there'd be
more deadly plants around, but the only stories we could get
were about fucking mushrooms. Which, you know, fine. It's
good to have a couple of bits about how some mushrooms

can be poisonous, but when you've sold a show to Channel 5 about Britain's deadliest plants? You can't just pivot to it being about Britain's deadliest mushrooms.'

I know this isn't glamorous work. I know there's nothing artistically satisfying about interviewing ten people, all with the same mushroom story, but I feel a surge of envy when she talks about it. She's still in the industry, still working her way up, still training her camera on the unsuspecting British public. Every day she hones her skill a little more, and moves another space away from me on the game board of our lives. Every step is a ladder for her, and I don't even have the drama and chaos of a snake.

'What about you, anyway? How's your dad?'

'He's . . . fine.'

I never know how to respond to this question. He is not fine. He is waiting on yet another round of chemo that will guarantee either a long, slow painful recovery or a long, slow, painful death. There is nothing *fine* about any of this, but in this new bizarre framework of parental illness, we have decided it's fine. He is not in immediate danger; he is not in torturous pain; he is not dying this week. This is what 'fine' is now.

She looks at me searchingly. 'How are you?'

'Also fine.'

'So you're both fine, then.'

'Is that so hard to believe?'

'Under the circumstances? A little, yes.'

A waitress appears and I am momentarily relieved of having to talk about my dad's illness. I try to shift the mood of our lunch into a more jolly upswing. We so rarely get to do this kind of thing any more, and I'm determined that it doesn't become one of those maudlin friend meet-ups where she feels generous for having met up with me but doesn't actually have a good time.

'Drinks, ladies?'

'We'll take a bottle of your cheapest, reddest wine, please,' I say, my voice trying for *AbFab* and landing somewhere in *EastEnders*. 'Two glasses.'

'Uhm ...' Laura is still looking at the menu. Since when did she become too good for the cheapest, reddest wine?

'We can spring for the second-cheapest bottle of wine if it means so much to you.'

'No, it's not that. I just don't want to get *drunk*, y'know? I have some editing to do tonight.'

I start to panic.

'But we're celebrating,' I blurt out. Both Laura and the waitress exchange a look, as if deciding who is responsible for me.

'What are we celebrating?'

'Bring us the bottle,' I say to the waitress, and she goes. Laura's eyes are on me. I feel a surge of power. I fish the crumpled letter for the Cork Film Festival out of my coat pocket. She reads it silently first, and then aloud.

'Well, *fuck*!' She says finally.

'Right?'

'If *Ireland* likes the movie ...'

'I know! Then it must be ... good, right?'

'Right,' she says. 'Or at least accurate.'

This is a tender issue for us. We have made a film about rural Ireland without setting foot in the country once, which didn't seem to matter so much to people in the UK, but we knew could go down badly with the Irish themselves. All through making it, I batted down questions about authenticity by saying that, as a half-Irish woman, I was more than capable of depicting this story. Plus, we had my dad. The only eyewitness you need, for a story like this. Who could accuse me of cultural appropriation? We were bulletproof.

But when it came to actually applying to Irish festivals, I

had stumbled over every line of my written testimony. Who was I to make this film? What did I know?

'We have to go,' Laura says decisively, and then stops herself. 'I mean, if you *can* go, we should go.'

'Please. Dad basically begged me to go. He said he'll even pay for flights. This means the world to him.'

The waitress returns with our bottle of wine, and Laura is whipping out her phone to sort dates.

'This is perfect,' she says, taking a big glug out of her glass. 'I don't start my new job until June, so May is ideal.'

'Wait, what? New job?'

'That was the other thing I wanted to tell you about,' she says. Laura takes a deep, exaggerated breath.

Oh, God. News. Why does she always have to have *news*?

'I've been offered a year-long contract, Charlie.'

'Oh? That's great.'

'In LA.'

For a moment, I'm totally speechless. The next year of my life unfolds in front of me like a paper fortune-teller, each tab revealing its own brand of isolation: Dad gone, Laura gone, zero professional prospects, a side-hustle in cheap porn and a mother who thinks working in a cafe is a shrewd career move. *Don't go*, I beg her silently. *Don't go, don't go, don't go.*

'That's amazing,' I say, my mind racing with accusations. *How fucking dare you? My dad is dying, you heartless cunt.*

She pulls a book out of her bag, a hardback with dog-eared pages and covered in Post-its. 'It's called *American Taste*. It's about ranch hands in Texas. Think *Sons of Anarchy*, but you know, cows instead of motorbikes. And in the 1930s.'

I hold the book, my wrists suddenly feeling so weak that I almost drop it. This book has prestige written all over it: it has that Dad Book air of importance and respectability, and is covered in quotes from the *Wall Street Journal* and the *New*

*York Times.* This isn't just a tiny show that Laura has been asked to be on. She has been asked to join a machine.

I want to vomit.

'This so, so, so amazing,' I say, and then I excuse myself to sit on the lid of the disabled toilet for as long as I think I can get away with it.

# 5

Right up until I see her at Stansted Airport, I am sure – absolutely, in-my-bones sure – that Laura is going to call and cancel.

As passionate as I am about this plan to go to Ireland, part of me wants it to go completely awry before it even begins. Laura could have a job that she can't turn down, or the Cork Film Festival could suddenly change their minds. Being around Mum the last few days has given me a sense of dread around the whole event, despite Dad's continued enthusiasm. He's home now, for the time being. Stable enough to sit, watch the snooker all day and take an enormous pill every three hours.

'Are you *sure* Laura is going to be able to make it?' Mum says, driving me to the airport. 'Just that, she's so busy, I'm surprised she can find the time.'

'She's coming, Mum,' I reply, but uncertainty creeps into my voice.

My brain keeps insisting on a kind of crooked logic where, if the Cork Film Festival never actually happens, then Laura and I won't be able to have our last hurrah. I'm not ready to have a last hurrah with Laura. This film was supposed to be our beginning, not our golden age.

I picture her 'year-long' contract in LA. It will be extended, of course, and her life will morph into a series of rituals that are totally unfamiliar to me. I can see it all so clearly for her. I can see her with a walkie-talkie and a baseball cap, her ponytail pulled smoothly through the back, organising extras on set as though she were hostessing a costume party. I can see her two stone lighter, her beautiful plushness all gone, sacrificed to hot yoga and matcha tea. I can see her typing frazzled, giddy messages to me – 'Skype soon!' – and I can see myself avoiding the Skype, because my room will never be quite clean enough and my achievements will never be quite good enough. I will make exactly one visit to LA, and then never go again. I will move further and further down Laura's Christmas card list, until one day I'll slide off it altogether, and on to her biographer's index.

Regan, Charlotte. Student film collaborator. Pp. 12–13, 17, 32.

But Laura, to my surprise, is actually excited about Cork. She slings an arm around me when she sees me.

'All right, pal,' she says, planting a big kiss on the side of my face. 'Ready for *Who Do You Think You Are?*, the no-budget, non-celebrity version?'

I smile, realising that one of the key upsides to this trip is that I'm spending four days with Laura. Even if it is more of a farewell than a celebration.

'You realise that my family's from Kerry, not Cork? That there's no *Who Do You Think You Are?* element to this trip?'

'Sure there is,' she says, pointing at the SLR around her neck. 'I'm making it into one. I'm going to get you looking at census records and crying about how "everything makes sense" now that you've returned to your ancestral homeland. Don't worry, I have it all figured out.'

She looks at my shoulder and spots that I am also carrying

my camera bag. Nowhere near as nice as her Nikon, but heavy nonetheless.

'Christ, what are we like?'

I laugh and punch her on the shoulder. I love how game she is. I spot that book again in her hands, *American Taste*. The bookmark has moved a good two hundred pages since I saw her last. She clocks me looking and crams it back into her handbag.

'Come on, I need to put my liquids into a plastic thingy.'

As we queue up for security, sandwich bags full of make-up clutched in our hands, Laura leans over to me.

'I bet you I get searched,' she says, conspiratorially. 'They always fucking search me.'

We watch the people ahead of us, who are all gliding through the metal detectors without incident.

'Look,' she says, pointing at a stocky woman in her late-forties with latex gloves on. 'I bet you she tries to feel me up.'

I shove her. 'Fancy yourself, much?'

She shrugs, a strand of ice-blonde hair falling into her face. She blows it off her nose.

'Old dykes like that *always* go for me.'

I actually gape at her, but Laura just laughs.

'Oh, like you're so surprised,' she says. She's beckoned forward, and slides her bags on to the scanner. I watch her unlace her boots and place them in a tray, still shocked she would talk that way. *Old dykes like that.*

*Like what?*

I step forward and start mechanically unzipping my bag, placing my laptop into the large plastic tray. Laura is queuing at the metal detectors. I keep flitting between her and the dark-haired woman in the latex gloves. It's so strange, this part of the airport, people padding about in their socks. It makes everyone look like they're at a big sleepover.

Every night was a sleepover when we lived together, in

that queen-sized bed in West Norwood. Two plug-in heaters, constantly turned on and turning the air stale. They did next to nothing to warm us, and they flared up Laura's asthma. *Feel how cold I am, Charlie. Feel.*

We took turns at who was the big spoon and who was the little one. Laura would complain that I was too thin, too many bones, and that made me a terrible big spoon. But I liked feeling as though I was protecting her. Like I was her scrawny little guard dog, protecting her from the draught coming in from the single-glazed windows. There was no question that she was the superior big spoon: all marshmallow curves and hair that would occasionally float over my shoulder so it looked like I had the kind of princess femininity that came so easily to her.

It's finally Laura's turn to walk through the metal detectors and, sure enough, the alarm goes off. She is asked to stand to one side and check her pockets for coins, jewellery, stray bits of tinfoil.

There came a day, probably a day quite soon after she decided that she was serious about Mike, that she didn't like joking so much about our living situation. She stopped laughingly referring to us as an old married couple, and stopped feeling that our arrangement was charmingly bohemian. By the time she had moved out, we weren't spooning any more. She had picked up a new phrase from one of her new work friends: 'not cute'.

Using leftover cereal milk for tea was not cute. Substituting shampoo with Fairy Liquid was not cute. Spooning your best friend to sleep was, despite previous assertions from our Clapham friends who thought we were adorable, *not cute*.

The woman in the latex gloves points at Laura to call her over. Laura puts out her arms, like Jesus on the cross. She looks over her shoulder at me and mouths: *Told you.*

The woman traces her detector along Laura's arms

dispassionately, then down the side of her body. I can feel my face burning red. She runs her hands under Laura's bra strap, around her back, and down her trouser leg. I walk through the metal detectors, hoping that I will also be searched. That would shut Laura up, I think. Who the fuck does she think she is, anyway?

I'm nodded through. I collect my things from the grey tray and decant them back into my luggage. Laura appears at my elbow.

'What did I tell you?' She says, triumphant. 'I don't know what it is about me. When Mike and I went to Athens, the two women on security both had a go.'

*Yeah, Laura, who knows what women see in you. What a mystery. What a huge fucking mystery.*

'Maybe they're just doing their job,' I say. 'Have you considered that?'

It comes out snappy, snappier than I ever am with Laura. She surveys me, and quickly realises that I do not find any of this funny. We walk in silence through the gleaming hall of perfume, whisky, watches and Toblerone.

'Do you want to have a look?' she asks, a hint of anxiety in her voice. 'I could buy us some travel sweets.'

'No, thanks.'

'Okay.'

Has she forgotten about that bedroom in West Norwood, or does she just prefer not to think about it? Does it matter, now that it's all over?

'You can buy me a pint, though, if you want,' I say, breaking the silence. 'Let's go over the plan.'

'There is no plan,' she responds, affecting an Irish accent. 'There is only destiny.'

The flight is so short that I am once again embarrassed at never having taken it before. This whole time, I could have been flitting between Ireland and London, getting to know my roots. My *roots*. It feels like an insane term to use. It sits in my mind, as foreign and waxy as a Hershey's Bar.

Europeans don't go searching for their 'roots'; Americans do. They lost their history in exchange for prosperity, and the especially rich ones pledge their summers in an attempt to swap back. They dump sacks of money on open-top London bus tours, Harry & Meghan china plates and, I suppose, Ireland.

It costs £10 more to sit next to the person you're travelling with on a Ryanair flight, so we're sitting apart. I'm sitting next to a couple from New York – 'New York *state*,' says the woman, with short grey hair and an Art teacher vibe. They are on their third leg of a trip that they have been saving for for a long time. 'Eight years,' she says cheerfully. 'Well, a little *over* eight years.'

I wonder what happened a 'little over' eight years ago that has fused the date so firmly into her mind. Did they have kids to worry about before that, and no money to spare on savings? Did she survive a brush with breast cancer, provoking a who-am-I existential crisis?

'Phil's people are from Limerick, but my family are Polish,' she goes on, and I can tell by the way her husband is crossing his arms and pretending to sleep that he would rather she didn't speak to everyone they met. 'So we went to the Warsaw ghettos, to see if we could find anything. A distant cousin, or anyone who remembered them, you know?'

I am about to ask her if she did find anyone, but she cuts across me, eager to skip the suspense of her inevitable disappointment. 'We didn't, but you know, we had a lovely time.'

'I hope you have better luck with Phil's family,' I say, and I mean it. Living in London has made me cruel towards tourists. Overly cruel, and if I'm completely honest, it's not just because they crowd the Underground in the summertime.

There's something cosmopolitan about hating tourists, and there's a tendency to lean into that hatred if you feel only marginally less lost in your city than they do.

I can't hate them now. I am one of them. My father is dying, and I am visiting Ireland before the dynamite fuse of blood connection burns out. It's embarrassing to admit, even to myself. You never hear of a French person trying to discover their heritage in Russia. They just call themselves French and get on with it.

Laura and I meet up again at passport control.

'How was your flight?'

'Okay.'

'I saw that woman chatting the ear off of you. I bet you *loved* that.'

'She was really nice, actually,' I say snappishly, partly defensive of Maureen from New York state, and partly furious about her 'old dykes' comment. Laura is perplexed that I'm still annoyed. I've never stayed mad at her for longer than five minutes before. She finds the Europcar kiosk and leaves me standing with the bags, watching people greet their returning family members.

The only thing that distinguishes Cork Airport from any other small airport is how much crying there is. Everywhere I look, there's a disturbing outpouring of emotion. Mothers clinging to their twenty-something children; fathers going misty-eyed; paper 'Welcome Home Sadbh!' signs being held by toddlers with puffer jackets over their *Frozen* pyjamas.

How can anyone muster this much feeling for a flight from London?

'It looks like Essex,' Laura says, and she's right. As we drive from Cork Airport to our hostel in the city, there's no doubt that it looks like every piece of English countryside I've ever seen. An initially promising spread of trees and shrubbery quickly melts into petrol stations, roundabouts and a sad-looking Travelodge. I sit in the passenger seat, willing myself to feel a connection with this anonymous landscape. Laura eyes me slyly, one hand on the steering wheel.

'Feeling at home, buddy?'

'Shut up.'

'Are you beginning to realise that Ireland, like every other white Western country in the history of ever, isn't so magic after all?'

'Shut UP.'

'Look, there's a sign for a McDonald's. Maybe they'll give you, like, a blood pudding Big Mac. With bacon and cabbage.'

That's the trouble with knowing someone as well as I know Laura. She remembers everything: every dumb thing I've said about how I can't wait to visit Ireland; every time I referred to myself as 'half-Irish'; every instance where I referred to it, half-joking but at the same time not-at-all jokingly, as the motherland. She's not spiteful, but she is amused.

When Laura and I moved into our Clapham house-share, she made fun of me for ticking 'White British' and 'Irish' on our tenancy forms. But that's how I felt. How I had felt my entire life, right up until the moment I boarded the plane. Now, I feel like a pretender. The only connection I have to this place is rotting in a hospital bed in Essex, and I'm *here*. I can feel my mum's wary disapproval radiating from across the Irish Sea. This isn't good daughterhood. This isn't good anything. This is going on a jolly.

Laura turns into the city. There's a huge classical-looking building, with Greek columns.

'Turn left at City Hall,' says the satnav helpfully.

'I guess the English built that,' says Laura. 'That's very much our aesthetic, right? Ripping off shit from the Romans?'

'Yeah,' I respond. 'Colonialism is a hell of a drug.'

I feel underwhelmed and nauseous, even though nothing

has happened yet. No one has been rude to me, nothing has officially disappointed me. It's not even had the chance to. But I had expected, in some silly way, to put my feet on the tarmac and to feel *something*. Some click, some tremor from the country to say that it had expected me and was glad that I was home. Instead, I saw tarmac and a Costa Coffee with the shutters half pulled down.

'Turn right over St Patrick's Bridge,' chimes the satnav, after a minute-long silence.

The evening is starting to draw in. There are young girls in tiny dresses, taking selfies in packs of three and four. There are couples nuzzling each other on the bridge, guys in suits hailing taxis after what is clearly one-too-many after work. It's not a bustling metropolis, but neither is it the chocolate-box city I was expecting. There's a tipsiness to the place, like everyone has had exactly one glass of wine, and is just thinking of finding something delicious to eat. Georgian red-brick buildings blend into all-night kebab shops, into pubs, into guitar shops, and then back into Georgian buildings.

Laura turns the car up a series of narrow hills to our hostel, a robin's-egg-blue townhouse with iron bars around every windowsill.

When we get to reception, a bulky girl with blonde dreadlocks hands us our keys and two laminated pages wordlessly, before returning to watching videos on her phone.

Wilkommen! Bienvenue! Bienvenido!
Valkommen! Welcome!
Wir hoffen sie werden Ihre Reise nach Irland genießen!
Nous espérons que vous apprécierez
votre voyage en Irlande!
Esperamos que disfrute de su viaje a Irlanda!

'Excuse me,' I say, 'but we speak English.'

'We ARE English,' says Laura, even though I told her not to say that.

'Oh. Hey,' the girl says, pained by this revelation, 'uhm, you guys are on the second floor. You have your own toilet but the shower is shared with two other rooms. Big towels are two euro, hair towels are one.'

Laura is about to ask something, but the girl with blonde dreads is mid-stream, and won't be discouraged.

'There are an array of local guidebooks in your room, which have an array of local pubs and, uhh, eateries,' she says mechanically, her eyes drifting back to her iPhone. 'There's a list of house rules on this,' she points at the multi-lingual sheets with a chipped fingernail, 'but the main thing is that you can't bring people back to the room unless they've, y'know, paid to be there.'

We look at the list again. 'So don't ride anyone,' she clarifies. 'Or, don't take them back here, if you do.'

Everything in our room is a faint brown, as though it were daubed very gently by a child with a teabag. The sheets seem clean. I flop on to them immediately. I close my eyes and picture tomorrow, and the day after. Dreading, slightly, just how little of this is planned. What are we going to do in Cork for a whole weekend?

'So, is there another room, or what?'

I sit up. 'What do you mean?'

'We're both supposed to share this one bed?'

I gaze back at her, incredulous that she could forget the two years we spent renting the same queen-size. 'Like that has ever been a problem before?'

'Just, when you said that it cost fifty-five pounds a night, I assumed you meant for a two-bed room. Or two separate rooms.'

'Forty euro, I said. Jesus, Ireland's not in the Soviet Union, Laura; what did you expect?'

She gives me an exaggerated shrug and crosses her arms. She scans the room, settling eventually on the right-hand corner of the ceiling.

'There's mould, there.'

I follow her finger to where she's pointing. There's a scabby grey watermark, its veins travelling down the wall.

'No, there isn't. And it's only for a couple of nights.'

Laura steps forward and strokes one hand over the bed-sheets. She pulls back the duvet and runs her hand along the sheet.

'Feel this,' she instructs. 'It's damp.'

'Jesus, you're in a good mood, aren't you?'

'It's my asthma. I don't want to wake up in the night hyper-ventilating because I've breathed in mould spores.'

'Christ, Laura. *Spores?* We're only here until Monday morning.'

'Hang on,' she says, and disappears from the room. I hear her ankle boots clattering against the staircase. It's amazing how Laura's asthma will go without mention for years at a time, and as soon as someone tries to make her do something she doesn't want to do, it becomes a national health crisis.

She comes back in again, ten minutes later.

'Right,' she says, the easy smile back on her face, 'I've sorted it. The room next door is free, so I'll take that. I've had a look. It's smaller, but it's cleaner.'

I narrow my eyes at her and hear her 'old dyke' comment rattling around in my head. I bite back my fury, and try to twist it into something resembling a joke.

'There's no spores in there, then? No old bits of fungi that are going to find you just too irresistible, and creep up on you in the night?'

She doesn't look at me, instead busying herself with a guidebook on the dresser.

'So, do you want to head out? I could eat. And I'm

excited to visit the 'eateries' that Ol' Dreadlocks seemed so excited about.'

I gape at her. 'Seriously, Laura?'

She pretends she hasn't heard me.

'I'm going to get changed. Meet you in ten, downstairs?'

# 6

She knocks on the door. 'Are you coming or what? Cork is waiting.'

If you had told me in Uni that one day Laura Shingle would be *knocking*, I would have laughed right in your face. I slide on my shoes anyway, wondering why I wanted Laura to come to Cork so badly, when now I have nothing to say to her.

The night before Laura moved out, we watched *The Craft* on her laptop. Her head sloped against my shoulder, two pillows propping up the ancient old Dell that she has since replaced with a MacBook. We were in that dazed, semi-conscious state that comes from having seen a film dozens of times. We weren't so much watching, as waiting for things to happen, and sighing softly when they did, glad that films could do this: run on the same endless track, hitting the same beats each time, playing itself out until the DVD started again after the legal print had come up in seven different languages.

Laura's hand was lying flat on the space below my belly-button, over my rumpled T-shirt. It was still, practically inanimate. I had forgotten it was even there, until it began moving. First, it was just a slight stroke of her thumb: the kind of touch you might administer to the dome of a cat's head. It didn't seem important. It didn't *feel* important. But the action spread through her hand and the tips of her other fingers until she was stroking, very lightly the skin on my stomach. The hem of my T-shirt had moved to my ribcage but I do not remember how it moved. I assume, like everything and everyone else, it had simply sensed Laura's wishes and acted accordingly.

I watched the schoolgirl witches fight on Laura's laptop and decided not to intervene. I'd had a crush on her when we first met. Of course I had. But it had waxed and waned accordingly, the way it does when your best friend is beautiful, charismatic, and very straight. By the time we were living together, the door in my head marked 'Laura' had been closed for so long that it was rusted shut.

Yet, here she was. The tips of her fingers on my pubic bone, her head still slumped in the crook of my shoulder. I couldn't look at her. I was embarrassed, even though I had done nothing. I had made sure, for years, that I did nothing. I knew what our relationship looked like. I knew what people said. There's a line, with female friendships – between what is acceptable and Best Friends Forever and will-you-be-my-bridesmaid – and what is, shall we say, *not cute*.

I didn't hang off her in public, like other girls did with their best friends. I didn't dance between her and the men who wanted her. I didn't take selfies, I didn't post pictures of us nuzzling and pouting, the way other women our age seem to behave with their best friends. I never wanted to seem like a liability to her. And when we spooned at night – *feel how cold I am, Charlie, feel* – I tried to accept that when Laura held me tightly she did it partly out of sisterly affection and partly because she was still working things out. She was straight as an arrow. I was sure of that. But she was still allowed to work things out, and if I were her friend, I would let her.

But I still did nothing.

It's not as if I'm a prude, or passive in bed. Quite the opposite, in fact. I often fall into phases of heavy promiscuity, followed by a season of celibacy. I use one-night stands like a steam valve, especially when hospital life becomes too heavy. I have been accused, more than once, of being too rough. I once heard two girls in the smoking area of a gay club refer to me as A Biter.

And yet there I was, lying still and pretending to be completely unaware of the heat developing between her hands and my skin, or of the ripening wetness that was gathering in my crotch. Maybe whatever Laura was quietly working out in those nights of being cold had developed into a theory, and now she was sharing that theory with me.

As her fingers worked their way upwards to the breasts I had spent so much of our life together complaining about, she looked up.

'Are my hands cold?'

'No.'

She held my gaze, checking. *Is this okay? Are you up for this? Will you hold it against me if I change my mind later?*

I nodded my approval, and she pressed her mouth on the bony equator in the middle of my chest.

*Such a weird place to start,* I remember thinking. *Who starts at the sternum?*

Laura did. Laura started there. She sat up and swung her legs over either side of my hips, grinding into me slightly as though I were a boy. I began to realise that this wasn't just her clumsily experimenting with being gay. This was her experimenting with *me*. She was curious about my bones, my limbs, my angles. She was curious about my small boobs and the puffy, bright red nipples that she ran her tongue across. When I realised that – that Laura was here for *me*, Laura loved *me* – I couldn't lie still any more. I sat up and drew her face towards mine, tracing my fingers along her lower lip. We held ourselves that way for a moment, hovering in our new shining reality. And then, I kissed her. Even her tongue felt like her: rounded and warm and pink, and surprisingly reserved when you got to know it. It was the most Laura a tongue could be.

*The Craft* was coming to an end: I could hear the witches screaming on the beach filled with washed-up sharks.

'You need to stop,' she whispered.

Just like that. She looked as though she had just woken up from a hypnotic trance. She jerked her head away from mine.

'What? Laura, you ...'

'Yeah, I know. I'm sorry. I thought ... I don't know. But I changed my mind.'

Goose pimples erupted on my skin. *Why was I the only one topless? Why is it so cold in here?*

'I love Mike, Charlie. I'm moving in with him.'

If we were men, we would have never spoken about it again. But because we weren't men, we talked about it the next morning, over breakfast.

'I think what it was,' said Laura, matter-of-factly, 'was that I was just a bit scared, you know, of commitment. Of settling down and being a boring old married couple.'

'You're not even engaged, Laura.'

'I know, but I was just reacting to that, I think. You know, what is my life going to be, now that I'm living with a guy? And such a great guy? It's hard, Charlie. What if I mess it up?'

And that was it. I, for some reason, was the one who had to console her, even though it was my body and my feelings that had been toyed with. Somehow, it had become a story about her and her boyfriend. She was wilfully forgetting everything – our mouths pressed together, her single kiss on my sternum, the rosy-gold light that seemed to fill us up when her face was in my hands – just so she could move in with her boyfriend unperturbed.

'I just felt that when you ... when you took my top off, and started kissing my ...'

'I know! And I'm sorry! But it's just, you know, there's so much pressure on me to make things work with Mike that I just acted out. It wasn't about you.'

'No, Laura, but listen, when you started touching me . . .'

'I am listening, okay? I get it.'

Laura's not an idiot. She's not a twenty-two-year-old who is playfully toying with the idea of bisexuality. She is a twenty-nine-year-old woman who is best friends with a lesbian, and has many more queer friends besides. She has heard – for years now – about the frustration of kissing a girl in a gay club only to find out that she wants you to have a threesome with her and her moron boyfriend.

We bumbled past it anyway. She moved in with Mike. Our lives have become separate. Months somehow passed, and now she is refusing to sleep in the same bed as me and is making cracks about dykes at the airport.

We walk around the city for a long time, hovering in the windows of pubs and restaurants, not quite sure what we are looking for because we do not know what Cork is. We trudge on, aimless and desperate, through the chilly waterways of the city. The whole place needs a paint job. Cork is prone to brief fits of grandeur – pretty, Huguenot buildings; red-brick art galleries; chic little restaurants – but lacks either the will-power or the resources to make the landscape feel consistent. Vape shops and grubby businesses that promise to 'unlock ANY phone €50!' feel as though they've sprung up recently, like shanty towns made permanent through lack of intervention.

Laura is determined to keep up a bouncy atmosphere, but I'm still too furious to engage properly, with her or Cork city at large. I limit my communication to either nodding or shrugging, and eventually her energy grows subdued. Her easy, chatty nature becomes exhaustingly try-hard, and soon she is reading signs aloud to pass the time.

'Merchants Quay. Merchants Qway? Key? Do you think this was a trading town, back in the olden days?'

And, 'Look they have a Starbucks here! Do you think they have the same stuff that we do? Do you want to go inside?'

And, 'Don't you just love exploring a new city, and watching the world go by?'

There's something very satisfying about watching her fail. If it were an ordinary day, and I were just being grumpy for no reason, she would prod at me to stop being a drama queen, or leave me alone to let me get over it by myself. But in this case, Laura knows she's the one in the wrong, and rather than just apologise, she's choosing to sweep her homophobia under the rug with Lonely Planet facts about Cork.

But *is* it homophobia? Laura knew who I was when we started sharing a bed together, after all. I want to laugh at how insane this all is. So she touched my tits! So what? So my best friend had a brief flirtation with bisexuality! So what? Why was it any of my business? What did I really care, anyway? She moved out months ago. And we've seen each other loads since.

All this fuss and panic over a *bed*.

But then I remember the airport, and the way she looked at that middle-aged woman on security.

*Old dykes always go for me.*

Is that how she thought of me, too? Just another woman desperate to touch her?

My hunger eventually breaks my resolve to be unpleasant to Laura and we find a Chinese restaurant with two plastic booths intended as a waiting space for carry-out customers, but the owner lets us eat in. Laura asks for chopsticks, while I take a small plastic fork from a basket at the counter. We sit down with two cans of warm Fanta and two identical meals: beef with black bean sauce, boiled rice, prawn crackers and a portion of spring rolls to share between us. It's the exact meal we used to order from Wah Moul, the takeout near our old bedsit. I like the fact that, despite everything, we still fall back into the same menu.

'Was Mike okay with you coming on this trip?'

'Mike? No. He's on a job in Glasgow anyway. He won't even notice I'm gone.'

I scan her tone, wondering if it's Mike who is the problem with Laura and me sharing a bed, though it's hard for me to imagine Mike with a problem. Or even an opinion, for that matter. After all this time, I'm still amazed that he's the guy Laura has declared her affection for. Everything about him is so flatly *fine*. He's handsome, but a regular, ordinary, six-foot-something kind of handsome. 'Don't you think he looks like a young Keanu Reeves?' Laura had said, on day two of filming *It Takes a Village*. 'In *Much Ado About Nothing*?'

That's what I called Mike, after that. Much Ado About Nothing. Laura found it funny until she decided that she was serious about Mike, after which I only said it bitchily, when she wasn't around. I see that book again – *American Taste* – peeping out of her bag.

'I've never seen you with a book that long,' I say lightly. 'Or, I've never seen you finish one.'

Her smile cracks. 'All right, bitch. *Ow.*'

I shrug her hurt away. 'I'm not wrong.'

And I'm not. Laura is many things – beautiful, funny, confident – but she's not a reader. She's the kind of person that refers to herself as 'street smart' as a way of apologising for the huge gaps in her general knowledge. The only time I've ever seen her sweat is when she had to locate the Gaza Strip on a map.

'I guess it's a period piece, then,' I say, pryingly.

'Yep.'

'Good luck with keeping all those history details accurate. And you'll probably get all these Texans who will be annoyed if like, a revolver design is off.'

'That's not exactly my role.'

'No, I know,' I say, then dig around in my food some more. 'Do you think you'll have time to say goodbye to my dad before you leave?'

'What do you mean? Of course.'

'No, I mean. You know. *Say goodbye.*'

'Charlie. Stop.'

'Stop *what?*'

I'm tired of people telling me to stop. People think that someone is only dying when a doctor says something final, like 'he has six months' or 'let's focus on making you as comfortable as possible'. The truth is, it's written on the wall for months, even years before anyone discusses it. They're talking about chemo again, but they also keep wondering aloud if my dad is 'strong enough' to take it. They are lightly introducing death as a subject so that we're not shocked when they finally tell us it's happening.

'You don't know your dad is going to die. He might get better.'

'He's seventy, Laura. Don't be naive.'

We're silent for a minute. I plan to leave it there, but I can't stop myself from speaking again.

'So, like I said, will you be able to say goodbye? It would mean so much to him.'

Why am I doing this? Why am I acting as though my dad would give a shit whether or not he sees Laura before he dies?

I can tell by Laura's forlorn expression that she has already thought about this. She knew that taking this job in LA would mean abandoning me while I sit back and watch my family disintegrate. She probably had long, terse chats with Mike where she kept repeating, 'What am I going to *do* about Charlie?' while fingering the ends of her hair. 'You're not responsible for her,' he would have said, repeating it over and over again, until Laura was convinced that the real proof of her friendship was being even vaguely concerned in the first place.

We sit and seethe: me hating her for leaving, her hating me for making her feel bad about it. Finally, she turns her big, wet blue eyes back to her rice.

'I just don't see how it's fair,' I say loudly, and to no one in particular. She looks up briefly, convinced that in her journey to meet my eyes she will come up with something good to say. She comes up with nothing. We watch each other, playing emotional chicken with our friendship, waiting to see who breaks first.

'I know,' she says finally.

We walk back in silence, and in the middle of St Patrick's Bridge, she slips her arm into the crook of mine. A boy on the bridge screams that he can see dolphins in the river below, and when we look to see if he's right, he starts vomiting a luminous yellow paste.

'Feel at home yet?' she says, trying to stifle a laugh.

'Starting to,' I concede, and I give her a dry laugh back, to show that I'm not going to be a bad sport about LA or the beds for the whole trip. We go to our separate rooms and, at some point, I fall asleep.

## 7

The hostel's breakfast options consist of a basket of mini-cereal boxes, individual sachets of instant coffee and Belvita bars. I load up a bowl with four different sugary cereals, mix myself a coffee and go back to my room. I have a WhatsApp message from Laura saying she couldn't sleep, and that she's gone to take some photos of Cork. This is how it's going to be, I guess.

I debated over whether I should put an out-of-office response on for LottieMinxxx@yahoo.co.uk. I decided not to in the end: there's something a bit fantasy-destroying about emailing a young nymph for paid nudes, and then receiving a 'Hello, I'm away from my desk right now . . . '

It's a good thing I did, too, because there's a new client in my inbox. Someone who saw the work I've done for my Michigan client, and wants his own set. He had sent the email only a few minutes before I went downstairs to get breakfast, offering me fifty dollars. I look at the time: if I'm quick, I could make it before lunch.

**What are you looking for?xxxx**

His response is immediate.

**I want to see you having a good time Lottie.**

And despite everything, I actually laugh.

I put on my usual mask of make-up and spread out on the sheets. They're cheap, but white, so will look more expensive in photographs. I arrange myself to look playfully rumpled, as though I've been up all night with someone who loves me. I start naked, and then reconsider. There's a pair of newish white knickers in my suitcase, so I put them on. I take them off again. I splash the crotch with lukewarm water. I put them back on. If I can make this guy a regular, that's an extra £200 a month I can add to my income. Tax free.

When the pictures are uploaded, I do some quick retouching on Photoshop. My eyes are darker, my underwear is brighter, box-fresh. I lighten my hair a couple of shades, so it looks more of a tawny blonde than brown. By the time I'm finished, I am the exact intersection between Madonna, schoolgirl and whore. I am the teenager on the bus that married men feel guilty about fancying. I am the intern who you're too professional to speak to.

When I send him the set, he pays me immediately, and adds a $25 tip.

Sometimes the worst thing about this job is how easy it is. I should have stopped, really, after Dad got better the first time. And I did, for a bit. When Laura and I were sharing rent and it was easy to get by on a barista's salary. But since she moved out I've started doing it much more. This is not out of choice. I'm just struggling to cover the rent on our bedsit, and I am getting significantly less money for porn than I did when I was twenty-four. Porn tends to be easiest when you can slide yourself into a category, and 'barely legal' and 'MILF' tend to be the easiest to market in. The closer I get to thirty, the more I slip into a sexless abyss.

When I leave the hostel, I decide to cheer myself up with a proper coffee and an almond croissant. Walking down Patrick's Hill and into Cork city, I find a chic little cafe with a twenty-person-strong queue. I peer at the customers, all in-between appointments at 11 a.m. on a Friday morning. I try to feel any sense of connection to them, or at least, any difference between them and the people I sell coffee to in London. There're heavy-lidded goth kids, tracksuit wearing adults, and vinyl-clutching twenty-somethings. The more I stare at them, trying to force a connection or some sense of recognition, the more alone I feel.

The bridge that separates the northern, older part of the city from the slick, commercial side stretches ahead of me; the sun's gleaming on the river, making it look like a scuffed marble. And then I see Laura. Her hair looks white in the sun, falling out from an unfortunate-looking red cap she knitted herself. She's taking photos of an old casino by the riverbank, where a bunch of teenagers in blue and grey school uniforms are smoking. Click, click, smile. Another click. She looks up, says something to them, and they quickly recalibrate, like pigeons reshuffling after a disturbance. She thanks them, then moves on. She turns to the green safety rail at the river's edge. Click, click, smile.

So much of her is performance. She can assess what a total stranger is looking for and, in five seconds flat, become it. When she ordered cocaine to our flat-share, she would always linger in the car with the dealer while I shifted my weight from foot to foot in the doorway. I used to watch her and think: *What could they possibly be talking about? What could they have in common?*

But it's not about finding things in common, with her. It's about eliminating all points of difference. Smoothing out every edge, brightening every shadow. A pillow person who invites you to sink in to them.

I see her, and I break into a small jog. I can't help it. If the next few days are going to be the last we're going to have, I want them to at least be good ones.

'Hey,' I say.

'Hey,' she responds, surprised to see me. She puts her finger on my face. I haven't taken off my make-up from earlier. 'You're wearing make-up! *And* you're in a good mood.'

'I am, you know. I'm excited to see the movie later. Want to get a pint?'

'It's not even noon.'

'So?' I say, throwing my face up to the bright blue chilly sky. 'I want to see you having a good time.'

And we do. We drink pints of Guinness and buy shots of ruby-red port to pour into them, like Dad does at Christmas. We piece together shards of Cork slang. *I will ya*, means 'absolutely not'. *Byore* ('like Eeyore with a b') means woman. Laura comes back from the bar with two pints and a packet of crisps between her teeth, triumphant.

'I found a new one,' she says. 'The barman told me.'

'Go on.'

'So he asked me if I was with *Yerone*. I don't know, I thought it was some kind of Celtic name. So I said, no, I'm with my friend, Charlie. So he said, no,' she pauses, to try out her sheepish little Cork accent, still too slow to be convincing, 'I said "y-o-u-r o-n-e". Like, the woman you're travelling with. Isn't that nice?'

'That *is* nice,' I say, a bit drunk.

'And,' she continues, delighted to have facts to share, 'if you're talking about a boy, it's "your man". If it's a girl, it's "your one". Isn't that sweet? Very sisterly, I think.'

'Very sisterly,' I say.

By the time of the screening, I'm pissed. The Triskel Arts Centre is, satisfyingly, in an old church. Laura and I glide past the festival organisers and the smattering of local press, still linking arms.

We smoke cigarettes in the graveyard outside, where people are milling around with plastic glasses of beer. We talk to strangers, some of whom are 'excited' to meet us.

Laura nudges me as we're filing into our seats.

'Charlie,' she says, 'I don't know if you've noticed, but there are some highly fuckable people at our movie.'

I laugh. I *had* noticed. I wonder idly if there's an after-party, and whether people will want to talk to us at it.

The room quietens and our titles come up. Suddenly my drunken high falls away and I feel frozen with nerves, solid all the way through with them. We're finally playing our film to an Irish audience, in Ireland.

*Please don't fuck up please don't fuck up please don't fuck up.*

### WRITTEN AND DIRECTED BY
### CHARLOTTE REGAN

The actress who plays the grandmother I never met appears on screen. Laura grabs my hand and holds it tightly. She lets me interlink my fingers with hers.

### PRODUCED BY CHARLOTTE REGAN
### AND LAURA SHINGLE

I watch my eight-year-old dad walk to school down a dirt road, carrying his books with a belt.

### *IT TAKES A VILLAGE*

My father sits in his lessons, leaning too hard on his pencil and snapping it. I look over at Laura and smile: we loved that pencil snapping, and I praised her about it endlessly. There's an eeriness to the way she put the shot together, as if the breaking pencil is a breaking point in itself, a sign of something changing for ever. A knock on the schoolhouse door. Mike makes a brief cameo. Laura and I look at each other again, and suppress a laugh. Most of the crew make up the non-speaking roles. Mike nods at the teacher and hands her a note.

'Colm,' she says, and everyone flips around to look at my father. 'You're to go home to your mother.'

Colm looks up from his broken pencil top. 'Why?'

'It says here she needs you to run an errand in town.'

The class titters at this odd boy and his strange, sad, widowed mother: always calling him home for no reason. 'It's because she has no one else to talk to,' says one snot-nosed girl, who will be dead by the next scene.

On the way home, Colm vomits into a bush. He has already ingested a near-lethal amount of carbon monoxide. He doesn't know it yet, but the note from his mother has just saved his life.

In the screening room, a shaft of light strips across. Someone has opened the door. Latecomers. I scowl. *Rude.* They are three men, and they sit a couple of rows ahead of me and Laura, looking a little tipsy as they do it. Maybe they just came from their own screening.

As the film ticks on, I'm reminded by how proud I am of it. Sure, we made it a year ago, on a £10,000 grant and every possible favour we could pull. Sure, I haven't had any paid film work since. But it's a good-looking movie, and nothing about it feels amateurish or film-school-y. I'm about to whisper that to Laura when I notice something.

The three guys sitting two rows ahead of us turn to one another and start gesturing at the screen. I squint my eyes and try to make out their faces. They're talking, during our film?

Wait, no.

They're *laughing* during our film.

I start to feel hot, my underarms prickling and itchy. This is the proudest moment of my entire life, and three strangers are laughing at it.

From then on, I can't concentrate fully on what's happening

on screen. I keep my eye trained on the three guys, all of them in their late twenties, to see how they're going to react. For a long time, they do nothing, and I begin to think I imagined it. I try to watch the film again: Colm has found out that there was a carbon monoxide leak in his one-room schoolhouse, and every single person in it – eighteen children between the ages of six and twelve, plus one school teacher – is dead. The town grieves: journalists swarm.

Laura's camera follows Colm as the sole eight-year-old in a grieving town, with nothing but grieving adults for comfort. He spends the day wandering the shoreline alone.

'Colm!' shouts his mother from the door of their house. 'Come in for your tea!'

The men in front of us completely lose it. They start stifling laughter again, pushing their closed fists into their mouths.

I know that laugh. It's not a joyful laugh. It's a laugh you only give when you're dying of second-hand embarrassment, when the only thing keeping you from jamming your fist into your eye socket out of mortification is the sweet, melt-on-your-tongue relief that this terrible thing is not happening to you.

Something happens, then. Something I'm so used to seeing in films and reading about in books that I can see its shadow creeping up on me moments before it lands. I am having an epiphany. That's what this is. This feeling that my heart has stopped beating, this dry, open-mouthed terror. I'm not just embarrassed. I am realising something, and that something is this: My film is bad.

This isn't insecurity. This isn't a crisis of confidence. These boys are forcing me to see my own work with new eyes, and now I am fighting the urge to tear those eyes out of my skull.

It's just *bad*.

It is bad because the dialogue is clunky and awkward. It is bad because it is full of tired, offensive clichés. But most of all it is bad because the whole story feels incomprehensible. It clangs with a sort of strange falseness, like one of those tinny pop songs you hear in a supermarket that is altered just enough so they don't have to pay royalties.

Laura nudges me.

'What the fuck is *their* problem?' she whispers angrily, pointing at the boys who laughed at us. I say nothing. My epiphany begins to morph into a panic attack. The actress playing my grandmother is on screen, telling the actor playing my father that God spared his life for a reason. That he was chosen, special, meant for great things. What bollocks. What insufferable, trite, nightmarish bollocks.

I remember the first time I showed Dad the film. Laura and I had managed to get the Genesis cinema in Whitechapel to let us have a 'premiere', a term we used semi-ironically, but my dad had rented a suit all the same. I sat next to him. I didn't know exactly what to expect, but I think a small part of me believed that if he liked it enough, he would never get sick again.

And he did like it! Even though he had criticisms. Even though he asked annoying questions, questions he didn't really want the answers to but just wanted to show that he had them so no one would mistake them for a parochial Irish immigrant who left school at sixteen. I caught him talking to Laura.

'The scenery was gorgeous, Laura. Gorgeous. Like Trevor Malick.'

'Terrence Malick?' she said automatically. The film student in her couldn't let a thing like that pass. She said it casually, as though she were talking to anyone, but Dad had stiffened. His Irish accent hid like a startled lizard.

'Yes, Terrence. What am I like? Of course. Terrence Malick.' He started going red, appalled at making a mistake in front of my posh friend. 'Trevor Malick! I've seen all his films.'

My mortification at watching the movie is as deeply out-sized as his reaction to the Trevor Malick gaffe, but I can't help it. Every new scene is fresh torture. Why did I ever think this was good? Why did the government give me money for this? I want to leave, but I can't. The seating is so tight in this ex-church that I would have to ask five people to stand up, and everyone would see the writer/director of this steaming shit pile of a film walk out, causing them to interrogate the steaming shit pile even further.

The actress playing my grandmother Kitty wraps herself in a shawl and stands at the water's edge, staring intently, thinking . . . Thinking what? I don't know. I didn't write any dialogue for this scene. The whole point was that we would rest the camera on her and just let her face do the work, let the emotional journey from relief to sadness to guilt play across her features as though they were moulding clay. But the reality is that I don't know how my grand-mother felt about the aftermath of the accident. I don't know what having the sole surviving son of an island does to a person.

I remember my interviews with my father, the tapes still lining the desk drawer of my old bedroom.

'What about Kitty?'

'My mother? What about her?'

'Well, did she socialise much? What was her life like on the island? Even after you left, what happened to her then?'

'She was a quiet person, Charlie. Socialising would never have been a thing for her.'

'But when she was all alone? Who looked after her then?'

'Looked after her? You must be joking. Those people wouldn't give you the steam off of their piss. No. I sent her money every month until she died.'

'Did you ever ask her to come to England? So you could have looked after her?'

'Leave Clipim? You must be joking. The only way that woman would leave the island was in a box.'

He took a long sip from his tea then banged his mug down, rasping the speaker. 'Which, eventually, she did.'

It didn't make any sense to me. In some stories, the people of Clipim were tender, funny and kind. In others, they were positively sociopathic: shunning my grandmother, isolating my father, making it impossible for either of them to get real jobs. Sure, I understand that people grieving after the accident might find Kitty and Colm Regan hard to be around, but outward cruelty? Why?

And then there was the whole business of him telling me that Clipim was a rock with three old men and four teeth between them. That's not true. I've known that for years. I've done enough research on the place to know that, while it is small, it has a thriving tourist trade. There are hotels, pubs, gift shops, museums, caravan parks. Even during Dad's childhood, Clipim was by no means an irrelevant speck on the map. In the early nineteenth century it was famous for being the last port of call before Irish ships left for America. Even the name 'clipim' is an English mangling of an Irish word 'chipín'. *Bain do chipín.* It means: cut your stick, get ready to go.

Which is sort of a round-about way of saying that there has *always* been money going through Clip. English money, sure, but the idea that it's this windy outpost in the middle of nowhere just isn't true. Yet, it's what my dad has been telling me for years, and it's how I styled it to look in the film. But why? Why have I been keeping up with this elaborate fiction?

The scene changes again. Different families are mourning their children. Some crying, some shouting at the sky, 'Why me?' Watching this is torture now. Is this normal? Is it normal to hate what you have created? I feel like it probably is. Scorsese doesn't sit around watching *Mean Streets*, does he? It's normal to hate your first film. It's a rite of passage.

*No, Charlie,* a stern voice from inside my own brain starts saying to me. *You hate it because it is bad. It is bad because it doesn't make sense. It doesn't make sense because the information you based it on is wrong.*

*And it is wrong because your dad, who you love, has been hiding something from you. And you, in all your glorious melodrama, have been letting him.*

Twenty minutes before the film ends, the boys leave.

# 8

After the screening, a few people who seem genuinely impressed with the film approach us. Some of them know of the Clipim tragedy, and some had never heard of it, and lots of them remember hearing about it at school as a case study for having a carbon monoxide alarm. A couple of people are a little alarmed that we're English filmmakers, but all seem soothed when Laura tells them about how my Dad was our script consultant, and everyone seems happy with that.

I want to scream in their faces, *I'm a fucking fraud. Can't you see how obviously bad this is? How offensively, incongruously shit?*

But I don't. I nod, and I smile, and I thank them. Because, after all, I am a twenty-nine-year-old woman and this film is still the most impressive thing I've done with my life, and that compels me to stand by it.

'The fucking *nerve,*' Laura suddenly says, pointing at the boys who laughed during our screening. 'They're still hanging around. After that.'

I shrug and say nothing.

'What? This doesn't bother you?'

'No,' I say quickly, but my eyes are filled with tears.

'Oh, Charlie,' she says, her voice thick with sympathy. 'Those fuckers have made you cry. I'm so sorry.'

They haven't made me cry. They merely triggered a set of realisations that I should have had years ago. I keep thinking about all the things my father has ever told me that don't quite add up. Sometimes he would tell me that he attended the funerals of all his classmates, and sometimes he said the funerals were too far away for him to attend, and sometimes he told me that his mother wouldn't let him. Questioning him was useless. He would just double down on whatever memory he was experiencing at the time. I eventually gave up, and just used whatever detail was the most cinematic.

'Well, fuck them,' she says fiercely. 'I'm going over there.'

'Laura. Don't.'

'Try and stop me.'

Laura stomps over. Only one turns around to acknowledge her, and hands her his empty glass.

'How'ya, thanks,' he mutters before returning to his conversation.

Laura is offended on behalf of both of us now. This *nobody* has just mistaken her for a caterer. Her! Laura Shingle! Laura Shingle of going-to-LA fame! She taps him on the shoulder and launches into him.

I watch them, worrying at the lime in my vodka tonic with my straw. I hear snatches of Laura's furious lecture. There's lots of 'how dare you' and 'what have you ever done'. To his credit, he does look genuinely bashful. It's hard to say what age he is. He has a weather-beaten look to him that could make him twenty-two or thirty-five. He looks like someone who surfs in the winter.

It all gets too awkward, so I just stare into the bottom of my glass. When I look up again, Laura is marching him over to meet me.

Oh, fuck.

'Hi, Charlie?' He is clearly mortified. 'My name is Nick Sheridan. No relation to Jim. My film was on just before yours. *Starving Hearts*?'

I nod, which he takes as a cue to continue. Oh God, please just let this end.

'Look, I just wanted to apologise for how I behaved. It wasn't cool. I should know better than to take the piss out of another filmmaker. And anyway, it doesn't matter. You've made a very . . . ' He glances across at Laura, who is still furious. 'A very accomplished-looking film.'

He takes a long drag of his rollie, then stubs it out on the back of a stone cross. He gives me a slow smile, revealing a set of lopsided, slightly chipped teeth. I want to die. Accomplished-*looking*. So it's not all in my head. The only thing even vaguely good about this thing I'm so proud of has nothing to do with me. It's all to do with her.

'It's okay,' I say, hoping he'll go away if I give him the validation he needs. 'Actually, you helped me realise some stuff about my family. So, thanks.'

I try to turn away from them, certain that I'm going to burst into tears if I stand there any longer.

'Realise . . . what stuff?' Nick asks.

'It's not important. Look, I'd rather just be alone right now, if that's okay. Laura? Can we go?'

'Sure, babe,' says Laura, concern etched across her face. She puts her hand on my shoulder, clearly sorry for dragging Nick over here in the first place.

'What stuff?' Nick repeats, his voice louder now. 'What do you mean your family? Are you related to the Clip kids?'

'Her dad was the subject of the film,' Laura stresses, watching his expression turn. 'He's the boy. The survivor.'

'What?'

'You would know that had you seen the credits,' she counters triumphantly, 'if you had not shown up late, laughed, and then left before it ended.'

'Jesus. No. Charlotte. I'm so sorry. Fucking hell, I'm a cunt.' Nick pushes his hair back, worrying at his hairline.

Which, I'm delighted to see, is beginning to recede. 'Wait. You have to explain this to me. Can I get you a drink?'

What was formerly a very detached apology suddenly becomes a frantic, worrying plea. His hand is on my shoulder now, his eyes scanning my face worriedly. He's no longer an amateur filmmaker who is throwing his weight around at a screening. He's a big-game hunter with a rhino in his crosshairs.

'Look, haven't you done enough, mate?' Laura pushes back. 'Leave her alone. She doesn't want to talk to you.'

'Tell me about your family, Charlie,' he presses. 'Let me buy you a drink. Tell me about your dad.'

'Why do you want to know about my dad? What do you care?'

'Because my dad has been trying to talk to him for nearly thirty years.'

## 9

We follow Nick to The Oval, a darkened fireside pub with maroon leather seats and a drooling candlestick on every table. It takes a minute for our eyes to adjust to the lack of light. He buys three inky stouts while we sit down, tugging off our jackets and scarves.

Nick sits down at our table and takes a packet of Amber Leaf out of his coat pocket, pinching a squat lump of tobacco between his fingers. Now that he's bought us drinks, the panic has dissipated from his voice. He takes on the demeanour of an elderly sea captain who knows the mutiny has been defeated and that we have no choice but to take his lead from here. Confidence slides back into his voice, plush and airy.

He rolls and starts to talk.

'First,' he says, flicking his grey-green eyes contritely at both of us, 'I want to apologise about the laughing. That wasn't nice. It wasn't polite, especially to treat up-and-coming filmmakers that way. And I'm sorry, from the bottom of my heart, I really am.'

Nick is used to having his apologies universally accepted. This one rolls around the table like a silver dollar we are each expected to squabble over. He sees no point in clarifying that further.

'It wasn't a complete accident, me being at your screening,' he says gravely. 'I mean, I was in town anyway, of course. The press for *Starving Hearts* has just been *mental*.

'But,' he puts his finger up at the 'but', carefully flitting his eyes between me and Laura, 'I've known about *It Takes a Village* for a while. So I wanted to catch it. It was *important* to me that I caught it. Do you know why?'

'Why?' I ask, resenting him for asking me that. This is a man whose ego expands to fill whatever space it's in. Even now, his determined eye contact and animated hand gestures feel like a pantomime of a person. It's all practised, all a production to show how good he is at talking to other people.

'My old man was starting out as a journalist around the time of the Clipim thing. And, you know, Ireland in the 1960s: there wasn't a whole mess of journalists around. It was a fairly small contingent of men taking trains up and down the country.' He traces his finger through the air, indicating the *up* and the *down*. 'Y'know, attending trade union disputes and conferences about butter and the like. So when the Clipim news broke – which was quite a while after it actually *happened,* you'll remember – they were all there. It was a huge story.'

'Yes,' I say irritably. 'I know.'

'My da, though ... this *thing* gets under his skin and it won't shift. Everyone knows there's something up with the story but no one knows what it is. But that's Kerry for you. They're not going to tell anyone a thing if you're from out of town, especially if you're from Dublin. They're hyper-aware of anyone who might be condescending to them, so they clam up.'

Nick takes a long sip at his pint. 'You might as well be English,' he adds with a wry smile.

'Thanks,' Laura says sourly.

'Well,' Nick shrugs, 'that's how it is. Not everyone's mad on the English here and don't expect anyone to feel sorry for you about it.'

Laura glares at him but doesn't say anything more. No one talks to her like this. She is trying to guess at how much arguing power she has in this conversation. She *is* English, and therefore the descendant of colonisers, so Nick, being from a nation of colonised, should have conversational right of way here. But she's also a woman, and therefore vulnerable, and therefore deserving of his respect. This is advanced privilege mathematics, the kind of social algorithm that comes naturally to Londoners like Laura.

'So a good few years later, when the dust has settled a bit, he decides he's going to rent a place on Clipim for a summer. This is the early eighties, now. He's still a single man at this stage, and he's freelance, a pretty respected reporter. He's covered the Troubles and all the rest of it. So he reckons he can get by doing some fieldwork for the farmers while gathering information on these people. He's convinced there's more of a story there, and that if he can get in with the locals it will all come out. So he does it. He gets a job in the lambing season and rents a little room in the village. Easy.'

Nick takes a long sip of his pint and a hole starts to open up in the pit of my stomach. One so wide that I'm sure my neck will fall through it. He is talking about Clipim with such certainty, such bravado, as if to him it's a real place: a place with rental cottages and odd jobs; a place with geography and texture and an internal clock that keeps on ticking. My Clipim is not like this. My Clipim is a dreamy landscape of hills and blanket shawls and people forever gazing seaward. My Clipim is the Clipim you see in the movie: a desolate rock that a cast of six people walk around in circles on, saying things that don't make sense and feeling emotions they never question yet cannot explain.

'And pretty soon, he begins to notice something interesting. First off, that most families emigrated after the schoolhouse thing. Which makes sense. Why would you stay, after all? So they sell up. And who do they sell to? John Foley.'

'Who is John Foley?' I ask.

At this, Nick holds his nose for a second, as if preparing to go underwater.

'You don't know who John Foley is?'

My face starts to redden. 'Look, I've done lots of research on Clipim. Reams of it. But I researched Clipim during the time my dad lived there. So, John Foley must have been ... after that.'

'John Foley isn't just a Clipim thing. He's not even a Kerry thing. He's an Ireland thing. He was this rich old farmer, died in the nineties, but he had about fifteen sons and sixty-five grandsons, and they're all over the country. Come on. The *Foleys*?'

It's clear we have no idea what he's talking about, and Nick takes great pains to slow down his speech.

'Let's go back,' he says. 'You're aware Ireland has, or had, quite a lot of farms, right? You know what a farm is?'

'I swear to God,' Laura says. 'I will tip this pint over your head.'

'So these farms and patches of rural land, Foley develops a taste for them. He starts buying them all up and consolidating them into big tracks. Then him and his sons either turn it all into grazing land, or they sell it on to international developers.'

'So? I mean, that's just capitalism, isn't it?' I say.

'You're fecking right it is. And it's the kind of shit that ruins this country. Have you read *Capital*?'

'I mean it's not *illegal*,' I say, keen not to stray too far into Marxist criticism. 'So where's the story?'

'Right. So the Foleys get more powerful. And more greedy. They start intimidating old bachelor farmers to sell them their land, blackmailing them sometimes. They have dirt on *everyone*, and they have friends in the Dáil. If you have so much as an outdoor tap that doesn't have the right planning permission, a Foley will find a way to tie you up in legal red tape so you'd have no hope of emigrating. There's stories that he stopped people getting their US visas, if they didn't sell to him.'

'And they're all over the country?'

'Well. Rural areas mostly. They get praised for revitalising tourism on the islands and all that, so people turn a blind eye. It's like the tax breaks for all the tech start-ups. The attitude is: as long as they're bringing jobs, it's all okay.'

'So they're the Mafia,' I say, amazed my dad never brought this up before. 'What you're describing is the Mafia.'

'And like the Mafia, people who are on the right side of the Foleys do very well. Jobs, money, you know.'

'And where does Clipim come into this?'

'Because Clipim,' he says slowly. 'Was one of John Foley's first big buys.'

Silence. Nick says this like this is world-ending, but I'm struggling to understand where it fits in, so I just say 'Okay.'

'This is actually quite privileged information,' he says, sulkily. 'I mean, not everyone knows this.'

'Well how did your dad find out, then?'

'When he was living on Clip. He had one hand in a sheep's uterus and one ear to the ground.'

Me and Laura flinch. It's always a surprise to hear the word 'uterus' in the pub.

'So he bought some land,' I say evenly. 'That just seems . . . opportunistic.'

'It does,' Nick reasons. 'But then John Foley dies in '91, and everyone finds out he was in the RA.'

'The RA?' Laura asks politely.

'The IRA, Laura, for fuck's sake,' I snap, still mortified at not knowing about the Foleys. I don't want Nick to think we're total morons.

'It transpires that he was secretly donating to the RA for years. It's a huge scandal. The sons go on the *Late Late* and say they had no idea, shocked as anyone else is, blah blah blah. Anyway it all gets covered up fairly quickly, but my da finally has a solid theory.'

'And his theory is . . . ?'

'Look,' Nick says, exhausted. 'A classroom of kids, half of them English, or half-English, or from families who are working for the English, gets wiped out. Then a certified RA man sweeps in and starts to make his fortune.'

I sit there, dazzled, my mouth hanging open.

'So your dad thinks the Clipim accident . . . was planned?'

'I wouldn't go as far as to say he believes it, but it's certainly a pet theory of his. For years, Clip was very West Brit. A bit of a pleasure island for Proddy aristocracy, y'know? Deer hunting and all the rest. So there were English kids, mostly servant children, in the school as well as Irish kids. He thinks old John Foley maybe . . .' He trails off.

'What? Killed a bunch of Irish kids just to off a few English ones? And poor ones?' asks Laura, incredulous. 'That hardly seems prudent. Like, it's not even economical from a terrorist perspective.'

Nick furrows his brow at her, clearly not charmed by her sardonic approach to his dad's grand theory. 'Look, there's stuff that happens down there that would make your head spin.'

'It does seem far-fetched,' I say carefully. 'With respect to your dad. And John Foley didn't die until years after your dad's lambing season on Clipim, right?'

'Right,' he agrees. 'But once he found out about John Foley's big buyout, people started closing ranks. No one ever confronted him or anything, but he was fired from the sheep job. His little rental room was broken into. His tyres were slashed. No one would serve him at the pub. They froze him out, until he eventually just gave up and left.'

We're all silent. I'm reminded, briefly, of a Children's Classic edition of *David Copperfield* I used to own. For years, I said that I had read *David Copperfield* with no conception that my book was an abridged, over-simplified one. A book designed to get children interested in classic literature, and not intended to be the end point.

'But,' Nick begins again, 'The revelation about John Foley in '91 stirs him up again. He thinks he can cover the story another way. By talking to the survivors.'

'Survivor,' I say weakly.

'Yes. Right.' And for once, he has the decency to lower his eyes in partial respect. 'Survivor. Your dad. But he always ignored my dad's phone calls and his letters. Then I hear about a film based on the life of your dad ... Well, you can see why I came to your screening.'

'And laughed at us,' Laura finishes sourly.

'Yes,' he agrees. 'But, once again, I would like to say that I'm sorry for that, and also, that I had a few pints on board at that stage.'

I try to visualise Dad refusing to talk to someone about Clipim. He loves mythologising his own past. It's all he ever wants to talk about. And yet, when a journalist contacted him he went completely quiet, according to Nick. Why?

'Well, what do you think?' Laura says to Nick suddenly. 'Do you think your dad believes Charlie's dad is covering something up?'

'I don't know,' Nick says, after a short pause. 'But the whole thing just smells bad, doesn't it? The fact that no one on the mainland knew for absolutely ages. No one reported it, or wrote to their relatives about it.'

'I know all that. It's in the film. I put that in there.'

'You put it in there, but you've chalked it up to some kind of deedily-didely small-town rural Irish thing. Like they were all so isolated and codependent that they never even thought to tell people. Charlie, this was the 1960s, not the 1860s. Most people had family and friends on the mainland. There was a boat that went there once a day, and people didn't know until weeks later. The schoolhouse thing wasn't ignored. It was *hushed up.*'

I'm speechless. I'm appalled that a total stranger could speak to me so baldly, but there's also a niggle of satisfaction in hearing him say all this. It makes *sense.* I've always accepted Clipim as a bedtime story, something beyond questioning. But the more Nick talks, the more holes in the story open up. The little surviving coverage of the accident is filled with local interviews and judgemental observations about the island, with very little on the mechanics of the event itself. Some articles mention that the heater was badly installed; others focus on the newspaper in the fireplace; others mention neither. The reports read like an anecdote that you keep remembering crucial details of too late. To hear Nick lay this all out makes me feel a resentful kinship with him.

I think about Dad, and the newspaper clippings stuck in his blue autograph book. How he will never go back again, and when he dies, the Clipim class of '63 will go from being a group of almost entirely dead children to a group of completely dead ones. What will the story even be then, with no one left to keep it alive?

'Tomorrow,' I say finally. 'We're driving down. Tomorrow.'

'Charlie,' Laura says gently, 'it's at least three hours away. And the festival prize ceremony is tomorrow night. We might win something.'

'I don't care about the fucking prize ceremony. We have to go, Laura. I have to know what happened. I have to.'

'Why don't you just ask your dad?'

'I've *been* asking him. I've been talking to him about this single subject for my entire life. Fucking hell, I spent the whole summer he was first sick making him recount every memory of Clipim, and he still never got his story completely straight.'

'Yes,' Nick murmurs, carefully observing me and Laura's dynamic. I wonder what we look like to him. Two women, almost thirty, bickering like an old married couple. Maybe he thinks we *are* a married couple. 'You should go, Charlie. The prodigal daughter. You're blood to these people. They'll trust you. You can find out what actually fucking happened. My dad's retired now, but he still has a little black book as thick as a tree trunk. Whatever the truth of this story is, it could still come out.'

'Don't be insane,' Laura counters. 'Even if we had the money or the time to take a three-hour road trip, why the fuck would they talk to some random English girl who pops out of nowhere? Why would they tell us anything?'

'Maybe they *won't!*' I say, my voice almost a shout. 'But all that stuff Nick was just saying about it being hushed up ... Laura, it's like someone telling you there's someone living in the attic when you've been hearing footsteps your entire life. Obviously it's disturbing, but y'know ... I'm also *glad* I'm not crazy?'

'You've never mentioned this. Not once.'

'But why would I?'

Because we've talked about basically nothing else for two years. I don't see how you could keep this to yourself. All these doubts.'

I meditate on this for a second. How can I explain it to Laura? How can I explain it to someone who has never been in the closet about anything?

'I'm very good,' I say hesitantly, 'at hidings myself from myself.'

Silence.

'That's mad,' she says finally.

I shrug. 'That's how it is.'

'I should go,' Nick says, having rolled another neat cigarette. There are three now, lined up on the table next to his pint like a boiled egg and soldiers. He tucks them into the breast pocket of his denim jacket and stands up. I think he is waiting for us to ask him to stay.

'It was . . . good to meet you,' I say lamely.

'Yeah,' Laura agrees shortly. 'Thanks for everything.'

Nick slides a business card out of his wallet. It has rounded edges and a black matte finish, and says:

NICK SHERIDAN
DIRECTOR CINEMATOGRAPHER
WRITER PERFORMANCE ARTIST

I take it from him. It is heavy with professional neediness. I am glad that I do not have a business card. A website, sure. But not a business card.

'Let me know if anything comes up. Or if you just want some filmmaking tips.'

Laura makes a face, but I shake his hand. I might not like him, but there's no doubt that meeting him has changed everything.

'I just have to see it, Laura. I have to see it for myself. And if I don't do it now, I'll never do it. Because my dad will be dead.'

'You don't know that!' She interjects instinctively. I put up a hand to stop her.

'Let me finish. He'll be dead, and it will be too sad to go then. I'll be too angry and too upset and my mum won't want it, and before you know it, I'll be fifty years old. I'll finally be brave enough to go and everyone who knew him will be gone.'

My voice breaks on the word gone. Because I am comfortable, now, with words like 'die', but not at all comfortable with words like 'gone'. You talk about death and you imagine the whole morbid festival of it: the funeral, the will, people bringing food to your house. But *gone*? Vanished? Nowhere?

I keep talking with tears sliding down my cheeks.

'This is my last chance, pal. Because I have a dad, and I have you, and you . . . '

I bite down on my lip hard, worried about what I have to say is a little too much for the Laura I have now, the Mike-adjacent Laura, the Laura who always has News.

'And you make me brave.'

There it is. The cheesiest thing I could have said, and I said it. The tears keep coming, hanging off my chin like icicles.

'Oh, Charlie,' Laura says. She wraps her arms around me, smelling that Laura smell of soap and cotton and good perfume. He voice is choked, but she keeps saying my name anyway.

'Charlie, Charlie, Charlie.'

## 10

So we're going.

Laura, in typical Laura fashion, has sorted our Clipim accommodation before I've woken up. We set out at lunchtime, the car loaded up with chocolate croissants and steaming-hot coffees.

Cork City is small, but the county feels huge. Every twenty minutes I check the satnav to see whether we are still in Cork, and every twenty minutes it confirms that yes, indeed we are. We watch civilisation peel away as we drive towards Kerry, and a sense of lightness enters us.

Straight, commuter roads that offered endless assistance – this way to Galway, that way to Lidl – become narrower, greener. The bars of reception on my phone go from five to three to one. Blue-grey mountains that blot the horizon begin to move closer to us, as if politely coming to meet us halfway. I gaze at the scenery, feeling like I am daring it to mess with me.

'*As I was going over, the Cork and Kerry mountains,*' sings Laura. '*Something something about a pirate, something else about a gun.*'

I laugh, and we go straight to the chorus together. '*What for, my daddy-oh? What for, my daddy-oh? It's whiskey in the jar-oh.*'

The appearance of cows is very comforting. Livestock in general is staccato in its regularity. We spot two horses, grazing companionably in a paddock, then six horses, then twenty. Three sheep, then nine sheep, then an endless cotton-ball sea of sheep, their bodies sprayed in protective blues and pinks. Laura pulls over and demands that I take out my camera.

'Get close,' I say, as Laura tentatively approaches a lamb with a velvety black face. 'Maybe it will let you pet it.'

She inches closer, but is nervous of touching it. She hovers her hand above its puppyish body, but doesn't let it settle. It's funny. Back in London, we would have no reservations whatsoever about rushing up to a dog and petting it. Here, the outside-ness of the animals and inside-ness of ourselves makes touching them seem like littering, or pollution. I picture myself as a toxic cloud, a ball of city gas. I don't want to subject the lamb to it.

We keep driving. Eventually, it seems, we are in Kerry. Bars become pubs, and pubs become Public Houses. We pass a two-storey house that has a petrol pump in the driveway and a black A-board boasting that there's shepherd's pie served inside.

'Imagine if *that* was your local pub,' I say. 'It's literally someone's house.'

'Should we go inside?'

I don't want to seem like a spoilsport, but because it is supposed to be my ancestral homeland I feel the urge to be gung-ho about everything.

'Sure,' I say. 'But who knows whether we'll be welcome. Being English, and everything.'

She nods, and we both silently recollect Nick's warning. *Not everyone's mad on the English here and don't expect anyone to feel sorry for you about it.*

'There's a town coming up,' says Laura. 'Waterville. Probably the last big one before Clip. Do you want to stop there for dinner?'

'Do you think I'm talented?' I suddenly ask.

As burdened as this new information about Clipim and my father is, there's something else I still can't quite shake. I made *a bad film*. For years, I have been telling myself that if I only had the resources, the team and the budget, I would make something truly, uniquely special. Not commercial, necessarily, but a film people could look at and say: This matters. It *matters* that she made this.

'Sorry, what?' Laura responds, briefly taking her eyes off the road.

'Talented. Do you think I'm an artist? Do you think I have what it takes?'

'Of course I think you're talented. Why else would I work with you?'

'Worked, Laura. You worked with me. Now you're moving to LA. *Village* will probably be the last thing we ever work on together.'

'Don't say that.'

'Why not? It's true.'

'I have a temporary work visa, Charlie. It will only last me a year.'

'But presumably if this TV show gets another season, it will get extended, right? They'll sponsor you, won't they?'

'I don't know.'

But she does know. She must know. If I see her destiny so clearly, then so must she. One of the big TV networks will give her a job, and then she'll guest direct a couple of episodes of some HBO series, and then, before you know it, she'll be directing a Leni Riefenstahl biopic and be on the cover of *The Hollywood Reporter*.

'You're talented,' I say pointedly. 'No one can argue with that.'

'Jesus Christ, Charlie.'

'What? It's true, isn't it?'

'Babe,' she says, shifting the gear stick, the action infused with rigid frustration, 'I believe the word you're looking for is congratulations.'

'I did congratulate you.'

'No, you didn't.'

'Well, then. It's implicit. Congratulations. I'm proud of you. That's obvious, isn't it?'

We are silent for a while then. We can't sync Spotify to the car radio, so we are stuck with what I have on my phone, which is mostly the songs that we listened to in our Uni days. We listen to the entirety of Florence and the Machine's first album, our tension suppressing our natural instinct to sing along. Laura hums.

'Let's stop for sandwiches in Waterville, or something,' I say.

She nods. The song changes.

'Charlie, what are you looking for in Clipim? I mean, really?'

I look out of the window. There's a roadside sign for a nearby nursing home. There are a huge amount of advertisements for elderly care in Ireland. They seem to have more old people than anywhere else.

'I think my dad has been lying to me,' I say slowly. 'And I don't know what to do with that.'

'Okay,' she says, nodding. 'Okay. We can work with that. You think he's lying to you. About what?'

'I don't know. The script always changes around what it was like for him and his mum on the island after the accident. He seems to have all this resentment for the people who live there, because of how he was treated as the last survivor or whatever, but then he will flip, and suddenly everyone has this noble Celtic spirit. Sometimes . . . sometimes I feel like even he doesn't know what happened.' I break off.

'You don't get it,' I say finally, gazing out of the window. 'No one's weird in your family.'

'In my family?' Laura says, laughing. 'May I remind you that Federica has a pet rock called Scarlett O'Hara?'

'No, but that's like ... kooky, charming weird. Rich people in the countryside weird.'

'Right.' She stiffens. She hates when I bring up her rich parents.

'But my family ... I don't know how to explain it to you. Do you know my mum has had three miscarriages?'

'Wow. No.'

'Two before I was born, one when I was seven,' I say, a little guilty for betraying Mum. Dad made her wait a long time for children, convinced that his past made him an unfit candidate for fatherhood. 'I thought I would be one of those awful overprotective parents,' he used to say. 'You'd be too precious to me.'

'When did you find this out?' asks Laura.

'Last year, from my Aunt Eleanor. We were up drinking wine last Christmas, and I made this crack about how I sometimes imagined myself as the middle child of four, with all these great crazy siblings. And Eleanor's face goes all dark and maudlin.'

'What? Why?'

'She started saying about how she was glad my mother had finally told me.'

'That she had three miscarriages?'

I prop my elbow on the car window and lean into it. 'Who knows, maybe I internalised the idea that I was supposed to have three siblings, or something.'

'Dee and Simon and Andrew.'

I smile at her. Sometimes it's nice to just know that some-one knows you.

'Right,' I confirm. 'I didn't know she had three mis-carriages. I don't know her *age*. It's all these weird, rotting secrets with them, and I'm the same. I mean, I never bothered coming out to my mum. She might know. She might have guessed. But we've never once had like ... a conversation about one another's internal lives.'

'You're right, that is weirder than Feddy's rock.'

'Yes, thank you.'

As we drive, I start thinking about my grandmother, and how it must have been for a widow with one son to live alone on an island. She wasn't even *from* Clipim. Her husband had been the native. When he died after falling off a roof, Kitty Regan's presence was felt to be extraneous. She managed to get odd jobs, cleaning for the hotel and the boarding houses, turning over barely enough to keep the rented roof over their heads, a trail of islander pity following her wherever she went. Pity that never quite extended to warmth, because not only was she not Clip, she was not *regular.*

Dad says that she's where I get it from. 'Quiet, clever, and a bit of a slave to misery,' he says. I asked him once if she were alive today, would she be diagnosed with depression. He said probably.

The morning of the tragedy, she had sent for him to come home, and that wasn't an uncommon thing for Kitty Regan to do. Nightmares kept her awake at night, and that sleeplessness added to her anxieties during the day. She would take him out of school, ostensibly for an errand, and then sit across from him blankly, trying to think of things for him to do.

We stop in Waterville, which appears to have more Charlie Chaplin memorabilia per square foot than any place on earth. We buy toasted cheese sandwiches from a Charlie's Cafe, which is next door to a Charlie Chaplin Film Centre. We unwrap them on a bench, staring at the irate grey ocean. There is no beach in Waterville, just some stones and a harbour. An older woman appears next to us, lighting up a cigarette.

'Visiting?'

Laura and I both say 'yes' at once.

'English,' she says, as if settling a debate with herself. 'Where are you two off to, then?'

'Clipim.'

She snorts, as if this is funny. She takes a long drag of her cigarette.

'Wedding?'

'No.'

'Most people now would only be going across for a wedding. Some lovely gardens there. Great for the photographs.'

We nod. I remember this from my research. Weddings are a big business on the island. Clipim, despite being roughly eight miles long, is an island of two halves. The west side of the island is the side where the ferry docks, and as a result, the historically more moneyed half. The fishing was good, the hunting laws were flexible, and so for a long time the English treated west Clipim as a sort of pleasure island. They built huge, Victorian manors, complete with sprawling grounds, red deer and rose gardens. The eastern Irish side lived in service of the western English side, and everyone – according to the historians who have covered the subject, anyway – got along reasonably well.

I peer at the woman sitting next to us. She's stoutly disapproving of us, yet chatty. Sociable because the only alternative would be to talk to no one. I keep tracing sketches of my grandmother over her, wondering how like this Kitty would have been.

It's in this abstract wondering where I suddenly remember something about my grandmother. Something I haven't heard in years, but is floating to the surface now like an old fishing net.

'Her father was in the war,' Dad told me once. There's no point asking which war. The War of Independence looms larger in my father's consciousness than either world war. He sees it as having more to do with him, despite it ending thirty years before he was born.

'Went on two hunger strikes. He was a bit tapped, after that,' he said, tapping the side of his temple.

'You mean starvation made him crazy?'

'Not so much the starving as the force feeding and the beating,' he said casually. 'Anyway, it turned him into a bit of a monster. His son left home to join the British Army, and you can imagine how *that* went down.'

'You can see Clip from here,' the Waterville woman says, pointing her finger to a humpbacked, blue mound in the distance. 'Not every day. The cloud would be covering it most days. But we always say that if you can see Clip, you can put the washing out, because it will be dry all day.'

I keep hold of this for a second, this little piece of local knowledge. It's nothing, really, a bit of trivia. A pub quiz question or a cryptic crossword clue: *What Kerry island can only be seen on a clear day?*

'It's so quiet here, you know?' she says, reapplying her lipstick. Her lips curve tightly inwards as she traces a wide oval shape. 'You hardly ever get the young people through here any more. They're all up in Dingle.'

'What's in Dingle?' I ask politely.

'A fecking dolphin,' she responds.

'Just one?'

'Well, there's a bit of controversy around that, now,' she says, before looking at us conspiratorially, as though she were merely confirming rumours we must have been hearing for months. 'They say that they switch out the dolphin every five years or so, it's not the original dolphin any more.

'Only now,' she continues triumphantly, despite no one responding to her initial comment, 'now the lads in Dingle are having kittens over Skellig Michael. Have ye been over to Skellig yet?'

'No.'

'Ah, now, you'll have to. They did the *Star Wars* out there.'

'Sorry, what?'

'*Star Wars*. Do you know the *Star Wars*?'

'Yes, we know *Star Wars*.'

'Well, they filmed it there. They turned the puffins into the porgs. They're only delighted with themselves over in Portmagee. *Porg*magee. Google it.'

We silently decide that she is insane, and Laura adopts her gentlest talking-to-an-old-lady voice.

'So, did Charlie Chaplin live here, or what?'

'Oh, no. Him?' she says, pointing at the Little Tramp on her T-shirt. 'He came here every year on his summer holidays. He stayed at that hotel.'

She points at the only hotel on the street, which is also called Charlie's. It is disconcerting to see my name everywhere. A welcome for someone else.

We drive on for another forty minutes, barely speaking except to murmur agreement on the music. We're on The Dresden Dolls now. All the music we used to listen to together is like this. Witchy, feminine, full of big gestures and circus make-up. I wonder if she listens to different music now, boy music, or worse, *couple* music.

Somewhere between the singing and the silence, the water comes into view. It's nowhere, and then it's everywhere. Ocean traces along the left-hand side of the car like an armed escort, and it makes us delirious with pleasure. The country roads loop and swerve around mountains, rivers and cliffs, making it difficult to drive through and absolutely breathtaking to witness. I roll the window down to touch the mountainside, trying to prove to Laura how narrow and close the road is. I pinch a handful of yellow flowers, the same yellow flowers that seem to grow everywhere in Kerry.

I rub my fingers over the satiny petals, and work on a

memory. Something has been coming together for me since we met the woman in Waterville. I am building on it like a bird builds a nest. Bits of family folklore drift into my consciousness, foggy and broken. I turn it around and around, putting it together, tearing it apart. I am searching my brain for things my dad said about his family, looking within memories for more memories. Something about the army.

An image of myself sitting in front of the TV with my homework open on my lap. My dad on the couch next to me. The material is a dark mustard, almost a dingy green. This is not the couch we have in our living room now. This is a couch from two couches ago.

There's a war on TV, and my dad is yelling about his favourite topic: young people dying for no reason. It must be the Iraq War, because I'm a teenager, and because he is yelling a lot about the British, and how they stick their noses into everything. My mum is furious with him. Not play-furious, like you see happy couples do, but genuinely irate.

'Don't put your ignorance on Charlotte,' she snapped. 'You'll teach her to have no British pride.'

Yes. That was it. That is why this memory is so clear to me. My parents, who were usually so mild with one another in his healthy days, were suddenly spitting. Dad stood up from his chair and turned off the TV. Mum and I shared a panicked look. Dad rarely lost his temper, but it was always for the most bizarre things when he did.

'British pride,' he spat. *'British pride?'*

He started ticking off atrocities on his fingers, ways in which the concept of 'British pride' had wounded him.

Laura suddenly turns down the music. 'You okay, babe?'

'Huh?'

'You haven't said anything in a while.'

'Oh, yeah?' I gaze out of the window and see that the landscape has changed once again. We are up very high now, on a road so narrow that it feels like we could topple into the valley below. 'I'm just thinking.'

I try to go back to the scene. My brain feels like it's breaking, but I keep worming my way through. He had a chronology of bad things that the British had done, and they had amounted to this: his grandfather, who he had never met, had been almost killed by the Black and Tans in the War of Independence. His uncle had joined the British Army and been killed in the Second World War, sending his grandfather into an insane, lifelong fury. A fury that he then took out on his daughter, Kitty, which then affected my father, Colm. The whole thing was a conga line of grief, one which he credited Britain for starting.

'If you hate it so much, why did you bloody come here?' My mum bit back, exposing the nerve centre of her hurt feelings. 'Why do you even *stay*?'

We pass through another village. Laura is clearly bored now, just reading signs aloud, each keen to tell us when the next market day is. I keep staring out of the window, the petals falling apart between my finger and thumb.

Then I remember it.

'Believe me, Sharon, if I could go back, I *would* go back.'

I don't recall what happened then. He might have stormed out. Maybe Mum did. Maybe I went to my room. It's quite possible nothing happened at all, and that we all carried on watching the Iraq War. But that sentence lodged in my brain like unwrapped toffee, hair and dirt sticking to it as the years piled on. That's when it all started, I think. That's when I started asking my dad about Clipim.

Finally, as though these memories were nothing more than a lengthy maths equation drawn across a chalkboard, I realise something. Something important. I had assumed that when my dad said 'if I could go back, I would go back', it was because my mum and I were keeping him hostage. That he was saddled with two British women, and if he wasn't he would be back on the island. But what if he literally *couldn't* go back? What if he wasn't welcome? What if I wasn't, either?

'The ferry port is just ahead,' Laura says cheerily. 'Three miles.'

I squint my eyes at the ocean. It has spent the last hour stretching alongside us, and has finally worked up the courage to meet us face-on. Clipim is right there, eight miles from the coast.

Eventually we reach a small car park, a dock and a converted shed that operates as a ticket booth.

Laura parks the car abruptly and takes a deep inward breath.

'Charlie, are you sure you want to do this?'

I worry my hands together, genuinely nervous now.

'Yes,' I say, after a few moments. 'Whatever's on that island, I'm never going to find out unless I go right now.'

'Are you sure?'

Another pause.

'Yes.'

Laura drives up to the booth, where a bearded man in a yellow windbreaker is doing a Sudoku puzzle. He gives us a blank, incurious glance, revealing the largest, greyest eyebrows I have ever seen. He pushes a button on his cash register.

'Four euros forty,' he says.

'Per person, or ...'

'Four euros forty,' he repeats, and Laura hands him over a ten-euro note. The cash register is empty, so he gets our change out of a locked iron box where he also appears to be storing two sandwiches.

'Do you want to go now?'

'Yes, please.'

He gives us one sharp tut, and puts his puzzle to one side.

'Two minutes, so.'

We watch him get out of his booth, slide on a pair of wellies, and walk over to the ferry docked in the pier.

'Is this a one-man operation?' asks Laura. 'Does he take the money, AND drive the ferry?'

'I guess so.'

The man pulls up the hood on his windbreaker, unties the one-car ferry from the bollard, and starts looking around, obviously irritated.

'Satan! Satan!'

Laura and I watch him, our mouths open in disbelief.

'Saaaaaaaaaay-tan! Satan!'

'Is he saying . . . ?'

'Satan. Yes. He's shouting about Satan.'

We sit in the car in silence, wondering if there's anything to be done about this new development, and whether we have enough energy to do it if there is. Then, a very small, very old terrier bounds out of a nearby field, leaps over the pier, and into the ferry. The man gets behind the wheel, reverses it to the carport, and beckons us on.

'Well, I guess that's Satan.'

The boat's engine sounds like an old woman clearing her throat. It takes a minute, then stops completely, then takes another thirty seconds before moving. Finally, the ferry begins puttering away from the mainland with Laura and me aboard it. Satan, his tongue to the orange sky, pants the whole way.

# PART TWO

On Raglan Road on an autumn day I met her
  first and knew
That her dark hair would weave a snare that I
  might one day rue;
I saw the danger, yet I walked along the
  enchanted way,
And I said, let grief be a fallen leaf at the dawning
  of the day.

*'On Raglan Road'*,
PATRICK KAVANAGH, 1946

**11**

Satan is much friendlier than his name might suggest. When we get out of the car at Clipim ten minutes later, he leaps up to greet me and Laura, burrowing his head into our legs, groaning slightly at the pleasure of having his ears rubbed.

'Why do you call him Satan?' I ask the ferry driver. 'He's so friendly.'

He bends down to pick up Satan, circling his arms around the dog, who immediately collapses with joy. The ferryman holds out Satan's left paw.

'What do you see here?'

'A paw.'

'Look closer. Look at his claws.'

I look at them, and then blink.

'Six claws.'

'How many are they supposed to have?' asks Laura.

'Five in front, four in back,' he answers. 'Satan has six. Six, six, six, the number of the beast.'

'Old Testament?'

'Iron Maiden.'

I decide in that moment that I like the ferryman.

'My name's Charlie,' I say. 'This is Laura.'

'Joe,' he says, and from under his eyebrows, I can make out that he's in his fifties. He was probably too young to be in school at the time of the tragedy. He might have had an older brother or sister in the schoolhouse.

'You've come at the best time,' he volunteers. 'Too early for tourists, but the sky is still nice and bright. Are ye here long?'

'Until the day after tomorrow. Our flight is from Cork.'

'Enough to visit the Button Museum then,' he says, with a sly wink. I laugh.

'Is it any good?'

'It's better than good,' he laughs. 'It's awful.'

Laura takes out her phone, and shows him her booking confirmation from the caravan.

'Do you know where this is?' she asks. 'Barrow Mews?'

'That's Benjamin Barry's place,' he says, rolling his eyes. He points to the narrow street running perpendicular to the ferry. 'Go up the Main Street, turn left, and there's a long lane. Left again, and you'll see a sign. He'll come out to meet you.'

'What if he's not home?'

Joe smiles, as if this were an incredible idea. We say good-bye and get back in the car, driving slowly to take in as much of the town as we can. The Main Street is everything I wanted from Cork, magnified. Two-storey brick buildings are painted mustard yellow, bright red and brilliant white. A shop selling wool jumpers, and only wool jumpers. There is the faint sound of whistle music coming from somewhere. There are two pubs – the tiny An Spailpín Fánach, and the more authoritative-looking The Fiddler. Both of them have TripAdvisor and Yelp stickers in the window. The Fiddler has an A-board on the street outside.

### TODAY'S SPECIALS

BACON AND CABBAGE
SEAFOOD CHOWDER

SMOKED SALMON W/ BROWN BREAD
REAL GUINNESS

And then, on the other side of the board:

**ALL-DAY BRUNCH:**

BOTTOMLESS MIMOSAS
PANCAKES
HOTDOGS

'Wow,' says Laura. 'I guess they know their audience. Yanks with money.'

We drive slowly past the new school, the Father Michael Fahy National School. It's beautiful, the kind of school you dream about going to: all yellow and white, with neatly planted posies lining the bright red iron gates. There's a silver-plated plaque hammered to the wall, and I crane my head out of the window to see what it says.

THIS SCHOOL WAS ERECTED IN 1964 AND
PAID FOR BY DONATIONS SOLICITED FROM
THE KIND PEOPLE OF IRELAND

WITH THE HELP OF FATHER
MICHAEL FAHY

'I never thought about that,' Laura says. 'That they had to get a new school after the old one ... '

'Yeah. Neither had I.'

I had seen photos of Father Michael Fahy: a square-shouldered man with the face of a dentist. *He* had given interviews. The type of interviews where the journalist takes special care to add adjectives to describe just how a person is saying something. *He says thoughtfully. He insists gently. He wonders sadly.*

'Did the Foleys have him in their pocket too, I wonder?'

'What, do you think the priest might have been in on it?'

What a sentence. I have to keep reminding myself that this is not a movie and I am not Humphrey Bogart.

There's a doll-sized fire station with two small trucks badly parked outside. There's a tourist office, closed now, its windows littered with advertisements for the equestrian centre and a seaweed-cooking class. Every business seems to have one thing in common – their windows are flashed up with stickers from various online review forums.

*People love us on TripAdvisor*

*Zagat guide 2004*

*Find us on Yelp!*

Each one is designed to give the business a competitive edge over its neighbours, but the whole thing is rendered void because everywhere has been blessed with the same honour. Every building is stocky and proud of itself, a gaggle of Boy Scouts each with the same badge.

One thing is clear: Dad couldn't have been more wrong about this place.

Laura spots a flier for a jellyfish photography class that happens once a fortnight, hosted by Benjamin Barry.

'Is that our Benjamin Barry?' she asks. 'Caravan Benjamin Barry?'

'Maybe there's more than one Benjamin Barry.'

But there is only one Benjamin Barry, and he is our Benjamin Barry.

Benjamin Barry is waiting at the front gate wearing wellies, shorts and the kind of hemp-woven hoodie that is between a purple and a moss green. Laura rolls down the window, and he crouches down to speak to us. His face is so far into the car that he could turn his head and touch the steering wheel with his nose.

'Charlie and Laura?'

We nod. Barry sticks his forearm into the car to shake my hand and Laura's.

'You must be Ben,' says Laura, attempting to match his enthusiasm.

'Benjamin, if you don't mind. Welcome, welcome, welcome!'

Benjamin Barry is about my dad's age, which immediately makes me think that he must not be from here. If Ferryman Joe and Dad are anything to go by, the Clipim personality is that of warm remoteness: of being apart from the herd, but enjoying the activities of the herd nonetheless. Benjamin's insistent welcome and faintly New Age air all smack of else-where, but my knowledge of Irish accents isn't good enough to know exactly where.

'Was the ferry all right?'

'It was fine,' I say, waiting for him to open the gate. 'We met Joe.'

'Joe!' he says, with far more enthusiasm than Joe was able to muster for him. 'Wonderful Joe. You girls must be excited for your stay. Clip is so beautiful this time of year, you know. Too early for all the tourists, but the sky is still nice and bright.'

'That . . . that seems to be the consensus, yes.'

'And you'll have the whole campsite to yourselves! Lucky ducks.'

I ask him, as politely as I can, whether the caravan is ready yet.

'Charlie!' Benjamin says, appalled. 'Caravan? It's a *mobile home.*'

Eventually he waves us through to the campsite and gives us the key to our mobile home, an odd rectangular structure that looks like a tin box from the outside and like the 1980s on the inside. Flowered wallpaper haunts the living-room-cum-kitchen area. The couches are covered in mock velvet the colour of walnuts. I run my fingers across it. There's a nauseous prickly softness to it that makes me snatch my hand away.

'Ah, you'll be nice and cosy in here, with the little electric fire on,' says Benjamin, who has insisted on showing us every single feature of the place, from the bedding cupboard to the kettle. 'Well, you'll see soon, won't you!'

He makes repeated insistences that he is going to 'get out of our hair', but he lingers on, telling us about Clip, about his jellyfish photography class, and about how he is currently in a dispute with the local farming community over some kind of plant. His skin has the just-boiled quality people have when they shower more often than their body would like them to, manifesting itself as a reddish sheen that intensifies as he talks. Laura and I blink heavily, eventually yawning so loudly that he leaves.

'Jesus,' says Laura. 'What the hell was that?'

'I guess he's lonely. He must be coming off the end of a long quiet season.'

'Quiet season? The bloke never shuts up.'

'Tell me about it,' I say. 'There're two bedrooms, though, so take whichever one you want.'

I say it lightly, to make it clear I don't care where she sleeps.

'Thanks,' she responds, matching my tone. 'So, when are you going to start asking questions?'

'I don't know,' I reply, kicking my shoes off and stretching out on the sofa. I can't stop thinking about my dad's assertion that if he *could* come back here, he would. 'I guess we need to find out what the IRA history is like in the area.'

'Nick said that Foley profited out of the tragedy. The land grab, you know.'

'Yes. The land grab,' I reply, trying to get it all straight in my head. 'Of course.'

Laura starts to laugh.

'What are you laughing at?'

'Nothing. I just hadn't realised how Nancy Drew this whole thing is.'

I can't help but laugh too. It *is* ridiculous. *'Nancy Drew and the Curse of the Gentrified Island.'*

*'Nancy Drew and the Mystery of the Bad TripAdvisor Review,'* she responds.

'You saw that too?' I say, glad that Laura and I still tend to notice the same things, without even mentioning them. 'They're *really* into their Yelp reviews here.'

Laura starts hunting through the kitchen cabinets. 'It's like you said, isn't it? They're really dependent on their tourist trade here. I guess if the thing you were most famous for was the death of a load of kids, you would cling to your positive online ratings, too.'

We walk into town, hoping to find a corner shop that will still be open at this time. On the high street, we find a well-stocked little shop, a cottage that clearly functions as someone's home. We peer through the door, willing someone to open it.

'It's shut,' I say, hungry and miserable. 'When does it open?'

'Uh . . . June,' answers Laura, pointing at a sign.

'What?'

'It's only open for the summer season.'

'That's ridiculous. Surely people need food all year round.'

She shrugs. 'Maybe the locals get food somewhere else.'

'*Where* else?'

Another shrug. 'Ocado?'

Eventually, we decide to eat in the pub.

The Fiddler is dark and cosy, and has a fire already going in the grate. The walls are filled with pictures: one of a boating race from 1933, a sponsored walk from 2003, a cycling event from last year. There are old clapboard toucans promoting Guinness, maps of Clipim bay, rosettes from local horse races.

There are many, many photos of President John F. Kennedy's visit to Ireland in June 1963: just five months before his death on 22 November. Less than two weeks after the Clipim disaster. There are headlines about his assassination, framed extracts from the piece Patrick Kavanagh wrote for *The Irish Times*.

Kind readers, I am here in London and as I write with a time lag of a week it will be understood that we are still darkly under the awful cloud of a murdered king.

There is nothing about the schoolhouse. There is only the kind of artful, comforting clutter that comes naturally to country pubs. I squint at the walls, pretending to look interested in the photo of a harpist from 1944, but really trying to see if there's anything even vaguely relating to my dad's childhood. There isn't.

Nothing about the school kids. Nothing about the Foleys. *Believe me, Sharon, if I could go back, I would go back.*

We grab a table by the fire and exchange comments about how nice everything is. We look at our menus. Holding court behind the bar is a girl of about thirty with black hair and skin the colour of bone. Every stool at the bar is filled, and it's clear from the way everyone's sitting in their seats that those are truly *their* seats, a position either earned or inherited. Constant as the fraying of the shoreline. I can't hear what she's saying, but every few minutes a swell of laughter reaches our table.

I assess the menu. I try to figure out how I can spend the least money without attracting any attention from Laura, who will offer to pay, which will leave me in the position of either refusing her, thus making a fuss, or accepting her, and then having to be grateful. I'm so sick of feeling grateful.

'I'm really in the mood for some soup,' I announce. 'I'm going to have the potato and leek soup.'

'Soup? *Really?*'

'Yes.'

A moment of silence while she considers challenging me, but it passes.

'Fine. I'll order at the bar.'

A silence falls over us when she comes back. A silence with a mother who I can't fully name. I can't stop looking at the people at the bar. How deeply comfortable they are, both with themselves and with each other. It makes my relationship with Laura feel shallow and strained. I picture life after she moves to LA. Will it really be that big a loss? Is there anything more to me and Laura than vague creative ambitions and jokes about Nancy Drew?

The longer we sit, the less comfortable the silence is.

'So,' she announces, after logging into the wifi, checking her emails, her Twitter and her Instagram. 'Have you heard from your dad at all?'

'No. I didn't tell him we were coming to Clipim, and I definitely don't want to tell him now. If he's been hiding this IRA thing my entire life, I don't see why he would suddenly unveil it.'

'Good call,' she says. She looks as though she's about to ask after his health, but remembers she's done that already today. She repeats 'good call' again.

The screech of a stool leg makes us both look up. A grey-haired man of about fifty stands up at the bar and places one hand on his stomach, the other on a beer tap.

With no warning or explanation, he starts to sing. His voice is huge and booming, reverberating off the decorative tin mugs that are hanging off the ceiling. It's not so much a folk song as an operetta. His singing lends itself to painted scenery and an admiral's hat, his face turning a rapid rose the longer he goes on.

*My heart is broken, but what care I?*
*Such pride inside me has spoken,*
*I shall do my best not to cry, by and by,*
*When the final farewells must be spoken.*

'Gosh,' Laura says, blinking in surprise. 'That's ... uh, that's something. Weird to rhyme "spoken" with "spoken".'

I can't help glaring at her. Someone is singing unaccompanied and in perfect tune, and all Laura can talk about is the rhyme scheme.

Just when we think he has finished, he downs the last milky glug of his Guinness and starts again. '*Goodbye! Goodbye! I wish you all a last goodbye.*'

The black-haired barmaid starts a response, waving a dishcloth like it's a handkerchief. '*Goodbye! Goodbye! I wish you all a last goodbye!*'

Everyone at the bar is doing it now. Half for themselves, half for the benefit of the tourists in their Patagonia jackets who are sitting and gawping. A man is surreptitiously taking a video on his phone, and for a moment, I'm sure that the man singing is going to wrench the phone away from him. I *want* the singer to wrench it away from him. I want this moment to exist only for the people in this pub, not to be given some glib caption online. It feels exploitative to collect a moment of someone's life as though it were a butterfly in a jar. I'm about to voice this thought to Laura, until I realise that it's exactly what *It Takes a Village* is.

But the singer walks over to the man, and sings directly into the phone's camera, winking and gurning. He throws his arm over the man's shoulder, and the camera is astutely switched to selfie mode.

I want to enjoy this. I know I'm supposed to be enjoying this. But there's something strangely scandalising about someone performing their national identity at you with such muscular pride. I feel like I should look away.

The two men turn to our table, the tourist mumbling, the Irish man singing for his life. For one terrifying moment, I'm sure he recognises me. The daughter of the boy who lived. For all I know, they've all been keeping tabs on Colm Regan and his progeny for years.

'*Then I leave behind and so, I go! To fight a savage foe!*' The singer grabs Laura's hand, dragging her into the pageant. '*Although! I know! That I'll be sometimes missed by the girls I've kissed!*'

Laura collapses into giggles, and everyone in the bar claps earnestly. An American accent pipes up above the din.

'So are you leaving or not, you show boater?'

It's the barmaid. The one with the black hair. American. There's a surprise.

'I'm off!' he announces. 'Don't bother tipping the cute hoor behind the bar.'

'Did he just call her a whore?' Laura says, as if this is the only shocking thing that has happened in the last ten minutes.

The food comes. I eat my soup and say 'mmm' a lot, to defend getting the soup in the first place. Laura has fish and chips.

'It's such a shame we have nothing like that in England,' she says, squeezing a lemon dressed in muslin cloth. 'People are too self-aware.'

'What do you mean by that?'

'What?'

'Self-aware. It sounds like you think that Irish people sing because they don't have the rational good sense to be ashamed of themselves.'

'Well, maybe they don't.'

I don't have time to pick apart what, exactly, is annoying about this statement, because a man at the next table starts talking to me.

'Sorry, girls, you aren't from London by any chance, are you?'

An English man in his late-thirties wearing a maroon corduroy jacket starts talking to us. The very fact of him feels alarmingly out of place. Like finding a River Island in the Kalahari Desert.

'Yes!' Laura smiles. 'She lives in south-east, and I'm in Shoreditch.'

'I work in Shoreditch!' He beams. 'Or, worked. My agency is still there but I work remotely from here. My mum's still in Leyton, though.'

'You live *here*?'

'Yep!' he says proudly, and an attractive pregnant woman who I assume to be his wife sits down next to him, all smiles.

'Kate! Londoners!'

The man has now fully swivelled around, making himself and his wife part of our table. Laura pushes two low stools out with her foot, inviting them to sit down. The three of them all say 'small world' at the exact same time. The conversation at the bar has moved on to the lambing season. Despite knowing nothing about lambs, I wish I was in their conversation and not this one.

'Oh Jesus, you won't shake him all night now,' the wife says, sipping at a Diet Coke. She's Irish, but not from here. 'Tobes, they're on their holidays. They don't want to be hanging round with two old losers like us.'

Nevertheless, we get the whole Toby and Kate story. They met in London. They lived there for ten years. They got married in one of the ex-stately homes on the island and loved the place so much they decided to live here. 'Everyone was shocked,' they laugh. 'And even more shocked when they heard we didn't have a shower for two months. We had to rely on Benjamin for everything.'

'Benjamin Barry? The caravan guy?'

'Not just the caravan guy,' Toby says. 'The estate agent guy.'

'He owns property all over the shop,' says Kate. 'He's

Clipim's resident house-flipper. You need a lot of odd jobs to keep yourself going here. The tourism trade is scant enough in the winter months.'

'Unless you're us,' Toby counters. 'The people bringing in the foreign money.'

This story has clearly been told many times, for the benefit of friends and tourists. This story is a relay race, the stick passed, endlessly and effortlessly, by two very nice people who have never been told that their stories are anything less than spectacular.

Toby buys a round and tells us how he didn't believe in marriage until three years ago.

'Just as well,' he says. 'What with Brexit, and everything. Actually, I just got my Irish passport in the post.' He slides the little red book out of a padded envelope, taps the harp on the cover, then kisses it. 'I love my wife.'

'You love the EU,' Kate pipes up.

'I can love both of you, can't I?'

I try, in all my Essex-born naivety, to imagine myself as an Irish nationalist. What would I make of the Tobys of the world? The people who are steeped in several generations of British privilege, who can languorously stretch one hand out and snatch anything from this little island whenever they feel like it. There's something inherently infuriating about it, and for a moment, I want to grab Toby's new passport and wallop him across the face with it.

And just like that, the feeling dissipates. I'm back to watching a man celebrate his wife and his new country. I'm back to being the liberal twenty-something who believes that people should live where they want.

We part ways outside the pub an hour later. Laura and Toby are still chanting the names of people they both know at each other.

'Laila!' Laura shrieks. 'You know Laila?'

'Laila Kahn? She was my intern!'

'She's my *manager*!'

The Clipim hills are a blue-grey band around the night, nestling us like small children. We yell 'bye' at Kate and Toby as they walk to their cottage on the west side. We go east.

'They were nice,' Laura says bouncily. 'Imagine, meeting Londoners on our first night!'

'Imagine,' I agree.

My stomach gnaws hungrily at me the entire walk home.

## 12

By the time we get back to the caravan, my stomach is so loud that Laura is actively annoyed at me about it.

'Why didn't you eat properly in the pub? I would have given you the cash.'

'I don't know.' I flop down on the couch and close my eyes.

'Well, now *I'm* hungry,' she announces, and I listen to her opening and closing cupboards.

'Weird, those two,' she says off-handedly. 'It's a weird spot in the map to choose to live in.'

'There's actually a history of it. Because it was the last spot people left before emigrating a lot of people who worked for the big ocean liners set up offices here. It was a proper Victorian market town.'

'You never mentioned that before.'

'Didn't I?'

'Not once.' She sits back down, munching on a box of Ritz crackers. 'So, people were, like, worldly.'

I remember again my dad's self-hating excuse about the oil burner, and how the people of Clipim would have been too ignorant to maintain it, or check for wear and tear.

'Yeah,' I say slowly. 'That's why so many English people were living here, remember? Hence Nick's dad's IRA theory, I guess.'

She crunches on and passes the box to me.

'Weird how people go backwards. How progress isn't always a straight line.'

'Yeah.'

I start loading my mouth with crackers. 'To hear my dad talk about it, you'd swear it was just a backwoods.'

'But you've always known that it wasn't.'

'Pretty much. Well, since I started researching it properly.'

'Huh.'

'Why "huh"?'

'"Huh" because I don't think you realise how weird it is to believe two things at once. You believed everything your dad said, while simultaneously knowing the other thing was true.'

'I guess,' I say, as if this has been the first time this has occurred to me. 'The funny thing is, now it's neither one thing nor the other. It's not a bustling market town full of poshos and their horses. But it's not a super-rural off-grid paradise either. It's ... TripAdvisor and people named Toby.'

'That would be a good documentary feature, wouldn't it?' she says. 'Small towns and super-niche tourist trades. We could talk to the Charlie Chaplin woman in Waterville about the dolphin in Dingle she hates so much.'

'And then we could find the woman in Dingle who hates the Charlie Chaplin museum,' I respond.

Laura starts opening more cabinets. 'Netflix would snap that shit up.'

'And they'd give it some self-important title,' I laugh. 'Like ... *A Yelp in the Woods*.'

'*A Yelp in the Woods*,' she repeats. 'That's funny.'

'Well, I'm very funny.'

'Oh, yesssssssss,' she says, suddenly triumphant. 'Come to Mama.'

Laura is holding a bottle of Jameson.

We spend the rest of the night lying on the floor in the caravan drinking whiskey out of mugs and eating crackers

with the electric fire still on. We talk about the Netflix doc-
umentaries we're going to make, the TV shows we're going
to write, the internationally-charting podcast series we'll host
and produce once she gets back from LA. All these conversations exist in the universe of Laura returning from LA in a
year, when we'll both be more experienced, and have more
clout to make the movies we want to make.

'I'll introduce you to Sayid at Channel 5 before I go,' she
says benevolently. 'You'll get a job as a runner or a researcher,
no problem.'

I don't ask her what has taken her so long to introduce me
to Sayid. I just say thank you, and fall asleep picturing the
next year of my life: a year of working night shoots, of eating
boxed lunches on set, of rapping on dressing-room doors and
saying, 'Five minutes till call time!' Maybe I will move out
of the room in West Norwood and get somewhere closer to
town, with housemates. It might be like the Clapham days
again, only with central heating. I'll finally be able to afford
some decent clothes. I'll finally be able to ask someone out
for a drink and not worry about having to pay for the drink.
I fantasise about meeting Laura in a year's time, in a pub with
my new girlfriend.

When I wake up, it's 4.35 a.m. and there's a cracker ground
into the shirt I'm wearing. Laura is next to me, her sleeping face pressed into her bracelets. I move her head on to a
cushion as gently as I can, so she won't wake up with bead
imprints on her forehead. I stand up, and the blackness of the
Kerry night through the living-room window weighs down
on me for the first time. It's the kind of darkness that your
eyes need time to adjust to, the extreme depth of it almost as
blinding as fluorescence.

I step outside, barefoot, and walk through the campsite.
I can smell the Atlantic, but I can't see it. The isolation of
my senses from one another makes the world seem distant,

something that begins a few feet ahead of me but not quite right now. It's like I'm not really walking alone at night, but playing a video game of myself. There are stars but no moon, caravans but no people. I circle the place, full of energy. I feel like the lone urban fox I sometimes see on my walk home from the cafe: quiet, fierce and curious.

The cold air hits me like a scythe. It makes me feel fresh, ready.

I eventually find grass, and my toes tickle with gratitude at the lush, long feel of it. I keep going, unsure of where, exactly, the campsite ends.

I expect to find a wall or a fence, but instead find myself swallowed by trees. The grass has given way to earth and branches, and rubbery needles stick to the balls of my feet – like pine, but less abrasive. It occurs to me that I'm no longer in a place for people. This is no longer a campsite, no longer a town, no longer a named history. This is a wood, one full of trees where the branches shoot out from every direction, reaching alternately for the ground and the sky. They arch above my head, wide as elephant trunks. They clutch at my T-shirt, slender as the wrists of children. My shoulder blades hunch together, poised for something. Seconds ago I felt like an urban fox, but right now I feel like an escaped pet rabbit.

There's a narrow path beaten through the trees, and this confirmation of humanity makes me release my breath, though I was barely conscious of holding it in the first place. I can't see the stars any more, just a web of branches and nee-dles. I spend a few moments standing perfectly still, my eyes closed. I breathe the trees in, the night wind hitting my lungs like metal. I feel hyperconscious of the small movements around me: of ferns waving, of animals moving, of every micro-transaction of energy that is constantly taking place. Around me, above me, through me. I remember how Dad said that people used to believe in fairies in Clip.

Then, all at once, there's the feeling of light playing on my eyelids, and I know I'm not alone, and possibly haven't been alone for some time.

'Is that Charlie?'

I open my eyes. Benjamin Barry is shining a torch in my face.

'Hi,' I say, covering my face with my arm, shaking off the strange waking-dream that briefly entered my head. 'Yes, it's only me. Sorry. I was exploring. I couldn't sleep.'

He chuckles. 'I thought that might be the case. But you can never be too sure, you know, especially now that it's May and gorse burning is illegal until October. They're all doing it under cover of night, now, so I keep watch.'

I try not to look confused, because I'm certain he mentioned this gorse fire thing before, but I was too tired to pay attention. Luckily, Benjamin isn't the kind of man who hesitates to repeat himself.

'You saw the gorse, didn't you? You must have, it's all along the roadside on the drive in from Waterville: yellow flowers on a sort of scrubby bush.'

'Yes,' I say, remembering the handful of petals I pulled into the car. 'They smell like coconut.'

'That's the one,' says Benjamin, leading me out of the wood by torchlight. 'And, you know, I do sympathise with the farmers who burn it, which is to say, practically *every* farmer in Ireland.'

He laughs as he says it, like he is saying something terribly droll about a dinner-party guest.

'But the danger it causes to the wildlife and the safety threat it poses to people is, well, bonkers. Especially because the fires always end up spreading. Thousands of trees burned needlessly last year in Killarney, and that's a National Park. Who knows what they would do to our lovely yew wood?'

'Is that what these weird trees are?' I say, gesturing to one that is folded over on itself like a hand over a limp wrist.

'Yews,' he says, patting it proudly. 'They're quite rare now, you know, and Clipim has one of the highest concentrations of them in the country. The most yews of any of the islands. Do you know why that is?'

'Why?'

'Because *I* take care of them. So you'll forgive me if I'm a little vigilant. They really are a fantastic tree.'

I wonder if maintaining the wood is a completely noble and ecological goal of Benjamin Barry's, or whether it has anything to do with his house-flipping. *And of course, this property backs on to our historic yew wood . . .* 'But you try telling the Foleys that.'

'The Foleys?' The name cuts through the night air.

'Sheep farmers,' Benjamin says, his voice edged with disdain.

'They're not just sheep farmers, though?' I say, then quickly jump to correct my use of the word 'just'. 'I mean, they're property developers. Don't they own half the country?'

'Do you want me to walk you back to your mobile home?'

I don't, but I get the feeling that if I refuse, Benjamin will put me underneath the Foleys on his long list of personal gripes. As we walk back, he talks endlessly about the yews, what they mean, and how gorse fires on neighbouring farmland is threatening Clipim's wildlife scene. How everything, virtually, is a threat to Clipim's wildlife scene.

'How well do you know your Irish folklore, Charlie?'

'Pretty well. My dad is from here.'

'Do you know the story of Deirdre of the Sorrows?'

I rack my brain, trying to remember all the Celtic storybooks my dad bought for me at car-boot sales. Weren't they basically all about sorrow? Weren't they all about someone dying a long and unusually painful death?

'Deirdre of the Sorrows,' I say again slowly. 'She was the beautiful woman who was separated from her boyfriend, right? Some king was keeping them apart, so he killed them both? Or something?'

'She flung herself from a chariot when she found out her husband had killed her lover. Her husband ordered that they be separated from one another for all time, so he buried them on opposite sides of the river. But a yew tree sprung up from both their graves, and the branches reached for each other across the bank. So they were together for ever, in the end.'

'Wow. Okay,' I say, because this conversation is a little intense for five in the morning.

'You could call the yew the tree of forbidden love,' he says, a wink just visible in the pale blue light that is beginning to break the morning. I do not know what the wink is supposed to mean, or whether it means something more because he is saying it to me outside the door of our mobile home.

'I better go inside,' I say. 'Laura might have woken up and be worried.'

He smiles. 'I'm sure she is. Well, I've loved our chat.'

'Thank you,' I say, opening the door. 'Good night.'

Laura is still asleep in front of the electric fire. I pull a blanket out of a cabinet, spread it over her, and go to sleep thinking about trees.

## 13

The next morning we walk down to the town in search of breakfast.

Laura is still very much into the Nancy Drew thing, pointing at door knockers or odd-shaped stones and then pretending to examine them with a magnifying glass.

'Look, Charlie, a clue!'

'And what clue is that?'

'The clue of this ... brochure for the Button Museum.'

'Jesus Christ, what is the deal with this Button Museum?'

Laura starts reading from the brochure. 'The Button Museum, formerly Stanworth & Sons Button Company Ltd, was established in 1981, eighteen years after the closure of the original factory. It now displays buttons and button-related curiosities to over 10,000 button enthusiasts a year.'

'What is a *button-related curiosity*?'

'The original factory was established in 1851,' she reads on. 'Providing employment and world-class buttons to the community of Clipim.'

'You're not going to read that whole thing, are you?'

'But it's a clue, Charlie! A clue!'

I eventually shove her, and ban her from uttering the word 'clue' any more on this trip.

We eventually find a shop Toby told us about, which is roughly the size of my mum's utility room and twice as crammed with canned food. A lady with owl glasses stands staunchly behind the counter, plastic boxes of jelly snakes stacked in front of her, a radio blaring traditional music at her side. We have only come in here to buy milk and bread but the whole place smells so strongly of sugar that I can't help lingering over the boxes.

'Hello,' says Laura, her big outsider's smile all wide. 'Just these please.'

'Era, this poor cratúir is after a snake, I'd say,' she says, beaming at me. I haven't heard that word – that funny pronunciation of 'creature' – since I was very small. *Cray-turh*. It was one of my dad's favourite words for me.

I smile back. 'I'm okay.'

'Ahhh, go on.'

We pluck out a snake each, gnawing on their yellow bellies like children as we walk down the road.

The Fiddler is opening, and the girl from last night is putting out the A-board again, topping up the chalk on 'pancakes' and 'hotdogs'. She brushes her hands off on the apron around her waist as she sees us crossing the street, irritated by having customers so early, hoping that we're headed down to the harbour and not looking for service. I smile at her as we go inside, trying to reassure her that we won't be difficult, demanding tourists who will ask a lot of annoying questions about buttons or bird watching. She tightens her raggy black ponytail and looks at us curiously. Her wide, pale eyes are the colour of jade.

'Do you guys want breakfast?'

We take two menus from her and sit down. It's just after eleven on a cool spring morning, but the pub retains the low, mahogany atmosphere from the night before. There's a smell of turf in the air. Being in The Fiddler makes it feels as though there's a storm happening just outside, and that you are lucky to be safe from it.

I tell Laura about last night, about Benjamin Barry and the trees. I tell her what happened, but I can't seem to communicate the precise feeling of walking through Clipim at night, the feeling of being part of the world while hovering slightly above it. Standing barefoot in the yew wood was enough to make me believe in shapeshifting, in past lives, in crystals.

I don't know how to explain it, so I just order breakfast.

'So people just light fires here? What did he call them? Gorse fires?'

'Apparently. That's his thing with the farmers. The Foleys, too. They burn the gorse to clear the land for grazing. They want to light fires; he wants to protect the trees from fire. As well as not wanting his caravan park burned down or his property values dented, I'm sure.'

'Did you ask about the IRA?'

'No. Why would I do that?'

She looks at me with the exhausted expression of someone whose puppy just won't grasp house training. 'Because that's why we're *here*.'

'I know, but you can't just come out and ask people shit like that. I mean, it's the IRA. For all we know, everyone who lives here is *in* it. Do you really want to become a walking target?'

The corners of her mouth start to twitch. 'Are you hearing yourself talk, right now?'

I don't blame her for being amused. It feels like earlier this morning, when we were talking about 'clues'. This is the trouble with being more versed in pop culture than in real life: when you're out of your comfort zone, you find yourself relying on old clichés. Other people's words fill your mouth because you don't have the language to deal with the scenario yourself. That's why I'm stalling, I think, and why I had secretly hoped that Laura would cancel this entire trip.

The waitress comes back with our food and Laura turns to her.

'Excuse me, can we ask you a quick question?'

She looks at us warily, as though we're about to ask where we can buy ketamine. But she nods.

'Do you know if the IRA are here?'

The waitress looks around. 'Like, in *this bar*?'

'No, I mean, on this island.'

At that moment, a compact man of about eighty walks into The Fiddler, a newspaper under his arm and a pint bottle of milk dangling off his finger by its handle. Satan the dog is next to him, a business-like stride in his legs. The man nods at the waitress while hoisting himself on to a stool, and she smiles back.

'All right Maria? How's the form?'

*Maria.*

'Morning, Tony. These girls want to know if there's any IRA on the island.'

'Any WHA?' He bellows, and Satan's huge ears prick up.

'IRA. Do you know if anyone's in the IRA any more?'

'Oh,' he says, and stops to think for a moment. 'Well now, let me think.'

He pauses for a moment, scratching the dog's head. He's treating the subject as though it were a pub quiz question.

'Some guns came in from America during the Troubles. They shipped 'em into Tralee and one or two of our boys drove them up to the border. You know. Tommy Devlin and his thick-as-shite friend Fergal. I don't know if you could say they were *in* the RA, though. They had about as much sense as two goats fighting over gospel.'

'What happened to them?'

'Nothing. Lost interest. I think they were just in it for the bang.'

'The WHAT?' shouts back Maria. 'THE BAND?'

There's a fondness between the two of them, as though they probably spend their whole day shouting stories at one another from across the pub.

'The bang. The craic, like. They were just after a bit of a day out. They'd bring sandwiches and a bag of cans. Who's asking, anyway?'

Laura gets up to introduce herself, pulling me along with her. 'Hello!' she says, sticking out her hand. 'I'm Laura, and this is my friend Charlie. We met Satan yesterday. On Joe's boat.'

Satan, as though he was there to appear as a character witness, stars licking Laura's knee in confirmation.

'You mean *my* boat,' he says, stroking Satan's head so hard that the whites of his eyes are visible. 'Joe took it over after my fall. My wife used to do it, too. She would take the tickets, and I'd do the ferry.'

Maria finishes the pint she had been pulling for Tony and places it on a coaster in front of him. She puts a light hand on his shoulder, and gives him a very specific kind of smile: the smile that I know well, from other adults giving it to my dad. It's a smile that says: *Yes, that's sad, but it was a while ago.*

'Did Joe ever drive guns up to the border?' I ask, and everyone looks at me sharply. It is clear that this is an inappropriate question. I bite my tongue. Why can't I ever talk to strangers properly? Why don't I ever know what an appropriate question is?

'No,' says Tony, giving the barmaid a 'who is this moron?' look. 'This was the seventies. He would have been a child.'

'And what about before that?' I press. 'What about the sixties?'

But he and Maria have already started talking about something and Laura and I return to our breakfasts. We eat slowly so we don't trouble our hangovers.

'So now we have Ferryman Joe and Grandferryman Tony,' says Laura, her voice low and laughing, her eyes on her bacon.

'Don't say it.'

'Say what?'

'Don't say it's a clue.'

'But what if it *is*?'

Maria comes back to clear away the plates, and Laura orders two pints of Guinness as dessert.

'You're starting early, aren't you?'

'Hey, if Grandferryman Tony is having one.'

As stupid as she's being, I do find myself fixating on Ferryman Joe and Grandferryman Tony. Between them, they must know everyone who has arrived and left this island for the last fifty, maybe sixty years. My stomach churns as I look at Tony, his stocky, thick build slouching towards Maria.

You must have seen their bodies.

You must have taken the coffins across to Kerry when the funeral parlour filled up. What was the admin of that? How many trips did you do? How many could fit on one trip? Was there someone at the other side, down from Waterville to collect them?

'After we finish these,' Laura says tentatively, 'I think we should try to find the schoolhouse.'

'Why?'

'Because that's why we're here.'

'Right.'

There's a silence before I speak again. I have been picturing this building my entire life. Am I ready to actually see it? Do I really want to open this particular can of worms on a full stomach?

'I'm not afraid,' I say unconvincingly.

'Charlie. You are. You are pissing yourself about confronting any of this stuff. You're terrified it's going to be different to how you imagined it.'

I bite my tongue and decide not to bring up all the things that Laura can't confront.

'Okay,' I say slowly. 'Okay, fine. Let's go to the schoolhouse.'

East Clipim is farmland, or cliffs made ragged by the Atlantic. There are mussel beds and periwinkles, but no beach. The old schoolhouse is smack in-between the two: a wide bungalow where you could see the vast grey sea from one window, and 500 head of cattle from the other.

The one famous photograph of the schoolhouse – the one that's always used, whenever anyone does a story on the tragedy – does nothing to make you associate it any less with the gloomy story that surrounds it. It's one dark building on a long, flat horizon, accessible via a thin path beaten through a field from the road. I've pictured walking up that path a thousand times in my head, felt my fingers curl around the brass doorknob, imagined my shoulder pressed against the stiff door. I've felt the cold grey wind, the desolate landscape. I've imagined it the way a Brontë sister imagines love, with perfect clarity and perfect drama.

What I had not counted on was nature, and its effect on a place that hasn't been touched in over fifty years. The building is still there, but there's nothing desolate about this place. The earth has seized the schoolhouse with both hands, with dead blackberry bushes surrounding it and thick bunches of pink fuchsia streaming through each window. Even from the road, you can see the fuchsia spilling out of the building in crimson, pink and royal purple, framed with sprigs of flame-coloured montbretia. It's an orgy of colour, like a Valentine's Day display that was knocked over by a child.

I hear Laura gasp beside me. She pulls out her inhaler and takes two quick puffs. Laura's inhaler is one of my secret favourite things about her: it's so wonderfully, woefully nerdy, so out of place with the rest of her. She points at the pink bushes again.

'Charlie, the *colour*. I've never seen anything like it.'

She snaps with her SLR camera, rotating around the plant life. I stop and wait.

The gate at the road is locked and chained up, but the low stone wall is so easy to swing your leg over that it seems like the most natural point of entry. The wall is deeper on the other side, and my leg goes straight into a thicket of bramble that clings to my legs and penetrates my jeans.

'Fuck!'

Three birds rustle and take flight at the sound.

'What's wrong?'

'Thorns in my fucking leg. Let me help you over.'

I take Laura's hand and lead her over the wall, steering her legs past the bramble and into a soft bed of wild ferns. I squeeze her hand to let her know she's safe. She squeezes back before letting go.

I find a stick, and start thrashing back nettles and ferns, trying to re-clear the old path. The door is split in two, like a barn door, and the lower half is almost entirely rotted. We duck underneath it, kick a few beer cans out of the way, and then straighten up on the other side.

We are in my father's schoolhouse.

I run my hands along the east wall. A line of coat hooks that barely touch my waist reach for me like unfinished question marks. There's a shadow where the blackboard has been ripped from the wall, and a dense grey rectangle where – judging by the loose fixtures and air vents – the faulty oil burning furnace used to be.

I crouch down at the fireplace. It doesn't feel like a fireplace so much as an altar: an altar to animal shit and pornographic playing cards and empty bags of crisps with fag holes burned in them. I lay my hands on the cool, moist red brick of the grate.

I tilt my head upwards, trying to remove my nose from the smell of fox poo. I look up the squat chimney to see that, incredibly, the newspaper that had helped close off the room's ventilation is still up there.

I wince, stretching my hand up the chimney, my arms just skinny enough to feel around and find something. A moist, papery mulch comes away in my hands, my arms suddenly heavy with stinking grey matter.

'Ugh,' I say, peeling it off my sleeve. It's the front page of *The Kerryman*, from 5 January 1960. I close my eyes and visualise them, shivering as each icy blast whistles down the chimney and into the schoolroom, being asked to take old newspaper from home to help keep out the draught. I attempt to unfold the filthy, damp paper and can just about make out a news item about the Irish Farmers' Association debating whether direct household water was 'strictly necessary, or a needless addition to the valuation of property'.

'Charlie . . . ' I hear Laura say. 'I think you better see this.'

I follow her voice to a little room that looks as though it might have been the teacher's supply cupboard. In the room, there is Laura, a pile of faded copybooks and an adult sheep staring blandly at us.

'Oh.'

'Yeah,' she agrees. 'Oh.'

We stand there for a second, watching it watch us, before it stands up and slowly walks out of the schoolhouse with the faint air of someone who has been pushed out of their regular cafe by visiting tourists.

We look at one another and begin laughing. Really laughing. Laughing because of the irritated dignity of the sheep, laughing because the pressure of being here is too huge, laughing because laughter is the only way to break the heavy, humid sorrow of this building. We start clutching ourselves in hysteria, tears coming out of our eyes, before eventually slumping against the wall of the teacher's cupboard, chewed-up exercise books beneath us, exhausted by the weight of things.

'I can't believe this is it,' says Laura eventually. 'I can't believe your dad went to school here. That we made a film about here. This building. Do you think it's haunted?'

I think about it. I close my eyes. I feel for ghosts. I don't find any. I pick up one of the exercise books, hoping to find something.

'See?' I say, half-laughing as I flick through the empty pages. 'They're blank. Extras from the stationery cupboard. They've taken out everything that belonged to the kids. There are no photos, no blackboard, no oil burner. They've taken everything. They don't want to remember this shit. There's no reason to keep it alive.'

Suddenly, I'm confronted with the memory of walking into my father's hospital room, a few days before he was last discharged. I remember him taking an extra minute to wake up, and how, for a second, I thought he was dead, and that this was it, and whether it was better to have the thing over and done with, and feeling like the worst person in the world for thinking that. Like thinking that way was tantamount to wishing cancer upon him in the first place.

And then I'm thinking about my father, dying, and his father, who died falling off a roof. I'm thinking about the endless stream of fathers and sons, and how they all end on me, a gay woman who hasn't had a long-term girlfriend since University. I can sooner imagine myself in a motorcycle gang than I can cuddling a small child.

'Charlie, are you okay?'

I don't say anything. Just kick another can, my hands shoved so far into my jacket that I can feel the seam on each pocket.

'Charlie?'

Laura can trace her family to the court of King James.

They bought her dad an Ancestry.com subscription for his birthday, and now every time you visit he presents you with an A4 printout of his latest titbit of Shingle history. It makes me feel stupid and petty, to be jealous that my family doesn't have the same. What comes before the hunger strikes that drove my great-grandfather insane? The famine. The famine happened. It's another one of those things – like Laura's and my giddy search for 'clues' – that feels like a punchline even though there's nothing funny about it. My great-grandfather's family were very poor and very Catholic and spent the latter years of the nineteenth century either fleeing the country or dying of starvation. It's one hundred years later and his closest living ancestor is living on the poverty line in a building where her post gets stolen.

*It Takes a Village?*

It takes an entire bloodline, apparently.

'There's nothing here, Laura,' I say, my voice choked and strange. 'Maybe if we were on a road trip of your family history we'd have discovered a knighthood by now.'

'We're here for your family, though,' she says, putting her hand on my shoulder. 'We're here for you.'

There is a freckle behind my ear that, when I rub a finger over it, feels like a tiny tumour. I start picking at it, catching it between my thumb and forefinger as though it were a spot. Laura snatches my hand away.

'You're picking,' she says tensely. 'Stop picking.'

I grant her a limp smile. She's right, of course. The freckle is always scabbed over, perpetually in a state of recovery from me digging my nails into it. I look at my thumbnail. Brown crust speckled with scarlet.

'What am I going to do?'

'About ... your dad?'

'About everything. About Dad. About Mum. About my career. Do you know, Laura, it took me sitting in that Cork screening with those boys laughing at us to realise that my movie is an absolute shitshow?'

And suddenly, I'm laughing again. 'I had to get on a *plane* to realise that the one thing – the one thing! – I've ever finished is terrible.'

Laura is too dumbstruck to reply.

'And I used the *government's* money to make it.'

'It's not terrible,' Laura responds. 'It's good. I wouldn't have made it if it were terrible.'

'You were humouring me. Go on. You can say it. You were humouring me because my dad was dying and you felt sorry for me.'

'We lived in a flat with no central heating for two years so we could get that movie made. Do you think I would have done that to be *polite*?' A tremor of anger is rising in her voice, clashing against her sympathy like two tectonic plates.

I shrug it off, thinking: *Well, it's not as if Laura's taste has ever been sky-high. Her favourite movie is* The Devil Wears Prada.

'I'm not going to be a director any more,' I announce, trying to wrestle back control of the conversation. 'Or, I'm not going to try.'

'Okay,' she responds, even and exhausted. 'What are you going to try to do?'

The thought is terrifying. I'm thirty next year, and qualified for nothing. Sure, I could try for producing jobs, but all my experience is on my own work, or on shorts directed by Uni friends. The only way to break into the industry at this point would be to go back to the beginning by resting on Laura's contacts: to take a meeting with her friend Sayid, and take the runner jobs that I found too bewildering at twenty-two.

The enthusiasm of last night's conversation ebbs away. A thirty-year-old runner. Is that really the best I have to hope for?

'Charlie, we don't have to stay,' Laura finally says. 'We don't have to stay if it upsets you.'

I stand there, clenching and unclenching my fists, unsure of what to say or how to say or how to feel while standing in the middle of the tragedy my dad escaped, only to run open-armed into tragedy fifty years later.

He *survived* this.

He survived *this*.

Surely he can survive anything?

'I think we should go,' Laura says.

Maria grins when she sees us walk back into The Fiddler.

'Hey, girls,' she says. 'Find any members of a terrorist cell on your travels?'

I flush.

'No IRA, I'm afraid,' Laura tries to joke. 'We actually walked up to the old schoolhouse.'

'Oh, man,' replies Maria, making a face. 'Cheery.'

'Have you been?'

She thinks about it for a moment, cocking her head. 'No, I haven't. I live over on the west side, and it's a real pain in the ass to get to, isn't it? Tourists always talk about what a let-down it is. Benjamin tries to discourage them from going. It's super unsafe. You have to like, jump a wall, and answer three riddles to a wizard or something, right?'

'No wizard,' I say, the first thing I've piped up with since walking in silence from the schoolhouse. 'Unless you're counting the sheep who lives in there, eating exercise books.'

'Oh, you didn't hear? The sheep *is* the wizard.'

We laugh and Laura watches me, surprised to hear me engage in small talk, willingly, with a stranger. But I like Maria. I like almost everyone who I've met in Clipim: I like Joe, and Tony and now Maria. Toby and Kate are fine, even if they are from London. It's relatively rare that I like three people at once, and it's a good habit to get into. We order two pints of Guinness. Maria pours half in front of us, then crosses her arms, waiting for the light brown liquid smoke to blacken.

'How did you end up here, then?' I ask. Then add, hastily: 'Being American, and everything.'

'Ah,' she says. 'There's a story. I got my heart broken in Dublin.'

'I'm sorry.'

'No, it's fine. I mean, this person, they really chewed me out. I was a wreck. We were supposed to be going on this year-long tour of Europe together, and Dublin was our first stop. We broke up on day three! Can you imagine?'

I tell her that I couldn't imagine, and Laura says nothing.

'So, they went on, and I stayed. My family were from Kerry, so I did the whole American tourist thing. Tried to track down my ancestry. I even got my mom to email me my family tree, and that led me to Clip. I never found them – I don't think anyone ever does? – but I liked Clipim. So!'

She finishes our Guinness with a clover in the foam and passes us our glasses.

'I think that's really brave,' I say, noting her use of the word 'they'. Not he or she. They. *They went on, and I stayed.* 'Well done.'

'Yeah, love sucks sometimes,' she says, shrugging. 'What about you guys?'

'Oh, we're not in lo ...' I begin, and then stop, because I realised too late that Maria meant how we got here, not whether we were in love. I shut my mouth. Laura raises her eyebrows at me, as though to say: *Well, considering you're suddenly so big on small talk*, and waits for me to re-start my answer.

'My dad is from here,' I say slowly. 'Actually, he was one of the kids who ... who, you know, the schoolhouse.'

Is it a good idea to tell her? To tell anyone? If my dad

feels like he can't show his face here, who am I to just announce myself?

Maria's pale green eyes widen, and she puts one hand over her mouth.

'Oh my God. He was *the* kid? The one that survived?'

'Yeah.'

Maria is the first person who I've ever spoken to about my father that is immediately aware of the context of my father. There's no 'the thing about my dad is' or 'the thing about Clipim is'. She knows. She lives here.

'That's huge. You should ... I don't know, tell someone. One of the older people. They would love to meet you.'

'Would they? Isn't it a bit ...?'

'Are you kidding? You'll be like a celebrity.' She walks out from behind the bar to a nearby table, where an old man is dipping some buttered bread into his seafood chowder. 'Hey, Enda! This girl here? Her dad was the schoolhouse kid. The one that got out.'

Enda turns around in his chair, his white hair sticking out at all angles, like Einstein. 'Kitty Regan's lad?'

'Yeah, his daughter. She's here. On that stool.'

She points me out to him, speaking loudly and clearly for his benefit, seemingly unaware that the rest of The Fiddler has turned around to look in my direction.

Enda eases himself out of his chair, his eyes the watery blue of imitation sapphires and hotel swimming pools. He is dressed in a collection of comfortable, grease-spotted beiges and is walking towards me with slow, heavy steps. He's huge, though: at least six foot five, and built like, as my father would say, a brick shithouse.

When he eventually gets to the bar, he sticks out a hand the size of a dustbin lid. I take it.

'Kitty Regan was my grandmother,' I say, my voice loud and nervous. 'Colm Regan is my dad.'

'Colm,' he says, taking time to form each syllable, saying it the way my father does: rounded in the middle, tongue pinching your front palate.

'I remember Colm. Little lad. Always going around on his own.'

'Yes,' I say, even though my experience of this lonely little boy is limited to the one I have fabricated. All I know is the adult who raised me, the man who treats his past like an arranged marriage that he has found a way to work within.

'We live in England now. He's ... uh, he's quite sick, actually.'

It never gets easier, for some reason. Maybe for people in their forties and fifties, telling people your father is ill feels more natural, like a thing that should happen to you at that age. Not so much at mine. You ruin someone's day just by letting them know.

Enda is looking at my face and holding my hand, and staring at me as though I am a deeply missed family member who emigrated years previously.

'Well, pet,' he says finally, 'I guess we better make you feel at home.'

## 14

The next few hours are a blur. There are pints, and crisps, and glasses of whiskey. We don't move from our seats at the bar, but gracefully receive people as though we were visiting dignitaries. I show people pictures of my dad on my phone.

I tell them how Dad moved to Liverpool when he was sixteen, and got work as a brickie. I tell them how he eventually moved to London, where he met Mum. I mumble my way through his early career, about how he works in an office most of the time now, and everyone is pleased to hear it. I tell them about how he and my mum are in a hiking club, and how they used to go to the Lake District every summer, and, sometimes, on long walking trips in Spain. I relay with careful detail how normal and well-adjusted my father is, and everyone reacts to it as though I were describing the life of a lottery winner.

People allow themselves to become sad. They talk about the years following the disaster as though they were the slow-moving stages of a nuclear fallout. They talk about the shock, and the grief, and the disappearances. Virtually all the parents of the dead children moved to the mainland eventually, in an attempt to put distance between themselves and their pain. The young people emigrated; the button factory closed; the farms struggled. The Foleys bought all the empty lots and turned them into grazing land and made a killing selling wool to the Killarney Woollen Mills.

Whenever certain words come up – *Foley, land, Kitty, accident* – Laura and I instinctively look at one another, silently noting the changes of frequency or tone when they come up. Then, I get nervous. If they see me constantly flicking my eyes to Laura, won't they suss that we're here looking for answers? I'm wary of giving myself away, so try to avoid looking at her completely.

I needn't worry, though. There's no hint of the secrecy that Nick's father apparently struggled with when he visited. People seem to babble on as if they've been waiting a lifetime to tell their stories.

'You used to get all sorts,' explains Enda. 'You'd go to the O'Connors for the eggs, Seamus for the spuds, the O'Sheas for the veg. We'd have been fairly self-sufficient. It was a big thing for us. We didn't need much, you know. Now the whole place is grazing for the sheep farmers and we have to get everything sent over from Waterville or Sneem.'

'Or Killarney,' chimes in his wife Mary, a smiley, chatty woman who is probably 4 foot 11 without her perm, but 5 foot 3 with it. 'And you wouldn't want to be paying Killarney prices for meat, sure you wouldn't?'

'And there's no use relying on the next generation. We still have to do everything ourselves. My grandson is eighteen, and if there was work in the bed, he'd sleep on the floor.'

The tight knot of Clipim residents all chuckle. It's very clear that, despite no one explaining what Enda and Mary do in Clipim, they have some level of social status that looms benevolently above the other residents.

'The social life was terrible, for a few years,' says Mary confidentially. 'There was no one around. Your poor old granny, before she died, God bless her, she opened up a little seamstress stall in town, sewing on buttons and fixing zips and the like. She wouldn't take a penny for it. Kitty Regan just liked a chat, the poor old thing.'

There's something strange about how my grandmother is spoken about. The phrase 'the poor old thing' is bandied around a lot, often sandwiched between 'God help her' and 'sure, wasn't she all alone in that tiny little house?'

The house is always described as being the 'tiny little house', so much, in fact, that I am beginning to suspect my grandmother lived in a sardine can.

'How small *was* it?' I ask eventually, but no one, except Maria, hears the question.

'It was probably fine.' She smiles reassuringly. 'Kerry people are just ... big on adjectives.'

'Kitty was an old dote. Mind, she liked a drink,' Mary says, patting my shoulder again and taking another sip from her own glass. 'A lightweight, though. God save her, she couldn't drink fog.'

'My dad often said that people ... ' I struggle to finish the sentence. 'Found her difficult to be around. Because of him. Because of his survival, I suppose.'

She briefly bristles at this, her face a map of hurt feelings that she quickly smooths back into an amiable, social one. Enda places a protective hand on his wife's shoulder.

'Ah, stop. You'll find no shortage of people with tall tales about this place,' he says. 'People looking for a bit of a story to tell. If they had any brains they'd be dangerous,' he laughs.

I laugh back, and then realise that he just called my father an idiot.

Scraps of story start building a new picture of Clipim in my head. Because everything had to be imported, the island became more and more expensive to live on. Middle-class hippies bought cheap in the 1990s, and they're *fine* – yes, everyone agrees they're *fine* – but they aren't old Clip, and isn't there something sad about that?

It feels as though the entire population of Clipim comes over to say hello.

I am introduced to a Pilates teacher, who is also a gardener. She tells me about how she sells natural beeswax candles on Etsy. A parade of yuppies pass in front of me, happy, fresh and dressed in colourful leggings. These must be Toby and Kate's friends, I think. The thirty-somethings with rustic fantasies of what it must be like to live on a pretty island off the west coast of Ireland, the last stop before the new world.

The ones who linger are all older. These are the seventy-, eighty- and ninety-year-olds who remember the old Clipim. They were the grown adults who watched it change, and they are the ones who sketch a new story for me.

And eventually, I pluck up just enough courage to tell them about the film, and how we're here for Cork Film Festival. I am careful and considerate, describing my father's illness and how we wanted a record of his memories before he ... well. People are graceful enough to not force me to finish the sentence.

I knock back another drink, and immediately, someone buys me another one. People want to know everything about the film. They ask about sequels, about interviews, about the festival, about Hollywood. Enda, in particular, makes me describe the entire thing, beat for beat.

'And then, Colm gets a message to the schoolhouse door to say his mother needs him at home.'

'Your grandmother. A gorgeous woman, Charlie. A lovely woman. Life was very hard for her. She had a tough time growing up, too. She wasn't a well woman, you know, even before the accident,' he says. 'She would be very proud of you, Charlie.'

Small knots of tourists come in and out. Maria pours them all pints of Guinness with clovers carefully imprinted in the foam. Pictures are taken. People look over their shoulders at Laura and me, wondering if we're local television stars. Eventually, we excuse ourselves for a cigarette. I take a look at my phone. Four missed calls from Mum. Christ, not now. Not when I'm finally having fun.

'Oh my God,' says Laura, when we step outside. The sun is going down, a fact that is dazzling to us, given we entered The Fiddler shortly after lunch. 'There are so many old people in love with us, I feel like we're the fucking Andrews Sisters.'

'Mate,' I say, shaking my head, 'this is incredible. I never . . . I mean, not in a million years did I think that people would be this happy to see me. To see us.'

Laura throws her head back and cackles.

'Ha! That's very kind, pal, but they're clearly happy to see you. They couldn't give two shits about me. I'm just your entourage.'

I grin into the creamy orange light of the evening, remembering how alienated we were last night, forced to the back of the pub with the tourists and the non-locals. Now we're sitting at the bar, the guests of honour. I can't stop myself smiling, already picturing the story I'll tell Dad.

'They seem very fond of my grandmother,' I say. 'I mean, they don't *sound* like people who think she was engaged in an IRA plot.'

'No,' she agrees, stubbing out her cigarette. 'And if they're so keen to hush up the whole thing, why are they being so nice to us?'

'I'm beginning to think that maybe . . . '

I drift off, my eyes distracted by the explosive peach light on the horizon. The mainland is just a shadow now. All you can see is sun.

'Go on,' she urges.

'That maybe all that stuff Nick was saying was . . . a load of shit?'

'What makes you say that?' she asks, but I can tell by her tone that she has been nursing the same suspicion.

'I don't know. People are so open and direct. And so affectionate. There's no reason for them to be nice to us.'

'No,' she reasons. 'None.'

On the way back in, we notice a poster on the door of The Fiddler.

TRAD BAND –
SING FOR YOUR SUPPER – 9 P.M.

'Let's get some food in,' she says, tapping her finger on the sign. 'This is going to be a late one.'

I'm glad we have seats at the bar, because The Fiddler goes from lively to packed between 7 and 9 p.m. The place is a mass of dogs and children alternately falling asleep under tables, of disorganised and highly dangerous games of darts, and of steaming plates of mussels being brought out of the kitchen every ten minutes. Laura and I order a bowl between us, sopping up creamy white-wine sauce in huge hunks of bread, too drunk to talk. Not that it matters: we can't hear each other over the sound of tables being dragged around and rearranged to create a stage area.

'If *this* is what the pub is like during the quiet season, what's it like in the middle of the summer?' asks Laura, amazed. 'I've only seen about a dozen tourists. If it gets as busy as they say it does, they must have to turn people away.'

'Not us, though,' I say, clinking my glass on hers. 'Never *us*.'

Eventually, I get up to go to the bathroom.

'Remember that *mná* means woman,' Laura calls out to me. 'Don't make the same mistake I did.'

I almost trip over myself trying to get there, and realise that I have been drinking for almost six hours straight. How did this happen? How am I still upright? And how didn't I realise, until now, that I am absolutely desperate for a piss?

There are only two stalls, and one of them is already stuffed to the brim with toilet paper and brown water. I hop from one leg to the other, half-convinced I'm going to wet myself, half-planning to squat over the sink. The woman in the cubicle is taking for ever, and eventually I knock on the door.

'Excuse me!' I say, trying to soften my English accent as much as I can, trying to make it into an amorphous non-accent that could belong to anyone.

No response.

'Sorry about this, whoever's in there, but I'm really really desperate. Do you think you could hurry up?'

Silence, and then the sound of the door lock being gently slid aside, with some effort. The door opens a crack and I see half a face, like how a witch opens a door in a film.

'Mary!' I say, astounded to see Enda's wife. I haven't spoken to her in a few hours, and I assumed she went home. 'I'm so sorry, don't mind me, I'll just go into the men's toilets.'

'Ah, Jaysus, tis only yourself,' Mary responds, her ginger perm barely visible through the door. 'Colm Regan's little baba. Now listen, I'm in an awful state here altogether. Come into me now and help an old fool.'

'Oh! In the . . . in the loo, with you?'

'C'mere now; the Regans haven't been living in England that long, have they?'

Well, there's not a lot you can say to that, is there.

'No,' I agree. 'Not that long.'

'So come in and we'll have none of that reserve.'

'Of course, Mary,' I say slowly. 'How can I help?'

She beckons me in and I see that her trousers are around her knees. She is holding them with one hand, barely gaining purchase with her thumb and forefinger, and pulling down her jumper over her waist with the other.

'You must think I'm an awful old fool but would you ever help an old woman get her knickers up?'

'Oh! Right! Okay,' I say, groping at the situation, knowing that however awkward this is for me, it must be far more mortifying for this eighty-year-old woman. Except she seems to be treating the whole thing as casually as if I were helping her take her washing out of a machine.

I ease her trousers up gingerly, her hand still pulling her jumper down, until Mary is able to grab at it.

'Now wasn't God very good to me when he sent you?' she says with instant affection. 'You're very good.'

'I'm not, really.'

'Era go 'way, you are. You come from good stock,' she says, carefully fastening the top button on her trousers. 'You're not English at all. You smell a' rashers and you probably bleed TK lemonade.'

I cackle. 'That's probably all the bacon fries I've been eating.'

'Your grandmother, God help her. A lovely soul. You're very good.'

It's on this second 'very good' that I realise that Mary, on top of having arthritis, is also quite drunk. There's a tang of wine off her breath, and I wonder if this is a regular occurrence for her. She seems to have recovered from me having to put her trousers on quite quickly, as though this sort of thing perhaps *has* happened before.

'Everyone keeps saying that,' I say. 'I wish I had known her.'

'She was like this. Always helping people out. She was even a friend to that bloody Emma Casey, though God knows why.'

'Sorry, what?'

'I suppose, Kitty being a widow and Emma Casey being alone in the world, you could see how they would get on.' Mary is washing her hands now, squirting too much pink soap into her palms. She appears to have forgotten that I am even there.

'And I pitied the woman. I did. I pitied her. But to make

her the teacher? It was a bad idea from the start. She wasn't fit. She had no training. Old news. Old, old, old news. Not important now, is it?'

'No, I ... I suppose not,' I respond, wondering how on earth you're supposed to deal with a drunk old woman you've just met and have already seen half-naked. She gestures to me to bring her one of the paper towels on the windowsill.

'I never had a thing against Kitty,' she says, as if answering an accusation. 'Not a thing.'

'Do you ... do you need me to walk you back to your table, Mary?'

Mary wipes her hands and straightens herself up again. 'Not at all, my love. Go and use the ladies now.'

So I do, and I try to make sense of what she just said. My grandmother and Emma Casey were *friends?*

I mull this over as I sit on the toilet. How come Dad never brought this up in his interviews? It would have added a whole new dimension to the story, a whole other layer of loss for Kitty. It made sense that they would be friends, like Mary said. My grandmother a young widow, Emma Casey a privately educated girl who was teaching on a tiny island. You can see it. Perhaps my dad simply doesn't remember. After all, do I know any of my mum's friends' names? Does my mum even *have* any friends?

When I sit back down I decide not to tell Laura about Mary. I don't want to take the piss out of her, and the simple act of telling the story will frame the whole anecdote as either pitying or cruel. Maybe that was what my grandmother was like, before she died. Old, alone, and with no friends or family to help her through it.

I look at Laura and think: *That can't be me. I can't be my grandmother. I can't be the person who relies on one friend, and then goes to pieces when she leaves.* And with that, I order another drink.

## 15

Maria finishes her shift, and immediately joins a group of young, beautiful, unwashed people who receive her as though she's lived on the island her entire life. Each of them has the kind of dirt smudges and perfect bone structure that you usually only get in a *Hunger Games* movie. Laura and I look like a Jack Wills advert in comparison.

The musicians arrive − a flute player, a violinist and a guitarist − and start playing. Some of the songs I recognise from the tape compilations my dad used to play in the car. 'The Star of the County Down' fades seamlessly into 'The Wild Rover', into 'Raglan Road', into '*Óró Sé Do Bheatha Abhaile*'. Shortly after they start playing, the energy of the room splits in two. The tourists, in their windbreakers and hiking boots, sit enraptured, clapping and singing along when urged to do so. The locals, meanwhile, appear to make a point of ignoring it. They carry on their conversations, raising an irritated eyebrow whenever the clapping gets too noisy. People like Maria − semi-permanent Clipim residents − opt for a polite middle ground of occasional clapping.

She grabs me on my way back from the bathroom, her hands tiny and cold and heavy with cheap silver. 'Charlie! Come meet everyone!'

'There's nowhere to sit.'

She looks around, and then shuffles her weight on to half of the low stool she's sitting on.

'There's room here.'

I bunch up next to Maria and meet her friends. I meet Dónal and Ciara and Stephanie and Aidan and Niamh, all of them just as gorgeous up close as they were from the bar. Maria introduces me enthusiastically, and with far less reverence than the geriatric quarter of The Fiddler had. Dónal was born in Clipim, while brother and sister Ciara and Aidan moved with their self-declaring hippie parents when they were children. These three seem to be the core of the group, and happily accept interlopers like American Maria, Dublin Niamh and Australian Stephanie as part of the lively ebb and flow of young, seasonal workers. They're making jokes about the band as I'm sitting down: rolling their eyes about how it's the same set every Sunday, right down to the order of the songs.

'This is Charlie,' says a tipsy Maria. 'Her dad was the kid that survived the schoolhouse accident. She's my new friend and she's a fucking miracle.'

I flush bright red.

'Fucking hell,' says Aidan. 'We used to go up to that house, when we were smallies.'

'I lost my virginity in that house,' chimes in Dónal, giving me a sly little wink. I can't help blushing. They're all gorgeous, but Dónal has the kind of dark curly hair and wide green eyes you only see on the covers of romance novels. Romance novels that feature stable boys.

'I lost . . . the *other* half of my virginity in that house,' says Ciara, all sass and side-eye.

More screaming laughter, more drinks. I look for Laura, but can't see her at the bar.

'We used to take turns dressing up as the nun,' says Dónal. 'We would take the little kids up there, and Aide would put on a long black habit and run around after them with a knife.'

'Where in the fuck did you get a nun's habit, Aide?' asks Ciara, nudging her brother.

'I got a shawl out of Mam's wardrobe most years.'

Everyone laughs, and I can feel the heat of Maria's hip juddering off my own as the sound comes out of her.

'Why a nun?' I ask, straining my ears to hear them over the music.

'I don't know. There was an old legend about a killer nun,' Aidan ponders. 'Era, I think it was an excuse to get into drag.'

'You'd think people would have enough to work with, given that they already had the ghosts of kids,' Maria says pragmatically.

'Well, nuns are just scary, aren't they?'

'Nuns are objectively scarier than priests,' Dónal reasons. 'Which is weird, because priests are the ones who do all the dodgy shit.'

'I had a nun teacher at secondary school once,' I volunteer nervously, dredging up my Catholic school memories. 'She told us that the altar was God's receptionist, and that if we wrote down our prayers and lay them there, He would answer them.'

'Did you do it?'

'I did,' I say, my memory slowly jogging. 'I wrote ... '*I ... am ... gay ...* '

The whole table starts to scream with laughter, the girls covering their mouths with their hands.

'What happened then?' asks Maria, who still has just one half of her butt on the stool. She turns her face towards me, her sharp jade eyes on me again.

'Well, Sister Josephine said she never read the prayers, but she never went *near* me again.'

Everyone laughs and starts comparing war stories from

their similarly bizarre Catholic childhoods. I grin along, feeling more at home with them than I have with anyone since Laura moved out. It's true that Sister J avoided me after that, but it's also true that she subtly discouraged anyone else from going near me. She tactically rearranged the classroom seating when she saw me get too friendly with another girl, and I always seemed to be the odd number when we were divided into pairs. I was either the hanger-on to a group of two or made to work alone. Sister Josephine worked under the understanding that while I was a lost cause, there was still a chance she could stave off infection in the wider group.

But look how easy it is to laugh about it now! The difference between a funny story and an upsetting memory is in how you shade it, and here, the shading is just right. Everyone understands the context for nuns and priests and how wrong they can be. Everyone wants to laugh. Everyone gets it.

I feel Maria nudging me.

'I once got caught fucking in a car in a church parking lot,' she whispers.

'You did not!' I say, my cheeks getting hot.

'I did. With my driving instructor.'

'No!' I reply. 'Hang on, don't Americans learn to drive at, like, fifteen?'

'Yep.' She shrugs. 'The priest told us we were defiling God's house. I don't think he understood that's what *made* the whole thing so hot.'

She laughs again, and the table laughs with her. I wonder if it's all that simple, though. Can anyone really be that casual about their own statutory rape?

Who *is* this person? Who *says* that to someone they just met this afternoon?

At that moment, Laura walks back into the bar, looking around quizzically for me. I wave a hand and get up to meet her.

'I've got a text from your mum,' she says. 'For you to call her.'

'Oh,' I say, pretending I haven't seen the missed calls. 'Okay, thanks.'

I get up, and Laura slides on to my stool. I watch Dónal clap eyes on her and wonder if she will indulge in flirting with him, even if it's just for one night. I've never known Laura to be so invested in a monogamous relationship that she'll turn down an opportunity for a man to tell her how beautiful she is.

I duck outside and call Mum back, hoping that it was just Dad wanting to know how I'm doing in Ireland. His phone is never charged so he often rings me from hers. I grin drunkenly into the night sky. He doesn't even know I'm in Clipim! His hometown! I gather all my anecdotes like eggs in a basket, excited to tell him about Enda and how much the island has changed since he left.

Mum picks up on the second ring.

'Hi, Mum,' I say, and at that moment a burst of tourists leave the pub and start jostling their way down the street, ducking in and out of the shops selling CDs of The Pogues and Celtic cross fridge magnets. A drunk tourist couple emerges from one, giggling about their bag full of shortbread. It's uncanny to see the shops so bright and busy against the darkness of the village, the whole street like a ripped-open advent calendar. Someone mentioned earlier that the gift shops all re-open on Sunday evening, trying to sop up the tourist trade before they go back to the mainland.

'Where are you? It's so *loud*.'

'We're in a pub.'

'A *pub*?'

My mother does not go to pubs and is amazed when she finds out that women are permitted entry.

'In ... We're in Clipim, Mum.'

Silence.

'It's really nice here, actually. Everyone's sharing stories of Dad when he was younger and Granny Regan. You'd like it here. It's cute, y'know? And everyone's so glad to see us. To see me.'

I can hear my mum's mouth getting smaller, more pinched. She starts talking like she's sucking the fluid out of an infected gum.

'I don't know what on earth compelled you to go to that . . . that *hole* in the middle of nowhere, but you need to come back.'

'We're coming back tomorrow, Mum. Our flight's at twelve thirty. We're leaving here at seven a.m.'

'Well, good,' she says, as if it was her that had convinced me.

'Wait, why do we need to come back?'

'Your father's having an operation.'

'An *operation*?'

'The drugs he's been on have messed up something in his liver. He had an X-ray and there's legumes all over it.'

'Legumes? Do you mean lesions?'

Dedicated as my mother is, she's never been very good at keeping up with what doctors are telling her. She tends to parrot whatever she's told by the NHS without necessarily understanding what's going on.

'Why are there lesions? What are they doing to him?'

'Cutting him open, Charlie. Cutting him open again.' Her voice is shrill now. High, worried and terrible. 'They'll put him under general anaesthetic, which of course he's just *delighted* about. He keeps shouting at them to just let him go home so he can die in peace.'

'Well, Mum, he's said that before. He says it all the time.'

'Maybe they should, Charlie. It would save me the hassle of having to deal with him.'

'Mum, you don't mean that. You need to calm down.'

'Would you like to deal with this, Charlie? Is this something you'd like to handle? Say the word and I'll step aside. I know you two have your little club and you can have a cosy chat about how old Mum is so stupid for worrying again.'

'How serious is this, though, Mum? Really. Because you've overreacted to things like this before.'

I try to say this as evenly as I can. It's true. Every time a schedule gets changed or a bed gets moved, she summons me to his bedside. Where, invariably, he turns out to be fine, and I will have just skipped out on a job interview to find that out.

'Like, are they just putting a camera in to see what the damage is, or ...'

'How serious do you need it to be to dig your head out of your arse, Charlie? Can you just stop being so selfish for *one* seco ...'

I take a series of deep breaths, telling myself not to rise to this. That she is angry and sad, and she is lashing out at me because there is no one else to lash out at. I try to detach, zone out from her. I try to see the task ahead and not the person giving it to me.

'I'll be back tomorrow, Mum. I'll call you with the details. Can you still pick me up from the airport?'

'Jesus, is *that* all you're worried about?'

'I'm not worried, I'm just asking.'

'I don't know. We'll have to see. I don't know.'

There's a silence as I try to think of something comforting to say to her, something comforting that isn't also outrightly annoying. Like 'don't worry' or 'he'll be fine' or 'this is just another one of those weird things'. I am mentally flipping through the pointless things people say to me and wondering which of them are okay to say to my mother.

'We're going to be all right, Mum,' I eventually say, the sea-salt breeze of the Atlantic hurtling its way up from the harbour.

'Oh, *you* will be all right, Charlie. I have no doubt of that.'

She hangs up the phone.

I stand and feel the chill, feeling the ocean and food, the music and stillness. Gazing at the sky, I wonder whether I would know the star names, if I lived here.

I would, I think. I would make it my business to know.

A burst of violin music escapes from the open door, gusts of warm gravy air coming out with it. Laura has come out to see what's wrong.

'Hey, you okay?' she asks, wrapping her scarf around her shoulders.

'Yeah,' I say.

'Is everything all right back home? Is your dad all right?'

I pause for a moment, considering things. Condensing things.

'Yeah,' I say again. 'He just wanted to know how we're getting on.'

'Did you tell him we're in Clipim?'

'I did,' I lie. 'He's really excited.'

She beams at me and puts an arm around my shoulder. 'Well, come back in then, weirdo, you'll freeze out here. Maria has bought you another drink. I'd say someone has a bit of a crush.'

'Shut up,' I say, pushing her. 'Do you think?'

'If we weren't leaving tomorrow, I'd say you were in there, mate.'

I blush and kick at my feet.

'Go on, Charlie. Go back for her. I won't mind. Fuck it; you can even take her back to the caravan. I'll put my Air Pods in.'

'Nah.'

'What's made you all shy?'

I don't know, exactly. I'm no stranger to a fling. In fact, with enough drink in me, I can be pretty good at them. I think girls sometimes mistake my awkward sullenness for a sort of Sapphic James Dean quality. Or at least, that's what one told me, and that I have repeated to myself pretty much every day since.

'I don't know,' I say. 'It feels a bit like shitting where you eat. Or, where your ancestors eat.'

We go back inside, and I see that Laura was right: Maria is standing there, jade eyes blazing, holding out a pint for me.

As one more drink turns into four more drinks, I start to convince myself that the phone call from my mother never happened. The memory of it feels like a dream that becomes less and less comprehensible every time I try to reach for it. There's something wrong with Dad's liver? No, that's not right. He never had problems with his liver before, and I refuse for a new body part to be implicated at this late stage in the war. The liver is neutral territory. The liver is Switzerland.

I don't mention it to Laura. I don't want her to know about the liver. I think about it, a pulsing cranberry flank, big as a cow's tongue. And the lesions. What do they look like? Raised bumps, like goose pimples? People are afraid of a word like 'lesions' because it almost always comes paired with words like 'brain'. But really, a lesion is just a fancy name for a bruise.

We're still huddled around the table with Maria's friends, and Laura is sitting on Dónal's lap. They are both pretending that this is due to a chair shortage, and nothing else.

'Jesus, but you're so *light*,' I hear Dónal saying to her, all twinkle, very aware that this kind of compliment is manna to her.

'I am not. Actually, if anything I've *gained* weight recently.'

'You have in your hole,' he says chidingly. 'We'll have to feed you up; you wouldn't last a winter here.'

'Are you serious? Look at these hips. These are what they call *child-bearing* hips . . . '

He jiggles his knees and Laura lurches forward a little, then playfully smacks him with a beer coaster.

'All right, Foley,' Aidan says, getting his cigarettes out. 'I'd say you're in for the ride, there.'

'Foley,' I suddenly say, through the mist of empty pint glasses and packets of Scampi Fries. 'You're a *Foley*? Like . . . those Foleys?'

The whole table erupts into laughter, and Dónal puts his hands up in mock defence.

'Christ, your family really *are* from Kerry, aren't they, Sasanach?'

Sasanach. It's a nickname they have for me and Laura. It means 'British person', and the boys say it with a short, playful hiss.

Dónal starts ticking off his fingers. 'Look, I cannot help you with your overgrown blackberry bushes. I refuse to make any calls about broken traffic lights, and I *will not* be going to your grandmother's funeral.'

Everyone laughs again, and I'm lost.

Maria puts her hand on my arm and tries to clear it up for me. 'Don's from a different branch of Foleys,' she explains. 'His grandfather was a big mover and shaker, but his dad's just a farmer. They're not rich but everyone always seems to think they are. Or wants them to be.'

'Oh,' I respond. 'So not the sheep farmers who bought up all the land after the accident?'

'What's that?' Dónal says. 'Who's got land? Look, I'm not going to inherit anything, so you two Tans can just stop trying to get your marriage claws into me.'

Laura rolls her eyes and says something about not being the marrying kind, and more jokes about Irish passports and EU memberships ensue. I keep thinking about what would happen if I mention the lesions. The light, flirtatious mood would vanish instantly. Everyone's body language would go from easy-going and open to cramped and tense, and it would be my fault. Even if I apologised for spoiling the mood, they would chide me and say, 'Relax, you're not *spoiling* anything', and we would all know it was a lie.

'Ladies and Gentleman,' murmurs the guitarist, 'we've got a little bit of a treat for you this evening. Enda O'Donovan, would'ya come on up?'

Quietness falls over the room and for the first time that evening, the locals are paying attention. Enda takes to the makeshift stage, sets down his pint, and squares his shoulders. I've never seen an octogenarian look so rudely healthy, so obviously in their prime of life. I glance around for Mary, wondering whether she's sobered up, and don't see her.

Enda puts one hand on his stomach, gestures to the violinist, and then opens his mouth for the opening verses of 'The Parting Glass'. It's my dad's favourite song, and Enda sings it in a chocolatey baritone.

> *Of all the money that e'er I had*
> *I've spent it in good company*
> *And all the harm that e'er I've done*
> *Alas it was to none but me*

Enda closes his eyes when he sings it, feeling every word, his palm flat across his chest.

> *And all I've done for want of wit*
> *To memory now I can't recall*
> *So fill to me the parting glass*
> *Good night and joy be with you all*

It's hard to listen to. Of course it is. It's a song about dying, and leaving the world behind, but being satisfied that you have at least lived your life fully and richly, having spent every kiss on girls who mattered and every penny on drinks for other people. And, for some reason, I'm angry. I'm angry that this is my dad's favourite song. Angry because I miss him; angry because I'm sorry I'm not there; angry because nothing about the song is reflective of the way he has lived his life. He never lived recklessly. He never had a lot of friends or girlfriends. He escaped a near-death experience, met my mum, had me, joined a walking club and got cancer. What kind of life is that?

What kind of life is that to go *back* to?

> *Of all the comrades that e'er I had*
> *They are sorry for my going away*
> *And all the sweethearts that e'er I had*
> *They would wish me one more day to stay . . .*

All of a sudden, the emotions pin-balling around my body rise and break into something new, and golden, and strange. For the first time in my entire life I *feel* Irish. It's a bizarre fact to even admit to myself, but I know it exactly as it passes through me. How do you know when you finally feel something innately, as opposed to knowing it academically? How do you know a hurricane from a storm?

I feel at home here, in this pub, with these people. I feel calm, and inside my own body, and I want to *keep* feeling this way. It doesn't matter what happened fifty years ago to a catalogue of people who either are dead or moved away.

I don't want to go, I think, tears gathering, my lips mouthing the words to 'The Parting Glass', knowing it's a song about goodbyes, and knowing that by tomorrow, a goodbye is all I will have left to give.

I want to stay and work on a boat, I think, and the recklessness of merely having the thought sends a spike of energy through me.

I hate London. I hate being quote-unquote creative. I hate my father's pockmarked liver.

I'm not mouthing, now. I'm singing. I can hear the words falling out of me even though I've never so much as done karaoke before. I'm singing, singing earnestly, singing with tears in my eyes and a light golden veil of clarity all around me.

I can feel Maria's presence behind me, sensing small, nervous movements. The pondering of touch. Then, she goes for it: she slings her arm around my shoulder and starts to sing in a way that we both know *looks* like a drunken new-found friendship but courses with electricity and bite.

Plausible deniability. No matter where in the world you are, you always, always keep plausible deniability.

'Goodnight,' she sings, turning her face to mine. 'And joy be with you all.'

# 16

I fall into bed just before 3 a.m., and wake up two hours later. My mouth dry, my teeth mossy, my jeans still on and firmly wedged in my vulva. There's a Club Milk biscuit smashed into the side of my pillow and melted chocolate on my neck. Maria put one in my pocket when she kicked us all out of The Fiddler last night, telling me to drop by in the morning before we set out for the airport.

'And if not,' she said, her breath grey and cloudy in the moonlight, 'well, then I'll see you next time.'

I should have kissed her. *Why didn't I kiss her?*

I stumble to the tiny toilet, my feet cold on the caravan floor. Blood running cold up through my ankles. I'm desperate for a piss, and when I finally sit down, the seat frigid, it gushes out in a long, aching stream. I put my forehead on my knees, simmering in my hangover. I have to get on a *flight* today.

Walking home from the pub, Laura and I had waxed lyrical in the freezing night air about how happy we were that we came to the island. How important it was to see everything for ourselves. And maybe we didn't find any big answers about what went on with the accident: but, by virtue of even coming, I had kicked open a door for myself in Clipim. A door that would remain open, regardless of what happens to my father. Laura had wrapped her arms around me, the moon bouncing off her hair. A milky, glittering gold.

'This is just the beginning, Charlie,' she had breathed. 'These are your people. And they *love* you.'

I knew she was overdoing it. You could tell that she was proud of herself for allowing me to take this detour, and in doing so, felt like she had palmed off the responsibility of being my friend to an entire island full of well-meaning Irish people. I could see her doing the maths in her head: *I'll have LA, Charlie will have Clipim. That seems fair. Appropriate. Proportional. I get the whole world, she gets an island.*

Still. I didn't mind.

'And do you think Maria ... ?'

'Charlie! She's clearly into you.'

'You think?'

'Babe, the way she looked at you all night? I *know*.'

I was highly aware, the entire time we were walking home, that this would be the appropriate time to tell Laura about Dad. I kept picturing what I would say, and how I would say it. 'Laura, I didn't want to say anything back in the pub, but ... '

And then it would all begin again. The hushed voice. The head tilt of sympathy. The rapid sobering up. Me and Laura's last big night out before she moves to LA would be transformed from a lively, bursting adventure into a mere preamble for another sickness story.

I look at my phone, currently on 3 per cent battery. We have to leave for the airport *in two hours*. I should have kissed her.

The one good thing about the freezing caravan is that the water is also extremely cold. I drink a huge pint glass of water and feel it juddering down me like liquid silver. I pour another glass and catch the sun slowly coming up, the pale white sunlight glinting off the dewy leaves. Everything looks like it smells amazing, and noticing my trainers kicked off by the door, I decide that before I leave Clipim, I will pay another visit to the yew wood.

There's a spongy, delicate wetness to the world outside, as though it had been painted overnight in watercolours and is still drying. Small brown birds hop out of my way as I pass them. They are neither alarmed nor particularly interested by me, but busy about like courteous commuters who don't have a moment to be distracted. It feels good to notice these things. It feels good to see birds and grass and the earth's big loafy body.

My mother has a front garden that is really just a lawn framed by a flowerbed, and it makes our house look like it belongs to an old person. Most of the houses on our road have adopted a semi-modern approach to gardening, going for either a zen garden – stone Buddhas are embarrassingly popular – or a kind of carefully overgrown Secret Garden effect, filled with wildflowers and tomatoes in artfully mismatched pots. My mother's pansies are tragically retro by comparison. In the summer Dad was first diagnosed, the grass became – by my mother's standards, at least – shockingly overgrown. First it came up to the ankle, then it was shin high. Dandelions everywhere; and the faint smell of hay. I liked it. Maybe because it was nice to know that wildness still existed in the world, and maybe because I knew she hated it.

I kept meaning to cut it for her, knowing that it would be the good daughter thing to do, but I was too intrigued by the social experiment of watching it grow. When would she notice? When would she care?

And then, for a short while, Dad went blind. It was just another one of those unexpected side-effects from chemotherapy that no one ever truly warns you about, and when the doctor told Mum, he relayed it as though it were nothing.

She lost it. She had prepared herself for a sick husband, even a dying one, but a blind one, too? After shoring herself up against every eventuality, the fact that something could still surprise her was enraging. So she came home and she took it out on the grass, screaming at me that I hadn't sorted it out sooner, pushing the mower around like a woman possessed. The bugs that had made the garden their home flew up and bit her on the face. Red welts started to show up all over her body as she hacked at the grass.

It was the end of the summer. It was not a time to disturb things. I got bitten, too, just watching the whole thing, the welts on my body turning quickly to hardened panels of pink flesh. I wanted to stick a pin in my legs and drain the fluid away, just like I wanted to dive into my father's body and cut away the cancer cells like an adventurer with a machete. It was such a satisfying thing to imagine.

Dad got cataract surgery in the autumn of that year, so the mosquito bites turned out to be for nothing. Illness is never supposed to be easy, but long-term illness with only my mother for support was impossible. I found myself resenting the pregnancies she'd lost, longing for the siblings that could have helped me share the burden of her.

I'm deep in the yew wood now, my breath hard and coarse. The long branches are eerier in the morning sunlight, catching the branches at odd angles, creating faces and shapes within the wood. I see patterns in the tangled web of tree. Human eyes that look like they are melting lava; a duck's face, its beak forced open by unseeing hands; a woman with a big pregnant belly, with big brown veins snaking across it. For some reason I keep walking through them, compelled to see how far I can go.

My phone battery is now on 1 per cent. It is almost 6 a.m. I have to be back soon. I should turn around now. Why didn't I kiss Maria? She wanted me to, I think. If she even likes girls, which she neither confirmed nor denied, and I suppose I could have asked her, but it never felt like the right time.

I picture Dad's liver, the lesions on its surface growing like mould over an abandoned cup of tea. Why does Mum have to make such a big deal out of everything? Why did she have to call me to say he was having surgery, when she knew I was coming home the next day? Did she have to pick a fight on my last night in Clipim? Did she have to make me feel guilty for going to Ireland in the first place?

The wood gets thicker, denser, and it's exciting to be at a part of the forest that looks completely untouched by humans. There's no beaten path here, no imprints from walking boots. Just me, my breath, and the sound of my heart pounding in my ears. The further I get into the forest, the more I realise that I don't know my way back. I have been pushing forward in random directions, and the ground is too dry now to leave a mark of me.

Dad wanted me to go to Ireland. It was his idea. There was nothing wrong with me going, and nothing wrong with me having a good time here. The fact that he suddenly needs surgery now is just bad timing, and not my fault, and not something Mum should be allowed to make me feel guilty about.

It is 6.45 a.m.

I'll find the road, and go back that way. If I just veer left, I'll eventually find the road. I'll sit down on a log first, catch my breath, and then find the road.

It is 6.58 a.m. A drop of rain falls on my head, like the polite knock from a policeman on a car window. Then another drop. And another.

Even if I *was* at home yesterday, what good would it have done? Would Mum have taken any comfort in me being there? Would she have acknowledged my presence at all?

It is 7.27 a.m., and it is raining, and I am still not back at the campsite. I am running.

I am running and I am not running towards the road. I am running further into the words. I am running so hard that puddles of mud splash into my trainers and I don't even slow down. I am running and I am running and I do not know where I am going to.

I am running away. I am running away. I am running away.

## 17

When I wake up, it has stopped raining, and everything is stone.

I cannot pinpoint the moment I fell asleep, but I know that the rain started, and that my shoes got too heavy and my breath too hard, and I had to sit down. The forest eventually bled into cliff-side grazing land, dotted with sheep shit and half-tumbled-down stone houses on the hillside. First one, then two, then eight. Some were half of a one-room structure. Others are just a few stones in the shape of a doorway. Structures that must have been here since the famine, that – like the schoolhouse – no one thought to clear away because they were doing no harm where they were.

I went inside one of them, roofless, but sheltered enough by a tree so that I was protected from the worst of the rainfall. I shivered into a ball, knowing with each passing minute that the likelihood of Laura and I catching our flight was getting slighter and slighter. At some point, the adrenalin wore off and the hangover kicked in, and my body grabbed at sleep like a greedy toddler.

I have no idea what time it is, where I am, or how long I've been asleep. I unfold my limbs and look at the sky to guess. A thin blanket of heat has settled on the day. I guess that it's late morning. Ten thirty? Eleven? Gazing at the sky, a new feeling takes over from the hungover muddle of sleepy limbs and violent nausea. It creeps out of the ground and grabs hold of my feet, the dark mud of it surging through my body and landing in my chest.

*What in the fuck have I done, and how in the fuck am I going to explain it?*

Panic rises like feathers on air. Laura and I have missed our flight. Because of me. Because I ran into the forest. Because ... because why?

Because the thought of going home to my parents, to re-start the whole process of illness and guilt, of barbed comments and blinked-back tears, was too much. When Mum called last night, all I could picture was another year of half-life: where Dad isn't sick enough for it to be an emergency, but too sick for me to have anything approaching a normal life. Because in the warmth of The Fiddler, I could feel myself starting to become someone, and it didn't feel fair to kill that feeling before it had even started.

I drag my feet through the stone village of broken houses that, at some point, must have been the main part of the village. Funny how the centre of power can pivot just like that: how people can pick up, move on, leaving their bodies and bad memories behind them.

Eventually, the ground levels out and I manage to fight my way through some trees and on to a dirt road. I try to orientate myself by standing on a five-bar gate, looking all around me for clues. There's a splash of pink in the road ahead, and I realise that I'm less than a hundred yards from the old schoolhouse.

Look. I'm in trouble *anyway*. Laura is going to be out of her mind. How many voicemails will she have left? Ten? Fifteen? She will have gone down to The Fiddler and raised hell, called my mother probably, and will have every right to scream at me when I get back. She'll yell, we'll book another flight, and this will be another item added to the great cosmic list of *Things Charlie Put Us All Through*. Why not go back to the schoolhouse and make my peace with whatever ghosts were left inside there?

As if Clipim itself were trying to mount a case for the defence, I then hear a short, sharp bark.

I look around, hearing a dog but not seeing one, and eventually follow the sound to the wire fence. Satan the dog has tangled his brown little head in some bramble and wire, and is crying miserably in protest.

'Oh! Satan!' I say, and look around for either Ferryman Joe or Grandferryman Tony. Satan whines on, scrabbling his feet against the mud, his six-pronged paws leaving frantic, six-clawed prints below him. Satan is not just stuck: he is stuck and lost.

I have no idea where either Joe or Tony live – they might live together, for all I know – and there are no houses around. I grip one hand on Satan's muzzle, and the other on his shoulders. I push him back through the fence, navigating his wiry, white body through the bramble. Finally, I pull him out and he yelps with relief, leaping eagerly to lick my face in gratitude. He has no collar, no tags, and I haven't the faintest clue what to do with him. I could take him back to the ferry port but it's a good hour's walk, and I'm almost at the schoolhouse now.

I decide to bring Satan to the schoolhouse with me. He'll ruin the sombre mood I was planning, but maybe that's a good thing. Satan likes this plan, too, and he trots alongside me without hesitation. I pick him up as I jump the wall, and we manage to avoid landing in the bramble this time. He runs ahead of me into the schoolhouse, and I'm grateful for his life and energy. In the rain, the schoolhouse looks even more desolate. It needs a dog, I think. Certain situations just do.

Satan shakes the rain off himself and bolts excitedly from

room to room, shredding up pieces of paper and sniffing at beer cans.

Everything is damp: the wood is a sodden, heavy, spongy thing, and the walls are greenish with mildew. I sit on the floor for a little while, watching Satan busy himself, waiting to feel something. A single strand of sunshine beams through the windowless frames. Maybe that's what gets me off my feet: it is spring after all. It's time for spring cleaning.

I find an old shopping bag and start putting rubbish into it, picking everything up with my thumb and forefinger. Satan starts jumping up at me, thinking this is a game, and I need to bat him away several times to stop him from snapping at the end of the plastic bag. He contents himself with headbutting a soft patch in the wall, where years of dampness have turned the plaster soggy.

There is, unbelievably, a battered old broom in the big cupboard where Laura and I found the sheep. I start sweeping up dust, ash and glass, but have no dustpan to put it into, so it stays in one corner of the room. The old newspaper I pulled out yesterday is still in the fire grate, drying out slightly, and I pull off a sheet as a souvenir, folding it into a small square before placing it in my pocket. I pick up some old chairs and stack them in the corner.

I don't know why I'm doing this. Maybe I'm trying to get myself into the mindset of Emma Casey, thinking of what her daily routine must have been. Probably this, I think, but with fewer beer cans. She probably swept the floor and stacked the chairs every day before she returned to the boarding house she lived in.

I start to think about Emma and Kitty Regan again. The reports that bothered to mention Emma at the time all had the same story: she was a young, unmarried woman of twenty-five who had been teaching for under a year. She was from Kenmare, a busy market town on the mainland, but had decided to take a job in Clip when the previous teacher had emigrated with her husband the year before. She was a good Catholic girl from a good Catholic family, and had a small flavour for adventure that brought her to rural Clip. I try to imagine her, this adventurous young woman, having a cup of tea with my shy and inward grandmother. What did they talk about? Being young? Being wholly without men, in a place that treated spare women as spare parts?

I try to picture both women waking up on 11 November: one to get her son ready for school, the other to go to work. To walk three miles to the schoolhouse while recovering from a bout of bronchitis that had had her off sick for days before.

This is the part that journalists referred to as the 'Swiss cheese' factor: enough holes lined up at once, and a whole generation slipped through. Perhaps if Emma wasn't so sick and weak already, she wouldn't have shrugged off the dizzy light-headedness as symptoms of her lingering illness. Perhaps she wouldn't have turned the heat on the oil burner up so high. Perhaps she wouldn't have kept all of the doors closed. Perhaps she would have joined the children outside at play-time, instead of sitting at her desk, desperate to keep warm, slowly being poisoned to death. The fire grate blocked, the big rectangular air vents in the walls stuffed with dirt and dust and paper.

A yelp from Satan pulls me out of my cleaning trance, and I turn around to find that he has disappeared, face-first, into the wall. The air vent in the top right corner shudders and rattles against its fixtures.

*This fucking dog.*

'Satan! Come on, get out of there.'

He wags his tail at the sound of my voice, but shows no sign of extracting himself from the inside of the wall. I clamp my hands around his hind legs and try to yank his barrel of a body out of the wall. Unfortunately his mouth seems to be wrapped around one of the beams of wood behind the plaster. He growls at my attempts to remove him, holding firm by the teeth.

'How are you not dead yet, Satan? Your entire life seems to be getting caught in weird places.'

The little dog gives me an insulted yap, and some more plaster crumbles away as he wriggles and gnaws his way into the wall. I lose my grip on him, and he takes the opportunity to delve even further into the building, wedging himself in the crawl space between the frame of the house and the indoor walls. It's only about four inches wide, but Satan is rangy, and apparently able to shrink himself down for investigative purposes.

I reach for him, leaning my shoulder up against the wall. The whole building rattles. I manage to wrap my hand around his leg, and it feels like grabbing on to a hairy chicken bone.

'Satan, I'm going to pull now,' I say, with as much tender concern as I can muster.

Satan whimpers in response. I can feel him trying to escape the building, but he can't turn around, and he can't walk backwards. He needs to be yanked. The wall behind my arm starts to crumble and fall away, and it begins to dawn on me just how old this house is, and how unsafe the two of us are inside of it.

'Satan, don't be scared.'

I pull back, quick, and as hard as I can. Satan emerges, screeching in pain. He comes out in a cloud of dust, stinking of dampness and insulation. The air vent – old, and embossed with the kind of swirly, fusty Victorian decoration you find on wardrobes – comes crashing to the floor. I shield Satan with my whole body, rolling both of us into a ball and sinking my head beneath my arms. The clatter of iron coming apart reverberates around the room, chalky dust billowing out of the broken vents.

I keep my body around Satan, who is whimpering softly into my T-shirt.

'It's okay, boy,' I say, kissing his rust-coloured ear. 'You're the prince of darkness, remember? Nothing scares you.'

I stand up, and brush the snow-coloured dust off of me. The school room, which I had just finished cleaning, is destroyed once again by the debris of the shattered air vent. I approach it cautiously, scared that I have just evicted a family of dormice from the cosy metal box.

But no – there's nothing here but metal, and tiny slats designed for air to filter through. I've read about these. Ventilation was all the rage in the nineteenth century. Everyone was convinced that if children had enough fresh air, they would become hardy, and therefore immortal. I wonder if it was a reaction to all those English children who had to be submerged into coal mines every day. *Force the clear air on your children. Show them how good they have it.*

As I kick it apart, wads of balled newspaper come loose. Of course. I always forget about the air vents, but they played a part in the Clipim tragedy as much as anything else. The choked-up fireplace was always first in my mind, but because I'm not used to even noticing vents, I barely thought about them. I live a vent-free existence. I start putting the newspaper in my trash bag until, in the piles of yellow faded scraps, I see a face. A familiar face. A face that, really, I've been seeing pictures of my entire life.

It's Paul McCartney's face.

A young, puppy-eyed Paul McCartney is looking up at me, his skin smudged with filth, and I'm so surprised to see him in my father's schoolhouse that I unfurl the piece of newspaper and study the story.

## MANY ARRESTED AS CITY CROWDS RIOT

More than a dozen men were arrested and taken to various Dublin police stations last night, when fights broke out while the Beatles, the Liverpool 'beat' singers, were playing at the Adelphi Cinema. Cars were overturned in Abbey Street and O'Connell Street; at least fifty people were treated for minor injuries, while three people were taken to hospital with fractured legs and arms.

Underneath the photo of Paul is a grainy picture of what I presume were the riots themselves, although all you can see are a bunch of men in dark coats being led away from the venue. Underneath, the caption reads: *On Thursday 7 November the Beatles played two gigs in Dublin, at the Adelphi Cinema on Abbey Street.*

My eyes flick to the top of the front page. The edition is dated Friday 8 November 1963. Three days before the accident.

I frown, and a thudding headache begins to grow at the front of my skull.

I reach into my pocket and unfold the piece of newspaper that I had retrieved from the chimney a few days ago. I study it, glad I had taken the front page. Yes, that was right: *5 January 1960.* The chimney paper had been up there for three years before the accident.

I lined up both scraps of paper alongside one another, the chimney one and the air vent one, convinced that I must be wrong. But no, it's right there, in black and white and sickly yellow. One paper is from three years before the accident, and the other is from three days before it.

*8 November 1963.*

Odd. The reports all said that the newspaper had been stuffed up the chimney for years, and when the oil burner suddenly broke, it had been the thing that helped suffocate everyone. It was a pretty simple if unbearably tragic story. But it becomes less simple when you factor in that the additional paper was stuffed up the vents only a couple of days beforehand.

I guess it was just cold. It got freezing on Clipim, I knew that. Dad talked about the long dead winters like they were Siberian hellscapes. But the weird West Kerry micro-climate, the gulf stream that hit the tip of the country, could change the sun's strange moods.

Wouldn't the dozens of reports have mentioned the extra paper? Everything was about the faulty burner. If the extra newspaper had been shoved up the vents only three days before the accident, wouldn't it have added to the whole tragic ballet of the story? *If only they hadn't used that extra newspaper! Innocent lives lost to a dozen sheets of print!*

Maybe they hadn't noticed. Maybe, in the context of dead children, it didn't seem very important.

I pick through the rubble on the floor while Satan wags his stumpy tail. I read through the scraps of articles that I can fix together. I find a photograph of some children playing outside, and for a moment, think it might be the children who died. It isn't. It's a gang of kids on a beach in West Cork, scarves and hats on, widely grinning into the lens.

*Reader's Pic of the Week: Children enjoying the rare November sunshine on Skibbereen. Photograph by John Mahon of Lismore. Please send in your photographs to be in with a chance of winning £5 and a year-long subscription to* The Irish Times.

They look happy. I feel a pang of resentment for the lives these children would go on to lead when, an hour away, their doppelgängers were destined to perish.

I flick through the rest of the newspaper while cross-legged on the floor. I still feel queasy, but most of that is just anxiety about running into Laura again. How is she going to react when she finds out I've stranded us here for another day?

Satan is bored. A shaft of sunlight streams through the window and he keeps moving so he can rest in it, following the warmth like an heiress follows the seasons. He splays himself out, an exhausted sow, then groans in irritation when the sun goes behind a cloud. I watch him, his little orange ears twitching. I'm not usually that into dogs, but Satan is extremely cute. Dad loves terriers. I'll have to get a photo of Satan to show him.

I can't stay here all day. I know that. Eventually I'm going to have to face up to Laura, and to my mother, and to the fact that I am hurtling into my thirties with nothing more than a bad film and a deep knowledge of hospital wards.

'Satan, we have to go.'

An annoyed groan.

'Satan, you sun hog, come on.'

He twitches and considers getting up, but instead just loudly licks his own penis.

'Gross,' I say, focusing my eyes back to the old newspaper. And as the shaft of sunlight yet again steals away from the dog, I see something. The weather report. Temperatures for 8 November 1963: highs of 14 degrees, sunshine; 9 November: highs of 13 degrees, sunshine; 10 November: highs of 14 degrees, some light clouds.

I flick back to the children on Skibbereen. They were on the *beach*. They have jackets on, sure, but you can clearly see the sun winking at them in the background. It was a warm week in November, the way bright, crisp, clear weeks in early November can occasionally be. My stomach churns.

Why would you put extra newspaper in a vent to keep out the cold if you were in the middle of a warm spell?

Satan finds the sun again and lets out a little moan of pleasure.

## 18

I sit on the step outside the schoolhouse, spitting hot, thick globs of saliva on to the ground. I watch it bubble. The dog sniffs at it, gives it a polite lick, and then wanders off to investigate a bush.

I try to retch, but nothing will come up. Why is vomiting so much easier for other people? When we drank too much on nights out in Uni, Laura would calmly disappear from the dance floor, and come back smelling of soft mints. 'I just made myself sick,' she'd say, shrugging. And then the night would resume.

I sit with a knot in my stomach and a warm feeling in my jaw. God, I wish I was vomiting. I wish I was doing anything else but sitting here, with this.

I wish Laura was here. She would tell me that I'm overreacting. I consider the possibility that I *am* overreacting. I try to think about the two newspaper dates coolly and rationally. It was just a coincidence, surely? Someone blocking out all the air in a one-room schoolhouse three days before the burner breaks down? In ... bright early-November sunshine?

That was perfectly plausible, wasn't it?

I clutch my belly button. The nausea of my hangover is turning to thick, black anxiety. It bubbles like a tarpit, starting in my stomach and spreading through my chest, across my shoulders and down my arms, every part of me feeling heavy. I clutch the doorframe. I don't feel like I'm going to vomit any more. I feel as though I'm about to shit myself.

I stumble out of the house and scurry into the overgrown grounds, my insides feeling as though they are about to rupture, like the blackness inside of me is going to break the levees on my entire body and melt the skin off of my bones. I pull down my jeans and squat into a mass of fuchsia plants, the petals brushing off the insides of my thighs and bursting through my knees like something out of a biblical plague. I close my eyes and feel the shit coming out of me like stale water.

I grab a handful of wet leaves to wipe myself, and gingerly stand up from the now destroyed fuchsia plant. I have never felt more disgusting in my entire life: hungover, rain-soaked and with splashes of diarrhoea stuck to the inside of my legs.

I have no choice but to crouch in the dirt, ease my jeans off and use my knickers as a rag, spitting on the clean cotton as I try to approach some form of cleanliness. Putting my jeans back on and throwing my underwear away, I imagine what the Lottie Minxx customers would make of this, and whether any of them would weirdly enjoy it. Humiliation is a big thing for some of them. What could be more humiliating than this?

I stagger to my feet and try to make sense of things. Nineteen people. Eighteen children, one teacher. But then there was the wider tragedy, the one that affected every person who set foot on Clipim island. The sorrow, the grief after the tragedy, the mass emigration, the lack of labour, the failing businesses, the toppled economy, the Foley monopoly, the new era of either destitution or mealy-mouthed tourism that served every shamrock-shaped Guinness head with a 'please rate us on TripAdvisor, won't you?'

I turn it over and over in my mind. Is there any feasible, logical, sensible reason to stuff up an air vent? The newspapers that had reported the tragedy had all made it seem that both the chimney and the air vents had been blocked for years, to conserve heat in the chilly seaside schoolroom. But having one blocked up from January 1960 and one blocked since November 1963 could change everything.

It's all too confusing, and I don't know enough, and even if I did know enough, I would have nothing to do with that knowledge. I'm not the police. I'm not a journalist. I'm just a stranger. A failed filmmaker whose only credit is a factually inaccurate and thoroughly bad movie that is in total service to the idea that this was an accident, not a massacre.

*Massacre.* Even the word.

I need to take Satan back to the ferry port. I also need to eat something and shower. I pat my coat pockets and grimace. No wallet.

Walking helps. I inhale huge mouthfuls of rain-soaked air, the full, green smell of wet things filling my nose. I keep walking, feeling the stones trying to poke through my trainers, feeling the layer of sweat that has formed on my scalp, making my hair sticky.

I spot a few tourists wandering around, some alone, some in pairs wearing matching Patagonia jackets, clutching their mittened hands together and grinning into the wilderness. 'Baby,' a woman says to her husband, looking at a brochure that is also a map, 'we're on the red trail. We need to follow the *red arrows*.'

This is what you want from an Irish holiday, I suppose. This is what I wanted. Breathtaking landscapes, bowls of soup, warm welcomes, an overabundance of the colour green. Last night the feeling of homecoming had throbbed through me as I sat in The Fiddler. Was it all an illusion? Is this simply what Ireland does? Casts a spell of familiarity over you, distracts you with smiles and fiddle music, while simultaneously choke-slamming its skeletons back into the closet?

When I finally get to the village, I duck into The Fiddler, hoping that Maria will spot me some breakfast before I head back to the caravan, where Laura is almost certainly waiting. When I get there, though, Laura and Maria are already outside. Maria is lifting the shutters of the pub with a long pole, setting out the blackboard, and doing, I realise, the exact same series of tasks that she was doing when we met her at this time yesterday. That Maria's days must be very similar to one another. I remember the long, unblinking stare she gave me during 'The Parting Glass' and wonder just how many pseudo-romances she has had with tourists. Girls? Boys? Does it matter when you're on island time?

I hear them before they even see me.

'You haven't see her *at all*?'

'No! God, where would I have seen her? I was at my house until ten minutes ago. Your guess is as good as mine.'

'You didn't tell her to meet you somewhere? Or imply she should stay?'

'I'm telling you, *no*.'

Their tone with one another is serrated. Both of them had a lot to drink last night and I imagine neither relishes having to speak to the other. I'm mortified that Laura seems to be telling Maria that the merest hint of encouragement from her would have made me ditch our flight.

'Guys,' I call as I get closer, determined to break this conversation up before I come across even more desperate. 'Hi, I'm here.'

Laura turns round, her lips bloodless, her face pale. She stares me down for a second before she opens her mouth. Satan runs up to Maria, leaping to lick her face as she crouches down to greet him.

'Just where the *fuck* have you been?'

'Look, I'm sorry. I'm really, really sorry. I've acted like a total asshole, Laura.'

Maria is still setting up outside, but is clearly taking her time, straining her ear to listen.

'Do you know what time it is, Charlie?'

'I don't know. Eleven?'

'It's eleven fifty-six. Our plane is in thirty-four minutes. Do you think we're going to make it?'

'Well, no.'

'OF COURSE WE FUCKING AREN'T, YOU DICK.'

The old woman from the corner shop across the street suddenly opens her counter window, designed for selling ice cream on hot days.

'*Language!*' she bellows.

'Sorry,' the three of us respond at once.

'Maria,' I say pleadingly, 'can we come inside, so we're not shouting on the street?'

'Sure,' she says, quietly excited not to miss the fight. She rattles the door open and gestures for us to go in. 'We don't open until one on weekdays. I'll give Tony a call and tell him that Satan is here.'

Walking into The Fiddler before it's open feels like disturbing an old Madame. Chairs on tables, the smell of stale yeast and toilet disinfectant hanging in the air, dimpled shadows from the shutters staining the floor. Laura glares at the pub, as if it were partly responsible for the situation we're in. She finally rests her eyes on me again challengingly, as if to say: *Go on, do your best.*

'Look, I got a call from my mum last night.'

'So?'

'She had some . . . news about my dad.'

Laura closes her eyes for a second, exasperated. She's probably thinking *Oh God, she's not going to pull the sick dad card now, is she?*

*Well, yes, bitch, I am.*

'He's gone back into hospital. The drugs he's on are doing something bad to his liver and they need to operate.'

'Well, I'm very sorry that's happening to him,' Laura responds evenly, her rage like a rabid dog she is keeping back with one foot.

'And ... I don't know. I couldn't. I woke up this morning and, I don't know if it was all the drinking last night or the fear of going home today, or both, but I panicked. I freaked out. I charged into the woods like a mad person.'

'So, you found out your dad was going into hospital, and instead of telling me, you ... *ran away*?'

I watch her face, as I have always watched her face, and realise that no matter how I try to explain my running away, she will never understand it. Never understand a person who doesn't follow protocol, and doesn't show up for flights, and isn't there for their sick family member, and resents their best friend for thriving. Laura is a person who has the right-sized reactions to things. And right now, the right-sized reaction is to be furious with me.

'Yes,' I say finally, giving up on her understanding, giving up on making sense. 'I ran away. I'm sorry, Laura. I'm so sorry.'

There is a tense, tight quiet. A silence gleaming with teeth. The only sound in the pub is Satan lapping water out of a bowl Maria has left for him.

'Maybe we should ... book another flight, then?' I say, desperate to break it. 'The next one? There's probably one this evening.'

Saying it is like turning on an electric knife.

'Yes, Charlie. Let's book a flight, shall we? I hadn't thought of that. I hadn't thought of just, you know, booking another flight.'

'Right. I'm sure you have, but maybe we should ...'

'Yep, I've just been sitting on my hands for the last five hours. I haven't been on the Ryanair site already. I haven't been looking at Aer-fucking-Lingus since nine a.m. What a good idea. *Let's just book another flight.*'

'I mean, there are at least four flights a day from Cork airport to London. It can't be hard.'

'Maybe it wouldn't be hard, if it weren't for a little something you might have heard of – the Cork Film Festival?'

'Oh. Shit.'

'Yeah, mate. This week is when it all kicks off. Colin Farrell's directorial debut *and* a *Star Wars* convention.'

'*What?*'

'That old woman we met in Waterville? Turns out she wasn't talking shit. There really is a *Star Wars* island, and J. J. Abrams is basically holding a *Star Wars* convention at the Cork Film Festival to celebrate it.'

The next part, Laura says through teeth so gritted that it feels like her words are abseiling through the cracks between them.

'So, you've chosen to skip our flight in the one week, possibly the one week in history, where flights in and out of Cork are actually worth something.'

Eventually, we manage to book flights for Wednesday afternoon. I suggest getting a flight home from one of the other airports, to which Laura irritably points out that we picked up our rental car from Cork, and we need to return it there or be hit with a huge fine.

'I'm sorry,' I say, as she punches in her debit card details into the Ryanair website. 'I'll pay you back.'

'*How*, Charlie?'

I realise she's mad at me, but does she have to be *this* mad at me? And more importantly, is she going to *keep* being this mad at me for the next few days? As we walk home from The Fiddler, I keep trying to apologise, but everything I say comes out slippery and insincere. I can't *sound* sorry enough. My mind is still firmly fixed on the mismatched newspaper, the unbearable fact of it beating like a heart under the floorboards. I just want her to stop being mad at me so I can tell her what I know, and she can happily explain away why it's fine that someone stuffed up the air vents mere days before nineteen people were killed from poisoned air, and I can stop feeling like I want to drown myself in a well.

Instead, once we're back at the campsite, I just start being a bitch back to her.

'I can make money,' I reply indignantly. 'I'm not totally helpless, you know.'

'*Aren't* you?' she says, rolling her eyes and walking into her room.

I hate her for being so superior. For having these little private jokes with herself, as if she is always giving a perplexed, world-weary look to a hidden camera.

'Sorry,' I yell after her, 'that I want to work in one of the most competitive industries in the world, and that in film-making it's all about *who you know*, not what you know.'

She turns around to look at me again, her hand still on her bedroom door. Her face says: *Don't say it, bitch.*

'If only I had a friend who *knew* someone, y'know? If only I knew anyone in the industry who could give me a chance.'

'Oh, for fuck's sake. This is it then, is it? Charlie, you really think that the reason you're not able to get work is because *I won't sort it out* for you?'

'I'm not saying you should sort it out for me. Just give me a phone number, an email introduction, anything. Jesus. Is it that hard? Am I *that* embarrassing to you?'

I'm quaking with rage now, spitting venom at her from across the caravan. Across the *mobile home*.

'You're not embarrassing, Charlie,' she says slowly, her fingers flexing in and out of a fist. 'But the way you flake on things *is*. You're the least reliable person I've ever known. All those job interviews you missed in the last few years? Did you *really* need to miss all of them? Fucking hell, the reason we're having this argument is because you ran into the forest.'

'My dad was dying, Laura.'

'I know, but . . .'

'No, no buts, Laura. My dad was fucking dying, and I had to be with him. You know *that*.'

She gazes at me coolly, white-blonde hair in her eyes.

'If you needed to be with him so much,' she says measuredly, 'then how come we're here?'

And then, incredibly, Laura leaves. I don't ask her where she's going. Part of me is offended that she could find things to do on Clipim that don't involve me. I have already started to think of Clipim as my place. Discovering the newspaper this morning has fixed that fact deeper in my heart. I *know* things about here now. Terrible things, but things nonetheless.

After Laura goes I manage to find a corner of the mobile home with passable wifi, provided I balance my laptop on the windowsill.

**Clipim Schoolhouse Disaster**
From Wikipedia, the free encyclopedia

*The Clipim schoolhouse disaster was a tragedy that led to the death of 18 Irish school children and their teacher due to carbon monoxide poisoning on 11 November 1963. The event occurred in Clipim, a rural island off the coast of West Kerry. The accident was caused by a faulty oil burner that was later deemed unsuitable for the building it was in. At the time of the accident, the community was widely criticised for the lack of structural safety of the school building, and the tragedy became one of the leading case studies in securing firmer public health and safety laws in Ireland.*

1. *Background*
2. *Cause*

I had tried, several times, to get my film added to the 'Legacy' section of the page. At the start of the year, I would check a couple of times a week to see if my addition was approved, and it never was.

I keep searching. I add words like 'murder' and 'conspiracy' and 'controversy' and 'air vent' to my original search term, but nothing comes up. After some fiddling around on the Met Éireann website, I manage to find some historical weather data taken from Valentia, the closest big island to Clipim, confirming that yes, the first week in November was a mild and sunny one. Would a concerned teacher or caretaker really stuff up the air vents if the weather was temperate and the burner was still working? It doesn't make any sense.

After my phone has been charging for a few minutes, texts start coming through. Mum asking what time I'll be home, and what time should she pick me up, and whether I will want anything to eat when I land.

*Fuck.*

It's almost one. She'll be leaving the house to pick me up at any minute. If I could get away with texting her, I would. Texting is a technology that my mum still periodically forgets exists, so there's only about a 60 per cent chance of her seeing it, despite her phone being on her at all times.

When she picks up the phone on the seventh ring, she already sounds frantic.

'Charlie! You've not landed already, have you? I have it here that you won't be landing until two.'

'No, Mum . . . I'm still in Ireland.'

'What? Why? Has your flight been delayed?'

'No . . . ' I say, before realising I have made the grave error of getting on the phone with my mother without a real alibi. I gaze out the window, where a seagull has just landed on the hood of our rental car.

'The ferry broke down.'

'*What?*'

'The ferry. Off the island. It's broken. They're looking to get it repaired. So, you know, it's awful, but it's the only way off of Clipim, so we're stuck here until Wednesday.'

'Until *Wednesday*?'

'Yeah, I know. It's bollocks.'

'Charlie, your father is having surgery *today*.'

'I know. I know. But I can't control it. It is what it is, Mum. I'll phone him. Does he have his mobile on him? Is it charged?'

'Darling,' she says, the spite draining out of her voice, 'he's in a coma.'

And for a second, no one says anything.

## 19

There was a time, a year or more ago, where I would have taken this information in a different way. 'He's in a *what*?', I might have yelled, spluttering over whats, whys and how-comes until the word 'coma' had properly taken shape in my mind. And then, as though illness were a jelly that needs time to set, I would have eased it out of its mould and presented it to others, telling Laura as though comas were the most normal thing in the world.

I don't do that this time. Screaming questions is a coping mechanism we seem to have outgrown. I wait for my mother to speak again.

'I didn't want to tell you last night. I didn't want to ... I didn't want you to be too upset while you were so far away. His liver has shut down completely so they've put him in a medical coma to monitor him before they operate on him.'

There is a crack, and for a moment I believe that we have lost signal.

'Mum? Mum? Can you hear m ... '

The sound of plastic hitting hard tile and rustling.

'Yes. Sorry. I just dropped the bloody ... the thing ... '

'The phone?'

The sound of a throat struggling with itself, and then my mother is crying.

'Look, Mum ... He'll get through this. He always does.'

I go on like this for a while, each word hollowed out and dull, clanging with uselessness. She keeps undercutting me – no he *won't* be fine, no it's *not* okay – and eventually, we run out of things to say to each other. We begin trading information, both of us exhausted by one another. We volley potential transport plans – I could get a flight from Killarney tomorrow morning, and Laura could get the flight from Cork on Wednesday? – before eventually agreeing that it wouldn't be fair on Laura, and that there's not a lot of rush when it comes to a medically induced coma. There's a silent understanding that the only person who really needs me home is her, if only to have someone to fight with.

Through her grief, she still manages to be mortified that Laura has had to book the new flights.

'And the extra days in the rental car. And the extra accommodation. I suppose Laura is paying for those too, is she?'

'I said I'll pay her back, Mum. She's on about two hundred pounds a day freelancing; it will be fine.'

I say this, knowing that Laura and I are 50 miles south of 'fine'.

'How are you going to pay her back, Charlie? Working in that café? If you just got a real job, I wouldn't have to worry like this all the time. Don't you think I have enough to be worried about?'

Biting down hard on my own lip, I reassure her that yes, I will get a real job. That yes, she *does* have too much to be worried about. By the time I hang up the phone, I hate her more than I ever have.

The fresh wave of hate gives me a teenage jolt of rebellious energy. Because the truth is I *can* make my own money. If I really put the effort in, I could pay Laura back in a single afternoon.

I open my laptop again and pull out my stash of nude

photos, studying each one carefully. Maybe I can resell some
to new buyers. So far, this business has been built on carefully phrased online adverts, accompanied by blurry, cropped
photos of myself. They promise the buyer a suite of custom
images, but there's no video chat, no dirty talk, no phone
calls. I want to keep this as coldly transactional as possible,
even though I know I could make more if I added flair to
my salesmanship. Shifting uncomfortably in the wifi-adjacent
window seat, I slowly load up the internet forums where men
who like girls like me go. This is the strange thing about the
world of porn: no matter who you are, or what you look like,
there's a fetish ready to exploit.

Words like 'teen' and 'barely legal' are merely industry
terms, peppered with amusingly quaint qualifiers like 'nubile'
and 'tomboy'. In my experience, there are two types of men
who buy photographs off someone who looks like me. One:
men who enjoy young-looking women but who spent their
own youth terrorised by the blonde cheerleader type who
dominate the 'barely legal' industry, and therefore take sanc-
tuary in a girl-next-door aesthetic. Two: men who are gay
and too closeted, even to themselves, to look at gay porn.
Curveless, androgynous-looking women are the closeted
man's gateway drug, or at least in the amateur porn world
they are. There's something quite funny and tender about
these exchanges, with their tentative requests for me to wear
a strap-on. A gay woman trying to help a gay man get off
by imitating heterosexual desire. What a swell party this is!

I always thought that the porn was okay, because it ena-
bled me to make 'real art'. It's jarring to realise that the porn
turned out to be realer than the art.

I go through my photographs: some cheeky, some big-eyed
and vulnerable. In one, I am sitting at my bedroom desk with
my legs open. God, if only the man who bought this photo
knew how hard I had to fight to get the computer desk in my

room. Mum had read all the stories about teenagers online and even though I was the only one in the house that could work our ancient PC, the idea that I could be alone with it, a whole floor away from the house's nucleus, frightened her. So many things do. Dad was the one who backed me up in the end, talking my mother round with the idea that if the computer was no longer in the living room, she could fit a new armchair in where it had been.

'Wouldn't it be good to have it out of the way, Sharon? Such an ugly old thing. And then we could fit a bigger tree in at Christmas! Sure t'would be beautiful.'

No one in the world says beautiful like how my dad says beautiful. Be-yew-ti-fell. Like beauty is a friendly concept, soft at every corner, and a little funny too. That's how he says it, and that's how he sees me. Delicate and delightful as a small brown feather.

I keep scrolling through my photos, not seeing anything, my wrists trembling. Wondering if anyone will share his definition of beauty and whether they will bestow it on me if they do.

Feeling the chill of the window, I plop my laptop on the coffee table and dig through my luggage in my bedroom. I only brought one hoodie, and it already smells like cigarettes, beer and the dampness of the caravan floor. After smelling the armpits and deciding that Maria would definitely pick up on it if I run into her, I dig out my deodorant and start spraying it liberally.

Walking back into the living room, I realise that I am no longer alone.

That Benjamin Barry is sitting on my couch. Well.

His couch.

The laptop is still open, but Benjamin is sitting in the corner seat, just out of view of the screen. My mouth goes dry. He can't possibly have seen, can he?

'Benjamin,' I say, trying to hide the panic in my voice. 'Hi.'

'Hello, Charlie. I hear we'll be having you for another few nights.'

'You spoke to Laura?'

I am trying to keep the tremor out of my voice, the frantic flight-or-fight instinct that is sounding like an alarm. *What has he seen, what has he seen, what has he seen?*

'I did,' he says, his face still glowing a scalded red. 'I take it she's not very happy with you right now?'

He smiles at me and I grimace at the thought of what Laura has been telling people.

'What did she say?'

'Nothing much. Just that you need to stay tonight and tomorrow night because there was a problem with your flight.'

'Yes,' I say, thankful that Laura remained suitably vague. 'Thanks for, er, accommodating us.'

'I suppose the main problem was that you were running through the yew wood at the crack of dawn this morning?'

'You saw that?'

'It's right in front of my property, so, yes.'

'Don't you ever *sleep*?'

Benjamin Barry doesn't answer the question, and instead stands up and starts fluffing the cushions on the sofa. I watch him punching and tugging the old flower-patterned squares, teasing them back into their former plumpness.

'Why were you running? I called after you. You must not have heard me. You looked very upset, Charlie.'

'I ... had some bad news,' I stutter, not wanting to lay out my father's medical history to a total stranger. 'I was quite upset.'

I try to leave it at that, but he keeps looking at me, staring me down, and I start to think that Benjamin Barry has not only seen my nude photos, but thinks that the fact they exist is reason enough to assault me. His eyes, hazel and round, are empty of light for a moment. I wonder whether he is breathing louder or if the fact that I feel so vulnerable around him has lit up my senses like a hunted animal. My ears twitch. There's a rattle in his nose, like he is getting over a cold and one nostril is still slightly blocked.

Taking a small step backwards, I start chatting nervously, hoping I can give him enough information to bring him back into the room.

'But we're really looking forward to staying an extra few days,' I say brightly. 'Getting to know the island better.'

'What did you find out?' Benjamin says, finally, taking a step towards me.

'Sorry?'

'The bad news you got. The reason you ran to the schoolhouse this morning.'

'How do you know I went to the schoolhouse?'

'Maria. She gave the dog back to Tony and said you were at the schoolhouse with him. I keep wondering why you went through the woods, though. Trying to keep off the main roads?'

I straighten up and decide that despite this being Benjamin Barry's property, I am still a paying guest. Would I take this shit from a hotel receptionist?

'Benjamin, I'm sure you'll understand that it was a personal matter to do with my family.'

Impressed by my own ability to sound adult, I move towards my laptop. I even manage to appear casual about it.

'Your family,' he repeats, still sounding remote. 'Like your grandmother?'

'My grandmother is dead, Benjamin. She has been for a long time.'

I am proud of my tone here. It's a tone that clearly says: *Now fuck off, please.*

'So, I'm just going to grab my computer,' I say breezily. 'I have some work I need to do.'

He catches my eye then and smiles from the corner of his mouth, the cushion still in his hands.

'Ah, *work*,' he says. 'Yes, we all need to get work done.'

## 20

After Benjamin leaves, I wonder whether I was being need-lessly paranoid. He's an odd guy, sure, and his understanding of social cues leaves a lot to be desired, but I feel guilty for presuming he was going to assault me. I mean, my social cues leave a lot to be desired a lot of the time. Shouldn't I feel solidarity with people like him?

If that were true, though, how come I still feel so unsafe in the mobile home? I had planned on taking a shower, but the idea of taking my clothes off here suddenly feels strange. There are too many windows, too many doors. The fact that this fragile tin can of a place is right in Benjamin Barry's sightline makes me squeamish and uneasy, so I spray another half-can of Sure under my arms, pack my laptop into my rucksack, and head to The Fiddler.

It's not until I reach the village, however, that I stop consid-ering Benjamin as a sexual predator and another much more disturbing thought enters my mind.

'Maria,' I blurt out when I see her behind the counter at The Fiddler, 'where was I this morning?'

'Hey!' she says sunnily. 'Uh . . . missing your flight?'

'No, but like, where was I? When I came in here earlier, did I tell you . . . what I had been doing?'

Maria starts picking up empty pint glasses with her fingers. Three, four, five, six in one hand.

'You found Satan,' she says. 'Tony picked him up, by the way; he says thanks. He said to tell you that your ferry ride back is free.'

'That's very nice of him.'

'But I don't know where you actually were, if that's your question.'

'It is,' I say, and then I'm silent.

Benjamin Barry followed me to the schoolhouse.

'Soooo ...' Maria is standing to attention, waiting to serve me.

'Oh, God, sorry. I don't know if I can drink again.'

'I don't blame you, after last night. What are you in the mood for?'

'Do you want the honest answer?'

'If you tell me will you have to kill me?' I look at her bleakly and she smiles. 'Okay, so we're not in a jokey mood today. What are you in the mood for?'

'A shower,' I say. 'And a cup of tea.'

It feels insane to me that I can still have petty needs despite the events of the last twenty-four hours.

'And ...' I begin, half-choked by tears, gazing at Maria pitifully. 'I don't know, a sausage sandwich on white bread.'

'Come to my house,' she says simply.

'What?'

'I have a shower in my house. And tea. I'm a vegetarian so I don't have any real sausages but there's some Linda McCartney ones there. They don't expire, do they?'

'I can't do that.'

Can I? I don't even know Maria. I can't be naked in her house, around her things. I fancy her too much. I would do something. Something would go wrong. I would get my period on one of her towels, or something.

'Why not? I have a clean guest towel, and everything.'

'Wow, you're so grown up.'

'I know; I'm even impressed by myself. Soon I'll have little guest soaps and everything. C'mon, I'm due a break anyway. I'll walk you there.'

Maria shares a little bungalow with Steph and another girl who is spending a long weekend in Killarney with her boyfriend. Steph is already at work, showing tourists the best seal-watching rocks.

'Nice place,' I say, and it is. It's tiny and colourful, and everything is warmly mismatched, the way they usually are in rental properties. A framed photograph of Pope John Paul II sits alongside an amateurish oil painting of a naked woman in the foetal position, each in an endless, unrelenting debate with one another.

'Thanks. Apparently it was originally the gatekeeper's house for one of those huge houses down the street.'

'I haven't seen those houses yet.'

'I mean, you don't need to. Seen one, seen 'em all, really. When there's a wedding I can sometimes see the guests walking past my window, all dressed up. I like waving to them.'

She shows me the shower en suite in her bedroom, leaning over to show me which way is hot, which way is cold, which taps are temperamental. Then she goes into the kitchen to see if Linda McCartney vegetarian sausages actually do expire.

And I am alone in Maria's bedroom.

It is amazing to me that, despite only learning about Maria's existence the day before yesterday, I'm already trembling with excitement at being left alone with her things. I repress, as much as I can, my urge to be weird. I do not go through her things, or pick up the cosmetics on her dressing table, or open any drawers. I decide that I will only look at things that are already on display, but look closely. That's all right, isn't it?

I wish we were still in an age of CDs and DVDs and film

posters. It would be so easy to get an idea of who she really was if I knew what she was into, and maybe even discover a few clues about whether she likes girls. *It's easier for men*, I think, for the millionth time. There are more social cues to announce that you're a man, interested in other men.

Maria has Herbal Essences shampoo and conditioner. That tells me nothing. Maria has a book by Anaïs Nin next to her bed. I don't know anything about Anaïs Nin, other than that she was a woman, so that's another point in 'possibly gay'. Maria has a purple bedspread. Are purple bedspreads camp enough to cite them as 'possibly gay'?

If there were fewer things to worry about, I think I'd enjoy the frantic energy of having a crush. It has been a long time since I've had a proper crush. Flings, yes. Frantic, sweaty episodes at Secret Garden Party or The Alex in Southend. But the sweet agony of a proper crush, where everything is infused with a blend of charisma and panic? Not for a long, long time. And certainly not since that episode with Laura.

I give up on trying to guess, and just take a shower. The hot water feels magnificent. I try to lather away the hangover, the diarrhoea, the newspaper in the air vent, Benjamin Barry following me to the schoolhouse. As far as he knows, I found out something this morning, and it led me back to the school. He has no idea about my dad's illness, I realise.

All he knows is this: a girl shows up calling herself a film-maker, talks to a few locals, and then abruptly cancels her flight in favour of running through the woods and towards the most inauspicious building on the island. *Trying to keep off the main roads.*

Benjamin thought I knew something before I even knew it.

My stomach churns again. If I just stay under the hot water, I can stave off reality for ever. If I can just get clean, I can stay out of this insane story. I keep washing, shampooing twice, conditioning the ends of my hair and waiting two minutes to rinse, when usually I wouldn't bother. I use a Neutrogena face wash, and a body scrub, and a moisturising body wash. When I'm done, I run a comb through my wet hair, my parting a shock of white skin against the murky brown. I'm just doing up my jeans when I hear Maria lightly knocking on the door.

'Everything okay?' she asks.

'Yeah, come on in.'

She slides around the door, averting her eyes at first, before noticing that I'm dressed.

'Was the shower all right?'

'Perfect. Thank you so much for letting me use it. Also, sorry, if I went a bit crazy on using your products.'

'That's fine. Do you want that tea?'

'I would love that tea.'

She walks back into the kitchen, where three drying racks are out, all sporting a variety of women's clothing. She flicks the kettle on.

'You're not choosy about tea, or anything? Being English and all.'

'Hey, I'm half Irish. And no, I don't care. Anything is fine.'

She laughs. 'Everyone who comes here is half Irish.'

I think of my dad, currently in a medically induced coma that he may never come out of.

'Yes, well, I actually am,' I say, grinning but defensive. 'Mary said I smelled like rashers and bled TK lemonade.'

She doesn't say anything, but takes out two mismatched mugs and some milk. And as though she were presenting a young emperor to its country, she hands me my sausage sandwich.

'Oh my God. You're amazing. Thank you, I want to cry with how happy I am.'

'I wouldn't go that far. I had to practically snap icicles off of those things.'

'Well, it's appreciated. Thank you, seriously.'

She watches me take three hungry bites and waits until I've taken a few sips of sweet tea until speaking again.

'So, what was up with your own shower?'

I take another long gulp of tea before answering, looking at Maria over the rim of my mug. She's not stupid, and she knows something is up.

'Benjamin Barry makes me uncomfortable,' I say finally. 'I felt weird being alone in the mobile home with him around, especially ... y'know. *Naked*.'

'Oh, Jesus. I mean, I don't know him very well but he is a little freaky, isn't he? Kind of intense. Did he say something to you to make you feel weird?'

'He let himself into the mobile home without permission. And ... I think he ... I think he followed me earlier this morning.'

'Where?'

'To the old school.'

'But ... *why*?'

'Why would he follow me or why would I go back to the old school?'

'Both, I guess.'

'I think because ... ' I begin, putting my head in my hands. There's too much to work out and it all feels jumbled up in the throb of my exhausted brain. 'I think because he's afraid of me finding out something about the Clipim disaster.'

'And ... *have you* found something out about it?'

'Yes,' I say at last. 'I have.'

## 21

I tell Maria everything. The conversation with Nick in Cork, his IRA theory, the newspaper in the air vents, the interrogation with Benjamin Barry. When I'm finished, I realise how bare everything looks when I lay it out in front of another person. The atmosphere between Maria and me changes. It's as though I were selling trinkets from a rug and she was happy to indulge in conversation, but grew awkward when I asked her to actually buy something. I can feel her turning away, patting her pockets, politely telling me that she will catch me on the way back.

'Sorry, go back,' she says, wrinkling her nose and lighting a cigarette. 'I don't get the newspaper thing.'

'So, obviously the chimney newspaper had been accumulating for ages. But the air vent newspaper was *all new*,' I say slowly, hoping her expression will change. 'From just a few days before the accident.'

'Couldn't that just be a coincidence? Like maybe it was extra cold a few days before the accident? Maybe they just stuck it up there because it was extra cold. Sure, it's dumb, but it's still an accident.'

'That's the thing!' I say, triumphant. 'It wasn't cold. I checked Met Éireann. It was super mild. Sunny.'

Maria takes a long drag, turning over the information like a raccoon with something in its paws.

'But if there is a big cover-up, from fifty years ago or what-ever, why would Barry be so invested in covering it up? He's only lived here for, like, a decade. He's not even from here.'

She exhales, then, laughing suddenly, says, 'He doesn't even *go* here.'

'Are you seriously quoting *Mean Girls* at me?'

'Yes. Sorry.'

'Good to see you're taking this seriously.'

'Sorry, sorry, sorry. I am. But this is pretty wild, Charlie.' She takes my plate away from me and brings it into the kitchen, plopping it in the sink.

'Hey,' she calls. 'What year was all this again?'

'The accident? Sixty-three.'

She pads back into the room and looks at me, her face a little bemused.

'And it's an IRA thing? Or, you think it is?'

'Yes. Well, that's the theory. The most plausible one we have so far.'

Maria eases herself back into the armchair. 'I don't know if that matches up. Date wise, I mean. The Troubles didn't kick off until 1969.'

She cocks her head to the side. Her expression is the same as Tony's. A sense of trying to remember a pub quiz answer, not a devastating history. She digs her phone out of her pocket.

'Yeah. Sixty-nine.'

She shows me a BBC webpage headline 'Northern Ireland: The Troubles'. I quickly read it, my face going scarlet. My eyes scan frantically for anything that happened before 1967, trying to pick out dates from the wall of text. Finally, I find mention of the year. Under the subheading 'background'.

*But for now, anti-partition forces had been neutralised and the unionists were firmly in control. There was little indication in 1963 of the turmoil that was about to engulf Northern Ireland.*

I read that last sentence out loud, trying to make sense of it to myself. 'There was little indication in 1963 of the turmoil that was about to engulf Northern Ireland.'

My face is burning with the mortification of having an American school me on Irish history. She knows it, too. She starts busying herself, asking me if I want any fruit or biscuits. After our little argument about being 'really' Irish, I now sound crazier and more deluded than ever.

'I'm not saying you're wrong, Charlie, and maybe the guy you met in Cork has his reasons. But it just seems . . . unlikely. That's all.'

I'm silent. I feel like a child, trying to jam a circle into a square on an Early Learning Centre toy.

'Unless . . . the BBC is in on it, too?'

She's trying to sound sincere, but the sheer ridiculousness of the sentence makes her splutter a little and I can't help but smile.

'You never know!' I say. 'They've done worse.'

'I guess,' she says playfully. We both look at each other and say 'Jimmy Savile' at the same time.

We laugh darkly. Anything to ease the tension.

'Also, there's one thing I haven't figured out. Why *did* you run into the woods this morning and miss your flight?'

It's my turn to act casually uninterested now.

'I got a call last night that my dad is really sick again.'

'No, I heard that this morning. But like, if he's sick, why wouldn't you want to be with him? When you were talking about him last night you sounded pretty close.'

'We are close. Very close.'

She gazes at me expectantly and I start massaging my temples.

'I don't know, Maria; have you ever just gone a bit temporarily insane?'

'Sure.'

'Well, I'm not sure how much I can explain it, apart from that. The idea of going home and starting the whole ... the whole *process* of terminal illness all over again just short-circuited my brain. And I was having such a good time with you, and with your friends ... I don't know, I just felt like I was in the right place for once. Like I was home.'

Maria stands up and stretches, supporting the small of her back as she does so. She takes my mug as a way of indicating that it's time for her to go back to work.

'Charlie, I know what I'm about to say is going to sound condescending, and you can tell me to fuck off if you like, but here it is. Ireland is *designed* to make people feel like they're at home. That's the whole deal. That's why thousands of people save up their whole lives to come here, even though it rains, like, 350 days a year. It's why every person you meet tells you their grandmother was from Wicklow.'

She starts rinsing my cup in the sink, her voice raised over the spurt of water.

'The whole country is set up, floor to ceiling, to make strangers feel like they can slice off a little heritage and take it home. No one who actually lives here *likes* those Sunday-night fiddle sessions. They put *up* with them. Do you know what *céad míle fáilte* means?'

'A hundred thousand welcomes.'

'A hundred thousand *welcomes*. Not a hundred thousand homes. Not a hundred thousand "stay here's". I mean, look at Direct Provision.'

'What's Direct Provision?'

She rolls her eyes. 'Asylum seekers are housed for years in these horrible centres that are owned by private businesses. It's basically the laundries, except it's supposed to be all okay, because they're foreigners, and aren't we good for letting them in in the first place.'

'I don't see what this has to do with ... '

'It's all temporary. If you feel at home here it means Ireland has *worked* on you.'

'How can you say that? You live here. This is your home.'

She breathes out a long, exhausted exhale. 'Yeah, it worked on me *extra* hard. But no one on this island is ever going to actually accept me, y'know? Like, I could marry somebody and live here for forty years, and I will still be a Yankee blow-in. There are things about this island that I will never be allowed to know, and I have to just decide to accept that.'

There's a slump in her shoulder as she consults the mirror by the door. She frowns at her reflection, and then shakes down her hair in clumpy black waves before tying it into a ponytail again. Her hair has a bump in it, the bump you get from tying your hair up when it's wet every day and you're just letting it dry like that. Despite how harsh she's being, I can't help but be desperately attracted to her. Every moment I spend with her she becomes less of a charming bar-girl and more of a human being, her skin more real, her face more touchable. It's like watching the contrast get turned up on a still image.

She zips her jacket back up and I stand, brushing sandwich crumbs off my legs.

'I get that, Maria. I do. And maybe I am being naive when I say that Clip feels like home, but you have to understand, I grew up listening to my dad talk about this place. I'm not just some art teacher from New York State who has an Irish great-grandmother. This means something to me. You get that, don't you?'

'That's what I'm saying, Charlie. Ireland makes regular people insane. But you . . . you come here with your sick dad and your big family legacy, and you . . . ' She shrugs, raising her arms in an exaggerated 'well, isn't it obvious?' way.

'What?'

'I have to get back to work, c'mon.'

'Are you saying that I have ... dreamed up a conspiracy? That I am ... looking for reasons to stay here?'

'Charlie,' she says, opening her front door, 'you ran into the woods this morning, kid.'

We bicker the whole way back to The Fiddler. Maria is being infuriatingly casual about her implication that I'm insane, dreamily reaching her hands out to the greenery that shelters the road. Every so often a car comes through and we're forced to press ourselves into the trees around us, the branches scratching at our faces.

'Do you see these?' she says, plucking a white flower. 'Hawthorn blossom. They only come out in May. You're lucky to catch them.'

I don't say anything. In this brief, intense friendship with Maria, I've felt so uncharacteristically relaxed around her, which is completely at odds with how I usually feel around strangers. Her gently telling me that I'm *imagining* this Clipim stuff feels like she's taken the head off her costume to reveal she was just like everyone else, after all.

'I love the way the trees arch around you here,' she continues. 'Like a chuppah. Do you have chuppahs in Europe?'

'No,' I say sulkily.

'They're like a Jewish gazebo thing you stand under when you get married. That's what this walk home always reminds me of. A big wedding chuppah.'

We walk on in silence. The walk to The Fiddler is only ten minutes, but it feels eternal. And then suddenly, she stops walking. She stands in the middle of the road, the afternoon light dappled on her pale skin. The sun brings out mauve shadows under her eyes and I see, for a moment, how tired she is. How tired she must constantly be. Yesterday she opened the pub at noon, finished her shift twelve hours later, and even then didn't leave The Fiddler until two. This morning she did the same thing. Her dinner breaks must be precious to her, and she spent today's with me.

'Look, Charlie,' she says, biting at her lip, 'I know how you feel.'

She has unusually uneven teeth for an American, her incisors protruding and jagged at each end.

'I came here looking for family, too, y'know.'

'And did you find them?'

'I got here,' she says quietly. 'My mother's great-aunt Nuala was supposed to have lived here. My great-grandmother moved to the States when she was a teenager, but *her* sister was only a baby at the time, and she lived in Ireland her whole life. I know it's a pretty vague connection, but I was interested, y'know? I thought I would find *someone* who remembered her.'

'Your great-great-aunt?'

'Hey, people have babies pretty young in my family. My Nana is sixty,' she half-laughs. 'White trash, I guess you might call us.'

We both go quiet, and Maria touches the pale blossoms again.

'People were polite at first. Just sort of, "sorry, nope", which I accepted, because you can't remember everybody, can you?'

She says this as if it's logic she has repeated to herself, over and over, long before I showed up.

'But then I went to the Button Museum. You know that shitty tourist attraction at the end of Main Street?'

'I've seen about three brochures for it since I got here, yes.'

'Well, I went there, and I saw her name! They've got these photographs up of women who worked there over the years, and I saw a photo of a few of them together. It was right there, written in the caption underneath. Nuala O'Shaughnessy. I was so excited, Charlie. She lived here! I was right all along!'

She takes her phone out and scrolls through for a few seconds.

'Look, I was so pumped. I took this photo straight away, sent it to my mom.'

Maria shows me a black-and-white photo of a few dour-looking women sitting at a workbench, a scattering of buttons underneath them. It's obvious that whoever was taking the photo was more focused on the sizes and shapes of the buttons than they were on the women who were working on them.

*Button covering was difficult and intricate work. Pictured: Moira Cronin, Aoife Nagle, Nuala O'Shaughnessy. 1959.*

'Wow,' I say. 'That's amazing, that you found that.'

'I know,' she says, stuffing her phone back in her pocket. 'I had been working here almost a year at that point. I had reapplied for an extended visa and it looked like I was going to get it. So, I was starting to feel kind of at home here, y'know? Like I belonged.'

Maria's voice tremors and cracks, and she moves her eyes away from the sunlight.

'So I started asking a few people, Enda and Mary and Tony. Y'know, oldish people who might remember, or remember someone who remembers. And suddenly, everyone got very, very . . . ' She breaks off for a moment, looking for the right word. '*Pissy,* with me.'

'Pissy? How?'

'Like, not talking to me when they ordered their pints, or going out of their way to order off someone else. I didn't understand. And then I sort of realised . . . this button factory that was, like, this whole industry for thirty years. No one ever talked about working there. None of the old ladies who I know on Clipim talked about it. Ever. They only talk about it as a museum, not as a factory.'

'So then what happened?'

'Then everything got kind of busy with my visa application, so I forgot about it for a few weeks. Maybe a month. But my mom kept pushing me about it, so I went back to the Button Museum to see if I could get more information from them. But the picture was gone.'

'*Gone?*'

'It was replaced with another photo of the building.'

'Did you ask?'

'The people who work there are all just, like, teenagers taking tickets. It's an audio guide thing, so there are no curators that you can just walk up and talk to. But eventually I talked to the manager, and he said that some of the photos had been sent to Dublin, to participate in an exhibition at Trinity.'

'Were any of the other photos missing?'

'A few? I don't know; I didn't really look that closely, if I'm honest.'

'Then what did you do?'

'Nothing.' She shrugs. 'I got my visa. I found out a couple of years later from one of those ancestry sites that she died in a convent on the mainland. So I guess whatever happened here was enough to turn her to Jesus.'

The sun hides behind a smattering of marshmallow-thick clouds and the road is shaded in a thick green chilliness. Maria puts her arms around herself, rubbing at her goose-pimpled arms. There's a pragmatic sadness to her in that moment, as if she has made up her mind, a long time ago, that certain things are not for people like her. No family saga, no deep history, no pre-destined fate. No great magic, and no great love affairs. Just a job, and a piece of paper that says she can stay in the country as long as she doesn't make a nuisance of herself. The inclination to refer to herself as 'white trash' to stop other people getting there first.

As if goaded by the branches clawing towards me, I put my hands on her bare arms. We have known each other for two days, yet standing this close to her feels like it has been an action that has been decades in the making.

'Hey,' she says, her voice hushed, her eyes scanning the top of my head, 'we're almost the exact same height.'

And the kiss is so huge that we don't even hear the car until it's beeping for us to get out of the way.

## 22

When we get to The Fiddler, Laura is sitting with Dónal at a table by the fire, the picture of cosy, made-for-TV hetero-sexuality. Her fancy Nikon SLR is out, and she's scrolling through, showing him her photos while he huddles in close. Trust Laura to bring a £3000 camera on a weekend trip. She's even brought the crazy expensive lens to match.

I realise, with a small amount of guilt, that I have barely thought about Laura since she stormed off after we booked our new flights. Dónal starts tipping the end of a bottle of wine into her glass, and she is pretending to beg him to stop.

'Stop, stop, stop,' she says, nudging her glass away towards him with her fingertips. 'You are *evil*.'

'Yeah, I'm the Antichrist,' he says happily. 'Fag and another bottle?'

'I suppose I don't have a choice.'

'No.'

'Go on, then,' she says, rolling her eyes at him. And, despite the fact I've just had one of the most romantic kisses of my life, my heart pounds with venomous jealousy. Have they been hanging out all afternoon? For once, I feel united with Mike on something. She's somehow cheating on us both.

Maria gives me a sly wink as she wraps her drinks apron around her waist. 'I'm off at ten. Let's hang out after?'

'Sure.' I smile.

'The kitchen door of my house is always unlocked,' she whispers. 'So if you don't want to wait at the creepy caravan park ...'

Laura finally sees me when she stands up to put on her coat.

'Hey,' we both say at once, before laughing awkwardly.

'Have you had a fun day?' I ask lamely.

'Yeah,' she says, her ragged, tipsy tone suggesting she would rather just press on with having fun than address the tension of earlier on. 'Dónal drove me around the island for a bit in the Land Rover. I saw the farm his dad owns.'

'She thought a Jacob's sheep was a goat,' cackles Dónal, looming over her shoulder with an unlit cigarette in his mouth.

'It had *horns*!'

'So do *lots of things* that aren't goats.'

I narrow my eyes at her, silently interrogating her the way you can only do once you've known someone since they were a teenager. My look says, *Does he know you have a boyfriend?* While hers says, *Don't fuck this up for me, bitch.*

'Can I talk to you privately for a second?' I ask Laura. 'After your cigarette, I mean?'

'It's okay, I shouldn't be smoking anyway. Don, you go out without me. I'm just going to chat to Charlie.'

*Don!* And I thought I was moving quickly with Maria.

We sit at her table by the fire, the embers casting a warm, burning heat on one side of my face. There's no chance we would have got this table yesterday, when it was still the weekend and the bar was crammed with tourists. Now, however, there's an emptiness to The Fiddler that makes me feel as though I am walking on stage. A few locals look up to study Laura and me, before gradually returning to their own conversations.

Laura's lips are stained from wine, and she starts picking at the dried, purple skin.

'Do you have any lip balm?' she asks absent-mindedly.

'No,' I say. 'Look, have you paid Benjamin Barry yet? For the extra nights?'

'Yeah, I transferred it to him on my phone,' she says. 'You can sort me out later, don't worry.'

'Right. That makes things ... difficult.'

'Why?'

'I don't know if it's safe to stay at the campsite any more. He was ... he was being really weird with me, earlier.'

'What do you mean? Like ... *sexually*?'

'I mean, he let himself into the mobile home, and he basically told me that he followed me this morning. After I ran away.'

She glowers momentarily, remembering to be furious with me, before mentally reasoning with herself that she was having a good time now, so what did it matter?

'Followed you where?'

'To the old schoolhouse. I went there for a sort of ... last look, and when I was there, I found some pretty dodgy-looking stuff. Stuff to do with my dad's classmates. Stuff that makes it seem ... *not* like an accident.'

'What do you mean? Like it was ... on purpose? Like how Nick said?'

I quickly explain the newspaper and my full interaction with Benjamin Barry. She squints at me sleepily, and I can see the wine is catching up with her.

'That *is* weird,' she says. 'But so is he. He's a weird guy. He probably freaks out everyone who stays in the caravan park. That's why there's no one else staying there, I'll bet.'

'So you agree we should stay somewhere else?'

She shrugs. 'It's only two nights. We're leaving early on Wednesday. What's he going to do?'

Dónal appears with another bottle and, to his credit, with an extra glass for me. He puts them down and presents three bags of nuts from his back pocket.

'What are you two on about then?'

'Benjamin Barry,' Laura says, seizing on the nuts. 'What, no crisps?'

'What's that old fairy up to now?' Dónal asks pleasantly.

'Is he gay?' I ask, slightly relieved that at least there was no danger of me being assaulted.

'Oh, I'd say so,' he says emphatically. 'Have you met him? There's a guy that *definitely* takes it up the arse.'

There's an uncomfortable silence as Laura and I exchange a look. One that says: *Oh, so Dónal is* that *kind of guy.*

But because Laura is obviously keen to preserve Dónal as a flirting partner, she laughs nervously.

'God, don't be such a homophobe,' she says, meeting my eyes with an anxious, apologetic look.

'What are you on about?' he protests hotly, pushing his thick, coiled curls back. 'I'm the complete *opposite* of a homophobe.'

'So you're a gay person?' I ask with faux-nonchalance.

'What?'

'Wouldn't that be the opposite of a homophobe?'

'I am *not* gay,' he says, narrowing his eyes at me.

'Don,' Laura says cautiously, 'you know Charlie's gay, right?'

'And that's fine!'

'Oh, I'm sure it is,' I snap, taking a purposefully long sip of wine. Dónal gives a panicked glance to Laura, his cheeks slowly reddening.

We eventually move on, Laura smoothing over the tension with stories about everything she has seen that day. I drink, observing the two of them like an anthropologist. Every now and then she punches him on the shoulder, or he finds an excuse to graze her hand. It's amazing to me that Laura can be so terrified to spend a night sleeping in the same bed as me, when we've slept next to each other for a thousand sex-less nights, yet is comfortable flirting openly with a stranger.

'So, Charlie,' he says, filling up my glass again, 'you went to college with Laura, then?'

'Uni, yeah,' I respond. 'We did Film and lived together after.'

'Ah,' he says. 'Old friends then.'

'Best friends,' Laura says, and it's the most tender she has allowed herself to be with me all weekend. I smile at her. We're not best friends any more, and probably won't be again, but it's nice to think that way.

'So ... did you two *ever* ... '

I look at him blankly, daring him to say it.

' ... get together?'

I raise my eyebrows and am about to say something terrible, until Laura cuts across me giddily. She's quite drunk now, the table in front of her a graveyard of pistachio shells.

'Well, *of course* we have,' she says, and the purr in her voice is so practised that I want to punch her straight in the throat. 'I mean, everyone experiments, don't they?'

It's too much. All of it. The whole thing, the whole day, the whole island. I stand up, my legs bumping the table and almost knocking the drinks over.

'I'm out of here,' I say. 'Laura, tell Maria I'll wait for her at her house.'

She snaps out of kitten mode and reaches for me.

'Fuck. Charlie. Stop.'

I burst out into the cold evening air and march back towards the caravan, hugging my hoodie tight around me. I remember Laura's lips on my sternum, her hand snaking over my ribcage when we pretended to watch *The Craft*. The dozens of nights where she whined softly about being too cold to sleep, spooning me in our freezing bedroom while the space heater clucked its tongue anxiously.

Within seconds, I hear the bang of the pub door and Laura's voice behind me.

'Mate!' she calls after me. 'Charlie, mate, I'm sorry. I'm drunk. I was being an idiot.'

'Why did you do that?' I screech, my voice cracking. 'Are you trying to make him think he can have a threesome? Because count me the fuck out.'

'I was just messing around. It was a joke.'

'He's an asshole, and so are you for entertaining him.'

'He's not an asshole. You don't even know him.'

'Neither do *you*!'

'Look, I'm not passing any judgements about Maria, am I?'

I shrug and turn around. 'I'm going back to the caravan park of suspicious homosexuals. You and your queer-bashing boyfriend will be very happy together, I'm sure.'

'Come on, Charlie. You can't be this angry. I said I was sorry for being an idiot.'

'Laura,' I splutter, shocked that she can be this clueless, 'two days ago, you were so scared that I was going to try to shag you that you refused to sleep in the same bed as me. Now you're here, casually trying to cheat on your boyfriend with this random guy?'

Her face softens and turns, to my surprise, to guilt. She looks at the pool of light coming out from The Fiddler's window.

'I told Mike about what happened,' she says, her voice barely above a whisper. 'That time when we kissed.'

'Oh?'

'He wasn't happy about it. He said I cheated on him.'

'Well, you did.'

She gives me a petulant little frown. 'But it shouldn't *count* if it's with a girl. And you're my best friend.'

'Why shouldn't it count?'

To her credit, she does think about it before she answers. 'Because you're not in competition with him. You're a different category to him. We love each other in a different way.'

I wince.

'What way do we love each other?'

'You know. Like sisters.'

'Do you kiss your sisters?'

'No, but – you know. It wasn't about him. It was like . . . it was like nostalgia. Like a goodbye. I don't know. It just felt like a one-time thing, something to . . . '

She starts chewing the skin around her nails as a way to avoid looking at me.

'Something to mark the end of an era, I guess.'

'Right,' I say. 'How charitable of you.'

'Charlie, don't be dramatic.'

'The only person who thinks this isn't worth getting worried about, Laura, is you. Your boyfriend thinks it's bullshit, and I think it's bullshit. Have you considered that you might be talking out of your *ass*?'

'I'm sorry,' she says lamely. 'I just had this vision of marrying Mike, and thinking: *Wow, I might never get a chance to be with a woman.* People experiment all the time. I didn't think it would be a big deal.

'Anyway,' she continues, 'we decided to have an open relationship after that.'

'Excuse me, *what?*'

'Both of us are on location so often, and we're both still young, and he said that my anxiety about marriage was coming from somewhere, and that he felt the same. So, I'm not cheating on Mike by hanging out with Don. It's all above board. I swear.'

I stand there, my mouth moving mutely. Of all the bombshells I've had to process in the last couple of days, this is the one that has burned my eyebrows off.

'So you have been in an open relationship since October?'

She nods.

'Why didn't you tell me?'

Laura purses her lips and makes a few false movements to speak.

'I suppose I didn't want you to think ... that there was a chance between us. I didn't want to get your hopes up.'

'And all this business with separate bedrooms?'

'Charlie, can you not see that after a certain point, it becomes a bit ... weird for two grown women to sleep in the same bed together?'

'No,' I say. Then quickly add: 'It's only weird if one of the women thinks the other is lusting after her.'

'Well ... '

Laura trails off, inviting me to fill in the blanks. We stare at one another for a long moment, ten years of dedicated friendship ricocheting between us.

'Right,' I say. 'That's that then. I'm going to ask Maria if I can stay at hers tonight.'

'You can't be serious.'

'Why not? You'll want your privacy with *Don*, anyway. And I wouldn't want you to think I was going to molest you in the night.'

I turn my back on her and charge back to the caravan, fling my laptop and some overnight stuff into a bag, and vow not to come back until it's time for our flight on Wednesday. Let her fuck Dónal in the caravan if she wants to. An open relationship. It was so infuriatingly *like her* to occasionally dip her toe into some form of alternative romance culture as a way of signalling that she isn't just a posh blonde girl with good teeth and rich parents. Oh, no, not Laura! She's a subversive.

The town is quiet when I walk back through it. I can hear my own rubber-soled footsteps tripping along the pavement. There's no fiddle music, no glass clinking, no one shouting 'G'wan ta fuck!' and no one descending into peals of drunken cackles. Just my own feet and the vague sound of a dog barking somewhere in the distance.

Last night a few of the small shops had stayed open late, sopping up the last of the weekend foot traffic. They're all shut now, and the lack of light on the street makes me feel exposed, as though this walk were not just a walk but a failing in military strategy. That's the difference between a Monday night and a weekend night, I suppose. This is what it would be like most of the time, if you lived here. Silent, and beautiful, and terribly, terribly lonely.

I pass An Spailpín Fánach, the sleepy-looking pub at the end of the street, and the only building apart from The Fiddler with lights on. I quickly peer into the windows, but the glass is too frosted for me to really see anything. As I reach the end of the street and start turning towards the lane that leads to Maria's house, I hear the door of An Spailpín open and close behind me, and feel a strange wave of gratitude at no longer being the only person on the street. A hunched little figure dodders out, hidden by a big coat and a ginger helmet of hair, and I smile when I see her.

'Mary!' I call. 'How are ya?'

Mary spins around and looks at me, her eyes squinting and suspicious. She probably can't make out my face in the darkness.

'It's Charlie,' I say, taking a step closer to her. 'Charlie Regan. From the other night.'

I suddenly feel a pang of shame. She must be so embarrassed, after the toilet incident in The Fiddler, so I quickly change the subject away from me.

'Do you and Enda live near here?'

Her face framed by the dowdy light of the pub, I can see that Mary is, once again, drunk. The slash of lipstick on her face looks as though it were applied in a dark taxi, her breath soaked with brandy and breath mints. I squint closer, and see that the lipstick is covering up a scab on her lip, one that looks fresh and just covered over by purpling blood.

'Your lip!' I say gently. 'You poor thing. Did you fall, Mary?'

Her eyes eventually register my presence, and the slow process of how and why she knows me begins to work together. She mumbles something, speaking into her left shoulder, her chin lowered like she has had a stroke.

'What was that? Mary? Are you trying to tell me something? Do you need to sit down?'

More mumbling. I ask her again what she is trying to say. She looks up, gazes directly into my face, and then over-enunciates her speech, like she's talking to someone who doesn't understand English.

'They should have died,' she says. 'They should have died in Glenderrig.'

And then, with no warning or fanfare at all, she spits on the ground in front of me, turns on her heel and leaves.

# PART THREE

For a time we tried to contact them by radio, but
    no response.
But then they attacked a town.
A small town, I'll admit, but nevertheless, a town
    of people.
People who died.

'BATTLESTATIONS', FIGHT LIKE APES, FROM
*Fight Like Apes and The Mystery of the Golden
Medallion* (2008)

## 23

I came out to my dad three months after he was diagnosed with cancer. I was twenty-two.

There had never been any need before that, as far as I was concerned. I'd never had a serious girlfriend, so the declaration would have felt redundant without proof. My mum, I'm sure, would have accused me of going through some kind of phase, and when it became clear that it wasn't a phase, she would have become unbearably sad. She has nothing against gay people on a private level, but believes that the world's prejudices – which to her are unchangeable, and a foregone conclusion – make a gay life a tragic one. I still don't know whether Dad has told her.

I gave Dad a long, handwritten letter and watched him read it in his hospital bed. When he turned over the last of the three pages, he smiled at me and stroked my hand.

'Darling,' he said softly, 'I love you, and this doesn't change anything.'

It was a good response. One of the better ones, in the scope of parental reactions. But I was unhappy anyway, because I *wanted* it to change something. I wanted the earth to move. I wanted to feel like I still had a stake in my own life, and like I hadn't just signed it away to observing my father's degradation.

I'd had one girlfriend at Uni. Her name was Andrea. She

was German, and serious, and had been out to her whole family since she was thirteen. People seemed very proud of us for getting together. An Economics professor who had never taught me squeezed my hand in the SU once, tears in her eyes.

'If the two of you need any support,' she said, her voice soggy with tenderness, 'if you get any trouble from *the institution*, you know where I am.'

'Okay,' I said uncertainly. 'Thanks.'

'Liz and Aisha don't get this,' I said to Andrea, bringing her our two hot chocolates.

'That's because Liz and Aisha are totally straight-washed,' Andrea explained patiently. 'They are so afraid of what people will think.'

English was Andrea's third language, and she was excellent at it. She had a hobbyist's love of words, and her favourites were: 'perspectives', 'systematic', 'queering', 'revolutionary', 'dismantle' and 'sensationalise'. She was also very fond of '-washed' as a suffix.

'They're happy going around, everyone thinking they are *gal pals*,' she said, wrapping her arms around my neck. 'While we put our crowbar in their perspectives.'

I loved the way she said 'crowbar', stressing each syllable with conviction. Crow*baawh*. I kissed her while the Economics lecturer watched, confident that I wasn't just doing it for me, but for some wider social cause that had been decades in the making. I had never felt so important in my life.

We went out for a year and a half. Of course, she dumped me. An English girl would have mumbled something about our lives going in different directions, but Andrea was crushingly honest.

'I just don't know if you are passionate enough for me, Charlie.'

'Oh,' I replied, dumbfounded. It felt particularly offensive given that we were in her bed.

'I don't mean sex,' she said, before course-correcting. Andrea hated all forms of dishonesty. She couldn't quite swallow it. She was like a person trying to convince themselves they like oysters. 'I don't mean *entirely* sex. I just don't know if I can go back in the closet with you.'

'But I'm not *in* the closet.'

'But you know what I *am saying*, Charlie.'

I knew what she meant. I was out, but I wasn't yet comfortable with the kind of gay life Andrea had been setting up for herself since her early teens. She talked dreamily about the all-female collective she knew in Hamburg, a situation that terrified me. I had no interest in growing my own food or in wearing a Mooncup, and in Andrea's opinion, that made me less of a lesbian. So did hanging out with Laura. Of course, they didn't get along. No two people I like ever do. Andrea would say arch, disapproving things about Laura ('She is like – I don't know, we have a word for this in German – a *soft egg?*') and Laura would say nothing about Andrea at all, confident she would win the war for my soul without so much as having to crack a knuckle. And she did. It was just us after that: her relationship fizzled out around the same time, and we resumed sleeping sexlessly in each other's beds, sharing sandwiches and inventing our future lives as Famous Millionaires.

There have been other girls. Kisses on dance floors. Coffee dates that seemed to go on for hours yet amounted to nothing. One-night stands that felt more like they were servicing some future anecdote about how wild my twenties were rather than facilitating any real passion.

That's probably unfair. There was passion. Of course there was. There have been phases, usually when Dad was at his sickest, where I would push myself to be as promiscuous and as cruel as my ever-diminishing standards of decency would allow. I fucked married women, and girls still at Uni, and women who assured me that their relationships were open when we were both perfectly aware they weren't. A summer with a girl who always wanted to do cheap, nasty cocaine and eventually abandoned me in a club for the keyboardist in an indie band. I got off with the same keyboardist a month later, just for the satisfaction of tying the whole thing up narratively. I had a character I could slip into: one of a flatly uninterested sex spider, a costume I invented for myself based on Shane from *The L Word* and biographies of Patricia Highsmith.

Being constantly poised for a disaster with Dad has prevented me from laying down any real tracks for a life of my own. I resented how having a sick parent made me come across. There seemed to be no way of avoiding the subject, and once it came up, no way of getting past it. I was constantly meeting sensitive young women who were brimming with empathy and a conviction that if *they* were the ones to make me talk about my dad, then that would inevitably project some kind of specialness on them.

Maybe that's cruel; maybe they were just nice. But I could always feel myself playing up to the image of myself as a caring daughter, making my voice catch on words like 'sick' and 'cancer' and 'day room'. I always left dates feeling like I had performed a version of myself, and Laura would tell me that this was simply what dating was. It frustrated me how much I depended on her, even then. I let all our Uni friends and ex-Clapham housemates fall by the wayside because she was the only one I truly felt comfortable around.

Our lives didn't change that much when she met Mike in the production company she worked at. He smiled gamely as we linked arms and held hands, and I was so confident in his featureless mediocrity that I was genuinely shocked when she told me she wanted to move into his flat in Shoreditch.

'Nothing will *change*,' she had said, shoving my shoulder. 'We're still us.'

Everything changed. We weren't us. And now, lying on Maria's couch, thumbing through her books, I'm not sure whether we'll ever be us again. Whether anything will be like it was.

*They should have died in Glenderrig.*

What was Glenderrig? I Google it. I pull out a map of the Ring of Kerry, folded in Maria's bookshelf. There's no evidence of it, and yet, the children of Clipim were supposed to have died there.

I call Mum a few times, but there's no answer. I haven't spoken to her since this morning, and there's a general feeling in the air of older women being unhappy with me. I text her to ask if there's any news, and then convince myself there's none. It's a medically induced coma, after all, not a real coma.

I fall asleep on Maria's couch with my phone on my chest, and wake up some time later to the sound of her microwave beeping.

'Fuck,' I say, mostly out of surprise. I can never usually fall asleep in other people's houses.

'Well, hello,' she calls. 'Look who's up.'

'What time is it?'

'Almost eleven. I closed up early. The place was *dead*.'

She passes me a cereal bowl full of spaghetti and green pesto, kissing me on the forehead from over the head of the couch. It's unnerving how quickly she clicks into domesticity. How often does she do this? Does she have a new fling every other weekend, and if so, are they all girls? Did she just seize upon the first lesbian to walk through The Fiddler?

'Maria,' I say carefully, 'not to be weird, and you don't have to answer, like, it doesn't matter and it's not my business, but ... '

Maria starts laughing and unscrews a half-full bottle of wine, smelling it to see if it's still drinkable.

'Why are you laughing?'

'Because I know what you're going to ask.'

'No you don't.'

'You're about to ask whether I'm gay, or bi, or straight and just messing around with you.'

'I . . . wasn't going to ask that,' I lie.

'Oh, well good, then I guess I won't have to tell you.'

'Fine,' I say, forking some pasta into my mouth. 'Bitch.'

Maria takes out a tin box and starts rolling a slim, tidy joint, before sprawling herself on the couch and lighting it.

She passes it to me and the taste is low, fruity.

'I saw Mary on my way here,' I say, my voice a splutter of smoke. I pass it back to her. 'She was really drunk.'

'Yeah, that sounds about right. Mary is drunk a *lot*.'

'Is she an alcoholic?'

'I don't know. You don't really say alcoholic around here, unless someone is violent or causes a car accident or something. You say: "He likes a drink", and you sort of put a wink on the end of it.'

She takes the joint out of her mouth and does a Kerry impression, sounding like an old man who has just walked into The Fiddler with a pig under his arm. 'He likes his *drr*INK.'

'Very good.'

'Thank you.'

'She spat at me,' I say finally. I had been shoving the incident to the back of my mind, keen not to analyse it too much. Mary was drunk. She didn't know who I was, and she certainly had no reason to spit on me. This is just another thing that drunk people do and feel embarrassed about later.

Maria doesn't say anything, so I say it again, this time with a laugh in my voice. 'I don't think she was trying to spit *on* me,' I chatter. 'Maybe she just had a weird taste in her mouth.'

But Maria remains quiet, and takes another drag.

'Well,' she says finally, 'I'm sorry that happened.'

'You think she *meant* it?'

'Well,' she says again, 'yes.'

'But . . . *why*?'

'It's complicated, Charlie. You know it is. Mary lost two nieces in the Clipim accident, and then her sister emigrated afterwards. That thing created a lot of long-term trauma around here that has never been resolved. There were a few . . . '

Maria glances off into the distance, hesitating a little, before wrapping an imaginary noose around her neck and sticking her tongue out to the side.

'I see.'

'And you can bet that no one's been to therapy, either. So when you show up, the kid of the only kid that survived . . . I guess some of the old people are reminded of the grandkids and nephews and nieces they're never going to have.'

'How do you know this?'

'I'm the only decent bartender in this one-horse town. When people are feeling morose, I'm the first person they talk to.'

She flicks her ash sadly, accidentally knocking the cherry off, and relights it. 'Sometimes the last person,' she says, and I'm reminded of the sticker ads for depression I saw in the bathroom of The Fiddler. TALK TO SOMEONE in bold letters with a Freephone number underneath.

'Is Mary the only one? Are there . . . *other* people who want to spit on me?'

'Possibly, yes. I don't know, though. I wouldn't worry about it.'

'She said something else. Something I can't figure out.'

'Lay it on me.'

'She said: "They should have died in Glenderrig."'

'Who?' she says, scrunching up her nose in confusion

before inevitably realising. 'Oh, the kids. Right. Where's Glenderrig?'

'I don't know. Have you ever heard of it?'

'Never.'

We don't say anything for a while, and Maria gets up to put some music on, plugging her phone into a little speaker. A thrumming tune comes out, active and giddy and filled with come-kiss-me energy.

Maria starts swaying to the music, singing along as she fetches some beers from the fridge.

'Look, you can't worry about it too much. Having a closet full of pointless secrets and things you're not allowed to talk about is very de rigueur here. A couple of years ago was the centenary of 1916, right? The big Irish revolution against the English?'

I nod.

'And I asked Dónal if there were any Clip people involved. Relatives of people I might know. And Dónal goes all dark and says he can't talk about it.'

Maria cackles loudly then, startling me.

'I mean, it was *a hundred years* ago! Anyone involved is long dead, and the whole country is celebrating, but Dónal won't talk about it. It's crazy. But it's what people are like here.'

'So that's why they hate me now.'

'Yes,' she says definitively. She sees my face crumple and pats me on the shoulder. 'I mean, no! They don't hate you. You just make everything a bit too . . . real for them. Anyway, you're leaving on Wednesday.'

'Yeah.'

'Will you come back, do you think?'

I look over at her, lying on the couch, her face tilted towards me. What does she *want* me to say?

'I don't know. Do *you* think I should?'

We sound like a couple of teenagers on a date. *What do*

*you want to do? Well, what do you want to do?* On and on, until someone does something to break the tension, raise the stakes, does anything.

'I think you should,' she says, her voice low now, her eyes downward. 'I definitely, definitely think you should.'

She passes the joint back to me, her hand grazing my knuckles. It feels different now, this small act, than it did a few minutes ago. We don't complete the pass. Our fingers stay touching for a moment longer than they need to, and for a second, we're both lost, both looking at our hands, both wondering what we're going to do next. I forget that I am holding a lit thing, a tiny spark of fire, and as the paper burns down it catches my skin.

'Fuck!' I say, splintering the moment. I withdraw my hand and start cradling it, when Maria stops me.

And then, like it's nothing at all, she takes the burned finger and places it, solemnly, in the middle of her bottom lip. She holds it there, closes her eyes, and makes one, single 'Mwah' sound.

I pull my hand back and Maria's face follows. Suddenly, she's sitting on top of the armchair, her legs astride me.

We don't kiss right away. Right in this moment, looking at her feels like enough. I run my hands along her, starting at her hips and working towards her shoulder, then the back of her neck. It's the slow, methodical process of trying to remember her before knowing her becomes impossible. Wednesday I'll be gone, and I'm not enough of an idiot to think that Maria is interested in a pen pal.

I love her body. She's only a few years older than me, but it feels like she lives in her body more than I have ever lived in my own. A curved pot belly from post-work pints. Strong, freckled arms that have lifted months', possibly years' worth of Guinness kegs.

She smiles down at me, showing her funny uneven teeth again.

'Do you always take your time like this?'

I laugh. She's good at this. Saying the exact right thing at the exact right time, like a heroine in a romcom, or a dame in a film noir. She's done this before, and I don't even mind.

'Complaining, are you?'

'Well, I *am* on the clock . . . '

That's it, for me. I kiss Maria, and it works. There's no fumbling, no repositioning of mouths, no wondering whether the other person is enjoying themselves. Everything clicks right into place. I could just sit here and kiss this woman for hours.

*What about Mary?*

*What about Laura?*

*What the fuck is Glenderrig?*

Fuck it all. None of it is my business anyway, and it all happened decades before I was born.

We both laugh when my T-shirt gets stuck around my head. Hers does too, snagging around her silver earrings. I keep pulling her closer to me, thrilled by her warmth, her realness. The closer we get the more it dawns on me how lonely I've been. I want to howl at the fat Clipim moon out of the sheer relief of physical contact with a person I actually *like*. You forget, when you haven't truly fancied someone in a long time, how your skin can come alive. The patch of skin below my belly button and above my underwear is suddenly an erogenous zone. My earlobe has its own eco-system. My mouth is its own planet. I keep pulling her closer, a hundred thousand nerve endings singing at once.

Maria's still sitting astride me on the armchair when she slips her fingers inside me, the heel of her hand awkwardly crushed up against my stomach. She gets up and leads me into her room.

And then, as though it were so easy and inevitable, there we are. On Maria's bed, trying to cram as much of each other into our mouths as possible. Her pace picks up, exploring everywhere, and everything starts to feel rushed.

It brings me out of the moment, and I can't concentrate. I suddenly start thinking about the men who buy pictures of me, and how they use those pictures. I think about the women I treated like human shields against my own sorrow, how I charged through them without really caring who they were.

'Hey,' I say, clearing the hair from her forehead. 'Hey, we don't need to rush this.'

'Oh, God. Are you okay? Sorry, I know this is quick, I thought . . . '

'No, no.' I laugh, kissing her, delighted to finally be the more confident one. 'It's just been ages, for me. With someone I . . . care about, I mean.'

Her eyes widen, huge and electric. Oh, God. *Too much, Charlie; rein it in, rein it in.*

'I just don't want it to feel like it's over before it starts.'

'If I was a dude, you know that would absolutely crush me, right?'

'But you're not, are you?'

She smiles with the side of her mouth. 'No . . . '

Maria delivers more of the long, slow, pouting kisses on my thighs that she gave to my burned finger just minutes before. Each kiss skitters around me, a long silver strand of light filling each corner of my body. A small, silly moan escapes my mouth and she moves in deeper, her tongue kneading the softest parts of me. God, she's good at this. It's easy to see why she teased me when I tried to figure out whether she was 'gay, or bi, or straight and just messing with me'. Whatever she is, this is certainly not her first rodeo.

My body is on fire. I'm torn between grabbing her face and kissing her or lying back in the hope she will continue on for ever and ever.

My teeth are about to break the skin on my knuckles when we hear the long, repetitive thud of someone banging on the door.

'Fuck,' we both say, at the same time. We look at each other as if the other person is expecting guests.

'Well, *I* don't live here,' I say. 'It's not for me.'

We stay completely still and listen. The thudding continues, rattling the door frame.

'Christ, whoever it is wants to get in *quickly*,' says Maria, throwing a robe on.

'My clothes are on your living-room floor.'

'Well then, stay in here.'

'What if it's not safe?'

'It's safe, Charlie. It's probably one of the lads looking to have a smoke.'

Maria pads out of her room, and I get under the blankets, in case anyone comes in. I have never felt more naked in my entire life.

I listen, my ears cocked. It's Aidan, one of Maria's friends from last night.

'Is Ciara here?'

His voice is urgent, strained.

'What? No. I haven't seen her all day.'

'Fuck. Fuck fuck fuck fuck.'

'What? What's going on?'

'There's a fire. Someone was up burning gorse by the nature reserve and it's gone out of control. It's fucking crazy. You can see the blaze from the town.'

'And you think Ciara is up there?' Maria asks.

'Her and Dónal and that English one went up to the old schoolhouse a few hours ago, but I don't know what they were doing. Dónal has had an acorn up his arse about the burning for ages.'

*That English one.* There's only one person that could be.

I grab a towel and swing the door open, and Aidan almost jumps when he sees me.

'You!' Aidan says, choosing to ignore, briefly, how obviously naked I am under my towel. 'Your friend. Have you seen her?'

'Not since this evening. What time is it now?'

'Half one.'

*Fuck.* How long have we been here? Maria is scraping her hands through her hair, trying to get her thoughts together.

'I don't understand. Why would Dónal take a *date* to a gorse fire?'

'I don't fucking know, Maria,' says Aidan. 'All I know is that no one can find my fucking sister. My parents are losing their minds.'

I put on my clothes quickly, barely caring if Aidan sees anything. *Laura. Laura. Laura.* If she is caught up in this, I will never, ever forgive myself.

If Laura is safe, I will never get mad at her ever again.

If Laura is safe, I will be a kind, loving, supportive friend who never resents her success or tries to hold her back.

If Laura is safe, I will never come back to this fucking island ever again.

## 24

I get to the town with the expectation that the entire thing is already engulfed in flames. That's what I want. I want The Fiddler in a ball of orange light, I want the Button Museum creaking and crumbling into ashes. I want to see smoke billowing out of the little shops that sell boxes of branded Clipim fudge.

The reality is different. The reality always is.

We get back to the town and a group of people are standing on the street, their hands covering their eyes, squinting into the middle distance. There's a plume of smoke coming from the hills. I take out my Clipim tourism map and hold it in front of me. I mark the hills with my thumb, calculating where, exactly, the fire is.

It's coming from the schoolhouse.

My breath starts coming short, and I feel Maria's hand on my wrist.

'It's okay. We have a fire brigade.'

At that moment, two dinky fire trucks come gliding past, shedding blue light over us. There is no siren on. Why is there no siren on? Isn't this an emergency? Does no siren mean something, in firefighter code? Is everyone already dead?

I ask Maria and her tone is hushed, patient, a little condescending.

'Sirens are for other cars to get out of the way. They don't need that here.'

I need to get up there. I need to find her. I can get there in twenty-five minutes if I run all the way.

'You can't go up there,' Maria says, tugging on my arm.

'Maria, it's *Laura*.'

'It's not safe. Stay here. Look, we'll . . . ' She starts tugging on my arm.

'Fuck off,' I snarl, snatching my arm back, ignoring her wounded face.

'You don't need to be so aggressive. We can work this out together. I know the town better than you.'

'There is no *together*. I don't even fucking know you.'

It is a pointlessly cruel thing to say. A relic from the 'I don't give a fuck about you' dating persona I've spent the last five years honing. It must be muscle memory at this point, something my body reverts to when threatened by the health of a loved one. And that's who Laura is to me. Like it or not, she is my most loved one.

I break away from Maria, and start running in the darkness out of town. The footpath slips away, and soon I'm on a rough country road. I can feel pebbles and sticks through the soft, cheap rubber of my trainers, each creating a rift in my foot. I keep running. The air is cool, steady. I'm bad at this, bad at anything physical. I spit on the ground as I run, my mouth hot, my throat ripped open by the cold air hitting it.

Laura loves to run. She runs at least three times a week, sometimes with Mike. She says it helps clear her head. How can anyone on earth have a clear head while running? Whenever I have to run, the same thought drums in my head, over and over.

'I hate running,' I say, my feet still pounding beneath me. 'I *hate* running, I hate running, I *fucking fucking hate* running.'

I don't have a body for this. I don't have a body for anything, really. My body feels like a pillowcase filled with sticks and peanut butter. My body feels like something bats are meant to live in. I think of Maria, who just twenty minutes earlier was softly kissing the skin on the inside of my leg. Maria, who felt the inside of me and made it feel like it really *was* the inside of me, not just the interior of a skeleton I was renting. God, I was horrible to her. Why was I so horrible to her?

I can hear the sheep bleating, wailing along like a Greek chorus. They catch the smell before I do. The crackling stench of burning grass. The smoke is getting closer, but the schoolhouse feels further away than ever. I stop and pant, both hands on my knees. My legs feel heavy, the way they do when you're being chased in a dream. Laura. Laura. *Laura*. Why did she go up to the schoolhouse? I crunch into a ball by the side of the road, winded by effort.

*If she dies, I will never forgive myself.*

I start to cry. *If she dies, I will die.*

My hair tangles into bracken and I feel eaten by the landscape. It's pulling me towards it, enveloping me in the coconut sweetness of the yellow gorse bushes. I try to wrench my face away, like a nose that is just about to disappear beneath quicksand. The thorns tear back, and just as I feel like I'm about to be torn up by the earth completely, the glare of headlights sweeps across my face as a car stops in front of me. I cover my eyes.

'Charlie! What the fuck are you doing down there?' comes a voice from the rolled-down car window. 'Are you in the bloody ditch?'

It's Joe, the ferryman who brought us over from the mainland. I unfurl from the tight little ball I had wound myself into.

'I was trying to get to the schoolhouse.'

'You know there's a fire up there, yeah?'

'I know. That's why I'm trying to get there.'

'You're a lunatic. Go home. Or go back to the town.'

I stand in the road, tears pouring out of my face.

'Laura is up there, Joe. My best friend is up there.'

He sighs at me, covers his hands with his face, and then looks up.

'All right; Jesus Christ, get in, you bloody old fool.'

I slide into the car, shaking. I gaze over at Joe, and he is wearing a reflective orange vest that says FIRE SERVICE across the arm.

'Wait a second, you're the fireman?'

'Volunteer. There are only two actual firemen on Clip, and they just sit in the station, or maintain the trucks. Everyone else is a volunteer. The rest are on their way up now.'

'The rest?'

'Twenty-two of us, in all. We have beepers. We must be the last people in the world that use beepers.'

I rub my tears away with the back of my sleeve and sit in silence.

'Charlie, it's going to be fine.'

'How will it be fine?'

'Because it mostly always is.'

'*Mostly*?'

'It's just a political thing, these fires. They need to burn it for more grazing land, and there's so much protected woodland around here, and so many rules over how the farmers can treat it. They hate it. You get little outbursts like this sometimes, and because gorse is so flammable, it spreads quickly. The Foleys have had their backs up about this for months, so I'm not at all surprised.'

'Who?'

'The Foleys. Seamus Foley and his three boys. Pat, Jim and Dónal.'

'Dónal is up there, though. In the fire.'

'He is?'

'That's what Aidan said.'

He grimaces. 'Fucking load of *óinseachs*, the lot of them.

They probably started something they couldn't control. The youngest one, showing off for his pals. Pricks.'

He slaps the side of the wheel in irritation. 'This is the Foleys for you, now. Jesus fucking Christ. I'm sorry, Charlie.'

'What do you mean? What's wrong with the Foleys? Apart from the gorse stuff.'

'They have more money than sense. They're all spoiled. Even the father is spoiled. They throw their weight around; always have to get their way. You should see them at town meetings. Always shouting about why they should be the ones to get planning permission, why their vote should count more than anyone's.'

When we arrive, the fire has already roared past the low stone wall of the schoolhouse, and is stretching out a hundred yards ahead. I've never seen anything like it: it's a wall of flames, hot and crackling, eating up the bracken and brambles. There are sheep in the middle of the road, screaming their disagreements like kettled-in protestors. Someone is trying to usher them into a van, but they're not budging. I can see the orange fire reflected in their shining black eyes.

This does not look like something that happens every day. I put my hands over my ears, to block out the bleating. This is *hell*.

The fire trucks are hosing down the flaming scrub, but everything about their efforts feels feeble and malnourished. There are too many people, too many men, and they all look like they're not doing enough. I want to scream at them, push them out of the way, kick them in the shins for just standing there.

'Where is Laura?' I ask, grabbing the first man I see.

'Eh?'

'Laura. The English girl. Blonde hair. She was in the schoolhouse with Dónal Foley and Ciara ... Ciara whatever her name is.'

He nods in the direction of a white transit van with the back door open. On it, Dónal and Ciara are sitting up, their shoulders covered in blankets. I run over. They look fine. Pale, dirty and harassed-looking, but fine.

'Where is Laura?'

'Charlie, let me tell you what happened first ...' begins Ciara. Dónal glares at me silently.

'Just tell me where my friend is.'

'The doctor is looking her over. Come on, I'll bring you over there.'

'So she's okay? She's like you?'

'She's ... she is *going* to be all right.'

Oh God, oh God. What was I about to see? Laura, with her hair all burned off? Laura, with third-degree burns on her skin? I had only had time to consider the idea of Laura being killed, not maimed or disfigured. Beautiful, beautiful Laura Shingle.

When I see her, I almost vomit in relief. Her hair is caked in mud, she's covered in sweat, and there's a gash on her head. Her face is red and there are black marks all over it, but she is sitting up, and breathing into an oxygen mask.

'Hi,' I say, as the doctor asks her to lean over so he can trace his stethoscope on her back. I can see her spinal cord protruding like the bones of a dinosaur. 'I'm her friend. I'm Charlie. We're travelling together.'

Laura looks up and gives me a pained smile.

'Laura, are you okay? What happened? Tell me.'

The doctor turns to me, putting a hand on my shoulder. He's about sixty, a big Santa Claus of a man with a belly snugly upholstered in a well-ironed shirt.

'I'm afraid she can't talk right now, and might not be able to for a few days.'

'What?'

'Laura's asthma and her exposure to the smoke have

damaged her vocal cords. She needs to be kept on oxygen, to make sure the airways are kept clear. We need to get her on bedrest immediately, and with the proper care.'

Laura is looking at me with huge arctic fox eyes, mute, terrified. I remember how much I hated her, earlier today. How I wanted someone or something to knock her off her perch, to stop her from believing in her own wonderfulness. As if there was a designated ration of self-confidence to be shared between the two of us, and she was hoarding all of it. And now, here she is: knocked off. I wrap my arms around her and Laura squeezes back tightly.

'Can you tell me what happened?' I ask over Laura's shoulder, facing the doctor.

'Gorse fire,' he says tersely. 'Foley was showing off to your friend here. It isn't the first time he's done something like this. Lights a fire he doesn't know how to put out; and then accidents like this happen.'

'Laura. Her name is Laura.'

'Right. They abandoned the fire, probably thinking they had put it out, and went inside. But it caught at the bracken, and the whole building was surrounded. The other two got out quick, but your friend took her time. They said she was looking around for something. Her purse, Foley says. That's how she cut her head like that. Bashed it climbing out of a window, then collapsed outside. It was Barry who carried her out of there.'

I pull back from Laura and look at her again, her face sleepy, her eyes unfocused.

'*Benjamin* Barry?'

'That's the one. He saw the smoke from the road and rushed over.'

I can't stop looking at Laura's cherry-red face. 'What's *happening*?'

Luckily, the doctor takes my existential panic as a question about logistics.

'Well,' he says, 'we'll have her at the surgery tonight. Una has done up the bed for her. She'll be perfectly safe. We'll look after her as if she were our own. My name is Dr Healy, and my practice is in the town.'

He must catch something like suspicion in my eyes, because he clears his throat and stands up straight. 'Please ... Charlie, is it? Please feel free to ask anyone in town. It's quite common to have patients stay at the practice. I'll be monitoring her throughout the night, make sure she's not concussed, or what have you. Then we'll move her to St Bride's in the morning.'

I nod. 'How long before she can travel? We need to get home.'

The doctor pauses and takes a long look at her. Laura looks like she's about to nod off. Oh, God. *Is* she concussed?

'She needs a chest X-ray, and her bloods checked. She was in that schoolhouse a long time. I don't know what it has done to her lungs, yet.'

I wait. He hasn't answered my question.

'But when can she ... ?'

'I don't know, simply. Can you call the parents? Any partners or other next of kin?'

I wince. I have to tell Mike that his girlfriend is being hospitalised. I have to tell the Shingles that their treasured eldest daughter can't talk. And I don't know how to tell them without making clear the truth: that this is completely my fault.

## 25

I have never been in a doctor's home before. He has a normal doctor's office, with scales and a blood pressure machine and even a long gurney with stirrups attached, but he seems to have no problem treating his entire home as a practice. His wife Una gave Laura a nightgown, propping her up in bed like she is her own child. She stitches up the wound on Laura's forehead beautifully, with neat seamstress stitches.

'Don't worry,' she says, smiling. 'I *am* actually a nurse. How about a nice ham sandwich and a lovely glass of milk?'

I'm suspicious about how many adjectives she crams into that sentence, but accept it nonetheless.

'Why does she need that?' I say, pointing at the IV drip she hooks into Laura, far too defensive of her.

'She can't swallow food yet. It's best we have her on nil by mouth until we know exactly what the damage is, anyway. You're going to need to bring some things, in the morning. A washbag, pyjamas, that kind of thing. Maybe a book, if she feels well enough.'

'Won't they want her in a gown, in the hospital?'

'What hospital, love?'

'St Bride's? Where she's going tomorrow?'

'Oh, pet, no. St Bride's isn't a hospital. It's a nursing home.'

Clipim, it turns out, does not have a hospital. The system is this: if you are sick but you can walk, you went to Dr Healy.

If you're sick and you can't walk, Dr Healy came to you, and if you needed some more care, he sent you to the nursing home. They have 'all the gear' there, Una says. It is 'as good as a hospital, even an X-ray machine, a small one, and better coffee than any hospital too'. If it's a real, proper emergency – a car accident, or cancer – you go to the mainland. This is the chain of medical care and it has served them very well, they are keen to remind me.

'Sure, who wants to go to a hospital anyway?'

*Yes, Una, but who wants to go to a nursing home?*

Somehow, Laura manages to fall asleep with the oxygen mask on. I want to sleep at the foot of her bed, like a dog. I have to do things, after all. I have to gather Laura's stuff, call her parents, call her boyfriend. 'And get a few hours' sleep yourself, my love,' says Una.

It's 4 a.m. by the time I get home. *Home.* Like Benjamin Barry's damp little hovel could be mistaken by anyone for a home. The air is colder in here than outside. I switch on the electric fire and sit in the sickly glow, a wool blanket around me, my clothes stinking of burnt wood. Breathe in. Breathe out. Tiny puffs of air float in front of me like fading ghosts.

My skin is starting to warm up now, my breath no longer visible in the frigid air. I'm still cold on the inside, though, my bones like milk bottles stacked on top of one another. I stand up to go to the bedroom, and I'm suddenly very aware of myself, and deeply conscious of how many windows and doors and cracks of light there are around me. I can see the moon and the ocean from one window, and the looming shadows of the yew wood from the other. I stand still for a moment.

I can look all around me, but I also am *being looked at.*

I can hear something: the crunching sound of gravel, faint at first, but growing louder. Benjamin Barry's form slowly emerges from the black of the wood.

He was there, earlier: one of the few people at the fire who actually seemed like they were able to do something. He even helped round up the stray sheep, driving them back towards the herd by edging them with his car.

He stops suddenly, seemingly to gaze at the close, clear moon, but then slowly turns around on his heel. I am standing up in a dark caravan, with only the faded glow of an electric fire for light, but Benjamin can *see* me.

I wonder briefly, dangerously, how long he's been out there. Waiting for me.

He stands still for a moment, the moon illuminating his short, stocky build. I can't see his face but I know he is deciding whether or not he is going to come say hello to me, to offer his condolences about the terrible evening that has just passed.

*Just fuck off,* I think. I am begging whatever cosmic deity has been assigned to my case to compel Benjamin Barry to turn the fuck around and go home. I'm too exhausted. I have too much to think about. I have too much to do tomorrow. *Just fuck off.*

It doesn't work. The gravel crunch comes closer. Benjamin Barry is coming in for a nightcap. I bet he uses that word, too: *nightcap.*

I open the door and hover, hoping that I can dissuade him by offering some small talk without actually inviting him in. I can see his teeth from ten feet away, beaming in the darkness, delighted to have company.

'Evening, Ms Regan,' he says. 'I didn't think you'd be up, still.'

'I just got home,' I reply. 'From Dr Healy's house. Laura is staying there tonight, and then they're . . . they're transferring her to a nursing home, tomorrow?'

Even though I don't like Benjamin Barry, I'm hoping he can at least offer me some reassurance that it is normal for a twenty-nine-year-old to be admitted to a nursing home. He just laughs.

'It doesn't seem so romantic here now, does it, Charlie? Country life all seems so charming until you're forced to compromise on the things you're used to.'

I give a short, awkward laugh, even though I don't think it's unreasonable to want proper medical care. I don't like his implication, either: that I'm some sort of spoiled city brat who only enjoys country living until it turns on her.

'Still thinking of moving here, Charlie?'

His tone is genuinely mocking now.

'I never said I wanted to move here.'

'No, but you were thinking about it, weren't you?' He smiles. 'Well, maybe you still are. Gosh, it's *cold* out here.'

Benjamin starts stamping his feet and makes a pantomime of hugging his arms. I say nothing.

'Do you know what, Charlie, I think I have a bottle of whiskey in the mobile home. In one of the cabinets. Maybe we could have a little nightcap?'

There it is. Nightcap.

Even though I'm bone-tired and would rather eat off my own fingers than talk to Benjamin Barry, Benjamin Barry is once again in my living room. It feels impossible to refuse: it is *his* living room after all. And he did save Laura. How does he not see how inappropriate this is? Does he think that, because he found me wandering around outside the other night, there's a precedent for him invading my space at strange hours? Does he think we're friends now?

I rummage around the caravan. There is a quarter left in the Jameson bottle that Laura and I drank on our first night here. I take it out of the cupboard and Benjamin clocks it immediately.

'Oh, naughty naughty,' he says, waving his finger from

side to side. 'I should have known if I let artists in here they would drink up my booze. Like fishes, aren't ye?'

'I guess we thought it was complimentary,' I say feebly. 'Like tea or milk.'

'Gosh, what funny ideas you have about the Irish, Charlie. Considering you're one of us.'

My cheeks burn. 'I don't have funny ideas about the Irish. I am Irish.'

But it doesn't sound convincing. Benjamin's scalded face looks cheerfully perplexed, as if trying to work out a logic puzzle. He puts his pointer fingers together, in front of his mouth.

'Funny,' he says. 'Funny.'

'My father and grandfather are from Clipim, Benjamin. I'm more from here than you are.'

I sound like a racist, but I don't care. I shouldn't have to defend myself to Benjamin Barry. Not at four in the morning, still smelling of ash.

He smiles at me, and takes the bottle of whiskey from my hands. 'I'll pour us two glasses, shall I?'

He goes into the kitchen and rummages around for clean glasses. I try not to be embarrassed by the sink full of mugs. Why is he here? I scan the room for exits. There's only one: the front door. If he were to try anything, I could probably duck past him and run, but as a plan it's ludicrously short term. He has a car. He knows the grounds. And in any case, it's 4 a.m., and I have nowhere to go.

The only thing to do is to be polite, and hope that he doesn't want to rape me.

'What's wrong with the film, then?'

'Excuse me?'

'Your film. *It Takes a Village*. What's wrong with it?'

'I didn't say there was anything wrong with it.'

Benjamin sits down on the U-shaped couch opposite me

and hands me my glass of whiskey. 'Ah, but Laura did. We had a chat at The Fiddler earlier this evening.'

My mouth twitches. I should probably just make something up, but I'm too exhausted, and too overwhelmed by the drama of the fire to be secretive.

'My dad always made me believe that the reason the schoolhouse disaster happened was because the building was badly maintained, and the reason it didn't get covered a lot in the press was because of the JFK assassination.'

'Mm-hmmm. But now, you believe different.'

'I don't know what I think. But I know it didn't go down exactly like that.'

'Do you have any proof of that, exactly?'

I don't know what to say. How can I bring up the newspaper now? I couldn't even convince Laura or Maria that the newspaper meant anything, and they're the closest people to me on this island.

'You found something strange in the schoolhouse, didn't you?'

I nod slowly. 'Yes.'

'I tried to get the property condemned, years ago,' he says ponderously. 'It's unsafe up there, as unsafe as it ever was. The walls tumbling down, things falling from the ceiling . . . '

He looks at me, and his face doesn't seem round and ruddy any more. It looks sharp, angular. We are both silent.

'I carried her,' he says, his voice softer than new honey. 'She had collapsed outside the window after hitting her head. I threw her over my shoulder. Fireman's lift.'

'Dr Healy told me,' I say cautiously. 'Thank you.'

'I kept wondering, why had she stayed in there, when the others had run out? Dónal said she ran back to get her purse, or something silly like that. But it wasn't her purse.'

He reaches for his trousers, and for a split second, I think that Benjamin Barry is going to show me his penis.

Instead, he takes out his wallet. Oh, God. Is he going to *pay* me to touch his penis?

He unfolds a piece of yellowed paper, and I instantly know what it is. It's a page from the copy of *The Irish Times* that I found in the air vent. I had only taken the front page, as proof of the date, but left the others behind. I was going to take Laura back there, once we had fixed our fight, but never had the chance. Laura had gone back to see for herself. It was just like her, too: you tell her something, she's instantly dismissive, but then later, she comes around to it on her own terms. She had asked Dónal to take her back to the schoolhouse to see if there was any truth to what I was saying. She cared what the truth was. She had been there when Nick told us there was something strange about Clipim. She needed to know, too.

I'm so instantly filled with relief at Laura's instincts that I forget the context that I am being shown them in. Why does Benjamin Barry have it? Why would he take it from her?

'We're a small community, Charlie. We're a bit like a family, that way. We might not always get on, but our values are the same. Can you understand that?'

He puts the newspaper back in his wallet before closing it and putting it back in his pocket. He doesn't wait for me to answer.

'And so when someone wants to hurt us, it's up to the people in positions of authority to stop them, to take action. I count myself as one of those people in authority.'

*You own a caravan park,* I resist saying. *You flip houses.*

'Hurt can come in many forms. You may not think you're hurting us when you poke around in old buildings, but you are, Charlie. You're opening up wounds that took a very, very, *very* long time to heal. Do you see what I'm saying?'

'Of course I do, Benjamin,' I say. 'That's why . . . '

He continues talking as if I haven't said anything.

'Look, Charlie. The school accident happened years before I even came to live in Clip, so I know you think it's none of my business. But there's a whole generation of people on this island who lost their children, their friends and their businesses because of that bloody accident, and most of them don't like being reminded of it. None of them want this beautiful little island to become known as some kind of grisly graveyard. Do you think people would choose Clipim as their wedding destination if the first thing they heard about it was that it is a death site? Do you think people would want to live here? Raise their kids here?'

'But it *is* a death site,' I say, tumbling over his awkward choice of words. 'Everyone already knows.'

'Charlie, I guarantee if you ask any of the tourists currently staying in Clipim, or any of the many wedding parties coming here over the summer, you would find that most of them are *completely* unaware of a terrible tragedy that happened fifty years ago. In fact, the number-one Google result for Clipim is this holiday park. Then The Fiddler, where your lovely Maria works.'

I hate how his voice sounds when he says Maria's name. He has no right to say it like that. Like she somehow belongs to him, but is merely out on loan to me. It makes me furious, and for the first time since he walked in, I have the strength to fight him.

'If it wasn't an accident, people have the right to know,' I say. 'People lost their kids and they deserve to know why. If there was a cover-up or whatever, then it's a bigger story than a few people picking a different wedding destination or a different summer home.'

'A different wedding destination. A different summer home,' he laughs. 'Do you know these things that you're so ready to cast off are people's livelihoods? This isn't Dublin. We can't just open a donut shop and wait for people to show up.'

'Benjamin,' I say quietly, 'what is Glenderrig?'

He looks at me for a moment, tilting his head to one side. The light of the glowing orange heater is bouncing off of his forehead. *You are a ridiculous man*, I think. His mouth twitches, halfway between a smile and a sneer.

'Goodness, Lottie, your curiosity knows no bounds. And to think, you've only been here a few days.'

My insides turn to ice. What did he just call me?

He stops to take a long sip of his whiskey, the first one he has actually taken since pouring the glass. He is enjoying this too much. Even more distressingly, he's so good at it that it makes me wonder how many conversations like this he has had: how many people has he cornered with a piece of uncomfortable information.

'It's really amazing, you know, how many ways there are for a young woman to make a living,' he says, smiling into his drink.

'You looked at my laptop.'

'I *saw* your *open* laptop.'

'That was private.'

'It was on *my* private property.'

'That's ridiculous.'

But it's not ridiculous. Not to him.

I keep opening and shutting my mouth like a trout, no idea how to come back from this. Benjamin sticks his hands in his coat pockets and produces his keyring, holding it up to the light, and I see a glinting USB stick. I instinctively lunge forward to grab it, and he snatches it away.

'Sit down,' he says, pointing to a kitchen chair. 'Now. Go on.'

I sit down, still clasping my glass tumbler full of whiskey.

'I was away from my computer for, like, five minutes. You couldn't have taken them,' I say, my voice high and shrill. 'You wouldn't have had time.'

He just smiles, looking at me like he's seen me naked. Which, I suppose, he has. How long has he spent lingering over the photos? Is he gay, like Dónal said, and found them exciting just from a blackmail standpoint? Or was he ... was he *using* them?

'I hope you sold the original batch at a fair price, at least,' he responds. 'Because soon they'll be so commonplace that they won't be worth a thing.'

An acute, desperate shame rises through me, and for a moment, I lose control of my body. My arms and legs go weak, and my whiskey glass falls right out of my hand, crashing to the floor. Benjamin Barry immediately starts cleaning it up, grabbing a roll of paper towels in the kitchen.

'Google Charlotte Regan, and they'll be the first thing,' he continues. 'The whole first page.'

My body is frozen. Could he really do that? Was he really threatening me? I think of the film career I've spent my entire life dreaming of, the festivals I still want to be admitted to, the jobs I still want to get. How could any of it happen if the first thing someone got when they entered my name into Google were photos of me masturbating?

How does *anyone* come back from that?

Benjamin is still cleaning up the whiskey. The glass has broken into three pieces, and he is gently gathering them into his hand while kneeling down in front of me. He deposits them into a package of kitchen towel and puts them to one side.

*I could kick him in the head right now,* I think. *I could murder him, maybe, or knock him out.*

He looks at me dead in the eye, as though I had said the thought out loud. He looks so stupid, on the floor, walking around on his knees like a child. What a stupid, stupid, terrible man.

Then, he touches me.

Benjamin Barry puts both of his hands on my knees and looks at them. Just looks at them, his grip getting firmer and deeper. He presses both of my legs together until I can feel my kneecaps grinding off of one another, sliding out of place.

I don't say a word. I am too afraid of him, too unsettled by what he might do or say next. Maybe if I just stay perfectly still he will go away and stop threatening to ruin my life.

He knows I'm intimidated, and he's curious about what he can get away with. He runs his hands up and down my legs, staring at my thighs. He is still kneeling on the floor, the top of his head level with my chest. I stay perfectly still, hoping that this is all it is: that all he wants to do is feel my legs a bit and go home.

His hands are getting warmer and warmer, and I can feel him disenfranchising my head from the rest of me. In this moment, I only exist as a lower torso. His fingers clamp around my thighs. Not painful, exactly, but pinching.

In the numb, hazy muddle one clear thought floats into my mind.

*Benjamin Barry is going to rape me.*

And before the thought has even landed properly, he does something even stranger. He lays his head down, folding his body over my knees. Benjamin's head is in my lap, like a child who has done something naughty. His hands grip the backs of my thighs, and I yelp with the sharp, sudden pain. It is the first noise I have made in ten minutes.

It breaks his trance. Slowly, Benjamin Barry gets up off the floor. He takes his glass of whiskey and rinses it in the sink, then replaces the bottle. He brushes himself off before standing up straight to look at me.

'Well, aren't you going to see me to the door?'

It's a ridiculous request, considering the front door is four steps from where I'm sitting, but I get up anyway. I go to the door, my movements mechanical and wooden.

'Goodnight, Charlotte.'

'Goodnight, Benjamin.'

He trudges into the darkness, gravel moulding around his feet. I close the door quickly behind him, but it's too late. The night chill is already in the caravan, and it doesn't leave all night.

## 26

Tuesday morning is heavy and white, the sky like a close grey cataract over the town. I wake up sweating and wearing two jumpers. After Benjamin left last night, I couldn't seem to get warm, so I layered my GAP hoodie over Laura's Bimba Y Lola jumper. It smells like fruit and Johnson's baby lotion and the kind of shampoo you can only buy at the hairdressers.

I dither over who to call first, and decide that, on balance, Chris and Anne Shingle are more positively disposed towards me than Mike is. Her dad has that old vaudevillian energy that makes you think Laura and her sisters were probably picked up and thrown around a lot as children, and her mum is the kind of robustly posh country woman who insists on leaving every window open to 'boost the immune system'. They are used to late-night calls and broken arms and trips to A&E.

My instincts turn out to be correct: after an initial 'pardon, what?', the Shingles are happy to chalk the whole incident up to 'well, these things happen sometimes, don't they?' Anne stays on the phone a little longer, telling me how glad she is that I'm with Laura, and that they'll transfer over extra money, if I need it.

'Oh, Charlie,' she says, 'if it were anyone else, I would be so worried. Hug her twice, from me.'

'Thanks, Anne. Would you mind calling Mike to tell him? It's just, the reception is really bad here, and . . . '

'Of course,' she says, not registering that the reception is good enough to call her, and therefore must be good enough to call Mike. 'I'll give him a bell, love. Keep us posted.'

Once I hang up the phone, I wander over to the only corner of the caravan that gets internet signal and my phone starts pinging softly. Between the spam and the newsletters sits an email from Nick Sheridan.

Hey Charlie

I found your email on your website and I just wanted to get in touch after our meeting at Cork Film Festival the other day. I feel really bad about how I talked to you. It wasn't cool. You made a really impressive movie and tbh if I knew how young you were I wouldn't have been so quick to take the mickey. I talked to my girlfriend (she is a feminist) and she said that it's important to support young female creators, and I agree.

Sorry again. Let me know if you need any help down the line.

Best

Nick

Nick Sheridan's dad came to Clipim, all those years ago because he was certain that something wasn't right about how the story was being told. He left when he couldn't get a word out of the locals, or so Nick said, but there must have been something else, too. If, half a century later, my questions are being met with threats and intimidation, what must Daddy Sheridan have been up against?

The IRA theory still feels like a lame one to me, especially after Maria was so easily able to dismiss it with simple, widely available historical fact. But then again, the Clipim disaster itself is a simple and widely available historical fact. The historian-approved version of something isn't always necessarily the truth, especially when it comes to a place as secretive as this.

I open up a new email to send to Nick and hover my hands over the keys like a nervous pianist before a great concerto. If his dad is still a journalist, or even still has connections in that world, I could have enough information to re-launch an inquiry into Clipim. But is that what Clipim needs? To have a sleepy tourist town inundated with journalists, TV crews, grief perverts and true-crime podcasters? I picture Mary with a camera in her face, spitting at the lens or doddering down the street, lopsided on brandy. I think of Tony and Joe and Maria and Enda, their quiet lives exploded by people who just *had* to know.

And as soon as the thought arrives, the past few years of Irish news headlines sharpen into focus. Stories that had always drifted around my field of vision, but always felt too shapeless and strange for me to ever get a hold of. At some point between learning about my Irish heritage and falling in love with the idea of Ireland entirely, I learned about Tuam.

In the 1970s, some boys playing in a field in Galway lifted a stone slab and found skeletons.

Without a ready explanation for the skeletons, the locals and the Gardaí decided amongst themselves that it was probably a mass grave from the famine. And then they did what Irish people do when grief meets logical inconsistency: they prayed, or they endeavoured to forget about it. A local couple tended to the grotto.

Forty years later, they gradually found out the truth. That the skeletons belonged to a mother-and-baby home in Tuam, and were the remains of hundreds of children who died there. Their deaths never registered, their remains disguised in an underground system designed to look like a septic tank, and many of their surviving counterparts having been illegally trafficked to America for adoption.

The story came out when Laura and I were still working on *It Takes a Village*. It's not often that a news headline comes out of Ireland and goes global. Two kinds of stories about Ireland get discussed in England: the kind that show how Ireland is limping its way into the future and the kind that measures the length of the shadows of the past. Tuam was the latter.

Because everyone on our tiny crew had their antennae up to anything Irish, the story cast a mood on set. No one could stop talking about it, and in a different sense, they couldn't start talking about it either. We edged around the topic by repeating the key facts within it.

'The *septic* tank?' The septic tank.

'Human *trafficking*?' Human trafficking.

'By *nuns*?' By nuns.

But despite the fact that we were making a film about rural Ireland, we couldn't find anything in the Tuam story to get purchase on. The story was a changeling that morphed every time you tried to catch it in your hands. How could it be real? It was the sort of thing that you could believe about a concentration camp in the Second World War. But Ireland? A place where so many of our parents and grandparents were from? Where Saoirse Ronan was from? A country that had Topshop and Nesquik and chemotherapy and gay marriage?

I felt like I was the virus that had carried this story in. By the end of the first day, I had found a little quip about it. 'If British colonialism hadn't destroyed Ireland, then the Catholic Church wouldn't have had such a fertile ground to work with.' I had read that sentence on the *Guardian* and I felt good about saying it. Blaming colonialism was easy because it was a way of half-blaming yourself. I blamed the English half of me for Tuam and pitied the Irish half of me for having to learn about it. I hated the Catholic Church and loved that

I was Catholic, because it gave me something sturdy and unbreakable to rally against.

That's what it comes down to, I suppose. I was obsessed with what I was, because I had no idea who I was. And worse, I still have no idea. I am sitting in a caravan wondering whether I'm the sort of person who looks into the pit of skeletons, or quietly recovers it with a stone. I open a new email.

**Hey Nick**

But that's it. That's as far as I get. I don't respond to Nick Sheridan or his (feminist) girlfriend. I stare at the blank email, wondering what on earth I could say that would make the smallest bit of difference.

When I get to the nursing home, a doctor notices me standing in reception right away.

'Are you with Laura Shingle?'

I can't help but feel relieved when I see how . . . well, how doctor-y she looks. She's a kind-faced woman with highlights and pharmacy-bought glasses and holding a patient chart.

'Hi,' I say. 'That's me. Charlie Regan.'

'Dr Denise Richards,' she says, and notices my expression change. 'Not *that* Denise Richards.'

'You must get that a lot.'

'Not as often as I'd like,' she responds, and I detect what I think is a Cork accent. 'So, Charlie, can I just confirm what your relationship is to Laura? Friends, relatives or . . . ?'

'Friends.'

'Great. Now, I'm sure you must realise, that Laura has had a lot of trauma in the past few hours. Normally, we'd send her home and get her on bedrest once her airways were clear and she was breathing on her own, but because she's an asthmatic, the damage to her chest is significantly worse. Her blood oxygen levels are dangerously low, and we suspect she may have hypoxia.'

'What's that?'

'It's when the body is deprived of an adequate oxygen supply at tissue level. It means she'll need oxygen for a little longer. You two are down at the caravan park?'

I nod, briefly remembering Benjamin Barry's head on my legs. 'Yes.'

'Too damp, the air in those tin boxes. She'll have to stay here until she's well enough to travel.'

'How long will that be?'

'It depends on Laura, really. It could be a day, it could be three.'

'Doctor ... ' I say, wondering how I can phrase this without offending her. 'Not that you're not ... a really good doctor, or anything, but wouldn't Laura be better off somewhere that isn't ... ?'

'A nursing home?'

'Yes. That.'

She laughs, closing her chart. 'I moved here a few years ago with my husband, and he thought the same thing. It's always strange when elderly care is more prevalent than everyday medical care. But honestly, we have superb facilities here. There's nothing we haven't seen. Or at least, I haven't seen. I worked at Whitechapel A&E for a decade.'

'That's around the corner from Laura,' I say, brightening at the mention of a familiar landmark.

'I know,' she says, tapping her pencil on the metal chart. 'I'm planning to speak to Laura's parents this afternoon, but really, there's no reason to worry. Laura's young and strong. I'm not allowed to guarantee things, but I have no personal doubt that she'll be back to her old self again in a few days.'

She leads me past a large, open space reserved for exercise classes and film nights and down a narrow corridor, where the door to all of the rooms are ajar and arranged so you can see the top of every bed as you walk. I guess it's the most convenient way for the staff to make sure everyone is still alive, but it feels like an invasion of privacy, as though every patient has been reduced to a tropical fish in a dentist's aquarium. There are twenty-two rooms in all, and as my trainers squeak along the waxed floor I catch a glimpse of approximately a dozen of their occupants. A woman snoozes with her teeth out, her face folded into itself like an old Halloween mask. A man is being helped out of bed by a nurse, his hands shaking as he grasps the bed frame, his white hair fluffed out around his ears. I walk down to Laura's room and it's a kaleidoscope of the elderly, a bouquet of wasting bodies and hourglasses running empty.

Laura is asleep with her oxygen mask on. I sit on the corner of her bed, the same way I've done with my dad's countless hospital beds. Slowly, her eyes open. Her face is red and puffy, her new stitches crusty and brown.

'Hey,' I say timidly. 'I brought your phone charger.'

She gives me the smallest nod, her eyes wet and crusted with sleep. She gestures to her phone on the nightstand, and I plug it in. An empty battery appears on the screen, and a sliver of red starts to show.

She doesn't deserve this. She only came to Clipim because I begged her to, and now she's lying here with a cannula in her nose and dried blood on her gown. Why does everyone I love end up like this? Before I'm done processing the thought, the answer comes to me: *Because everyone in the world ends up like this.*

'I'm so sorry, Laura,' I whisper. 'I don't know what else to say. I'm so sorry I brought you here, and I'm sorry for fighting with you, and for storming off so you had to spend an evening with that fucking idiot.'

Laura gives me a delicate, bleary smile and I wonder if she's on drugs. She opens her mouth and a puff of failed language falls out. Her voice is strangled and raspy, as though she's been wrung around the neck.

'Laura!' I gasp, bringing my hands to my face. I had been determined not to cry, regardless of what scenario I found Laura in, and here I am. Weeping at her attempts to communicate with me.

She sits up and reaches for her phone again, gesturing me to sit upright on the pillow with her. After a few minutes of waiting for it to boot up, she opens her Notes app and starts typing: *I told you we should have gone to the awards ceremony.*

I yelp in grateful gulps of laughter. It really isn't that funny, but the fact that Laura is here, awake, making sarky comments on her phone is enough to bring me back into the world.

'You're right. We should have gone to the awards ceremony. And hey, maybe we won something. Maybe our award is in the post right now.'

She rolls her eyes, the perfect summation of: *I'll believe* that *when I see it.* She picks up her phone again.

*I believe you,* she writes.

'What do you mean?'

*I saw the newspaper.*

I'm about to open my mouth to speak again, but Laura keeps typing.

*When I showed it to D he got very shirty about me asking. Territorial. He went completely off me.*

'Do you think he knows something?'

She thinks for a while before responding. *I don't know exactly. I think he was more annoyed that I would question Clip at all.*

'So did you push it?'

*He got annoyed and left. I stayed. That's when the fire started.*

She closes her eyes, exhausted with the effort of typing. I consider leaving. She should be sleeping, not straining herself by talking to me. She flicks her eyes open again and starts to type.

*I know they're saying the fire was D's fault, but I think it was BB who started it.*

'I thought it was a gorse fire they had started?'

*No. He brought me up there because I wanted to see it. We didn't go up to burn anything.*

'So there were no fires lit by Dónal? None?'

She pauses for a long time. I'm still not clear on how much head trauma she's had, I think, eyeing the stitches in her scalp.

*I don't know,* she writes. *We had been smoking weed on the walk up, in the field bit.*

She stops again, and thinks.

*I remember D being very casual about it.*

'Do you think that he might have flicked a joint into the grass, or something?'

*Maybe.*

'He said you went back in for the something. Why?'

She wrinkles her nose.

*I didn't go back in. They left me there. We had a fight.*

'What?'

*I just thought he was being stupid. Ciara too. Clearly something is fishy about this whole story but they didn't want to acknowledge it and they kept telling me to shut up. So they left and a few minutes later there was smoke everywhere and they were running back, trying to get me out. BB was there. He pulled me out.*

Laura's slow, laboured typing is giving me ample opportunity to visualise the entire scene. Dónal was born here. His parents are the richest farmers on the island, which – according to most of the people in the pub on Sunday night – is an indirect consequence of the economic crash that followed the accident. Small farmers sold up and left, the Foleys acquiring more and more plots until the entire island became mostly grazing land. The family aren't exactly spoken of in glowing terms. At the fire last night, everyone was more irritated by their involvement than concerned for anyone's health.

Then in crashes Laura, with all her directness and intellectual vigour, asking Dónal whether the accident was planned. Dónal, who has probably been hearing whispers about his family's farm since he was born, probably didn't care for the interrogation. I can picture him storming out, leaving a tipsy Laura to herself with a *fuck that bitch* on his breath.

But would he start the fire? To show her a lesson? To silence her questions? To destroy evidence?

Laura seems to think not, but Laura never wants to suspect evil motivations of attractive people. Hotness represents moral virtue, in Laura's book.

'Do you think he could have been angry with you? That maybe ... he wanted to scare you out of asking questions?'

She considers this, her fingers hovering above her keypad.

'I mean, judging on my one meeting, he seemed like a pretty quick-to-anger guy. And ... I know that you fancy him, so sorry, but not particularly bright. He could have started the fire to show off.'

*I guess. But it happened so quickly. It couldn't have been D.*

'But it *could* have been Benjamin Barry? Mr Eco-friendly?'

I say it, and instantly remember that Benjamin Barry is currently threatening to ruin my life. I open my mouth to explain this to Laura, but can't quite find the strength. She can't hear about the porn. Not now.

*Maybe he saw Dónal and Ciara leave and thought the place was empty. I mean, why was he there to pull me out?*

## 27

A nurse comes in to tell me that Laura needs rest, and I instinctively head to The Fiddler. After a few days, my body seems to simply propel me there.

The last of the weekend tourists have been truly sopped up, and dense shadows have filled the corners where people once were. Maria isn't here, either. I ask a grey-haired man behind the counter who I've never seen before where she is, and I'm abruptly told that it's her day off. I realise that this is probably the owner, whose existence up until now I was only vaguely aware of. I always just presume this to be Maria's pub, run by her and the scattering of twenty-year-old glass collectors and bartenders that do her bidding.

'What'll you have?'

'God, I don't even know what time it is,' I laugh exhaustedly.

The owner looks at me blankly, clearly not in the mood to discuss what time is appropriate to have what drink.

'Look,' I say, still smiling, 'is there any chance I could have a coffee?'

'We only have instant.'

I know this isn't true. That, when we had our breakfast at the weekend, we were given steaming cappuccino cups full of Nespresso-filtered coffee.

'That's fine.'

As I wait I start scanning the walls again, letting my eyes rest on the framed article by Patrick Kavanagh about the death of John F. Kennedy. It's about 800 words along, but Kavanagh was too much of a typical poet to stick on the one subject. Towards the end he starts breaking off in vignettes; observations about himself, about death, and about the assassination heard around the world but ricocheted around the Irish ear with a sharp ding.

*Everyone here has been saying the same. These old ones are steal-ing the show all the time. But let nobody think that I believe in old ones and old things. I believe in spring and the sun rising, shining on the dew-wet grass and myself on a hill aged twenty-one.*

I am given a narrow mug of black coffee, the water splashed messily over the brown granules. When I ask for sugar, a bag of it is placed on the table with a dessert spoon wedged into it.

'Thanks,' I say, wondering if this is really the same Fiddler that I've been in and out of for the last few days. The handle is so narrow that I burn my knuckles off the side of the mug.

There are only three other people in the pub, all men. Two of them are reading newspapers, the other staring at a fixed point on his own table, breaking his gaze only to take a long sip from his pint. The whole room chimes with the smell of disinfectant and stale yeast.

After a few minutes of this, a blast of light and cold air comes in from the street. Enda walks in with two young men trailing behind him, each carrying crates of food from the mainland.

Edna exchanges a 'how'ya?' and a 'how'ya keeping?' with the men tending their pints. The two boys are pointed into the kitchen. Satisfied that the job is taken care of, Enda sits down and orders himself a pint.

'Hi, Enda,' I say. 'How are you today?'

Enda fixes his swimming-pool-blue eyes on me, and suddenly the sweet, doddering old man that I first met is a stranger to me.

'Charlotte,' he says stoutly. 'You're still here, I see.'

'I am,' I reply. 'I suppose you heard about the fire.'

'I was there at two in the morning putting it out,' he says. 'This has been an exciting trip for you, hasn't it?'

It's phrased like a question, but nothing in his inflection demands an answer.

'Let's see,' he says, stretching out one huge hand. 'You have interrogated my wife,' he ticks off one finger. 'Set fire to valuable land,' he ticks another. 'Destroyed a remembrance site, and have shown absolutely no respect for the history of this community.'

Enda grits his teeth and picks up his Guinness.

'I hope this documentary you're making is worth the hassle, Charlotte.'

'Enda, no,' I say, reeling in confusion. 'I'm not making a documentary. I made a feature film. I told you this when we met. And I didn't interrogate your wife. The fire wasn't us, either.'

'My wife,' he says, looking straight ahead as though addressing the dusty bottles of gin on the back wall of the bar, 'is a very sensitive woman.'

The two boys that came in with Enda are now standing by the door of The Fiddler, looking at me with mild interest.

'We're done now, End,' the shorter one says, and Enda lifts one hand. A silent indication to wait until he's finished his drink.

My instinct is to use the word boys to describe them, although I know that isn't correct. They could be anywhere between the ages of eighteen and thirty-five. Their flushed faces appear ruddy and energetic at some angles, but piggish and boiled in others. One of them starts slouching against the windowsill, and takes out some rolling tobacco. The other just stares. The compulsion to call them boys comes from, I think, their utter deference to the much older man.

'I don't know what Mary has told you,' I say slowly, 'but I think someone's got the wrong end of the stick here. I've only met her twice. I helped her in the ... in the ladies' loo, the second night we were here. And then I met her on the way home last night.'

I decide to leave out the spitting. The boy with the rolling tobacco by the door starts to snigger. 'The wrong end of the *stick*,' he says in a pantomime of the Queen's English.

'She came home to me crying,' Enda barks at me. 'She came home upset because she said you were drilling the poor woman for information. Presumably for this documentary you're making.'

'I'm not *making* a documentary, Enda. I can't stress that enough.'

'You thought I was an old fool,' he says, louder now, his voice practically a shout. 'Coming in and sitting up at the bar and taking advantage of only poor old people. You know, as long as there's been a Kerry there's been people like yourself. People who look down on us. Thinking we're only simple. Well, I can tell you now we're *not*.'

His last words echo around the bar and the room falls silent. The only sound is a cigarette paper being licked and turned over. I want to leave. This pub, this island, this version of my life where I'm treated like a wanted criminal by total strangers.

I'm struck with the feeling that, if I approach the door of the pub, I might be physically stopped. My stomach drops as I picture Enda's boys suddenly springing into action, acting as armed guards.

I get up from my stool, leaving a couple of euros on the bar for my coffee. Squaring my shoulders, I make my way through the bar, feeling like every eye in the room is watching me leave. As I move towards the door, I try to find the courage to keep my head up, and to maintain eye contact with the boy who made fun of my accent. He's unfazed by me, his stare large, looming and bored.

'They certainly have a lot of gear with them,' the other lad says. 'For people who aren't making a film.'

He smiles, and my determination to seem strong breaks. I look at the floor as I shuffle out of the bar, closing the door firmly after me.

I consider going to Maria's house, but decide that I can't inflict myself on her again. I've ruined it now, with her. The way I snapped at her last night, pushing her off me like she was a drunk eighteen-year-old in a club. The Biter came out. Maybe she always will, eventually.

I can risk Benjamin's campsite. A few hours' sleep, some lunch, and I'll go see Laura again. Or go to the Button Museum. Anything to pare down the hours until Laura's doctor says we can go home.

I wonder what the boy means by this – the word 'gear' – until I get back to the caravan and see a shiny black lump swaying by our door. Rushing forward, I think it's a crow that has tried to get inside but has instead collided with the frosted glass, damaging its wing in the process. There's an excitement to this. A living thing I could do something good for. The urge to put my hands on its dark feathers, the bird's heart beating underneath. I run towards it, and the closer I get, the more I realise it's not a bird. It's not a living thing at all. It's Laura's camera, hanging by the door handle from its leather strap, and almost completely smashed beyond recognition.

The last time I saw Laura with her camera was only a few hours before the accident. She was showing Dónal her shots of Cork city. Did she drop it back to the caravan before going back out? Or did someone find it at the fire and bring it back here? I turn the broken thing over and over in my hands. It's a magnificent camera. The kind of equipment that Laura and

I used to make fun of people for having. Whenever a boy at Uni showed up with a brand-new Nikon, she would nudge me and say: 'What on *earth* does he think he's going to do with that?'

We considered it bougie and trite to have a nice camera, and anyone who had one had to go out of their way to prove to us they weren't a spoiled poser. But in the same way that there comes a point in your life where you start congratulating your friends on being pregnant rather than commiserating with them, there came a point where people started getting nice cameras and *needing* them.

The door of the caravan is still locked, which does almost nothing to comfort me. The place was already a mess before I left, strewn about with my pyjamas and Laura's make-up wipes, so it's hard to tell whether anything has been moved or tampered with.

My laptop is still in my bedroom, hidden under my pillow. My camera is nowhere to be found. Panicking, I start pulling apart the caravan. My SLR is ten years old, bought in the January sales with a combination of Christmas-present money and babysitting funds. Even then it wasn't considered especially top of the line. But it's *my camera*. My first tiny step towards being a proper filmmaker. At the very beginning of the memory card is a thirty-second film of my dad poking around in Jessop's, adjusting his glasses as he considers whether or not I need a tripod. I don't know why I never deleted it, but the more time that passed, the more I found myself coming back to it. My dad, still with some colour left in his hair, during a lost age where driving me to the shops and picking out a camera wasn't an expedition that required a permission slip. It was just something we did together.

And now it's gone.

I crumple on to the bed, holding my knees protectively. The urge to scream and kick and cry surges through me. The urge to run into the town with my arms flying, screaming, *I want my daddy.*

I dial his number and, of course, his phone is off. I dial it again, just for the comfort of hearing his answer phone message. I listen again. And again. A medically induced coma. What *is* a medically induced coma? The entire time I've been here I've told myself that it's something like a cryogenic sleep, an optional nap that Dad can be woken from at any time.

I still have no idea when the surgery is, or how long they're observing him before they operate. Maybe they have already. I've told myself that Mum is making a big deal about nothing, and that him being in a coma would give her a chance to catch up on errands. The reality of the situation – that Mum has likely spent the last forty-eight hours glued to his bedside, a scarf over her eyes to block out the many tiny red and green lights of the hospital room – has been stamped down like a pizza box crushed into a rubbish bin.

I curl deeper into a ball, clutching Laura's ruined camera to my stomach. Rain starts to bounce off the roof of the caravan, the water sounding like rocks on the corrugated metal. Maybe they are rocks. Maybe being buried under a heap of stones is exactly how stories like this are supposed to end.

## 28

I wake up covered in sweat and with the firm instinct to flee. The rental car keys are on the coffee table, so I quickly pack up everything we own and load it all into the boot, pressing the car fob until I hear the satisfying click of the doors locking. I pack my laptop, my wallet, my various chargers and a spare pair of underwear back into my rucksack and vow that I will only come back here when Laura is well enough to drive us out. It doesn't matter where I stay: whether it's Maria's house or in the Button Museum, or in the burned-out schoolhouse.

I'm still nervous of approaching Maria after last night. Even if we were on good terms, there's no guarantee she'd hear what I have to say. She loves Enda, after all. She had an easy affection with him at The Fiddler and seemed defensive of Mary when I told her about the spitting. Is it such a good idea to go running to her now?

By process of elimination, I finally end up in the Button Museum.

There are no free buttons with the Button Museum factory tour. The ticket says it clearly, and the girl at the ticket office is explicit about it.

'Just so's you know. There's a gift shop at the end, with lots of lovely buttons, but there are no free buttons. No samples.'

'That's fine.'

'I just like to say, because sometimes people are very disappointed. I don't know why. You wouldn't go to the Ford factory and expect a free car!'

This is obviously a line that she says a lot, but is still amused by nonetheless.

The Button Museum is one of those tourist attractions that is just about on the cute side of shitty. There are shiny-faced yellowing mannequins, their fingers all poised elegantly as if about to press a lift-call button. The first room is just female mannequins dressed up in different button-centric looks from the Victorian period to present day. 'Present day' has been visualised as a woman wearing a construction worker's hard hat, and a blazer with huge buttons.

A placard informs me that a 'popular misconception' about the Button Factory is that the buttons were actually made here. No. The decorative button coverings were merely *sewn* here. When I wander into the next room, I find a handful of sewing stations, all attended by mannequin women with shawls over their heads. Two of them are bent over their work, threads and bright fabric locked into their cramped plastic hands, the colours lurid against their long black uniforms.

'Stanworth & Sons was well known for its hand-sewn, brightly coloured covered buttons,' reads the placard next to them. 'Each button took up to ten minutes to make, but quicker seamstresses could manage it in less than five!' Then, below that: 'Speedy seamstresses were highly valued by Stanworth, who were often paid up to a pound more a week for their quick work.'

Another two mannequins are next to them, having what's supposed to look like a conversation. These women are younger, as evidenced by the strands of horse hair curling out of their caps, and their big, frightening smiles.

'Button covering was highly social work, and many of the seamstresses went on to be lifelong friends!'

I roll my eyes. God, no wonder the locals find this place so funny. It really is a shit museum.

I scan the photographs of the real-life seamstresses, all lined up in choir positions, dressed in stiff-looking black uniforms and white shawls. There's a new photo for every five years or so, and for the first couple of decades, you can see sisters, and mothers, and sometimes daughters. At first the photos are ten, twelve, fifteen women at a time: huddled together, long dark dresses and aprons. Their names are printed below, and soothingly similar to one another.

*1935 L–R, BACK ROW: Mary O'Shea, Kathleen Cavanagh, Eile Cavanagh, Aileen Walsh, Patricia O'Donoghue*

*1945 L–R, BACK ROW: Mary O'Shea, Eile Cavanagh, Pauline O'Toole, Tara Fleming, Ann Fleming*

The 1950s, apparently, were boom times for buttons. The factory staff triples in size. Names stop appearing below the photos. I find myself even more drawn to these women, though: the nameless newbies. Where did they come from? Who were they? Who comes to Clipim, of all places, as a young woman?

I wander around. The historical relevance gets thinner and thinner with each display, most of them not even bothered with Clipim, but with the history of buttons as a whole. There's a room about button collectors, and another room about military buttons. I am invited to take an interactive quiz to test my newfound button knowledge. I decline, making my way to the cafe and gift shop, both of which are staffed by a lone teenage girl who is propped against the coffee machine, mutely Snapchatting dog ears on to herself.

I buy a black coffee and a handful of giant souvenir buttons and a picture calendar, hoping that they will somehow be enough to allow Mum to forgive me. I have been texting her every few hours, all met by fraught, short responses. Updates that consist of the phrase 'no updates'. I call her from the cafe, but she doesn't pick up, so I begin retracing my steps through the museum, seeing the whole history in reverse. I come back, again, to the photos from the 1950s. Maria had been puzzled by these, too.

*No one ever talked about working there. None of the old ladies who I know on Clipim talked about it. Ever. They only talk about it as a museum, not as a factory.*

Where did they *come from*? Who were they? We spoke to dozens of people about the history of Clipim. Statistically, at least one of them should have worked here, but the only person who seems to have is Maria's great-aunt Nuala.

It doesn't make any sense. The population of Clipim was only a few hundred back then. These women would have had children in my father's school.

And it's exactly like that – exactly as the word SCHOOL forms in my head – that I see her. Her wide forehead, her face the egg-shape of an old Tudor. She's so familiar that at first I think she's a friend of my mum's, or an old relative, or someone who takes my bus. But she's none of those people. Sitting among thirty other women in a photograph marked 'SUMMER 1961' is Emma Casey.

Emma Casey worked at the button factory. Emma Casey, the only adult victim of the schoolhouse disaster, began her career in Clipim sewing expensive fabric on to cheap buttons. At a place where all the women seem to be curiously missing.

Why has no one ever mentioned this? The mysteries in Clipim are piling high now: the newspaper in the air vent, the missing photo of Maria's relative, the fire last night, the sudden labour explosion in the button factory, and now Emma Casey's history there. The facts, though disconnected, don't feel like they're unrelated. Otherwise, why would Enda and Benjamin be so determined to scare me?

With Enda, it seems like a simple misunderstanding. He's convinced that I'm making a documentary about Clipim, and that I tried to use his alcoholic wife as an interview subject.

Mary, last night, drunk and spitting at me. The old woman with the big perm and the cut on her lip. *She came home upset because she said you were drilling the poor woman for information.*

Why would she say that? It's clear that Mary thinks she told me something of value, and that Enda . . . that Enda punished her for it.

My stomach buckles at the thought of it. Could the smiling old man with the swimming-pool eyes and the voice like honeyed smoke really hit his wife? I can feel myself trying to resist believing it, my head shying like a horse refusing a bridle. Everything else, I can take. I am ready to believe that the schoolhouse was a conspiracy, a cover-up. That is accept- able to me somehow. But the notion of a man like Enda, who practically *swooned* when he met me, raising a fist to his diminutive wife is . . . too much?

No, not too much. Just enough. That was the problem. It is what you expect an old Irish man to do; at least, that's what all the most disgusting and thoughtless clichés tell us. I'm not ready for everyone I've met and everything I've fallen in love with this week to become another cliché. A souvenir as tacky and brittle as the ones being sold in the Button Museum.

I try to remember everything Mary said to me on the night of our toilet encounter, but I was so drunk myself that it's a muddle. Something about my grandmother. My grandmother being friends with Emma Casey. Was that information really so precious? I had treated it like it was nothing.

But Mary hadn't. Mary told me and was frightened she'd said too much.

*But to make her the teacher? It was a bad idea from the start. She wasn't fit. She had no training.*

The realisation comes to me so suddenly that I have to put a hand to the wall to steady myself. My grandmother got Emma Casey the job teaching. Mary had told me so.

Emma had been slaving away at the button factory and somehow struck up a friendship with my grandmother, Kitty. Kitty recommended her for the teaching position. All of Emma's students died, except one.

Kitty's son.

## 29

*So what you're saying is, Emma did it.*

'I don't think I'm saying that,' I respond curtly.

*Right. You're letting me get to that conclusion myself.*

'Do you really think it's that simple?' I ask Laura, who is typing away on her phone frantically. The dried blood has been swabbed away from her forehead but her voice is still scratchy and dry. She has to keep her mask on so that her blood oxygen levels can get back to normal and we can go home. The nurse seems to think she could be well enough to travel on Wednesday morning.

*I think we're talking murder-suicide.*

This is why I need Laura. I can simmer in soupy grey feelings for days and weeks at a time, and she will kick the door in with simple statements. I baulk at the text.

*Emma put the extra newspaper in the vents.*

'But why? You can't just call it murder-suicide, like we're on *CSI*. This is real, Laura. This is real people's lives.'

*Revenge.*

'Revenge for what?'

Talking to her like this is like talking to a Ouija board. This is the kind of thing you normally puzzle out for hours, chatting over every angle with conversational softeners. Softeners like 'what if . . . ?' and 'have you thought of . . . ?' and 'obviously not this, but something like this'. This new, text-based version of our friendship has stripped all the nuance out, and Laura's natural bluntness feels like other-worldly wisdom.

*Go in my bag and get my book.*

'What? *American Taste?*'

She nods vigorously, and I hand it to her. A glossy piece of yellow paper falls out, something she has obviously been using as a bookmark. I squint at it, and see that it's the bro-chure for the Button Museum that she picked up on the first day. I let out a short bark of a laugh, remembering how she had paraded it around, mocking me about the 'clue' she'd found. I start reading it aloud again.

'The Button Museum, formerly Stanworth & Sons Button Company Ltd, was established in 1981, 18 years after the clo-sure of the original factory,' I say, still in a mocking voice. 'It now displays buttons and button-related curiosities to over 10,000 button enthusiasts a year.'

Laura starts tapping on her phone again. As I watch her, I realise that she's not in her Notes app any more. She's on her calculator.

1981

−18

=

1963

I bite my lip. The year the Beatles came to Dublin. The year JFK visited Ireland, and was killed less than six months later. A year where the country swayed on a pendulum between an old world and a new one, and eighteen children and one adult teacher were killed in a carbon monoxide acci-dent in rural Kerry.

*Emma works at the button factory. Your nan gets her a job at the school. Everyone dies. The button factory closes.*

'Everyone dies, except my dad.'

*Exactly.*

'That's a fucking wild theory, Laura,' I say, running my hands through my lank hair. 'Revenge for *what*?'

She shrugs, and gives me a 'you figure it out' look.

'It could have closed by coincidence,' I tell her, but my tone is unsure. The secrecy around Maria's great-aunt Nuala suddenly seems justified. Also, why would you wait eighteen years to turn the factory into a museum, unless you were truly desperate for something to sell tickets to? If there was something wrong with the button factory, they clearly thought the heat had died down by 1981, and another Irish economic recession had rolled its way around.

*That's why you have to be careful, get as much information as you can, and get the fuck out of here.*

'Laura, they smashed your camera. They stole mine. And now you're telling me to get *more* information?'

Laura blinked back a few tears when I told her about her beloved camera, but bristled past the implied threat and instead went straight to reality. Her camera was insured, after all. She'll get a brand-new one for nothing.

*They're just trying to scare you. They can't actually do anything.*

I bite the edge of my lip, gnawing at a dried piece of skin that is flaking upwards. It tears away, revealing a red wetness that's painful to touch.

'The thing is . . . they can. Benjamin can.'

She looks at me quizzically, her big arctic-blue eyes and confused expression making her look like a young Goldie Hawn.

'Benjamin . . . knows something about me.'

Is this really how I tell Laura about the porn? Because a caravan-park owner is threatening to leak my nudes if I reveal the potential murder in his town?

It occurs to me then just how sick I am of keeping secrets,

and of having them kept from me. I made *It Takes a Village* in an attempt to understand the world my father came from, and instead I've solidified a myth. Because of me, Clipim will remain a sad story about an unsafe building. The truth – whatever it is – will eventually disappear for ever, as each key player dies off and each puzzle piece becomes more faded. Another chapter of Irish history that mud is kicked over until someone bigger and braver than me is able to unearth it. Someone properly Irish. Someone who has the cultural right to uncover things – not some English upstart who made a film about Ireland without setting foot on Irish soil.

I feel a gentle tap on the shoulder, softer than a cat's paw. *Are you okay?*

'Laura . . . ' I look at her as a way of steadying myself. I'm sick of it. Sick of myself, sick of feeling guilty, sick of cloying on the outside of an identity, sick of feeling marginal even to myself.

'I sell porn.'

Every card is laid out, now. I officially have no secrets left from Laura Shingle. The adrenalin rush of having told her has made me pace wildly around the room as I explain more and more precisely how I make the rent, and how Benjamin Barry was blackmailing me with the information. The further I get into the discussion, the more relieved I am that Laura still can't talk. I only have body language and the whites of her eyes to go by, along with the occasional typed message.

It's endearing to see just how many of her questions are business-focused. Every time she starts typing stuff like 'Don't you find it degrading' . . . she gets tired and realises that the question isn't worth the effort.

Instead, it's: *So how much money are we talking? Do you meet these guys? Did you have to register as self-employed with HMRC?*

It's strange how much we seem to have been keeping from

one other: her with her open relationship, me with my porn career. There's a sharp little thrill in the whole thing. We're both discovering that we're more sexually illicit than the other one has let on. What could have been depressing now feels almost funny.

She's visibly more worried when I tell her about my clash with Benjamin.

*He assaulted you.*

'Would we call that assault, though?' I say, hesitant. I remember his head on my legs, his hands gripping my thighs.

*Charlie.*

'He didn't touch my vulva, or anything.'

*Charlie. He assaulted you.*

And then: *Stop saying vulva.*

'Vulva. Vulva vulva vulva vulva.'

Laura starts typing again, her nostrils flaring around her cannula.

*If he was willing to steal from you, assault you and threaten you,* she types, *then he must have been willing to burn the school-house down.*

It's an upside-down kind of logic, but I see where she's coming from. Laura is much more fixated on the fire than I am, which makes sense, given she could have died in it. But there's something more to it than that. There's been a shift in our perspectives somewhere along the line. Laura still sees the island as a group of individuals, one of whom may be an arsonist. From her makeshift hospital bed in the retirement home, the whole situation is a logic puzzle waiting to be worked out. For me, the person who still has to eat and sleep and walk around the island while she convalesces, Clipim has become a heaving, unified mass, a wall of energy that's slowly falling on top of me.

'I started an email to Nick – I thought I could ask him for his dad's contact details,' I say finally. 'I thought ... that maybe, if he re-opened the case, something could happen. Justice could . . . happen.'

*Now you sound like you're on* CSI.

I snort. 'More like *Law and Order*.'

At that moment, Laura's nurse walks into the room to signify that visiting hours are over.

*You need proof,* Laura types furiously. *You need Mary.*

## 30

The inside of An Spailpín Fánach feels like death and looks like the sea. It's about the size of one of Benjamin Barry's mobile homes but every spare wall is taken up with fishing paraphernalia. A huge pike is mounted above the bar, its mouth gaping open as though it's trying to see whether an oncoming bus is headed in the right direction. There are fish-hooks gleaming under glass, rope diagrams of sailors' knots and detailed prints on how to properly de-bone a trout. In a larger space, all of this might be charming. But the white-washed stone walls are peeled grey in places, and it's too cold to be comfortable, too dark to feel friendly.

From the moment I step inside I feel off-centre and unmoored, drunk just from standing there. Which could be to do with the fact that I'm here to run into Mary, but on inspection, has a lot to do with the pub itself. As I stumble up to the bar I see that half of the building juts out over the Atlantic, hanging out over the sea like an anglerfish's under-bite. There's a little balcony outside for smoking, the kind of place you can imagine a sea widow standing and gazing from while she waits for her husband.

The pub is practically empty, so I order a pint from the old man behind the bar and find a dark corner to sip it in, hoping that just because I saw Mary outside here yesterday evening I might find her today, too. I drink, and I doodle on a notepad, and I turn over the same questions over and over again. Was Emma Casey really capable of killing herself and a classroom full of children? Was my grandmother capable of befriending a murderer? And my dad – the spared child who refused to return to Clipim for his entire adult life – could he have known all along?

I step out on to the smoker's balcony, the sea wind high and cold against my cheek, and I call Mum. Partly to see if there are any updates, but mostly out of a rarely felt need to hear her voice. She sounds tired, but glad to hear from me.

'Hello, love,' she says wearily.

'Hey,' I reply. 'Just thought I'd check in.'

'Are you still . . . there?'

'I am. Did they operate?'

'They did.'

'And what are they . . . ?'

'They said he's responding well, but I have no idea what that means. He isn't awake yet. But they think they will be able to discharge him next week. They said . . . they said he will . . . '

She coughs. Clears her throat.

'They said he will come home again.'

We are both quiet.

'Right,' I say softly. 'And . . . you? How are you? Are you home?'

'No.' She sighs. 'Not for a good while yet.'

We lapse into silence and for a few seconds her breathing syncs with the sound of the ocean beneath me.

'I hear music,' she says finally. 'What music is that?'

'Oh,' I respond. I open the door of the pub and a stream of music flows out. 'Is that what you're hearing?'

'Yes. Is that The Dubliners?'

'I think so. It almost always is over here.'

'We went to see them once,' she says. 'Colm and me. A reunion tour. Not with Luke Kelly, of course.'

'No,' I agree. 'Luke Kelly collapsed on stage in Cork and Dad had ...'

' ... had a ticket to the show,' she finishes.

We both laugh at that, before settling back into quietness. I remember in the car last month, when she had told me not to fill up my old iPod with Irish songs. She said it would be too depressing for him. Maybe it was just too depressing for her.

'I better go, love. The doctor has just come in.'

'Okay. Kiss Dad for me.'

'Yes.'

'I love you, Mum.'

'And ... yes. I love you too. And love to Laura.'

I decide not to tell my mum what has happened to Laura. Never tell someone who is exhausted by hospitals that someone else is in hospital. It makes them feel like illness is a tacky franchise. The mortality equivalent of: *Ugh,* another *Starbucks?*

Mum rings off. I breathe in a deep gulp of ocean air, cold salt hitting the back of my lungs and reverberating with something that feels like hope.

When I go back inside I'm surprised to find that Maria is there, waiting for me at my table.

'Hi,' she says, smiling shyly. 'I thought I might find you here.'

'How did you know?'

'Because you weren't in the other three places I tried, and one of the good things about living in a place this small is that there are limited places you can be.'

I laugh. 'I'm so sorry about the other night. What I said to you after ... after Aidan showed up.'

She grimaces slightly. 'Thanks.'

'Not to sound like a complete cliché of a nineties man, but I've got some, ah, intimacy issues.'

A wry smile. 'You didn't seem to have any issues *before* he showed up.'

Maria leans in to kiss me, and I back away out of instinct.

'Sorry,' I say. 'It's just ... in a pub? Won't he mind?' I gesture to the ancient landlord with his newspaper splayed out on the bar.

'John,' she calls, 'you have any problem with me kissing this girl in here?'

'Hmmmmh?'

'I said: DO YOU HAVE ANY PROBLEM WITH ME KISSING THIS WOMAN IN HERE?'

He briefly looks up from his paper. 'Sure, didn't I vote for the gays?'

'You did, John.'

'And the Taoiseach's a gay.'

'That's true,' she agrees good-naturedly.

'There we are so.'

I can feel my ears turning pink. I return the kiss. We sit and drink for a while. She asks about Laura and the fire, but seems curiously keen to keep conversation light and breezy. It's her only evening off, and she seems to want to spend it bouncing her charisma off me, lassoing my adoration for her own amusement. I'm glad to play along. This is the role I'm used to with Laura, being the mirror for the other woman to see herself in, and it transposes well on to dating.

There's a reason that all of Maria's friends are seasonal workers, and that she's chosen to live in a seasonal town. Everything is temporary for her. As she buys me a second drink I feel delighted at the prospect of everything being temporary for me, too. Emma Casey and troubling phrases like 'murder-suicide' begin to fall out of my head as Maria's hand creeps into my lap. It's the first time I've seen her on a non-work day, and I'm slightly thrilled when I detect the small efforts she has made on her appearance. Nothing major: a dab of lipstick, a smudge of eyeshadow the colour of milky coffee. She's wearing an oversized denim shirt stitched with light, colourful embroidery and mismatched beading.

'This is so cool,' I say, rolling the beads between my fingers.

'Thanks,' she says. 'I got it in Mexico, like ten years ago. I've had to replace all the beading myself, but it's still my favourite thing.'

'Holidays?'

'My mom and I lived there for a year,' she says shortly. I'm about to ask more, but her hand suddenly grazes the bare skin of my inner wrist. 'Hey, have you been out on the balcony yet?'

I nod, and she leads me back out onto the balcony.

Everything is navy blue outside now, the sea a noisy dark line, more sound than sight. Every couple of minutes the water sprays my face, making it impossible to smoke. Maria watches me and starts laughing, yanking the damp cigarette out of my mouth and sliding it behind her ear.

'Come here,' she says, twisting her hands into my hair, pulling my mouth towards hers.

The first time I kissed Maria, we were standing in the middle of the road. The kiss had been so full of loneliness that I felt like I was in the presence of a woman who was hearing herself speak after decades spent alone. The second time, there was a silliness to it. An awkwardness we were both aware of and trying to push past even as we were enjoying ourselves. Now, Maria is all intention, all id, all desire.

She pins me to the wall of the pub, inches from the door, and keeps an occasional eye to see if anyone's coming. She pleats kisses down my neck, her right hand lightly on my throat, her left inside my jeans and grabbing at my ass. I have never, not once in my life, felt this sexy, this desired, this wanted by another person. Despite her dominance, it makes me feel in control. Like she would do anything for me at this moment.

'Your hands are fucking *freezing*,' I gasp.

She says nothing, but cocks her eyebrow and I feel her sly smile spread over my neck. Maria slides her hand around to the front of my pants and I yelp as her icy fingers glide over my clit.

'Jesus,' I whisper, grinding against her, suddenly aware of how wet I am against her cold hands. 'Jesus fucking Christ.'

I pull at her shirt, the old buttons and battered denim falling open easily. It never gets old, being with someone whose body is so different to yours, especially when you've spent so long miserable in your own body. There's a gorgeous roundness to Maria, a softness that spills out into my hands and mouth and makes me feel wildly envious as well as painfully turned on. It's a strange thing, being attracted to women while simultaneously being conditioned to compare your own body to every other female body in the world, and something about the crossover makes me snap my teeth at the skin below her collarbone.

'Fuck!' Maria yelps, before laughing and pulling me to her neck. 'Oh, we've got ourselves a *biter.*'

My entire back is wet from being pushed up against the wall, a fact I was happy to ignore at first, but becomes more uncomfortable the longer we stand in the smoking area. Maria clearly feels the same, because she presses my hands to my face and suggests we go back to hers.

'Sure,' I say, buttoning her shirt back up for her. 'We probably shouldn't get naked in the Spailpín. I think that would test even John's liberal politics.'

She turns back to the pub door while clutching my hand, and I suddenly feel her freeze and drop it.

'Shit,' she says, peering through the glass. 'Dónal, Ciara and Aidan are in there.'

'So?'

'Look, how about you stay out here, and I get rid of them? Then I can meet you at home.'

'Why?' I say. 'Are you not out to them?'

'No, that's not it,' she says, her voice quavering. 'It's just you're not very popular around here, Charlie.'

'Well, I knew that,' I respond snappily. 'I have three thousand pounds' worth of destroyed camera equipment to tell me that.'

'What? Who destroyed your camera?'

'Laura's camera. It was Enda and his weird cronies. They think I'm . . . '

' . . . making a documentary. I know.'

'How do *you* know?'

'Charlie, the whole town has been talking about you. Apparently Laura really pissed off Dónal yesterday, before the fire. Shooting her mouth off about how he was being deliberately ignorant. The whole "city mouse telling all the country mice how dumb they are" routine.'

Oh, God. That sounds like Laura all right.

'Honestly, I've never known Clipim to be so united. People . . . people want you *gone*, Charlie.'

'And you? What about you?'

If she had taken even three seconds less to respond, I would have stayed in the smoking area, waited for them to leave, and then joined Maria at her house. If she had kissed me, or told me they were all crazy, or even said that all she cared about was a decent fuck before I disappeared for ever, I might have followed her plan. But the fact is, she just stood there.

'You're a coward,' I say slowly. 'You're a fucking coward, Maria.'

## 31

It's hard to stand your ground, but it's even harder when you're not on home turf, and the person you're standing against is impossibly attractive. I don't care if that's shallow – it's true. The moment I'm standing in front of Dónal, I feel as though his eyelashes have won the battle before it's even begun.

'What the fuck is *she* doing here?' he snarls at Maria.

'She has every right to be here,' Maria responds, with battered confidence. Clearly she's keen to undercut my accusation.

'Does she?' he says, standing up from his chair. 'More than the people who live here?'

Dónal, who one day ago was just an oafish idiot sitting next to Laura in the pub, now seems intimidating. He's like a cat that's been snoozing by the fire all day and has suddenly decided to unfurl his limbs and become a mountain lion, peering down on me from a great height. He's well over six foot, his body long and strong and solid all the way through. His big green eyes, his curly dark hair, his obvious *prettiness* should make him less threatening, but for some reason it only makes him more so. The way a dictator is scarier when they're being nice to you, Dónal's perfect Cupid's bow and the smile he bends it into sends a chill through me that's colder than the thrashing ocean outside.

'Jesus, we can't be rid of you, can we?' he says, still smiling.

'We all sussed you day one, you know. Coming in with the whole prodigal daughter act. Snapping photos and acting like we're idiots. Like we don't see you. If you had brains you'd be dangerous.'

'So Laura asks a few questions and *implies* you might be in denial and your reaction is – what?' I splutter. 'To burn her *alive*? Is this the fucking Salem witch trials?'

'You think *we* started the fire?' Dónal snarls. 'Oh, I see. You might be only here five minutes but you've sure picked up on the whole "blame the Foleys for everything" theme. Properly ingratiated yourself, haven't you?'

His eyes flicker to Maria. 'I mean, I *know* you have.'

'Don,' Maria says, 'stop. You're being a douche.'

'She *told* me,' he says slowly. 'How you grilled her about the town. That's all you've been doing since you showed up. Butting into everyone's business. Well, maybe keep your nose out of our lives and wedged firmly in Maria's gowl.'

'*Gross*,' Ciara suddenly exclaims, without looking up from her phone. Aidan stays silent, his eyes batting between me and Dónal, but he saunters to the door so that there's a man standing on either side of me.

'DON,' Maria shouts, 'don't fucking talk about me like that. And don't be such a homophobe.'

'I love how everyone's so concerned about how I feel about gay people when there's literally Tan cunts who have rocked up out of nowhere, telling us what to do. Jesus Christ, wasn't eight hundred years enough for you lads?'

I decide to ignore the eight hundred years comment. It's a bit like bringing up Hitler on the internet: at that point, the argument has lost all logical sense. It's the first place my dad goes whenever he's pissed and an English person is rude to him. Instead, I whirl on Maria.

'What did you *say* to him?'

'*Nothing*,' she stumbles. 'After you went to Laura last night

everyone came to my house. Don said that Laura was interrogating him, and I said that you ... that we ... that you had
talked to me about your ... suspicions. That's it. That's all.'

'That's *all*?'

'I was hurt when you just ... pushed me aside like that.
You told me to fuck off. You literally pushed me off you like
I was hot garbage.'

'My best friend was—'

'Yes, I *know*, I do, but you're just so clearly in love with her,
and you had *just* spent the night with me. You didn't even ...
like, kiss me on the cheek or tell me that you'd be back. You
didn't even *call* to say everything was okay.'

'Maria,' Dónal snaps, 'you agreed with us. We asked you
if there was something shifty about Charlie and Laura and
you said yes.'

'I was drunk,' she says defensively.

'You were honest,' he counters.

'I bet I know why you were in here,' Dónal says smoothly.
'You thought Mary would be here, and you wanted to get
her plastered and dig some more dirt out of her, didn't you?'

Maria's eyes widen with terror and I realise that she really
did tell them everything, down to Mary spitting on me
outside the Spailpín last night. Then she shows up, twenty
minutes before Dónal, Ciara and Aidan do, nervously groping at me and refusing to talk about anything more serious
than the weather. Was she trying to get me to her house
before Dónal showed up?

'Look, Dónal, you hate me. I get that. I'm English and I'm
a lesbian – whatever. But even you have to see that something
is wrong with the schoolhouse story, don't you? Finding the
different dated newspaper was a bit of luck, but then ... the
fact that Emma Casey worked in this button factory that has
all these women that no one has heard of – Maria's fucking
aunt worked there, and they got rid of the photo when she

asked about it – and then my grandmother gets her a teaching job, and then my dad survives? It's not as simple as just an unsafe building, is it?'

'Yes, it fucking is, you idiot,' he says, grabbing my shoulder hard. 'You don't even have a story. Just some random bits of information you've forced out of people by being a spoilt entitled Brit.'

'If it's all so idiotic,' I say slowly, looking at him in his beautiful, terrible face, 'then how come you're so scared of me?'

That's what does it. That's what sends Dónal over the edge, away from simple hatred and into pure rage. For a moment, I think he's about to hit me across the face, but instead he grabs a handful of my hair into his fist and brings my eyes to his.

'You're a little cunt,' he says, his face contorting with rage. 'You're an evil fucking cunt.'

And then, quite suddenly, we're on the balcony again.

'DON,' Maria screams, the sea catching her voice and throwing it into the horizon. 'STOP it. STOP that right fucking now, I swear to God.'

Dónal and Aidan exchange a look, and Aidan grabs at the collar of Maria's denim shirt, picking her up like she's a pup. He shoves her back into the pub, then drags a heavy table in front of the glass double doors of the smoking area.

I'm alone with two men and the Atlantic Ocean.

'Is this it?' I screech. 'You're going to beat up a girl?'

'I don't hit girls,' he replies, and grabs me around the waist. For a split second, I think he's going to kiss me. Like he thinks that making a gay woman kiss a man must be the greatest punishment of all, like my skin will melt if he touches me.

But no.

Dónal lifts me off the ground, and shouts to Aidan behind him in Irish. I know so few words that it only adds to the sense of terrified helplessness. This, I realise, is the point.

'*Cos*,' he yells. '*Cos!*'

*Cos*, I think. I know that word. What *is* that?

As Aidan steps forward and grabs at me, I remember.

*Feet.*

Aidan grabs at my ankles while I scream and beat my fists against Dónal's back. I feel my centre of gravity shift and the crash of the sea get louder, the blood rushing to my head as I'm flipped upside down by the two men and dangled over the side of the balcony.

They are going to drown me.

My hair is short enough that I feel the first strand hit the water and tingle all the way to my scalp.

'Please stop,' I scream, gulping through panicked tears. 'I'll go home!'

At that moment, a wave crashes against the rocks and my face is under. My body screams in fear, the water rushing into my ears and eyes, turning the whole world dark. I feel a solid weight shifting in my jeans, and then a splash. My phone. My phone has just fallen into the water.

A second later, the sea settles again and just the tips of my hair are touching it, coiling like rat's tails. I can hear the boys, singing and laughing.

'For eight hundred years, we fought you without fear . . . '

Another wave hits against the rock and washes on to me, turning me deaf again. I can feel the tune of the song vibrating on the water's surface, the song so familiar that, despite everything, I finish it in my head. *And we will fight you for eight hundred more.*

When the water clears again, I start to feel a trickle of warmth spreading from my crotch and running toward my waist.

I have somehow pissed myself without noticing.

'Dónal!' I scream again. 'I will leave this fucking place tomorrow, just let me go. LET ME GO.'

I can hear the rising of the water, the sound of another wave making its way to the rocks.

Then, a crash. Not of seawater this time, of something else. Of broken glass and battered furniture. A brief mutter of voices, then a woman's voice. I am lifted out and dumped on the balcony, a shivering, crying, piss-stained mess.

'Charlie!' Maria screams. 'Don't move. There's glass everywhere.'

She's right: Maria has thrown a bar stool through the balcony doors and barged through. I can see tiny crystal shimmers in her hair where the glass has caught, and her wrist is starting to bleed where she must have groped for the handle.

'Come on,' she says, holding her hand out. 'We're leaving.'

## 32

I sit under the shower in Maria's house, my numb skin gradually warming up as my blood starts to circulate again. When I get out, Maria has made a plate of scrambled eggs on hot, buttery toast and places it on the coffee table.

'No, thank you,' I say, my voice barely a squeak.

'You have to eat something,' she says, putting on an old lady voice. 'You'll catch your death.'

The thought of eating makes me nauseous. It feels like there's a thick ice cap sitting in the middle of my chest, crushing my internal organs and making me very, very still.

'Do you want a tea?' she nudges, having already made the tea.

'No,' I respond shortly. 'Thank you.'

'What do you want to do?'

I think about it for so long that Maria is opening her mouth to repeat the question.

'Sleep,' I say at last.

She takes me into her bedroom, the room half covered in shadow. 'Do you want a toothbr—'

I've already crashed into her bed, naked and groping at the thick duvet. She smiles.

'There's an electric blanket, you know.'

I give a small murmur of appreciation and close my eyes. There's a click, and then the gradual heating of the panel under me. The whole bed is the temperature of blood.

'Hey,' I say finally. 'It's really cosy.'

'I know.'

'Do you want to . . . ?' I begin, and she nods.

She climbs in, tugging off her clothes. I feel the bandage on her hand. Her whole arm smells of disinfectant cream.

We lie like that, curled up in each other like brother foxes, her arms wrapped protectively around my chest.

'You were so brave,' she whispers, just as I'm about to drift off.

'So were you,' I respond.

'No, I wasn't.' She sighs, her breath blowing my hair. 'I never am.'

We sleep.

Dreams wake me every few hours. Dreams about water, and oceans, and Emma Casey. Dreams about being in a rowing boat and my arms not being strong enough to lift the oars. Dreams about falling under the waves and emerging in different places, choked for air. The Fiddler. The schoolhouse. My mum's bedroom. The Fiddler. The button factory. My mum's bedroom. It's the kind of sleep that never settles or deepens, like lying in a rock pool with the tip of your nose breaking the surface.

Maria didn't pull the blinds down the whole way when we went to bed, and I'm grateful for it. I keep my eyes on the three inches of exposed world, waiting for the sliver of pale blue light to touch the room. When it finally comes, escorted by cooing of wood pigeons, I get out of bed and pull my clothes back on.

While the kettle boils, I step out into Maria's little garden. From her front step, I can see the spot where I first kissed her. How long ago was it? Two days? Three? How can it feel like years in the distance? How can you fall in love with someone and also have them betray you in such a minuscule amount of time?

I roll my big toe on the wet grass. I have to go today. Every time I think about staying I feel the sea in my ears again. I have to get Laura, and we have to go. If Dónal is willing to half-drown me to teach me a lesson, then what is he going to do to her, the person who *really* pissed him off? The Foleys have the whole town in their pocket, after all. Between them and Enda, there's no limit to what they could do to us and get away with.

I hear footsteps on the flagstones in the kitchen, then the sound of clinking mugs.

'Morning,' I say as she steps outside.

'Morning.'

'How's your hand?'

'It's fine,' she says, handing me my mug. 'I woke up to a few texts from Don.'

I don't respond, but take a long sip of the too-hot tea.

'He says that his dad really laid into him yesterday. Daddy Foley thinks the fire was all Don's fault. I think we met him fresh from a fist fight with his older brothers.'

I turn around to look at her face.

'And what does that have to do with me?'

'He was drunk, too,' she continues. 'I don't know if you could tell, but he was. I think he'd had, like, eight pints in The Fiddler beforehand.'

'Uh-huh.'

I know what Maria is doing. She is telling me this because she wants me to forget about last night. About the threats, about the shouting, about my feet being held as I was turned upside down into the water. She wants to have her cake and eat it; to keep Clipim on side and have some kind of relationship with me at the same time. What does she even *think* that relationship would consist of?

'I'm leaving today,' I say. 'Thanks for letting me stay last night, but I have to get Laura and get going.'

'Get going *where*? It's not even six a.m. The nursing home won't be open. The ferry doesn't start till ten.'

'I can't stay here, Maria.'

'I know you can't stay here . . . '

'No, I can't stay *here*. With you. In your house. Not if you're going to convince me that Dónal is actually a really nice guy, not if you're going to report everything I say to people who want me dead.'

'No one wants you dead. They were just having fun with you.'

'Maria,' I snap, my neutral tone dissolved, 'they tried to drown me last night.'

'They weren't trying to drown you, for God's sake. They were just trying to frighten you. I'm not saying that's okay, it's completely fucked up, and I'm going to chew him out for it, Charlie. But I just want you to understand that there's a context for everything.'

'Is that what you were doing when you told Dónal that you thought there was something wrong with me?'

'No!'

'Which, by the way, there is. I'm an amateur pornographer who hates her mother and ran away from her dad's hospital bed to be here. There's no one in the world whose motives you should be more suspicious of.'

'Can't you understand, though, that not everything's about *you*? What *you* want to find out, what *you* need to know? Like, ultimately, none of this is your business, Charlie.'

'These kids died, Maria. And there's good reason to think they were murdered.'

'Do you actually care, though?' she snaps. 'Beyond . . . beyond it being some loose end you need to tie up between you and your dad? This story is part of your past, but for some people, people like Mary . . . it's their present. They have to live with this every day.'

I'm dumbstruck by this. That, after all this, Maria could think that I could be so flippant. I push past her and head back into the house to grab my rucksack. When I come back into the kitchen, she's sitting at the table, smoking in her dressing gown.

'Don't leave,' she says shortly. 'I don't want the last time I see you to be ... to be this.'

'And I can't stay here and have you pretend that all this is nothing. That these threats, that Dónal last night ... that all of it is some harmless joke and that I'm perfectly safe. How can you not get that?'

'I do get that,' she says, baring her teeth. 'But maybe if you got the absolute *shit* beaten out of you every day you would understand that getting your face wet isn't the end of the world.'

Silence. Maria stares at me. I stare back. In the short time we have known one another we have shared virtually nothing about our real lives, our real histories. I knew she had a break-up in Dublin and that, in a previous life, she was a hairdresser. I knew she had no intention of going back to America, and that's all I knew.

'Your ... parents?'

'My husband.'

My jaw drops. 'Husband? Present tense?'

'I mean, we haven't spoken for two years.' She shrugs. 'I don't know if you could call that a husband. Technically, I guess I deserted him.'

'Fuck. I'm sorry.'

And I am. I'm astounded anyone could bring themselves to hit Maria, while at the same time being strangely unsurprised by it. Of course that was where she was coming from. Of course she loved quickly, intensely, and only people who are destined to leave. Of course she keeps a low profile on a tiny island, pulling pints and dyeing her hair. Partying all summer,

reading all winter. I try to remember every detail of our first
real conversation in The Fiddler.

*I mean, this person, they really chewed me out. I was a wreck.*

'When I met you, you said you got your heart broken
in Dublin.'

'My heart,' she replies, looking into her cup. 'And my
collarbone.'

'I'm sorry.'

'It's fine.'

'No, really.'

'I know.'

'And you came . . . here?'

'It was supposed to be our honeymoon. That was our big
European trip. That was actually true: we got married and
spent eighteen months saving for our honeymoon, which is
exactly the length of time it took me to realise I was married
to a fucking asshole.'

'Why didn't you leave him in the US?'

'Because I knew he would find me,' she says, finally meeting my eye. 'I knew my mom would be useless. There was
no place to go. He knew the salon I worked at. He had all
our money. It was all fucked.'

'So you waited until Europe.'

'I just knew it would be easier to get lost. To start again. So
I did it. I ran, and I ran, and I ended up here. It was the only
place in Ireland I knew about, because of hearing about my
great-aunt. I thought, like you probably thought, that there
might be family here.'

Silence. I don't know whether I should go and wrap my
arms around her or stay exactly where I am. I wonder how
many people have heard this. Whether I'm the first of her
holiday romances to get the unedited version of Maria's story.

'And y'know what, Charlie? People were really fucking
nice to me when I got here.'

'I'm not saying they weren't.'

'Not just nice, either. People are smart. And funny. And *fun*. Me and Tony are in a poetry club together. We all get together and do readings of Irish poets in the Spailpín. Did you know that?'

'No,' I say. 'But I don't see what that has to do with ...'

'I've been down this road. Not the exact same one. But trying to pry information out of people who don't want to give it is a dangerous game in this part of the world. But I let it go. I stayed. Dónal's dad sponsored my visa, along with Tom who owns The Fiddler. And for the first time—' Her voice cracks at this, and hot, angry tears start spilling out of her. 'For the first time in my entire fucking life, I felt safe.'

'I'm sorry,' I say again, although I'm not sure quite why. Am I sorry for thinking the truth is important? Or am I sorry because, despite everything she's telling me about the grace and the compassion of Clipim, I still want to run for the hills?

I wrap my arms around her shoulders and nuzzle my face into her black bottle-dyed hair. A few more croaking sobs come out of her, but eventually she goes quiet. We stay like that for a long time. Swaying in her kitchen, two broken girls.

Finally, I break away and reach for my bag. I take out the calendar I bought in the Button Museum yesterday, presenting it to her with an embarrassed flourish.

'I thought you might be interested in March,' I say simply. She flicks to it, the glossed paper squeaking between her fingers. When she gets to March, her hand flies to her mouth.

'It really is a shitty museum,' I say half-heartedly, 'if no one buys anything in that fucking gift shop.'

Nuala O'Shaughnessy's photo might have been removed from the display, but not from the archives of whatever printing company mocks up the exact same calendar for the museum every year. Maria stares at the photograph for a long time.

'Thank you,' she says finally. 'I'm going to send this to my mom. She's going to be really happy.'

She twists her lip with her fingers, as if afraid to smile.

'I can't believe I'm one of those people,' she says at last.

'What people?'

'People who get all emotional about finding their ancestry in Ireland. It's so ... I don't know. It's so done. It's just ... people like me don't usually ... we don't *get* things like this. I spent the first four years of my life in a trailer, Charlie. I've never lived anywhere long enough to have roots.'

'Roots are ... overrated,' I respond eventually.

She laughs softly and closes the calendar. 'I really like you, you know. I've really liked ... this thing we have. I hope you do, too.'

'Maria, this is the most I've *liked* someone since I was nineteen. "Like" isn't a good enough word.'

She smiles at me wanly and strokes my hand with her thumb. 'Would you say you're fond of me, then?'

'I would. Very fond.'

'I would, too. And maybe I'll visit you in London some time. If you'll have me.'

'I will. Always. And don't ... don't feel like you're stuck here, Maria. Get out when you need to.'

As I kiss her goodbye on her front step, I'm afraid for her. Afraid of what she'll do to stay here, of what she'll ignore to keep her life simple. There're a lot of things that can happen to someone this beautiful and this frightened.

'Please,' I say, my lips on her forehead, 'tell me where to find you if you lose your way.'

## 33

There is a T'ai Chi class happening in the day room of the retirement home. According to the bulletin board in the corridor, it is a 'sunrise stretch', but it is – very clearly – T'ai Chi. It's strange to see the place so robustly busy so early in the morning. Maybe old people are just livelier at this time of day.

'How'ya, Charlie,' I hear a voice say. 'Jesus, you look like a turnip with the top cut off.'

I turn around to see Joe in front of me, all smiles. I scan his face quickly, the way I do with everyone I meet on the island now. But there's nothing in Joe's grey shining eyes or matted hair but friendliness. He does run the ferry, after all. By necessity, he spends most of his time with his dog on the mainland. He might not even know the town consensus on me and Laura.

'Joe!' I can't stop myself from hugging him. His whole body stiffens, entirely unused to this level of affection from tourists. 'What are you even doing here?'

'Dad's here for the exercise class,' he says, gesturing to the back row. Sure enough, Grandferryman Tony is trying to maintain serenity while looking thoroughly embarrassed at Joe's pointing to him. 'They open up their classes to the whole community, free of charge.'

'That's nice of them.'

Joe shrugs. 'I suppose. Most people end up in here anyway.

The very old people here don't tend to have much family around. For ... well, obvious reasons, I'm sure you'll agree.' He finishes with a grimace, and then looks around the room. 'They get their money in the end, anyway.'

I nod, and we watch the class in silence, twenty people gliding their fingers through the air in perfect unison. No wonder the medical service in the nursing home is so good. *Most people end up here anyway.* What must it be like, hurtling towards very old age with no children, grandchildren, nieces or nephews to take care of you? To mourn the children as they died, but then to mourn them again because the adults they were supposed to become never materialised. The adults who were supposed to look after you, so you didn't end up in places like this.

'I have to go see Laura,' I say quietly. 'But we're leaving today. Are you going to be on the ferry later?'

'Sure am. Ten twenty is the first one, then every forty minutes after that.'

'Cool. I'll see you then.'

I wave to Tony, who is in the process of a very slow wave himself.

When I get to Laura's room, the door is already ajar. I rap my fingers lightly to make sure she isn't with a nurse or something, but when the door opens, there's no one there.

Laura is gone.

Her things have disappeared, and her bed is stripped bare. There is no trace of Laura ever having been in this room.

I flag down a nurse in the corridor.

'Excuse me,' I say, trying to keep the note of panic out of my voice. 'Laura Shingle's room is empty.'

'Who?'

'Laura Shingle. The girl. The only young person in this place.'

'And who are you?'

'Charlie. Charlotte Regan.'

'Are you next of kin?'

'I'm sorry?'

'Are you next of kin?'

'No. But I've been with her this whole time.'

'Were you with her when she was signed in?'

'What?'

'Were you here with her when she was signed in?'

The nurse's face is completely placid, patient to the point of ignorance.

'No, but I've been visiting her,' I respond, and she continues to look at me blankly.

'Have you changed her to a different room? Is that where she is?'

She says nothing, merely peers at me in my dirty clothes that smell of sea water and cigarettes. I start walking up the corridor, pushing at the ajar doors of the patient rooms, looking for Laura.

'Excuse me,' she says, her voice getting louder as she follows me. 'EXCUSE ME. Madam, MADAM!'

Her voice drifts away as I open the doors to more and more rooms, most of which are empty. The ones that aren't have sleeping people in them, none of whom move when I come in.

'MISS!' the nurse says, putting herself between me and the next door. 'Can you please stop? Our residents are very fragile and can't be disturbed. Many are managing very sensitive heart issues and *don't* appreciate shock.'

'Where is Laura?' I say. '*Where*?'

'I'm afraid if you're not next of kin, we're not allowed to—'

'Why? You're not even a *real* fucking hospital!'

There are two more nurses now, plus the receptionist from the first day. 'What's the problem here?' and 'you're going to have to calm down' echo around me.

'What have you done to her?' I plead, tears in my eyes. Did Dónal check her out, masquerading as her brother? Did Benjamin have some kind of authority over the retirement home? I remember Dr Healy, the GP from the first night, who assured me Laura would be fine here. He was old Clipim. Born here. Who knows how many people have showed up, asking questions, before me?

'I'm afraid I can't tell you anything, unless you're ...'

If someone says next of kin again, I'm going to scream.

'... next of kin.'

It must have been so easy for Emma Casey. Stuff up a few air vents, kick a pipe loose on an oil burner. Wait. Watch everything around you dissolve into a woozy calm, a warm layer of sleep thickening over the small bodies around you. For what? Revenge? Insanity? Or just an everyday idiotic mistake?

It would be so easy to kill Laura. Especially in a place like this. Anyone can just walk in and out under the guise of attending an exercise class or visiting an elderly relative. Anyone could have yanked out her oxygen mask. Filled the oxygen tank with something that would kill her. Hell, put a pillow over her face. If she died from asphyxiation in her sleep they could write it off as a symptom of her asthma. Her asthma makes her the most highly killable person in this place. All of it would be so easy to explain. Much easier, in fact, than the death of eighteen children.

'Miss, if you don't calm down, we're going to have to escort you out.'

How am I going to explain that? To Chris and Anne Shingle? To Mike? To everyone who was counting on Laura to be the great, white-blonde hope of our graduating class?

I close my eyes and press my forehead to the wall, trying to think without the bulging eyes of the nurses inspecting me. *Keep yourself together, Charlie. Whatever they've done to her, you'll need to calm down to find out.*

'Charlie.' I feel a light tap on my shoulder, and think, for a moment, that it might be her.

'Charlie, it's me, Dr Richards. We met yesterday?'

I turn to her, blearily remembering who she is.

'Charlie, if you'll just come through to my office, I can explain to you what happened.'

*What* happened *to Laura, or what you* did *to her?*

'No,' I respond, my hands shaking. After last night with Dónal and Aidan, I have no intention of being in a confined space with anyone on this island again. 'No, tell me here.'

'I don't want to discuss this in the open,' Dr Richards says crisply, nodding her head to the T'ai Chi class that is still going on – with some distraction – five feet away. 'It's private patient business.'

'Just tell me. Tell me what happened. Tell me what you're hiding.'

Dr Richards lowers her voice. 'Look,' she says, clearly irritated now, 'Laura's X-ray showed a few shadows on her lungs, and I decided it would be best if she were to be transferred to the University Hospital in Tralee for a CT scan. Now, it's very probably nothing, but sometimes shadows can indicate pneumonia or even tuberculosis. And if it's either of those things, Laura is a risk to our other patients. So, you see why we needed to transfer her quickly.'

I can't seem to keep hold of the information she's telling me. I catch words, but they slip out of my brain, like coins into a fountain. I know these words, of course. I know them from years of taking diligent notes at the hospital while my mother twisted a plastic bag full of almonds in her fingers.

'It's nothing to worry about,' she follows up quickly. 'But we'd hate for it to turn out to be something more serious. We transferred her yesterday evening with the permission of her parents.'

'I don't believe you. They would have called me. She would have called me.'

I remember then that I don't have a phone, that it fell into the water last night, but it doesn't do anything to soothe my panic.

'If you come into my office, you can call the hospital. I can put you on the phone and they can confirm what I'm saying is true.'

'No, I'm not going into your fucking office.'

I have been taken into small rooms before. Small rooms where doctors push pamphlets on you that are heavy on phrases like 'manage' and 'care'. I cannot start another cycle of small rooms. Not here. Not with Laura.

A few of the women in the reception booth are disturbed enough by my presence that they have ushered in the largest porter they can find, whispering in cat-like hisses what the problem is. They're pointing at me, practically pushing him towards me. He's about twenty, huge, and holding a step-ladder. He's probably related to the boys who smashed our cameras, probably friends with Dónal and Aidan. Probably does odd jobs for Benjamin Barry.

'I'm going to have to ask you to either come with me or leave entirely,' Dr Richards says sternly. 'You're not next of kin, and so I've told you more than I'm supposed to already. I'm not actually legally required to tell you anything.'

The stepladder boy looks lost, unsure what he's supposed to stop, or start.

'Stephen, could you come here please?' snaps Dr Richards, showing the whites of her eyes now. 'Could you show this woman out?'

*This woman.* I was the prodigal daughter, a few days ago.

'Why? Why are you trying to make me leave?'

'Stephen,' she says again. The T'ai Chi class isn't even pretending to go on now. Everyone is peering at me. A thousand old eyes, curious yet enthralled by this filthy girl with the English accent, screaming at their staff.

Stepladder Stephen comes towards me and places his hand on my back, the weight of it attempting to steer me towards the door.

'Don't fucking *touch* me!' I say, pushing him back. Suddenly I'm reminded of the night I met Laura. The man who picked me up and wouldn't put me down. The way Laura lunged at him, biting at his face like a rat. I imagine her being held down, her teeth snapping, her eyes widening.

'You're going to fucking kill me, aren't you?'

Joe is walking towards me, his bearded face dark with disapproval. What's he going to do to me? What can he think of that hasn't been done to me already?

'Charlie,' he says, through gritted teeth. He puts his hand on the top of my spine. 'Charlie, I don't know what you think you're doing, but—'

'You're going to fucking kill me,' I screech. 'You're going to fucking kill me like you killed those kids.'

It's the first thing I've said that has shut everyone up: Joe, Dr Richards, the panicked nurses. Stepladder Stephen is looking around him in shock, utterly unused to scenes. I've said the thing you don't say. The thing you must never say. It feels so good that I say it again. And again.

Those kids. Those kids. Like you killed those kids.

By the time I've said it the third time, Joe has grabbed me by the shoulder and is dragging me out of the nursing home. As I'm being propelled out, a round man in a blue tracksuit comes up to me. He looks like a retired Santa Claus: ruddy and well-fed, someone predisposed to smiling. He's not smiling now, though, but gazing with repulsion.

'*Our* kids,' he says.

Our eyes meet. They are the same glassy blue as Enda's, a cerulean that seems to come to the eyes of everyone over eighty. Babies are all born with blue eyes, apparently. Maybe everyone goes back to that, eventually. Ashes to ashes, blues to blues.

He repeats himself, tears filling his eyes.

'*Our* kids.'

And for a moment, I wonder if he's related to Connor Cronin, the pudgy boy, who made for a pudgy corpse.

## 34

'I'm going to make a deal with you, Charlie.'

I am sitting in the passenger seat of Joe's car. Satan is here, rootling around in the footwell and trying to jump into my lap. Joe waits for me to stop crying before he speaks.

'I'm going to make a deal. You're going to take my phone, and you're going to call Laura. Then, you're going to get on the ferry, and I'm going to drive you to the hospital in Tralee.'

I don't say anything, my mind still ricocheting between utter shame at having caused a scene and the certainty that something has been done to Laura that I can't control.

'No,' I mumble. 'No, I won't let you.'

'Why not?'

'Because I don't trust *any* of you. I've spent the last few days being ... being ...'

But my words are lost again. I can't even speak about my head in the water without my tongue freezing on me. There's no way of explaining it that will convey the blindness of your face going under, the horror of your nose filling up. As for Benjamin and Enda, it's starting to feel like a dream. Did he really steal photos of me? What was he going to *do* with them? I keep trying to tell Joe why I can't possibly trust him, but every attempt begets fresh tears, my arms quivering with adrenalin.

I don't know how long we sit in his car for, parked in the

nursing-home driveway. Satan eventually curls up on the backseat and goes to sleep. Me crying, Joe gazing at his lap and occasionally casting worried eyes over me.

'You won't go with me,' he says softly.

I shake my head.

'But you can't stay here.'

'I can . . .'

'It's not a question, Charlie. You can't stay here. Not if you're so determined to whip up a lynch mob for yourself. Jesus Christ, if I didn't know your da, I would be throwing stones at you myself. The things you said in there, Christ . . .'

'You know my dad?'

'A little. I remember him, like. He didn't have any friends his own age, as you probably know. He was just this lonely old soul, hanging round by himself, the worst kind of celebrity. It was better in the summer. Boarding-school kids would come home; there was more of a sense of youth about the place. A liveliness. You'd almost think . . .'

He gazes out of the windshield and rubs his beard with the knuckles of his hand.

'You'd almost think nothing ever happened. When I was about . . . seven, I'd say, Colm came to my da and asked him for a job selling tickets for the ferry. And of course Da says: Why would I need anyone selling tickets? He drove the boat and Mam took the tickets. They didn't need anyone else. And your da said . . .'

Joe spreads his fingers over the wheel, his nails remarkably short and well cared for.

'Your da said,' Joe rushes, trying to suppress a lump in his throat. 'Your da says that he wouldn't have to pay him. He just wanted to sit in the ticket booth on the harbour all day, so he wouldn't have to be on Clip.'

'But why . . . ?'

'And my father, you know, he has a soft heart. He felt for

him. So he came home that night and said to Mam, would we think about it. That maybe she could go down to three days a week, so we could let Colm do it. He was a good lad, Colm. Trustworthy and well-built, you know, and could come in handy with deliveries and repairs and all that. He made his case. Anyway, Mam said no.'

'Why?'

'She said that ... she said over her dead body would we give Colm Regan a job.'

My fingers dig into my palms as I try to steady myself.

'I never knew that. I mean ... I always sort of suspected that maybe things were ...'

'The kids who lived, Charlie,' he cuts across me, 'the kids who survived, who were away at boarding school, or, like me, were too young to have gone to the school ... they were the most loved children in the world. We had the best of everything. The girls were having their hair brushed by their mothers well into their teens. Mine gave me the biggest cuts of roast beef on a Sunday, even better than Dad's. But Colm ... you'd rather have died yourself than have been Colm. It was like he was death himself.

'The reason I remember it is because it's the only fight I remember my mother and father having in front of me,' he murmurs. 'And it's also when I first knew that something was wrong with the whole story.'

I look at Joe, my mouth open in shock.

'Charlie ...' he says slowly. 'As soon as you set foot on the ferry, I'll tell you everything you need to know.'

## 35

The thing about ferries is that they move so slowly that some-times it feels like you aren't moving at all.

But we are, definitely, moving.

I called Laura off Joe's phone, her thin, cracked voice full of laughter when she realised how worried I was. Relief floods through me at the same time as acute mortification. What did I *say* to those people?

We got the car from the caravan park, fear clinging to me despite Joe's presence. Benjamin was as ever-present as always. He was placid and friendly in Joe's company, but didn't break eye contact with me once. I'm trying not to let it bother me. If he's going to leak the photos, he's going to leak the photos. It could ruin me, but I'm beginning to wonder what's left of me to ruin.

I gave him the keys. His hands were red, chapped and clammily warm.

'Don't be a stranger, Charlie,' he smiles. 'Don't get lost in the woods.'

I sit in the car while Joe drives the boat and think about my father. *The worst kind of celebrity.* Being a parent is a form of celebrity in itself, I suppose. You love them like you love a boyband, which is just a quest for love in return. For years, I've wondered about my dad's comings and goings, his patchy and hidden inner heart. The way he talks constantly about

Clipim, and at the same time, never says anything about it at all. All I have ever had is one version of events, playing on repeat like a folk song, immovable in its consistency. *I survived; I left; I had you. Genesis, Exodus, Leviticus.*

Part of me thought that if I could be the courtroom stenographer of his life, the head of his fan club, the expert on everything that's ever happened to him, then I could somehow dissipate the thick fog at the centre of our house. That giving our lives some artistic merit would turn our family from a pathetic one into something of value, or at the very least, something of interest.

I get out of the car, zipping my coat up to my face. There's a strong wind coming off the grey sea, whipping my hair all over my face. Keeping one hand on the prow to steady myself, I stagger towards Joe at the front of the boat. I try not to look in the smooth grey water. Satan is patrolling the area, his sea legs firmly in place.

'What do you call this bit of the boat?' I ask, attempting to make conversation. Shy, suddenly. Knowing that he's going to tell me something and that knowing will end a chapter and begin one at the same time.

'A cockpit.'

'I thought that was just for planes?'

'No,' he says shortly. 'It's a cockpit. It's the same.'

We're silent for a few minutes until eventually the chugging, whirring sound of the boat stops, and we're at the harbour on the other side. It's alarming to me how short the journey was.

'Now,' he says, 'you're going to sit down, and you're going to listen to me until I'm done.'

'Yes.'

'You're not going to interrupt, and you're not going to ask questions. At least not until I'm finished. Understood?'

'Yes.'

Joe produces a folded beach chair and instructs me to sit down on it, and plugs in a travel kettle. He hands me a steaming mug of black tea with the bag still in.

'I'm not stupid. I know that, once I tell you this, there's nothing I can do. But I'm trusting you, Charlie. I'm trusting you the same way you trusted me when you got on this boat.'

I nod, my fingers firmly clamped around my mug.

'Do you know what an industrial school is?'

I shake my head. I am trying to keep my promise to stay quiet.

'An industrial school is a place where, for a long time, the Irish government put children. Children that no one wanted. Or children they couldn't care for. Which ... Ireland had a lot of them, Charlie. A lot of them. And one of these schools was a little place near Kenmare called Glenderrig.'

I bite my lip, choking on the familiarity of the word. Glenderrig.

Joe talks, and as I listen my mug gradually grows colder.

Glenderrig was an industrial school for girls, a sort of reformatory run by nuns. It had a Magdalene Home next door, run by the same congregation. The approach was this: girls were admitted to Glenderrig if they were orphaned, too poor, deemed to be living in unsafe conditions or somehow at risk. When new girls were admitted to Glenderrig, the attending priest and jury of nuns would decide whether or not the girl was 'beyond saving' – Joe's choice of words – and if she was, beyond saving, that is, she was siphoned off to the Magdalene Home. Being 'beyond saving' could mean anything. It could mean being pregnant; it could mean you were once raped; it could mean that you walked with a sense that you knew your own body.

If you qualified for the reformatory school, your life was hard, but it was saveable. You learned some basic skills, some sewing, maybe even got to work outside growing food. You

learned to read if you didn't know already. Girls who grad-
uated were often offered the chance of emigration, and a lot
of them took it. Australia, mostly. Yes, you were subject to
beatings from the nuns. Yes, you could find yourself sum-
moned to the Mother Superior, who would cut your long hair
off with kitchen scissors. A priest could touch himself while
you whispered confession to him, shuddering with spite as he
came and called you a sinner. But there was an exit strategy.
A purpose.

That's *if* you got into the reformatory.

The other girls ran the laundry. Half-starved and almost
bald. Covered in lice. Tuberculosis outbreaks were frequent,
and deadly. They took in laundry for local hotels and boarding houses, their only contact with the outside world the boy
who delivered it in a van every Wednesday. If they spoke to
him, they were whipped. If they pleaded to get a message to
their lost children, they were put in isolation for weeks at a
time. Their life was penance, and it was profitable. It made
money. That's important. These places were set up to save
women from prostitution, Joe says. To save 'fallen women'.
But the more profitable they became, the broader the definition of 'fallen' became. Any woman could be fallen, if a
powerful man described her as such.

But then, something happened.

Washing machines.

I choke on my tea at this. '*Washing* machines?' I splutter.

'Washing machines,' he confirms. 'Shut up and let me finish.'

Thousands of rural homes still didn't have electricity, but
enough hotels were fitting industrial washing machines that
the Magdalene Home's business suffered hugely. They tried
to make up for the profit loss elsewhere by taking on sewing
work, but while most of the women were pretty competent,
there wasn't the same level of demand. Eventually, some of
the Magdalene Homes had to close down.

But Glenderrig still had a reformatory school to run. It couldn't afford to lose the laundry, at least not if it wanted to remain a respected and useful institution.

It was a problem.

A problem that was solved by the intervention of Stanworth & Sons. The factory, which was a small, English-run business on a tiny island off the west coast of Kerry, had been limping along for years, employing local women to produce extraordinarily ornate button coverings that were sold to English dressmakers at a huge mark-up. But the margins were small, and they too were on the verge of having to close.

'I don't know how it happened, exactly,' says Joe, raking his hand through his wild hair, 'but somehow these two struggling enterprises ended up finding each other.'

Glenderrig agreed to loan their workforce out to Stanworth & Sons, on the proviso that the women would be highly supervised, live in monitored housing, and that their contact with the rest of the islanders was kept limited.

This went on for a couple of years, and despite the strict conditions, on the whole the women tended to fare better. Less of them were dying, in any case. They lived together in a boarding house, overseen by a couple of elderly nuns who had a distantly benevolent relationship with their charges. They attended mass along with everyone else. A woman from the community came in to cook their evening meal. Some of the women kept window gardens, and a few managed to send letters to their children. There were luxuries. At least, luxuries compared to what they were used to.

There wasn't a lot of hope, or happiness, but neither was there outright cruelty. There was peace, at least in an outward sense. The mistake, Joe thinks, happened when people mistook the peacefulness of the Glenderrig women for contentment.

Then, something changed. The old school teacher decided

to emigrate with her husband, leaving a vacancy that no one seemed to want to fill. The woman who cooked the evening meal for the Glenderrig women eventually suggested that one of the Button women – Emma, her name was – would be a perfect candidate for the role.

I was still honouring my promise not to speak, but at this point, I allowed myself a sharp intake of breath. Joe puts his finger up. 'No,' he says firmly.

Kitty was a widow, and not from the island, so was inclined to sympathy towards the women who were also outsiders. Working at the boarding house was a good job for her, the steadiest income she'd had in years, and she was drawn towards Emma's soft-spoken intelligence as well as the fact that both women were originally from Kenmare.

Kitty pleaded Emma's case to the parish, playing up the most sympathetic elements of her story. Emma had been training to be a teacher before she was raped by her uncle, gave birth to a child that was wrenched away from her, then stuck in a home to rot. She wasn't a hard person to feel sorry for. Her plain, white, quiet face in a perpetual pose of marbled modesty, her eyes downcast. There was nothing sensuous to her at all, that was clear. She was just a woman who had been very, very unlucky.

Emma became the teacher. And for almost two years, everything went well.

Until one day in November 1963, Emma, after a week off with a chest infection, came to work for the last time.

## 36

*They should have died in Glenderrig.*

My mistake was to assume that Mary was talking about the children. She had been talking about the women. The button women. Maria's aunt, who disappeared from Clipim and was reported to have died years later in a convent.

The dog begins to cry softly, not for any great physical distress, but for the pure psychic weight of the conversation. Satan can feel the mood in the cockpit, and he doesn't like it.

'So you think it was revenge?'

'Revenge,' he considers, sipping from his mug. 'Or sheer madness. Or both. This was a woman who was abused from the day she was born. Never given an ounce of authority, not the smallest degree of control of her own destiny. Raped by her uncle. Beaten by the nuns. Sold into slavery, which is the only thing you can call it. Indentured slavery. Right here in the Ring of Kerry.'

'You sound like you're on her side.'

'I'm not on anyone's side. It was a terrible, horrible thing that she did. Unforgivable, by God or by anyone else. But I also understand how Emma felt that she was deserted by God. I understand that she was smart enough to understand her situation, and sick enough to abuse it. I think a part of her thought she was . . . I don't know. Saving them. From life. From the life she had to lead.'

'*Saving* them?'

'Well, no. That doesn't hold up, does it?' he reasons, scratching Satan's ear. 'Because if she thought she was saving them, she wouldn't have spared your dad, would she?'

'You really think she saved him? Out of respect for my grandmother?'

'That's what I think. That's certainly what your grandmother thought.'

'She did?'

'There wasn't much of a life for your grandmother after that. It's a wonder she didn't leave the island when your father did. But she sort of believed that she had to live out some kind of penance, you see. She did everything for people. Picked flowers, mended clothes, minded your children if you had to pop out. Eventually ... people forgave her, I think. For being spared. It was like hers was the only door painted with lamb's blood, and it takes a long, long time to forgive that.'

I nod.

'But, Joe ... you can't be the only *one* who saw through the story. We can't be the only two people in almost *sixty years* ...'

He sighs. 'I don't know,' he says grimly. 'You have to understand, Charlie. We're very good at picking up pitchforks when it's English landowners and all that, but when it comes to the Church ... if they said something, people just ... accepted it.'

'So they just ... accepted what the Church said? With no further questioning?'

'People were in mourning. They were grieving, lighting candles, giving masses. The place they were relying on for comfort was the same place that was pulling the wool over their eyes. Hard to question the Church when you've got the Infant of Prague on your mantelpiece. In their grief, the explanation of a faulty burner ... it was enough, I suppose.'

He sighs again and rubs a hand over the dog's skull.

'And it's not unlikely that the Church were ... going to extremes to keep people quiet. Which worked.'

'But ... not you. Or Mary.'

'Me? I'm quiet as a mouse. This is the first time I've ever talked to another person about it. And Mary drinks.'

He stares out of the window of the cabin.

'I'm an awful coward, really.'

The motor on the boat hums, the water sloshing beneath us.

'I had to figure all of this out myself,' he says after a moment. 'I don't think most people even knew where the Glenderrig women were from, or that they weren't receiving any wages for being there. They preferred to be in the dark. They took the explanations given to them.'

'And the families? What happened to them?'

'Oh, Stanworth paid up to all the bereaved families. They filtered it through the Church, of course, through a charitable donation.'

'But surely at least a few people ... '

'Charlie, you have to understand,' he says, massaging his scalp, 'this has taken me years to put together. Trips to Glenderrig, and all the rest of it. All Glenderrig will tell me is that at the end of the fifties, they absorbed their Magdalene Home into the reformatory school. They won't even admit to loaning out women to Stanworth. I've even spoken to organisations that work with victims of these horrible homes. They were disappeared, after the accident brought so much publicity to the island. Sent abroad, probably. Never heard from again. Any of them.'

I remember Maria's great-aunt Nuala, who died in a convent.

'But ... why, Joe? Why did you care so much, when no one else seems to?'

'It's not that they don't care, Charlie. Their lives were

destroyed that day. No one forgave. No one forgot. Even people who were able to swallow the parish line on the whole thing knew deep down that something was wrong. I'm sure of it. But kick enough dirt over something and eventually, it gets buried. And it stays buried.'

'So you do all this work, and ... for what, Joe? So you can tell me?'

Satan groans again, rubbing his ear against his master's leg.

'I thought ... I don't know. I thought that maybe I could make it right. Involve the press. Shame the government. Something like that. There were all these abuse inquiries a few years ago, but nothing good ever comes of them, Charlie. They shove a camera in people's faces, splash a big story across *The Irish Times*, someone writes a book. There's a court case and any compensation these families might get is eaten up by the lawyers. It always comes down to the same thing: the government won't put legal pressure on the Church to release any of these records, and so all of it just remains hearsay. Everything I just told you, there's no actual written proof of it anywhere. There are no available records for any of this. You just have to take me at my word, the same way I had to take all of this at the word of the people I've talked to.'

And just like that, I'm all out of questions. The last few days, I have been so convinced that I was blazing a trail for truth and justice, when the whole time I was merely plodding in Joe's footprints.

'But as I say,' he reasons, 'I'm just a coward. Maybe I'm too close to this island to be the one who brings that level of misery to it. Maybe this stuff needs to go public; I'm just not the person to do it.'

He looks at me, like this is my cue to say something.

'Are you implying that I should be the person to do it?'

'Yes. No. I don't know. I'm almost sixty, sweetheart. If I

knew the right way to live a life, I wouldn't be driving my dad's boat with only a dog for company.

'But,' he adds, 'if you are going to go public, you have to know what it will do. The hate you'll get. You'll never be able to come back to Clipim, you know, prodigal daughter or not. The media will eat it up, and most of the people your age; but there are many that will be hurt by this. And now that you know them, you need to ask yourself whether you can do it.'

'Right,' I say slowly. 'And how much good it will even do.'

'Sure.' He shrugs. 'There's no bringing anyone back.'

'No.'


Joe says he will drive me to the hospital in Tralee, even though I say he doesn't have to.

'Yeah, fucking right I don't have to,' he chuckles. 'You can't drive and you can't just leave your rental here.'

'That's a good point. But how will you get back?'

'I know a guy in Tralee who will give me a lift. Don't you worry. We'll make it back.'

'Thanks, Joe.'

It's amazing to me how this man, this stranger, feels – in a strange way – like family. Like my imaginary siblings, Joe feels like a long-wished-for uncle that has finally materialised.

Satan waits for a break in the conversation before he leaps, all four legs in the air, off the ferry and on to dry land. Joe and I give him a round of polite applause.

'What about your da?' Joe asks, scooping the dog into his arms. 'Are you going to tell him?'

Satan takes a long farewell lick to my fingertips and I mull it over.

'I don't know.' I shrug. 'He's so sick, and . . . I don't know.'

I try again. 'What if he's known something was wrong

with this story for years, but needed to bury it to ... to survive the fact of it?'

'He wouldn't be alone,' Joe says quietly. 'He certainly
would *not* be alone.'

As he reverses the car off the ferry, I take a long look at
Clipim, and wonder whether I'll ever see it again, or whether
Maria will ever leave, and if I'll ever see her again when
she does. It's amazing how somewhere so tiny can come
to mean so much, to hold so many memories both painful
and euphoric.

'Last look?'

'Mm-hmm.'

'What do you think?'

'I knew something was going to be wrong about this place,'
I say, because it's true. 'Even before I suspected it, I knew.
My dad ... ' But then I stop again, because there's no point
talking about Dad now, what he told me or didn't tell me,
how he raised me or didn't raise me.

'But I didn't expect to love it like I do. Because I do still
love it, Joe. I love Ireland. I love Kerry. It's horrifying and
beautiful and so fucking sad. Everything I learn about being
here makes me question just ... who people are, and how
they can do these things to each other, and how they survive
them after they do. I hate it, but I love it.'

'Hey, congratulations Charlie,' he says, giving me a pained
smile. 'You just officially became Irish.'

I burst out laughing, and Satan gets on his feet. 'Fuck you,
I've always been Irish.'

'Fuck *you*, and get in the car.'

Satan jumps into the backseat, and Joe makes a big stink
about making sure he stays sitting on a blanket pulled from
the ferry. ('He'll only get hair everywhere, otherwise.') I call
my mother using Joe's phone, to tell her I'll be home sooner
than expected. I ask her how Dad's doing, and she says he

has pulled through. There is a 'this time' in the addendum, a 'this time' that goes unsaid and is communicated purely by tone. There will be no more weekends away, her voice seems to say, until there are.

As the car curves around the mountain and Clip finally disappears from view, I stretch my hand out of the car window again and tug at the chunks of yellow flowers growing by the roadside, bringing a petal to my face, inhaling the joyously improbable smell of coconut. Who could bring themselves to burn this?

'*Slán go fóill*,' I say.

Joe chimes in. '*Slán go fóill*.'

And I'm grateful, in that moment at least, that when Dad taught me how to say hello in Irish, he taught me how to say goodbye, too.

# LATER

The wake was well attended and catered for superbly, so people had high hopes for the funeral. No one was disappointed. Guests were invited to 'light refreshments' that were served at The Fiddler. Anyone who knew the dead personally wasn't expected to work so everything was prepared the night before. The bar was managed by two bewildered trainees who Maria had taken on in the beginning of February.

I helped with the sandwiches. Two hundred and twelve of them. We had a little supply line going. Steph did the butter and mayo; Maria did the filling; I cut them into triangles. Ebba, the Swedish girl who replaced Niamh in Maria's houseshare at the end of the previous summer, was in charge of cling film. Then we started on the sausage rolls, chicken skewers and vegetable samosas.

There was a late panic about whether The Fiddler had enough bottles of slimline tonic water, to which Joe gamely agreed to take the boat to the mainland to stock up. He returned just before 1 a.m., me and Maria on the verge of collapse at her kitchen table.

'Are ye ready for tomorrow?' he asked, surveying the apocalypse of food in front of us.

'Depends what you mean,' I said, not taking my eyes off my samosa folding. 'Do we have enough food? Yes. Am I ready? No.'

'She invited you, Charlie.'

'I know,' I said, standing up to massage the ache in the small of my back. 'I just don't fully understand why.'

I should have been worried about Dónal, about Aidan, about Benjamin Barry, but I'm ashamed to say that all I remember worrying about that day was the sleeping arrangements. Maria and I had tentatively texted, sure, but we hadn't actually seen each other since the morning I left her at her doorstep. She said I could 'crash' with her for the funeral, but what did that mean, exactly?

In the end, I didn't need to worry. I fell asleep on the couch while watching her ice a coffee cake.

I was jumpy all the next day. Terrified of someone swivelling a judgemental eye on me and asking why I had come back to Clipim, and why now, and whether I had done enough damage the first time around. But no one said anything to me on the day of Enda's funeral. Nobody saw me at all.

I remember noticing, as the coffin was carried in, how naturally the room segregated itself into waves of age and status. Clipim's oldest took up the top pews, having claimed their spots by waiting around after morning mass. Behind them, the older locals like Joe; next, the middle-aged farmers; then a scattering of the residents who had bought land in the nineties; and finally, the young. I kept my eye trained on the front row. It was bizarre that the people who had been hurt the most by God would still choose to sit closest to him. Eventually, I landed on Mary, her face still, her hands twisting.

*Why did she invite me?*

I spent most of that afternoon arranging trays in the kitchen of The Fiddler so that Maria would be free to grieve Enda accordingly. It was a relief to be hidden from view. I didn't know how to approach the death of a man who beat his own wife. But equally, I didn't know how to refuse an invitation.

So I glided as silently as possible from room to room, refreshing drinks and avoiding eye contact.

After a while, grief's natural tendency to one-up itself settled in like a game for long-distance drives. You knew him ten years? I knew him twenty. He was your godfather? He was my uncle. The Clipim kids, the ones who had been away at boarding school or were fractionally too young when the tragedy hit, all came home to roost that day. I couldn't stop looking at them. These people, my father's would-be contemporaries, lounged around with the confidence of celebrities who insist that they never forgot where they came from. Their kids were there, too. And grandkids. The Fiddler had a sign outside that said 'Closed, for Private Event', but the afternoon had none of the rigidity that privacy demands. It all felt very fluid. Girls played with their dolls under pub tables, and boys chased each other around with pool cues.

When the room had thinned out and the best of the food had been eaten, I tried to position myself so that Mary could talk to me. If she wanted. I wasn't vain enough to assume that she would. Her husband had, after all, just died. But there must have been a reason that she invited me back to Clipim: why she asked Maria for my address, why her short, shakily written note had said that she would be 'much obliged' if I came.

Maria found me with my arms in the sink, rinsing stale cream off a cake tray.

'Hey, grab your coat. We're going for a walk.'

'Now? What about everyone still here?'

'They're not going anywhere. Trust me, this will be a late one. I need to get some air while I can.'

The wind whipped at our hair as we trudged through the village and into the backroads that led to Benjamin Barry's caravan park.

'Don't worry,' she said, seeing my face. 'No way are we going there.'

She grabbed my hand and navigated us through woods, fields and bridleways until, eventually, I began to recognise the route.

'Oh, no, Maria. I don't want to deal with all that right now. Not today.'

'It's not what you think,' she responded, a rueful glint in her eye. 'It's something different. I swear.'

The building was gone, the nettles and bramble burned out and cleared away. The only thing that remained of my father's schoolhouse was the low stone wall that I had climbed over with Laura. The land where the school once stood had been smoothed over, a huge stone disc fixed in its place. On it, an inscription, written in both Irish and English.

'They spent months debating what to write on it,' Maria said. She hung back to let me explore the stone by myself, knowing that this was a finale of sorts for me.

'In the end, they opted for simplicity.'

TO THE CHILDREN OF CLIPIM WHO
PERISHED HERE IN NOVEMBER 1963:
YOU WILL BE REMEMBERED

In the end, I never spoke to Mary. I never really got the chance. As the widow of the dead, she had the pleasure of being fussed over from all sides. I noticed an attractive middle-aged man with an English accent who seemed very attentive to her. Later, I found out that this was the son of the sister who emigrated, brought up in London with a dim, mythical knowledge of his two older sisters who died in the schoolhouse. She went to live with him shortly after that. I'm told she had a very happy few years spoiling her grand-nephews and -nieces. We received Christmas cards for a few years until, eventually, we didn't. We took that as its own conclusion.

Tony went a few years after Enda. By that stage, Maria and I were living in Glasgow. I had got a job at a Scottish film production company and Maria started doing hair again.

'Glasgow?' Laura had asked us, over Skype. 'Why *Glasgow*?'

'Name a better place for a creative person who hates London and loves Ireland,' Maria answered.

'Fair enough.'

We reported back for Tony's funeral, and Joe spoke to us about selling the ferry business to a young couple who thought that owning a one-car ferry would be a cute idea. 'Let them think that,' he chuckled. 'Be my guest.'

Satan spent the wake under Tony's stool in The Fiddler, his head between his paws.

Gradually, the elderly residents of Clipim started to dwindle. Maria takes each passing like a shard of glass to the heart. That's the thing with her. She gets very committed to people. She's like a stray: you feed her once, and she follows you home. I tell her this a lot. 'I think that's a bit rich,' she says, 'considering *you* were the one who originally followed *me* home.'

Every funeral I tell her I'm too busy with work to go with her, and every funeral I end up going. It's easier now, going to Clipim as Maria's partner rather than as Colm Regan's daughter. I've established a context for myself. Maria flutters around and hugs people, and I do the trays. That's the good thing about funerals, I think. If you feel self-conscious, just pick up the nearest tray and start walking.

But no matter who the funeral belongs to, every trip ends in the same way. There comes a point when the sandwiches run low and the guests start to go home that Maria comes to find me in whatever socially inept corner I've chosen to hide myself, and asks me if I want to go for a walk.

The walk is always the same, and so is the conversation that follows it.

We talk about the women of Glenderrig. We wonder

where they are now, and whether any of them are alive. We try to estimate the kind of trauma they are living with, and then we give up when it becomes unbearable. We talk about my grandmother. We make plans to visit my mother. Maria will sometimes voice a wish to have known my father better, and I tell her that she knew him pretty well. I tell her that he was a hard man to know. We talk about Laura, and what she's up to these days in America, and how desperately jealous Maria was of her on the weekend we all met for the first time. Invariably, Maria will remind me about how we asked her if she knew the IRA.

And eventually, we talk about the stone. The stone, and what it stands for, and what, precisely, was meant by those four carefully chosen words: *You will be remembered.*

Not: *we remember you.* Not: *you are missed.* We ponder 'You will be remembered' and its undeniable future tense.

It is an instruction, and we take it seriously.

When the time is right. When it's no longer possible to further hurt the people whose lives were defined by the murder this country was complicit in. When this wave of funeral-attending settles into its inevitable quiet.

Then. *Then.*

We know it's coming. We know this can't stay a secret for ever. We know what might happen after the truth gets out, and we wonder whether we'll be welcome here afterwards. Sometimes she tries to make a case for not doing it, but she loses her faith in her own argument before she's had a chance to complete it.

And then, before fear and the future can snatch her away from me, I wrap my arms around her. I tell her that I love her. I tell her that she's the only person I ever want to love.

And eventually, when there's nothing left to talk about, we begin the long journey home.

# ACKNOWLEDGEMENTS

This book is about a woman who makes bad art because no one has the heart to tell her otherwise. My first duty is to all the people who had the heart to tell me when and where this book was bad. Thank you to my editor Sarah Savitt, my agent Bryony Woods and my eternally patient first reader, Ella Risbridger. If anything here is good, it is because you three muscled it out of me. Special thanks to Ella, who is the only person of the above to not be financially reimbursed for her editorial work on my books, but who deserves it nonetheless.

To my parents, Peter and Noelle, who have been forcing me into the car for the long drive between Cork and Caherdaniel since 1994. A trip I hated you for then, but am eternally grateful for now. Thank you for the most beautiful place on earth. Thank you for Kerry.

Thanks to my brother, Robert O'Donoghue, for sitting at my kitchen table and reading from my manuscript so we could get the voices just right. Thank you Jill for being stronger than any woman alive; thank you to Shane for inevitably flogging copies of this book at the Audi dealership.

To Gavin Day, whose questions and insights as an Englishman discovering rural Ireland inspired most of the observations made by Charlie and Laura. Happiness is eating brown-bread ice cream with you in a parked car in the rain in Killarney. To Sylv, who inspired Satan, and made me realise that if a chapter needs spicing up, just throw a terrier into the mix.

Thanks to everyone at Virago, in particular to Rose Tomaszewska for your notes in the book's final stages. Thank you to Nithya Rae for her eagle-eye on both this and my previous book. Thank you to Grace Vincent for being the best in the business. Thank you to Sarah Maria Griffin and Jeanne Sutton for your eleventh-hour rescues of both this book and my sanity.

This book is fictional. The island of Clipim does not exist and neither does the button factory. However, many of the story details are inspired by real events. The following works were extraordinarily helpful in the creation of this book: *Do Penance or Perish* by Frances Finnegan, *The Deserted Schoolhouses of Ireland* by Enda O'Flaherty and *Sex in a Cold Climate* directed by Steve Humphries.

The last Magdalene laundry closed in Ireland in 1996. However, the mass warehousing of people in Ireland still continues today. With this in mind, thank you to those working to end Direct Provision and fighting for the rights of asylum seekers.

# CREDITS

Page v The dedication is an extract from *Brother of the More Famous Jack*, by Barbara Trapido (Viking, 1983).

Page 103 The lines from 'On Raglan Road' by Patrick Kavanagh are reprinted from *Collected Poems*, edited by Antoinette Quinn (Allen Lane, 2004), by kind permission of the Trustees of the Estate of the late Katherine B. Kavanagh, through the Jonathan Literary Agency.

Page 225 'Battlestations' by Fight Like Apes, from *Fight Like Apes and The Mystery of the Golden Medallion* (2008).

# Don't let the
# story stop here